Under The Canopy
Of Heaven

Under The Canopy
Of Heaven

Georgina Hutchison

First published 2018

Author's note

This story is based on recorded events in Huddersfield from 1812-13. Nearly all the names (character and place) and significant events in the novel are based on information from primary historical sources (newspapers, Home Office records, private correspondence, maps, parish records, etc). All the locations, routes and geographical features are real, and as accurate to the period as possible. A short glossary of West Riding dialect appears at the back of the book, in case any reader should need it. Though this is a work of fiction, I have endeavoured to be as historically accurate as possible, and so for any errors, I apologise.

I could have happily continued researching this topic for years, but to quote an excellent local author, Dr George Redmonds, whose detailed and extensive research into Huddersfield's changing landscape has been of enormous help to me, 'I offer this view...as tentatively as most researchers offer their work, fully aware that I may come to regret certain assertions, but having reached a point where some sort of statement needs to be made.' This novel is not an apology for the Luddites (for in my opinion they need none) but an elucidation of their plight, purpose, bravery and continuing relevance.

GH
October 2017

For my Mum and Dad

Prologue

Shades of night encompass his failing vision; the hem of a greatcoat sways in and out of focus and a boot, not a hand's span from his eye, turns by a few degrees. Up close, he can see the pattern of scuffing on the leather, a ridge of dried mud on the stitching, then the boot shifts and a voice comes from far above - 'Let's lift him up.'

The shadows fall in, flickering, upon him. A hand raises his cheek from the clammy stone floor and the sharp pressure against his left hip bone is gone, as if rather than being lifted from them, the slabs have instead fallen away beneath him. The deposit is swift; the wraiths are panting as they swing his heavy frame onto what passes for a bed. They spread upon him a gaol blanket held together more by filth and oil than by the weave, and - by God! - his left temple throbs as though a hammer were striking it over and over; clanging, beating, smashing his skull and brains to a pulp.

'Look at him shaking,' says a different voice from the first, and a breath comes, rancid and damp over his face as his wrist is grasped, pressed.

'A brain fever?'

'He may not survive the night.' His wrist is dropped.

These deathly crows twitter their alien language, but he is receding. The distant gaol cell stills and narrows but for a single, sputtering puddle of candlestick. He turns his head with spasms of effort away from the dying array.

Speckles of light dance upon his retina, trapped on the

underside of his closing eyelids. He counts seven, bright as stars, their soft wings folding in upon themselves before all the world turns black.

1
Lads Of High Renown

The platform stands tall, made of rough and choppy boards of weather-worn timber still slick with morning damp and reflecting the sky's forlorn January pallor. Before the prisoners stands a sea of people, motionless, as if in the eye of a storm. They face the high castle walls that rear up behind the drop. Between the platform and the swell of observers, the cavalry holds the line - horses resigned to blinkered immobility under the saddles of wary militiamen who hold primed muskets and train their eyes on the crowd. The awe, the fear and the horror are palpable, paralysing, as though no one is capable of action; as though events are rolling under force of inevitability alone and no one can do more than witness the unfolding of a great calamity. Below, flooding St George's Field, are hundreds of people. The sound of their shuffling and murmuring is thrown into relief by the unnatural quiet of the castle mound and its ghastly ritual; the watching crowds are straining to catch the words of the Ordinary as he recites the mandated prayers, the grim set of his jaw rendering a tone, perhaps unintended, of hesitance, of distaste. Mellor fastens himself to the words and pictures the simple pulpit of the chapel on Buxton Road and the pews of familiar faces.

On the platform, to his right, Thorp swallows - an audible, gulping effort - and Mellor looks sideways, very slightly and slowly so as not to alarm the guards. He softens his eyes - not a smile, but an authoritative assurance. Thorp blinks and - ever so fractionally -

nods. If one must face it, both can. This is, Mellor knows, what dragged him back from his terrible fever and collapse in the night, from the dark tunnel and the dancing stars; the thought of William and Thomas, up here without him.

He is being directed to step forwards, to accept his chance to pray. The Ordinary, his voice dropping to a private whisper, says 'Speak up my lad, say what you've to say.' A ripple of anticipation eddies the crowd, hands rising to mouths to stifle involuntary gasps and moans, heads dropping at the unbearable sight of Mellor's fiery chestnut hair, the line of his jaw a perfect flourish above the rough woollen shirt, collarbone achingly visible. He kneels down on the rough boards and lifts his hands to join them together in prayer, and the jangle of irons sets another peal of sympathy in motion. A woman below exclaims 'Irons! As if they could get away now,' and spits towards the troops. 'Shame,' someone cries. 'Mercy.'

'Lord, our Father, who art above in heaven and can see all and shall judge all - hear this, my final prayer and please God, be wi' us now.' The people halt their own lamentations and fall deathly still. Even the Ordinary cranes down to hear the kneeling man. 'Lord, I pray for mi brethren, for those who stand beside me, for those who've been brought to this place bih nobbut desperation. Lord, take William Thorp into thy care, swift as thi can-'

William Thorp, long bones and heavy muscle, towering, rollicking, swilling ale, sweat at his temple with the shears in his hands; Will Thorp, boy - running, laughing, calling 'George, come on little George,' disappearing through tenter fields and town ginnels, stick waving, cut-down shirt flapping, grazed knees under broadcloth breeches - William Thorp, Guilty, I sentence thee to hang - Uncle William, lift me up - William, you take the second division - William, what do the men think o' me? - William, are they friendly or not? Friendly or not-

'No idea, don't know 'em up in these parts,' Thorp answers. Mellor studies the faintly glowing cottage where a householder has abruptly closed his door, but not before leaking a sudden shaft of light across their path. It shouldn't matter. There's no law up here at Hartshead, on the heather-blanketed moors and the hard-earned parcels of intake land; the magistrates are far away, nestled in their huge ashlar houses, the patchwork of the hills a sight they admire from a comfortable remove - on horseback or through their picture windows. In any case, he and Thorp are simply two men, of respected profession, passing over the tops on their way to The Shears. They're not breaking any laws, not yet.

Thorp, as tall as Mellor but broader, his fair hair thick and kinked under his hat, hops up over a stile. He betrays no sign of fatigue from their walk through the bitterly cold night. Behind him, Mellor grabs the wooden post and hoists himself over. They plough on, following the footpath through the fields, seeing below them the faint, shifting lights from dotted homesteads.

'How many tonight?' Thorp asks.

'Whoever Hall can rustle up. And John Hirst, he's a good lad. He'll have brought a fair few. John Walker'll be over, you can bet on that.'

'Getting big now, in't it?'

'Aye, but maybe not big enough.'

'George Mellor, tha's nivver satisfied!'

'Happen not.' He doesn't mind these pointless conversations with Thorp who, at twenty three, is a year older than himself. They've grown up together, played together, sat squashed in the Chapel pews together and now as adults they work in the same trade. They've been best friends for so long, they hardly bother to think or to check their utterances before they speak, confident - though it will remain forever unarticulated - that the instinctual expression of their deepest selves will be entirely acceptable to the other. It's very different when they are together in company. Around other people, Thorp becomes more rowdy, adept at drunken banter, while Mellor has been accused of being careful, moody, reserved - sulky, even. Somehow, though, he is the type of person from whom others seek approval. From the women who eye his curled copper hair and bulky biceps and forearms, to the men who lean in close with lines of concentration on their foreheads, and nod while he speaks, there's barely one he doesn't get on with.

Finally, after their miles of walking over towpaths, tracks and moorland, they see The Shears public house, up on the road, stolidly perched among a run of cottages

'Thank the Lord,' says Thorp, rubbing his hands together, 'Time for a pint afore we've to be out marching!'

He picks up his pace, near-bounding to the large white-washed establishment from which bleats of laughter and a throb of voices emanate, the clunk of

6

pewter and the ebbing discourse spilling irreverently into the peaceful night. Mellor follows his friend through the slim doorway, into the lit passage and then into a crowd of men, all florid-faced and expectant, drinking and jostling and parting fluidly to swallow Mellor and Thorp within. At the back of all the fuss, Mellor can see Lister, the pub landlord, serving behind the bar, and he clocks three heads he knows, supping up front - Brook, Hall and a kid called Mitchell. Over in the corner near the oak-encased clock is John Walker, as he'd both hoped and expected, and around him a knot of men, probably from up at Joe Jackson's cropping shop on Aquilla Lane. John Walker is from Huddersfield, but he makes friends easily and he likes the Liversedge croppers. A man from the periphery of that group turns and grins with recognition.

'George, lad,' he says, lunging across and bringing a walloping hand down on Mellor's right shoulder. 'Tha's here at last. Lister! Pass us a pint.'

'Evening John,' says Mellor, digging under his coat for money.

'None o' that,' John Hirst orders. 'This one's on me.' William Hall pushes through the crowd with Mellor's pint as Hirst hurls a coin over at the Landlord. It hits the back wall and Lister points a finger of warning at the laughing men before he picks the coin from the floor. Mellor finds himself in the corner encircled by the raucous Liversedge men. He grins and nods and goes along with their conversation but all the while he's scanning the room, counting men and assessing them, working out who and what they are. He can tally the actual croppers with ease; he just needs an unobstructed view of their wrists. There are other

7

clues of course - the croppers are usually big lads, tall and broad with arms like tree trunks, but a miner can be built like an outhouse and even a clothier gets strong, shifting cloth about. What you really need to look for, and what Mellor takes pleasure in counting on this January night in The Shears, is the ridge on the right wrist - the hoof of gristle built upon the joint like a mark from the devil himself. A young lad, an apprentice, might not have it yet, but he'll have something there - a callus, an angry red mark, an open wound, maybe the rust-coloured staining of day-old blood. By the time you've finished your seven years as an apprentice, that hoof is on you for life. There's no hiding what you are.

When Mellor sees a lad with his wrist all blistered and the cuff of his sleeve soaked crimson, it takes him back to the days when every heft of the shears was torture; back to the burning ache in his upper arms, the strangled, half-numb response of his tortured limbs as they fought with fifty pounds of brutal metal; the groan of his muscles as his left hand depressed the nog simultaneous with the sharp bloom of pain in the right hand that held the lower blade steady against the action of the fulcrum and then- a slight relief as the blade sprang back up and he pushed the shears forwards over the cloth. He spent years with the blades yawning and grinning at his feeble efforts, his left hand on the nog and his right managing the handle on the lower blade, cutting, shearing, over interminable lengths of woven woollen cloth, trying to get that perfect finish, being careful not to smear blood on the fibres. Falling asleep at night, he dreamed of the nap, standing on end, waiting for the

8

cut, and in his dreams the blades slid effortlessly under the iron grip of his hands and the finish of the cloth afterwards bore the closest touch, the keenest eye, and John Wood said 'Well done, son.'

Mellor drains his mug of beer. He wipes his upper lip with the hard, hoofed wrist that hurts no longer. He's been a year out of apprenticeship. Mile upon mile of the finest cloth lays behind him. His scarred right hand can steady the blades of the heaviest shears in the West Riding.

Besides the throng of croppers, there are miners and weavers drinking in The Shears. There's a blacksmith, a few dyers, a maker of healds and slays - if he doesn't know someone, he taps Hirst or one of the others and finds out the stranger's name. Some of the men filling the room are just there for a drink, or to satisfy a dangerous curiosity, but most are waiting for someone to shout 'Friendly Society, upstairs!' When that happens, all the croppers and quite a few others will parade up to the first floor room, clattering on the steps so that Lister's wife, in the kitchen at the other side of the passage will shake her head and shout to her husband, 'Them lot's trouble, James!' and he'll stick his head through and yell back, 'Them lot keep you in new shawls, woman!' and the men still in the bar will laugh and raise their pewter tankards in a respectful hello to Mrs Lister, glimpsed through the doorway, while Lister himself will eye the beams above his head thoughtfully.

Mellor has been here often enough now to know how it plays out. He's been a regular visitor since last year, when the rebel breeze from Nottingham first blew in, sailing the wave of shocked newspaper reports and lifting the hairs on the back of the croppers' necks. Wood was in Mellor's ear too, always talking about the Damned Repeals and the Cursed Orders. His step-father's contempt for the Government is palpable and over the years has finally rubbed off.

Someone has rung the bell, given the shout, and the procession upstairs is underway. Mellor is jostled along between John Hirst and John Walker. Walker, now there's a man Mellor understands! He'd happily sink pints all night with this fellow Longroyd Bridge cropper. They'd have walked over together except Mellor and Thorp were late finishing up and thirty-one year old Walker won't wait for anyone if there's ale at the end of his route. Someone knocks Walker's arm on the stairs and his first instinct is to bring his tankard towards his lips to rescue the sloshing ale.

In the upstairs room, chairs surround a long, thin table, and as these coveted spaces fill up, men squeeze in and line the walls behind them. Thomas Brook has pushed to the head of the table and he stays standing there, while a couple of men hitch their chairs in to let Mellor pass.

'Na then,' Thomas says, in greeting.

'Where's James an' John?' Mellor asks.

'Shop's busy. Left 'em working.' Thomas's brothers are in their twenties, but Thomas, like John Walker, is about ten years older than Mellor. The men defer to him because he's a master cropper. He runs the shop at Lockwood and rules his two brothers, his wife and his children with a diligent undercurrent of taciturn force. He carries on his face a look that suggests he's ever about to reveal something important, and yet so often he keeps quiet. Tonight, though, he's planning to speak. He clears his throat a couple of times, a gesture that one might mistake for nerves if they didn't know him. Mellor steps back behind him, through a cloud of smoke from Brook's long pipe. The room is fit to bursting. Brook hits the table with inch-thick knuckles and a silence drops.

'Evening friends,' Brook says, opening the meeting of the local croppers' Sick Club and Friendly Society. 'Have we all brought our subs? On't table, if yer will.'

There's a jangling of coins such as is never heard these days elsewhere in the West Riding, as the cream of the cloth trade dig into their pockets and pull out what they can afford. The metal is slammed down onto the table. It grows into a pile, and Thorp, who has made his way close to where Mellor stands, opens a leather pouch and slides the heap of shillings and pennies into it. He slings the bag to John Hirst who will log the takings as the meeting proceeds.

'And now,' says Brook, 'I'm of the feeling that something has got to be done. I had word the other day that yon felly, Cartwright, has got frames due to be sent out to Rawfolds.'

'He's got frames already,' someone chips in.

'Aye, an' don't we know it,' says Brook. 'But more are coming and it'll si thee out o' work. How long'll Jackson keep running, if that queer devil rams any more o' the blasted frames into his mill?'

Jackson's cropping shop, up on the hill above Rawfolds mill, is where Hirst works, along with a fair few others in the room. More shearing frames at Rawfolds means dwindling trade in the cropping shops. But it isn't just the croppers getting nervous - Mellor is watching the clothiers too, their heads

11

shaking at the news that Cartwright's manufactory is growing. They know what this means - more change, more uncertainty. No one knows where it will end, nor what the West Riding will become if the manufactories keep on growing.

'Na then,' Brook says, tapping his pipe and clearing his throat again, 'You all know the Leeds men fired Oatlands,'

'Oh aye,' nods Walker, rubbing his hands together. 'I bet it were fair toasty when it went up.' There is laughter around the room.

'We're no strangers to that kind of action,' says Brook, and men nod, thinking of a mill they set light to just a few weeks since. 'And let's not forget, it's the *only* action we can take. We've been forced to this.'

At the back of the room, there's movement as a new figure pushes inside. Men budge up and let Ben Walker squeeze in. He catches Mellor's eye as he finds a spot against the wall and gives him a wide grin whilst patting his belly. Mellor shakes his head, smiling. They work together at Wood's cropping shop and the last Mellor saw of Ben today was when the latter headed home for tea with his mam and dad. Ben's dad is a dandy known as Buck, and consequently Ben is rarely called by his proper surname. Everyone calls him Ben O'Bucks instead.

'You've to ask,' Thomas Brook is continuing, 'how bad does it have to get afore we make 'em stop? If thi took a rag an' dipped it in't mill goit and then rung it out as hard as thi could, then that'd be akin to what the poor o' this county is suffering. There's not a drop left to ring out.'

Brook's jaw is clenched. The hand that grips his

pipe is white on the knuckles. Anger fair crackles from him and Mellor catches a tingling quiver of angry excitement between his own shoulder blades.

'Well, by ummer, lets make 'em stop,' says Hirst. 'Cartwright'll not get those frames. If he's to bring 'em up over Hartshead, he's not got a chance.'

'Aye,' agrees William Hall. 'We'll find out when they're coming and have a band o' lads up here waiting.'

Hall is another of Mellor's workmates but has the added connexion of also being his bed-mate. While Ben Walker still lives at home with his parents, William Hall shares an old wooden double frame with Mellor in a small upstairs bedroom at John Wood's house, adjacent to the shop. Will's heart is in Liversedge though, and he'd be over here still if he could find a job over this way. He lost his position at Jackson's - a victim of the down-turn in trade - but over in Huddersfield, thank God, men like Mellor's step-father are just about clinging on to their customers.

'If that's the plan,' Mellor says, 'then we need a man on t' Huddersfield end to let us know when they're coming. I'll talk to a mate o' mine and get that sorted out. So, who's in for breaking these frames up then?'

A dozen or more voices answer - the obvious ones: Hirst, Hall, Thorp, Walker, Ben o' Bucks, that kid Mitchell, Bob Wam who's nestled at the back getting slowly stoked up. Mellor pays more attention to the ones who haven't answered: that Pule, who works for Cartwright and might be double-dealing, John Booth who's looking out of his depth - a saddler in a sea of croppers - and some of the older men, with more to lose.

'Aye, that'll do.' He says, pointing to exactly who he wants, one after the other. 'I'll send word, when we've a date. Tha shall need to bring kit from this end - we can't be lugging hammers out all this way. An' fetch a coil o' rope. I don't have to tell any o' thee to black up or wear a mask - or better still, both.'

'Well George, thanks for taking it on,' says Hirst. 'We know you've enough to deal with over your way.'

'It's all't same,' says Mellor. 'Let a weed grow an' it'll spread. Doesn't matter where we hit 'em, as long as we strike a blow. We'll have 'em all running to take down their frames.'

'We're all brothers in this,' says Walker, 'and fair glad we are to be united.' Mellor laughs and some of the men cheer. John Walker can be a sentimental fool when he's got a belly-full of ale, but Mellor likes him for it. He brings some levity and morale to a situation which weighs heavy on them all.

The meeting breaks into separate conversations, the formal business over. Mellor squeezes through to John Hirst.

'How's tha want to play it, then?' Hirst asks, with a nose-clearing sniff, his slim, intelligent face turned sideways on, watching the room as well as attending closely to Mellor.

'I think you should wait up t' track.' Mellor says. 'Keep out o' sight. We'll wait in't woods. That should give us chance t' hear 'em coming. A cart carrying a pile of iron is going to be rattling, in't it? We'll get behind 'em on't road. You come out in front of 'em.'

'That'll work,' nods Hirst. 'But what if there's guards, extra men, what if they've all got guns?

14

'We'll fall back onto t' moor an' run like blummin' ummer. You're going to have to trust me, John. You won't see us coming up behind, but I give me word we'll be there. As soon as you bring the cart to a stop, we'll block 'em from behind.'

'Send one o' thi men up to find us, once tha's in't woods, just so's we know you've not been taken up or owt daft.'

'I'll send Will Hall up,' agrees Mellor. They shake hands, Hirst's skin like warm, weathered leather in Mellor's hard, tendon-strung grasp.

'Time to go out,' shouts Bob Wam over the throng of voices. He has downed his ale and risen to his feet, and fidgets in the doorway.

'Aye, I'd say so,' agrees John Hirst, stowing the money in a hidden pocket of his breeches, where it bulges awkwardly. Mugs are hastily set down on the table. The grating of chair legs and heavy tread of men back out through the little doorway and onto the stairs alerts Lister, and possibly all the residents within the adjoining cottages, that his clientele are leaving. He sees them out at the main door.

'Take care now,' the Landlord orders, and he gives Mellor a hard stare.

'Allus do,' Mellor says with an affable wave. One of these days, Lister - a Sheriff's officer, no less! - is going to take serious issue with what's being planned in the club room of his own establishment, but tonight, only weeks after the hopeful beginning of this new year of 1812, he lets it go.

Outside, the cold air assails Mellor. Having been hemmed into a room full of hot-blooded, thick-limbed men, the icy temperature makes him take a hard

15

shallow breath. He should have had another ale. Most of these men, breathing warm fumes into the sapphire atmosphere, will have drunk four or six pints easily. They smell like a brewery. Mellor stamps his feet a few times and walks to the front of the crowd. Thorp hurries alongside him, lifting his hat to rake back hair that is getting in his eyes, before pulling it back on straight. A little way along from the pub, across the slim road, is a stile. Mellor and Thorp drop down over the cleft in the dry stone wall and walk for about half a mile, a comfortable distance away from the houses. Behind them, the rest of the men walk briskly, in twos and threes, allowing their large mass to dissipate into something less threatening. Where Mellor halts, the winding trail ravels into knots of men, gathered on the moor under faint starlight.

'Company One,' Mellor calls, and a group assembles to his left, shifting into line. 'Company Two. Company Three.'

He waits until the three lines are formed. It takes about half a minute, shadowy figures side-stepping and pushing one another out of the way

'Company One, present!' he calls.

The men in the first line rattle off their numbers, one after another. It goes one through to seven, then nine through to seventeen.

'No Hartley?' Mellor asks, and is told no, Hartley hasn't come tonight. Eighteen and nineteen are absent too, but that's because they've stayed up on the road. If eighteen or nineteen hear some trouble-maker clip-clopping in this direction - that militant bloody vicar, Roberson, or one of the magistrate's men - they'll whistle out a warning and the three companies will leg

16

it off down the fields and away. Mellor has become more cautious recently - a lad was picked up after the last firing job and now he's pinned for it at York Castle. Mellor won't let that happen again if he can help it. He repeats the roll-call procedure for his second and third companies, with similar results. A couple are missing, but that's normal. Wives and children keep men back, or they've to work. It's rarely a full turn-out, but he watches for men who are away twice in a row.

'Company Three, double up. And... left march.' The line of men concertinas into a paired column and sets off across the rough ground, left foot first. Mellor calls out commands to the other two lines and makes the whole lot of men parade around on the moor like some tiny army, though he is careful never to raise his voice above the necessary volume. He makes them march and run, gets them into formations, lines them up again. They obey his commands without hesitation. Mellor knows he must get them working as a unit. They think they can set light to mills and break frames and then high tail it over the moors or into the woods, but Mellor knows that unless they are prepared and trained, then running away won't be enough. Mellor has plans greater than just smashing the odd cartload of frames on the highways, but it will take skill and strategy to break the grip of the manufacturers. The high roofs of Rawfolds, the towering walls of Bradleys, the dense mass of Ottiwells, these metastasising manufactories of the West Riding put him in mind of a pack of fighting dogs, their teeth set against the world, their chests heaving against the constraints of domestic production, slavering all the time for more profit, their tight collars held fast by men like Cartwright, the Atkinson brothers, and Horsfall, who sit high on their horses and preside over market dinners and hold fancy meetings of local militia regiments and think they can trample the people who have helped make their fortune. Mellor knows both William Horsfall and Thomas Atkinson and he likes neither. It's not that they are wealthy and he's envious, but that they are complacent and arrogant, as if they were baronets or lords, when they are neither. They are just a warped form of merchant clothier. They are fulling millers gone despotic. They are black ticks in the wool, fat on the blood of innocent sheep.

On the way home, after all the marching is done and morale is up, young John Booth catches him up. He falls into step beside Mellor, with William Hall and Ben O'Bucks up ahead and William Thorp and John Walker some way behind.

'How are thee, Booth?' Mellor enquires.

'Reit well, aye,' says the lad. He's nineteen, but you'd take him for younger than that. He's got soft skin and big eyes, a slim build, but his arms and legs are wiry and he must be strong enough, working as a saddler and learning to be an iron-monger. Booth's father was a cropper, but cuts his cloth in the pulpit now, a curate out at Leymoor. Booth the younger is a sensitive lad who might have suited God if he'd a mind to it - but of all the trades, it surely wasn't going to be cropping with that slight figure.

'How's Wright, business good?'

'Aye, aye. He's good to work for. Says I'm coming on well, that iron work suits me.'

'That's grand.'

'I hope tha dun't think badly o' me, not raising me hand for t'Hartshead job.'

'Nay lad, there were more didn't shout up than did. Tha's not alone.'

'It's not that I'm flaid,' Booth says. 'I just think we're doing it the wrong way. The problem's wi' t'upper classes, not the men making t'frames, or even men like Cartwright who are buying 'em. The problem is men like Armytage, sitting in his mansion, an' Justice Radcliffe, climbing on t'backs o' t'people to make his name.'

Mellor considers this. He doesn't dismiss Booth out of hand because he knows the kid's got a fair bit of learning.

'Maybe them at top have got more than their fair share,' says Mellor, 'but taking them out'd still leave men like Cartwright, wringing us dry. Whereas, take out men like Cartwright, and we'd go back to the old way o' trading, where people would have enough to live on.'

'Get rid o' t'upper classes and the whole system would change,' Booth insists. 'Say we had no King, no bloody regent, say the Church couldn't hold sway over all a man did - then we'd have something new, where everyone got a fair deal. I've been thinking, from what I've read, and it in't just us in't Riding - there's men all over t'country who'd join us. Look at Ireland - the papists there'd be happy to see an end to t'King an' his son. An' there's the weavers up in Scotland that's been protesting, an' all them in t'cotton country. We could raise an army, bigger even than t'King's own.'

'Now hang on,' laughs Mellor, 'yer sounding like a

Republican. That kind o' talk'll get thi hanged. Who's going to lead yer revolution anyway? Fancy inviting Napoleon across?'

Booth colours and dips his head, features obscured by the brim of his cap. He admires Mellor and is eager not only to impress, but to forge a closer friendship with him, and in his pleasure at having caught a chance moment alone with the enigmatic cropper, he has allowed his mouth to run away with his thoughts - thoughts which involve such complicated and controversial reasoning that he has rarely tested them aloud, and therefore can't fully express to Mellor what he means anyway.

'I'm not saying yer wrong, lad,' says Mellor, taking pity on him. 'Just - one step at a time. Let's get these frames broke and keep a few men in their jobs a while longer.'

Booth nods.

'I'm in then,' he says.

'Thanks, lad. We'll be reit for this job, but I'll remember thi for another.'

'Aye, fair do,' Booth concedes.

They walk on in silence. Mellor feels Booth is still slighted but there is nothing he can do about that. The kid needs to toughen up a bit and learn when to bite his tongue. The rights or wrongs of wider society won't sway minds around here. What sways men is what will keep their bellies full and their children alive. They've got the heart for taking apart the machinery that is slowly killing them, but there's no heart for real revolution - for blood in the streets and heads in buckets. People just want the good old days back.

Only a few generations ago, Huddersfield was just a one-street place, flagged by tenterfields and nestled in away from the world. Cloth was made, cloth went out, money came in; a perfect circle of existence. The whole of the West Riding was a place of peace and money. Wood told him stories when he was a kid, of fields that stretched where the canals now run, of meadows and ings where roads are being laid, of all the hillsides ablaze in cloth, the fabric stretched out on posts to dry in the golden sunlight. When men left the Riding and came back, they talked of how ill it was received, not to doff your cap in the presence of your betters. Betters? In the West Riding, such a thing did not exist, and there was no doffing of caps. Why would the man who milled the wool, or the man who wove it, or the man who sheared it or the man who traded it, doff his cap to the man who preached in church or the man who bought the cloth or the man who sat idly in a grand house bestowed by his ancestors?

Woollen cloth had made this town rich. People measured themselves by their cloth and their place within its creation, not by the social hierarchy that existed outside the West Riding valleys. The scribbling and fulling mills were just that - places where a clothier would take his wool to be scribbled before hefting it home again to be spun and woven; and take it again, as a piece of cloth, to be fulled, before market day, when the clothier would arrive at the Cloth Hall to make a sale. And as for cropping - that didn't even happen until the sale was made. The trader, having bought the piece from a clothier, would pop into his chosen dressing shop and have the nap sheared. The very idea of a manufactory, doing all these jobs in-house, is still an unpleasant novelty. The really big mill owners might still put out a bit of spinning, and even weaving, to the clothiers on the hillsides, but what they really want is to be able to scribble, spin, weave, full and crop themselves, inside the high stone walls of their own mills, with great machines that churn incessantly, if not skilfully.

Mellor is beginning to see two great problems that must be overcome - firstly the use of machines that steal men's jobs (and, infuriatingly, produce poorly finished cloth) and secondly, the gathering in of what was formerly a domestic process under the auspices of the mill owners, where men are beholden to tyrants - where journeymen are no longer inspired and motivated by a realistic dream of one day owning their own shop and being a true master of their own fate. Whatever the merits of Booth's Republican-flavoured arguments, Mellor cannot afford to be distracted from his goal. There are things he can accomplish, and things he cannot. He may never unseat a corrupt Prince, nor redistribute the astronomical wealth of the few amongst the deep needs of the many; he does not fancy himself as Robin Hood. But there is a line which he must hold here in his cherished and native land; he must defend what remains of the way of life he knows and believes in. The manufactories must be held at bay and the frames must be destroyed. This, Mellor can do; this, he believes he can achieve.

Late on a February afternoon, Mellor, Thorp, John Walker, William Hall and Ben O'Bucks make their way along the footpath towards Bradley Wood.

They've come in good time - as soon as the barge was in sight of the Huddersfield basin, Jonathan Dean sent a man out to Liversedge and his own eldest lad over to Longroyd Bridge with the word. Mellor, Hall and O'Bucks dropped their work, leaving John Wood to manage Tom Smith and the other apprentices in the shop, and then called over the road for William Thorp and for John Walker. But although the five croppers are now making their way to the edge of the woods, from where they will have a perfect view of the cart approaching on the track from Huddersfield up over Hartshead, they have no idea how long they will have to wait; and out there on the moor, nestled into some blackly towering dry stone wall beside a remote sheep pen, the Liversedge men can only watch the slow clouds gathering, and wonder at what appointed hour they will have to leap up and charge onto the track. They have their weapons stowed in the hedge at the place they hope to ambush the carters - hammers and axes and some rope in case the carters are difficult.

Mellor's group reach a sheltered clearing. They tuck in amongst the thin trunks and leafless saplings and begin to cover up their faces, drawing mucky lines on their cheeks and foreheads with small lumps of coal and smearing the sticky dust in until they wear greasy masks of dark grey.

'Go on up and let 'em know we're here,' Mellor instructs Hall, and William Hall leaves them in the woods, crosses the footbridge over the gushing Calder, and walks up the fields. He keeps close in to the line of the stone boundary walls, passing through the edge of land belonging to the Armytages over at Kirklees Hall. A lone figure, a woman, comes into view, trudging with a basket down the track that runs parallel to his own route. He keeps walking in the fields, with his head turned away and his hat pulled low over his dirtied face and the woman disappears from view with only a cursory glance in his direction. Only a little further up he finds the concealed Liversedge men - John Hirst, Bob Wam, and Mitchell - and he sits down with them in the lee of a wall. It's a good spot that they've found - they won't be seen from the track, but they should hear the wheels grinding up it well in advance.

'Mellor down there?' Robert Whitham checks, and Hall nods in the affirmative.

'Mellor, Thorp, Bucks and Walker,' he confirms to Wam. 'They're in place.'

The weak sun blots out behind a rolling bank of cloud and the day darkens. Down in the woods, Mellor pulls his greatcoat tight around him. John Walker paces in the crisp twigs. Ben O' Bucks is twitchy, sat on a mossy stump, but rocking about and pulling up grass, unable to stay still. Only Thorp is solidly immovable, feet planted hard on the dry soil as he watches the track. Mellor wonders what it would take to make Thorp twitch.

He stands beside his friend, eyes fixed in the same direction. Now that the weather has turned, the day is fading quickly. It looks as though it might be dark when the cart comes past. This means that the carters are not expecting trouble - if they were, surely they'd have left much sooner and so given themselves the presumed safety of daylight to pass through? Better still, no one from Rawfolds has passed this way towards Huddersfield - Cartwright hasn't sent his own men to escort the cart through. Mellor smiles. Cartwright probably expects that if his barge-load of shearing frames can make it through the heart of Huddersfield, they'll make it up here no problem. He bets that the Taylors, who have made these frames for him out at Marsden, have told him that tales of the Luddites are exaggerated anyway. He's heard it told, by some quite sincere gentlemen in the pubs in town, that it's all a myth - there's no oath, no gangs of men meeting up to parade about. Sometimes, those that say they've seen dark armies marching in secret on the moors are laughed at. And it's in the Taylor brothers' interests to give this impression to their customers. They don't want the mill owners getting skittish and cancelling orders of the iron frames that James and Enoch work so hard to churn out of their Marsden foundry.

'Does tha think the Taylors have got their money out o' Cartwright yet?' Mellor wonders aloud.

'That canny Enoch?' Thorp laughs. 'Aye, I would a' thought so, George. Ever thought we should pay them a visit?'

'The Taylors? Nay. Who'd make hammers for us then?'

They all laugh at that. It's a running joke, that the biggest hammers they have come from the same foundry that is trying to supply all the local mills with frames. The huge blacksmith's hammers work almost as well for breaking cast iron apart as they do for moulding it in the first place.

'Enoch Taylor, he's an odd felly,' Mellor continues. 'Did thi know t'church hates him? He dun't believe - not in any of it. They say t'only thing he does believe in is a good lump of iron. I heard tell at the market dinner one Tuesday that the Vicar of Huddersfield himself said that Enoch Taylor was well-placed in amongst his foundry furnaces, as it should better prepare him for where he was headed.'

John Walker grins and spits. Ben O' Bucks laughs out loud, flashing teeth in his coal-dust face.

'Some even say he's got Republican ideas, an' that his other brother ran off abroad as a dissenter,' Mellor says, 'but I don't know about that.'

'Well, let's hope, since he's such a good lad, that he's been paid then,' jests Thorp. 'Or God knows, he'll get nowt out a' Cartwright for a pile o' smashed metal.'

The light is fading. The men are hungry. They watch the track restlessly, except for Bob Wam up on the moor, who, being more mature in years, has perfected the art of napping in adverse conditions, while the others sit grumbling in the damp air. Spots of rain are starting to fall and Hall, Mitchell and Hirst pull up their collars and pull down their hats. In the woods, Mellor, Thorp, Walker and O'Bucks watch the distant thickening clouds disperse a thick shower of dismal grey, far away over the hills in the twilight. Under the trees, they are protected as a thin rain bites at Hartshead. Darkness falls. Ben murmurs something about wanting his supper, but no one answers.

Finally, on the breeze they catch the low, grinding sound of cart wheels chewing up muck and stones, overlaid with the faint bang and rattle of iron thumping against wood. Mellor holds his breath as the cart rolls along the track and the volume of noise increases. There is no escort - just a single cart carrying two men, forming a shape coloured deeper black than the dark night around them, growing in size on approach, the churning of the wheels increasing in gritty clarity as the carters drive the horses forwards and on, up towards the moor. Mellor leads his group along the edge of the woods, making for the track. The cart is rumbling ahead, oblivious, as they silently follow its progress.

Behind a high wall further on, Hirst has shaken Wam awake, and the pair of them are scrambling up and over the wall, closely followed by Hall and Mitchell. Mitchell is shaking. He grips his hands into fists, swallowing hard against the nervous clench of his own throat. The four press in against the wall, slightly stooped. Given the curve of the track and the late hour, the carters won't see them until they're almost level.

Wam, shoulder to shoulder with the trembling Mitchell, whispers, 'What are we?' and the others in unison whisper back, 'Determined.'

The cart rounds the bend. The two carters have their hats pulled low, their focus on avoiding ruts and keeping a steady pace. One of them gives a full body jerk of terror, like a dreamer brought abruptly to consciousness, as a black figure races out of the darkness, jumps up the stepping board onto the cart, and pulls him from the seat before he can even shout aloud. His partner raises his whip to crack the horses into speed, but Hirst is upon him, even as Hall is dragging the first man down from the other side. Mitchell clambers onto the still-moving cart and grabs the reins, pulling the horses steady, while Wam and Hirst pin one carter down, and Hall rolls about, fists flying, with the startled driver who has begun to recover his wits. Mellor's group is there within seconds, John Walker sprinting to help Hall disable the fighting carter.

'Where's the gear?' yells Mellor, and Mitchell jumps down from the now stationary cart and runs thirty feet along the hedge to where the hammers and axes are stowed. Mellor grabs the rope and runs back to the carters, while Ben O'Bucks, Thorp and Mitchell lug the tools.

'Keep still an' you'll see home tonight,' Walker is grunting at the man on the ground. On the other side of the vehicle, the second carter is sat motionless, shock glazing his features. Mellor ties up the troublesome one first and they lay him in the ditch, then Walker takes the rope and ties up the other man.

At the back of the cart, O'Bucks' eyes gleam white from blackened sockets as he and Thorp pull the canvas away to reveal a stack of iron frames and rollers, complete with sets of shears. Mellor and Thorp climb up amongst the machinery and Ben moves to one side as they pit their weight against the metal carcasses, shoving them out of the back of the cart and onto the dirt track, where they land with a disgruntled clatter. The horses whinny and tap their feet. Walker leads them forward ten paces, to give Mellor room at the back to push the rest of the machinery out onto the track.

Mitchell hands Ben O'Bucks one of the hammers, and O'Bucks goes at it, swinging the long-handled tool and bringing the iron head down onto the frames. Hall and Hirst keep watch over the carters while the other men, all six of them, put their backs into smashing the shearing frames apart. They take turns with the two large hammers - it's heavy work, taking cast iron apart, and they want to do a thorough job. Walker gets one of the rollers loose, and sends it off down the lane with a vicious kick and a burst of laughter. In the ditch, the carters keep their heads down. One of them is shaking and Hall bends down, keeping his blackened face averted. He says 'Na then, it's nobbut frames we're smashing tonight. Settle thee down. But 'appen tha'd best tell Cartwright tha's none fetching frames for 'im no more,' and the carter jiggles his head up and down in nervous, shaking compliance. Mellor notices this and is pleased. He won't have anyone say they're thugs - he won't have a man harmed in these breakings. He's told them all, time and again - no punching, no poising, not even any insults. All that men like this need is a kindly warning not to have anything to do with the shearing frames or the gig mills. If they don't comply, if they repeat their mistakes, perhaps a good poising is in order then, but Mellor thinks they'll do as they're told. They don't need much excuse anyway - there's hardly a man in the West Riding, save for the clutch of big manufacturers and their eager foundry-men, who really wants this new machinery.

The work's near done. Mellor takes the hammer from Thorp and gives a few more blows, just for the fun of it. The frames lie crumpled and bent in the wet lane. They can stay there until some poor bugger has to scrape them up and cart them off, Mellor thinks. Maybe it'll be this sorry pair in the ditch that get the job of taking all the mangled iron back to the foundry. He hopes Cartwright sees it first, before it's disposed of.

'Reit lads,' he calls, 'Good work. Careful going

back. Si thi soon.' He hands one of the hammers to Wam. There are nods all round, then the hammers are thrown over before the eight of them climb the wall into the field, so the carters won't know which way they head.

'Yer can't just leave us here,' yells the pluckier victim, but his friend manages to fetch him a kick on the ankle.

'Let 'em be off,' he says, and begins to stretch his wrists, working at the rope that still binds him. Now that he's safe, the carter feels elated. Tomorrow, when he tells his story to all his friends and neighbours, the Luddites will have grown by a foot, and they'll be fast as lightning and twice as many, and it will sound to his listeners almost as if he admires them.

The Liversedge men break away into the dark. The Huddersfield men have the longer walk home, and they split into two groups to do it. Mellor takes Thorp and Walker. William Hall and Ben O' Bucks follow a different path.

The rain has petered out, but they're damp, exhausted and hungry. Tomorrow morning, they'll all be up for work at the crack of dawn. Mellor knows his step-father would let him have another hour or so in bed if he really needed it, but the truth is, Mellor isn't sure he'll even be able to sleep. He's bone-tired and his head aches, but his mind is racing. He's thinking that now they've done this, there'll be no one in the pubs saying the Luddites are phantoms. It'll prove to everyone that there's a real fight going on. But that, in itself, brings problems. They've all sworn not to betray each other, but will it hold? Will everyone keep their mouths shut? He could hear Ben O' Bucks chellping on at Will Hall for a good few minutes after they'd parted - he almost ran after the daft sod to tell him to quiet down - proof enough that even the most assiduous Luddite may have issues with preserving discretion. And if word gets around, which it surely will in the next few days, that the Luddites are laying ambushes, then will the magistrates increase their judicial efforts?

Mellor has spent months worrying and preparing but this is when he will find out if he's got it sewn up or not. If there's a dropped stitch, it won't take long for the whole lot to unravel. So he knows what they have to do - they have to hit fast and hard, they have to take out as many frames in as many manufactories and shops as they can, and they have to implicate as many of the sworn Ludds as possible. Yes, he'll take Booth up on his promise. He'll set Hey onto rounding up Hartley to drag him along. He'll get all of them out smashing, so there's not one that'll be able to speak against another, without having his own name turned in. But where should they strike? Should they all go together and hit Bradley's Mill, one of the biggest manufactories, run by the Atkinson brothers? Or should they split into gangs and attack the smaller shops? They have the advantage - just - of surprise. He's willing to bet Thomas and Law Atkinson aren't really expecting an army of Ludds to storm their mill yard, but on the other hand, the Atkinsons are rich men - worse still, they're dedicated militia men. They have weapons and they have guards. The big mills will be difficult to get into in the first place, never mind getting the frames broken. The cottage shops are an easier target - they can take out maybe a hundred frames within a month, without being at serious risk themselves, but will that have any real, lasting impact?

For the whole way home, Mellor is chewing this over, even when Thorp and Walker strike up a low-key conversation, picking their way though blackness without even a japanned lantern to light the way. Nearer town, the cobbles underfoot guide them to safety and light flickers from pub windows. They're strolling past The George, Huddersfield's fanciest pub, which presumably puts Walker in mind of an ale, because he asks them both if they fancy The Brown Cow for a few. Thorp agrees readily enough, his stomach rumbling audibly, and Mellor shrugs. He supposes he should get a bite to eat - truth be told, he feels dizzy from not having eaten.

He follows them from the dark market square that smells of ammonia and rot, into the brightly lit pub in the corner. This place is small - not like the huge pubs on the other sides of the square. The George Inn and The Queen's Head have yards alone that are twice the size of The Brown Cow, but Mellor likes the smaller pub, and as soon as he's in through the door, he spots his workmate, Tom Smith, over with the barmaid he's been seeing. The kid's never out of here these days. At the bar, they get their ale and Walker's off, chatting to some other mates, leaving Thorp and Mellor to fill Smith in on what's happened.

'Did thi get 'em, then?' Tom asks, supping his ale and glancing over Thorp's shoulder at Nan. His girl is scraping old porridge on the bottom of a pan, mixing in some milk and a bit of left-over bacon as a supper for Mellor and Thorp. Walker has already declined - he'll take his sustenance from the rich, malted beer.

'Aye,' Thorp answers, draining his mug and putting it back on the bar to be refilled.

'I'm fain, I am that,' grins Tom.

'Say no more,' Mellor murmurs.

Tom nods and the three of them stand quietly for a moment, but three croppers standing quietly is suspicious in itself, and so Thorp gives himself over to a loud and rowdy examination of Smith's courting of Nan while Mellor sinks in grateful repose against the bar. Nan, rolling her eyes at Thorp, puts the pan on the wooden bar-top next to Mellor.

'Eat up,' she says, giving him a spoon. 'Tha looks fit to drop.'

'I've 'ad a busy night,' says Mellor, with a wink, and Nan blushes uncertainly at this unclear intimation and goes off to serve more pints. Tommy Ludlam, the pub landlord, is a reasonable man and knows the value of a barmaid who'll chat to the customers, but she can't be idle, or he'd send her packing. Mellor swallows a mouthful of the porridge, then another and another, and the life spills back into him. Thorp takes the spoon off him and ladles some into his own mouth.

'By 'eck, Smith, tha'd do well to hang on to her, she makes a lovely supper!' he says, shovelling in more as he speaks and chewing around his words. He puts the spoon back in Mellor's hand. 'You finish all that, I'm fair full.'

'I thought the way thi stomach were carrying on, thi'd crammed a lowing cow in there already.'

'I wish to God I'd a cow to put in me stomach, George. This'll not see proper meat till Sunday!' Thorp slaps his flat, hard belly twice, and then belches.

'See, it's trying to get out,' laughs Mellor.

'Eat up, afore tha wastes away,' Thorp says, turning his attentions back to Tom, who is alternating between joining in the banter and making eyes at Nan.

'Another beer,' Mellor calls, lifting his mug above his bowed and tired head. The heavy clout of iron hitting iron on a cold, lonely moor is suddenly very far away. Mellor drinks three more pints of thickly silted ale, and starts to feel that he will sleep tonight, after all.

2
The Fair and Free Creation of Heaven

Tom Smith is behind him, next to William Thorp on the platform. Tom, whose gentle snores Mellor fell asleep listening to, night after night in the room they shared with William Hall, and who rose from the single cot each morning looking over to Mellor and Hall in the double bed with the kind of sleepy smile that made you wonder what he'd been up to in his dreams. Who would have expected tentative young Tom to be up here, facing such an end? Not Nan, who for all Mellor knows might be out there in the crowd, crying and watching as her lover gazes mystified at the irons that bind him. There was hope for mercy for a time - hope that Tom's more limited part in events would be held in his favour. Ben O'Bucks did at least, in his given evidence, try to save Tom. Perhaps even now, some gangling, ridiculous clerk is running through the corridors, waving a signed paper, pushing past the guards, to emerge at any moment with a breathless reprieve. What foul haste the magistrates have shown, to step from verdict to sentence within two days. Mellor and his friends are charged with further crimes but they will be dead before those cases are even tried. Will they be convicted posthumously of those deeds, even as a college surgeon is sawing apart their unwilling bodies? Deep within the castle walls, so many friends languish, awaiting the trials and sentences of this Special Commission, and Mellor will never on this earth know who lived and who died and who was shipped to the vicious labour camps of Australia.

'Save Tom Smith too,' he whispers, from his kneeling position on the drop, 'who never once hurt a person and only by his sworn oath has come to this. Please God, forgive our sins and let us meet again in heaven, all of us.'

The Ordinary shakes his head. He bites at his bottom lip and fixes his attention on the blackbirds and starlings that decorate the crenellations, drawn by the spectacle and the attendant promise of crumbs. Not for the first time, he is experiencing grave discomfort with regard to the Bill under which men are now being hanged. He has no doubt that Mellor shot that poor man, and should face the rope, but the other lad? The one who everyone agrees never fired a shot? One hang, all hang - the judges made that quite clear. Tom Smith will hang simply for being there, for being present, when other, more hardened men did the deed.

In the coming weeks, as the Ordinary is all too aware, he will stand on this same platform with men who have never, to the court's knowledge, injured a soul. Those men will hang for breaking window frames, for beating machines with hammers. He's not a stupid man; he reads the papers and he understands the terror and disorder these Luddites have caused. But he also sees the paupers on the streets, the miniature shrouded bodies passing under lych gates and the widows begging in the gutters, and he reads about parliament's useless response to the starvation all around - heavily pregnant women being shot dead by the militia when they clamour for potatoes at affordable prices, for heaven's sake! He possesses, though it would be a terrible and dangerous thing to show it, some sympathy for these reserved and mannered men beside him and has come to believe, in his brief time spent around them, that they are not violent in nature, that they do not share the petty-minded aspirations of the common criminal. Yet, the law is the law - and Thou Shalt not Kill is God's law. They have been warned over and over - even the editor of the paper most friendly towards the Luddites pleaded, months ago, for them to cease their activities. The Ordinary recalls the eminently sensible advice - that they were waging an unequal war with the military power of the country and should stop before it was too late. Well, too late it now is. The Ordinary can do nothing. It isn't his fault. And a man did die - most horribly according to the papers. The pounding of his heart slows, reassured by his mental rationalisations.

'For Christ did forgive all, ' Mellor says. 'He forgave thieves and liars, cheats and idolators, fornicators and adulterers. He even forgave his murderers. And Luke says forgive, and ye shall be forgiven, so I forgive fully any that have wronged me. And now, as thee promised, forgive me, Father, for all me weakness, and me mistakes, for the hurt I've caused and those I've left behind. Make mi sins as white as snow, though they be red as crimson, they shall be like wool.'

It is a favourite of Mellor's, this verse that exhorts the reader to plead for the widow, to relieve the oppressed, that casts fury on the princes who revel in the company of thieves, seeking self-reward with not a care for the destitute. When Isaiah, in his first chapter, talks of the rebellious and the murderous, it is the corrupted, frivolous rich that he surely means. When he exhorts willing obedience, he means to the principles of Godliness, not to the laws of a sinful nation. Under lowered lashes, Mellor looks out upon the people. They are waiting, straining, lips slightly parted, heads cocked. Except for one figure.

She stands far to the left, two-score deep in the crush, but, unlike the rest, she isn't looking at him. She's watching the sky, head tipped upwards, hands down by her sides and the enormity of what he has done comes rushing in once more, crashing against his now inconsequential body. The hand raking hair, the brusque cleansing rub of spit and finger, a voice in the depths of night when he was young and afraid, arms wrapped around him to keep his tiny limbs warm. He looks for his mam, but there is no sign of her - no lowered, familiar bonnet - just his sister Betty, alone and erect; taller, in her desperate desire to fly up and away, than any of the bowed and shaken spectators around her. Will she watch when he hangs or will she keep gazing heavenward? He can picture her, standing there alone, when everyone else has filed away and only the creak of the gallows breaks the silence, and no one is left to take her safely home.

Oatcakes hang flaccid over the flake, still warm from the rising heat of the hearth. Mellor takes one down, being careful not to disrupt the rest. The soft circles of griddled doughy mixture drape in rows on the strings of the bread flake up between the ceiling beams, but the wooden frame that holds the now sagging lines is blackened with grime and claggy crumbs of old oatcakes. He'll lift it down for his mother later so she can clean it and tighten the strings. In the corner, Wood is sat with a drink, chewing on his own piece of oatcake and looking through an old newspaper. Mellor's mother, Mary, is cleaning the pan in a bowl of water, scrubbing hard and pausing every now and then to stretch out her aching arm. She wears her long gown tucked up in front, the petticoat underneath acting as an apron to catch all the drips and splashes from her work.

'There's butter in t'bowl,' she says over her shoulder and Mellor looks and finds the thick yellowish lump under a square of flannel.

'Leave some for t'others,' Wood jokes, but Mellor, who has a mouthful of oatcake and rich, thick butter, doesn't bother to answer. It isn't likely he'd ever take food out of the mouths of his siblings. Of the nine children Mary has borne, only four are still living in the house. William has gone to an apprenticeship and Mary-Ann to live-in as a maid-servant. Elizabeth at fourteen will likely be next to leave to find work and Daniel at twelve has a few years under Wood's roof yet. Betty - his full sister - is at twenty-five years old still toiling for their mother. The rest are dead - three girls, all gone. Watching the others, born, raised, some dead, some grown, all within the frame of his own lifetime, gives Mellor a lonely, aerial feeling of separateness.

When Betty has gone, as surely one day she must be, this sense of isolation will increase. She, like him, remembers a time before their mother was married to Wood. He cannot clearly remember his real father, but the fact that Betty can is reassurance enough. She makes their dad real, bringing him into blurry focus along with the laughter, the high bounces into the air, a particular scent of sweat and leather. His mother, in these instinctive primal impressions, is a smiling, warm figure but Betty is closer. He stands alongside her, both of them tiny, both looking out on the scene from the same childhood plateau. She anchors him to older, safer times, while his mother sails in the present, shifting only forwards in the tides of her expanded family's life. He doesn't want Betty to leave, but she's getting old now, passing the age when she should be marrying, having her own babies.

'You out tonight?' asks his step-father, from behind the paper. Mary's head jerks up and she looks first at Wood and then at her eldest son. Elizabeth dances into the kitchen and snatches herself an oatcake.

'Aye.'

'Back late?'

'Aye.'

'Look after thi sen.'

'I will,' Mellor replies to Wood, and he gives his mother a sideways grin from which she takes no comfort. She goes back to scrubbing the pan with a frenetic action that shakes her shoulders. Elizabeth flounces onto a stool and pulls it up alongside her older half-brother.

'Are thi going out wi' a girl, George?' she asks slyly, chewing on her breakfast, and he fetches her a light shove to the shoulder.

'On wi' thi,' he answers, winking and pushing himself up from his chair. He shoves the last of his oatcake into his mouth and starts rolling his sleeves up, tight over his biceps.

'Si thi in t'shop,' he says to Wood, leaving the small kitchen and crossing the tiny stone yard. The terraced houses stand in a U-shape around the yard and, completing the square, Wood's cropping shop stands parallel to the River Colne, with a good view of the bridge that spans it. Mellor swings open the door of the shop and steps inside, tightening the strings of his apron. Tom Smith is over in the left-hand corner, checking the state of the teasels in the handles for use that morning, and Hall is already lining up a piece on the nelly. Both men ate earlier than Mellor - Mary would have fed them either oatmeal porridge or oatcakes, while George was still abed. As the boss's step-son and shop manager, he has some privileges, but he's still only ten minutes behind them.

'No Ben O' Bucks?' Mellor asks, crossing the shop floor to where the cropping boards stand, in front of a glorious stream of harsh morning sunlight.

Tom leans over the table full of teazels and cards and peers out of the window.

'That's 'im, coming now.'

Sure enough, several minutes later, Ben Walker comes through the door.

'Yer beat me again,' he says to Mellor. 'It's mi mam. She won't let me go till she's sure I'll none be clammed during 't day.' He rubs his full stomach in a show of discomfort.

'Never mind, Ben. I'm only just in.'

'Be glad thi mam's got so much food to give thi,' Hall comments.

Mellor watches Ben set straight to work. One of the apprentice lads is in the room to the right, cleaning flock off handles from yesterday and the other is out filling a watering can for the piece they've to leck. Everything is in order. Mellor can relax as he unfurls the cloth that's waiting for him on the cropping bench.

Hall has helpfully taken this off the nelly - the wall-mounted frame with rollers at the top and bottom, to which you fix a piece of cloth in order to wind the fabric from one roller to the other, raising the nap with the teasel handles as you go. The raising of this piece is done. Now Mellor must work his magic.

He runs his hand over the nap. It's a bit flattened from being left overnight, but it'll do for a first shearing. This piece will take a second go - maybe even a third. He spreads it over the bench, attaching it to the hooks and letting the length cuttle on the floor. It lies heaped, in folds, ready to be drawn up at intervals. With the cloth in place, Mellor walks around the cropping benches and takes his shears down from the wall. He checks the blades, turning the four-foot, sixty pound contraption in his hands.

From behind him comes the raking, brushing sound of teazels over cloth, as Hall starts raising the nap on another piece. Mellor casts a glance over the new piece on the nelly. It's a cheap one, they could have got away with just using the cards - curved square pieces of wood with nailed cards attached. The best way is undoubtedly with a handle - a device holding about twenty teazels; those teazels with their little hooks will draw up a nap to perfection. But handles cost more than cards, and they're harder to clean, hence the use of cards on cheap cloth. Still, they're in front with the work and Hall may as well do a good job if he wants. And the card stocks are low anyway. Mellor needs to order new ones in from Brighouse.

The back door grates open and Wood steps in, with a throat-clearing cough.

'Morning John,' the men call out and Wood calls a

convivial good morning back to them.

'What's t' lad doing out getting that watter?' Wood asks Mellor, as one of the apprentice boys returns with the watering can. 'I sh'll tan that Daniel if he doesn't get out an' help when he should.'

It must have been a rhetorical question, because Wood doesn't wait for an answer from Mellor. He merely goes back to the doorway, sticks his head out and yells loud enough to wake any neighbours still fortunate enough to be in bed, 'Dan, get thi fat, lazy sen out'a that bed an' into this shop!'

Mellor settles his shears onto the cloth and tests the feel. He adds a couple of lead weights to the resting blade, so it pushes down into the pile, then with his left hand he takes a firm grip of the nog on the raised blade and begins to cut, drawing the top blade down to meet the other and shaving off the raised nap in a soft, fine smattering of fibres. He moves the resting blade along the piece with his right hand, the hoof on his wrist pressed up against the shaped wooden handle on the bow of the shears.

Over and again he draws the nog down, pushes forward, draws down, pushes forward. The cut nap drifts in wisps over the sheared cloth. When Mellor reaches the end of the section, he places the shears on the free end of the bench, unhooks the fabric and draws it up and over. The sheared end hangs down the other side of the bench, falling in cuttle on the floor, and Mellor hooks the new section in place before commencing with the shears again. He has unhooked and re-hooked the cloth twice more before Daniel enters, a truculent smirk on his face and his sleeves rolled up ready. Wood gives him an appraising glance and sends the boy in to sweep the flock from the floor in the other room.

'Leck that piece afore tha cuts a second time,' says Wood, looking over at Mellor's bench.

'I were thinking that.'

'Well be sure tha does it, lad. Now Daniel,' he says, slipping through the back, 'I want thi to run a message up to one o' the jaggers for me.'

The last Mellor heard, Wood was thinking about apprenticing Daniel with a dyer over at the corn market. Dan had been angry at first - he wanted to be a cropper like his big brother and his dad - but Wood talked him round. There's money in dyeing, Mellor had heard Wood say, and none of us know whether there'll still be money in cropping in ten years time.

Mellor himself has no doubt that there'll still be money in cropping. How can it be otherwise? These cropping frames of iron that the Taylors are building don't give a finish as good as a flesh-and-blood cropper can. He's broken enough of the cumbersome creations by now to know about how they work - pairs of shears mounted on an iron shell, drawn along by cords and cranks, rollers and pulleys, the jerky motion of the shears, opening and closing, the tumbling rollers pulling the cloth along the bench. The machine proceeds uniformly, blindly uncaring and indifferent, with the inflexibility of iron and wood. It breaks with the same disinterest, splintering under hammers and axes, the iron-work ringing hollow and soulless under the blows. A thing such as that can't take the place of men, but he understands the old man's fear for his youngest son. It's too late for Mellor; the hoof is there, the apprenticeship passed.

44

Just after midday, Mellor is sat on the riverbank, eating a hard crust with some cheese and one of the last apples from the winter store, when Joseph Kenworthy plonks himself down beside him.

'Kenny,' says Mellor, 'How are thi?'

'Grand,' says the wool card merchant, tugging his long woollen coat under his bottom to stop the damp soaking into his breeches.

'I were just thinking earlier, about how we need some new cards.'

'Aye, yer felly inside said as much. I'll 'ave 'em for thi, soon as. He alright, thi man in there?'

'Who, Ben? Aye, he's sound.'

'Twissed?'

'Aye.'

Kenworthy nods in approval. Men who aren't twisted in are a danger to him. With all the shops he visits, it would be easy to slip a word to the wrong person, forgetting they weren't sympathetic.

'Well lad, it's definitely on for tonight. Midnight at Rashcliffe, just like y'asked for.'

'Well done, do yer think they'll all turn out?' Mellor takes the final bite of his apple and hurls the core across the river to the opposite bank.

'Aye, everyone's straining at the bit. Expect abaht thirty - fifty if tha's lucky. Anything more tha needs?'

'Nay, I think it's all in hand. Yer got the guns over to Lockwood, din't yer?'

'I did, that! And no one's short of a ball or two.' He guffaws at the double meaning. 'Reit, well I'd best be off. Ave a care won't thee?'

'Allus do, Kenny.'

The wool card merchant pushes himself up from

the grassy riverbank and smooths down his greatcoat. Mellor watches him disappear through the gap between the Wood house and shop, crossing through the small yard and out towards the road and bridge. As he slips out of view, Elizabeth sidles out onto the banking.

'How's my best girl?' he asks her.

'Tired,' she yawns, taking the place that the travelling merchant has vacated and leaning into the hard wall of his upper arm. He's sat with his knees drawn up in front of him, arms wrapped round them. 'What did Mr Kenworthy want?'

'I'd t'order new cards.'

'He settled that wi' Ben,' Elizabeth says, quick as a flash.

'Aye, well everything in t'shop comes through me an' all, Lizzie.'

'Nay, that weren't about cards.'

'Oh aye? An' how would you know?'

She shrugs, then says 'Where are thi going tonight?'

'Nowhere you've to worry about,' he answers. He lets her stay there a moment longer then he drops a kiss into her hair and nudges her off him, his break over. She watches his broad body filling for a second the gap that leads into the yard. The low winter sun throws his shadow onto the cornerstones of the house, slipping away after him into the shop.

Whatever his mother had suspected before, she knew for sure after Hartshead.

'It were you, weren't it?' She'd said, well into the next day, when news had spread about the breaking on the moor, and he'd known better than to lie to her. He

46

had answered sincerely, 'Aye, it were me, mam,' and she'd fetched him a hard clout to the side of the head. Mary was only a small woman - she'd had to reach up to do it - but she left a bruise around his ear.

'Yer'll get yer sen into York, lad. Is that what tha wants? Leaving us wi' a man down, and t'kids wi'out their brother?'

Daniel had come in full of curiosity when he heard the fuss, so Mary had kept any further commentary to herself but he'd heard her laying into Wood later.

'How can thi let 'im do it?' she'd shouted, 'He's mi first born son.'

'He's a grown man, he'll do what he thinks is reit.'

' Aw, I'm having none o' that John! He's like thee, all ovver again, getting worked up about what he cannot change. Yer need to talk 'im out of it.'

'I'll none do it, Mary. The lad's a cropper an' the croppers are all in it. Yer can't stop 'im. He's twissed.'

'He's taken an oath? My lad's taken an oath wi' them rascals?'

'He's not just taken an oath, lass, he's given it to t'others. He's in it up to his neck.'

'Oh George, what has tha done!' she'd wailed, and pausing on the stairs, Mellor had fingered the raised lump behind his ear and experienced an unfamiliar, unwelcome slice of guilt.

So it's no surprise tonight, barely a fortnight since Hartshead, when he pulls on his hat and his greatcoat at gone eleven o'clock, that his mother blocks his way with her hard, rabbit-round eyes. He waits for the blast of her anger, for a bitter remonstration held in low tones so as not to wake the children upstairs. He is not prepared for the hand that touches his cheek, nor for

47

the slight nod she gives as she steps from his path

'Night, George,' she says, turning her back on him and picking up the firepote to give the embers a stir.

'Night mam,' he says, and he feels a part of himself break away, settle down there in that cosy, poky little kitchen. Stepping into the cold night with a pistol strapped to his waist and a scythe-bladed sword concealed under his coat, his shadow remains in the warmth, feeling the last burst of flame from shrunken nuggets of coal and wood.

When he catches up with Hall and Thorp, and they march up the streets to the meeting place, hearts full of anger and determination, that imaginary part of himself rests back in the wooden spindle chair under the flake and the beams, with nothing more to think about than whether the little ones are sleeping soundly, and how many shearings that fresh piece is going to take tomorrow. By the time the gang is all together, the sensation has faded, and he's truly there, out in the blackness and the cold with the starry sky above, ready to inflict Luddite justice. But the one thing he can't get over is how she touched him - right on his cheek! No one touches like that, not in these parts. Kisses and cuddles, anything approaching affection, draws mockery. He's pushed to remember when his mother last touched him. It must have been when he was a small child, he thinks, and then he realises what it means to her that he's out here, and how it must hurt, and how hard she fought herself to move out of his way. He has a silent prayer to his mother on his lips as he arrives. The press of her fingers is on his face still, and he knows not the route he took to get here, nor how his feet found their way while his mind was so entirely elsewhere. He enters the field and surveys the forty or more men standing around in the darkness, spectral and still in the faint starlight. They cluster as they see him arrive, coalescing in the centre of the rough grass so that he can speak to them without shouting too loud.

'Evening lads.'

'Where are we tonight?' calls a voice - Mark Hill, maybe, but it's hard to tell with everyone's faces blackened, or dark cloth covering their mouths and noses.

'Hirst's,' he says, without hesitation and there is a mild groan of frustration that masks general relief. They want to make that great bid for glory but they know that Bradley Mill is just too much for them - there's not enough men and they've only ten or eleven pistols between the whole lot of them. Joseph Hirst is a far more modest target. He runs a shop at Marsh, and Wood's told Mellor they've at least a handful of frames up there - and Hirst is set on getting more. Not after tonight, Mellor's willing to bet. It was Wood who suggested Balderstones, too. How his mother ever thought she could get John Wood to turn her son back from Ludding is a mystery to George Mellor. Wood's in this up to his eyes, can she not see?. This is his bloody field they're meeting in, for crying out loud! The only difference is, Wood keeps his face clean. No blacking up and breaking for him - just a gentle bit of organising on the side. Mellor's friends and workmates think he is lucky. He landed on his feet, they say, when Wood married his mother all those years back. To get the big man of Longroyd Bridge for a step-father- and look at him now, twenty two and running the shop. Oh aye, Mellor knows he's got a lot of things to thank Wood for, but he can't help feeling sometimes, that being fatherly is not one of them. Wood is his mentor, his employer, his master, but would Mellor's real father have lined him up for this? And if the Luddite cause was a worthy one, then why has Wood sent his natural-born eldest son away? William Wood will be nineteen now - the perfect age to wield old Enoch - but he's out of the action, in a different trade altogether, safe, distant, law-abiding. Never mind, Mellor thinks, I had a father but he's dead now, and this is the life I have.

He assembles the men into their three companies and is about ready to lead them out of the dark field, when his attention is abruptly caught by a disfigured face so awful that his head snaps back sharply to stare. The ghoul laughs at him, and raises the flap of his red and white spotted face.

'It's calf-skin,' comes the unmistakeable buttermilk-rich voice of John Walker. 'Made mi sen a mask to wear. Does tha like it? Appen I can fashion one for thee.'

'I'd skaddle mi sen,' says Mellor, shaking his head and showing barley-white teeth in his blackened face as he grins. He fastens a large kerchief over his nose and mouth. It's his mother's, an old one, the type she'd wear around her neck, but it's badly frayed and won't be missed. 'Company one,' he calls, and leads the men out towards Marsh.

Trust Walker to come up with that horror. When Mellor looks back on this evening, he'll find his memory is punctuated by flashes of that stained, distorted calf skin. On the way to Marsh, they pass a drunkard who stumbles out of their path and waves his cap in their honour, but Mellor catches the moment his flaccid face tightens and his eyes grow large. The drunkard, who sobered up quickly at the sight of Walker's mask, is the only witness to that march - at least, the only witness any of them see. In the houses they pass, men whistle loudly and women strike up needless conversations, blotting out the traipsing thump beyond their walls where dangers march abroad and the greatest risk to their own selves is to bear witness.

Despite the lateness of the hour when they draw up outside Hirst's, a worried face presses up to the dirty window pane and stares out, the light behind him illuminating his hair into a fuzzy mess. At the sight of Mellor striding to the door he makes a belated attempt to bar the way.

'Come on now, no sense in making this hard,' says Mellor, forcing the door ajar, with half of his first company tightly packed in behind him. 'Tha's not going to get hurt. It's just t' frames we're after.'

'Nay, there's no frames here,' insists the miserable man inside, and Mellor sees two lads beyond him, cowering at the back.

'No frames? Oh well, then tha won't mind me coming in and looking,' says Mellor and he pulls out his pistol, lines it up through the crack and points it at the man. After that it's easy to heave the door fully open, allowing six men behind him to burst through. The first wave takes care of the man and the two apprentices - no need for rope tonight, they just pin the first man to the floor and make the two apprentices lie down beside him, then they keep loaded and primed pistols pointed at them. In comes company two, obediently equipped with hammers and axes. They swarm over the shop, and out into the back and within minutes, they've found seven frames.

'Oh dear,' says Mellor, bending down to the man on the floor. His sword scabbard scrapes a line in the fine, woollen dust. 'Thi must have forgot abaht this new machinery. Well, no harm done. We'll take care of it.'

The smashing sounds are already rattling through the premises, and the boys on the floor are covering their ears and shaking. Mellor glances round at the activity, catching sight of Walker again, a demon - red, white, deformed; hammering bloody hell fire out of one of the frames, the blows chiming the seconds. They've to be in and out of places like this, because you never know whether some rascal will take fright and send down to the magistrate. He's not so bothered about Scott out at Woodsome, who'd not likely stir from his bed till morning, but Radcliffe down at Milnsbridge is always looking for a fight. That old rotter would be on his horse and up here as fast as his fat little legs could carry him. There's barking outside from an angry dog, then the harsh retort of a couple of shots being fired. He sees a frame buckle under Tom's hatchet and the man on the floor tenses, tries to raise up.

'Stop that bloody shooting!' Mellor yells through the open door, then, laying a firm hand on the man's shoulder, he says 'Nay, you just stay there. Na then, tell Hirst not to go replacing these frames, or we'll be back here again, an' 'appen we'll forget our manners that time. How are we, number five?'

'Abaht done, General,' gasps Jonathan Dean in the

corner, pounding for all he is worth against a set of shears that lays pinned to a broken frame. He gives them a few more blows for good measure, twisting them into scrap, then whistles and waves at the men around him to fall back.

'Yer an army man?' asks the man on the floor, gazing at the whites of Mellor's eyes. Mellor laughs, the sound muffled in his handkerchief.

'Aye, an' this is mi army,' he replies. 'Now stay down till we're gone.'

Mellor straightens up and surveys the mess in the shop. A bar of iron rocks unsteadily where it has fallen and shards of debris are clumsily kicked by the last men out, sent skittering on the dusty floor to fall, severed and silent. He walks to the door, his head ringing in the sudden quiet. Outside, some of the men who haven't had the chance to come inside the shop are converging on the building, their hands full.

'Now for t'windows!' yells one, and a couple of heavy stones come flying through the dark, shattering glass and clipping the window-frames. Mellor notices the body of a dog, laid up in the shadow of the wall.

'Halt,' he shouts, 'Companies assemble! This place is done, leave it alone.'

They obey immediately, and Mellor gets out in front of them.

'Company, march,' he yells and, stashing his unused pistol back into his waistband, he leads them off. They'll go down through Longroyd Bridge and up towards Crosland Moor, where he hopes to find frames at James Balderstone's place. The three companies have fallen in behind him and he has, as usual, William Thorp alongside, leading the first

53

company. Thorp is whistling a little tune.

'Did thi see Smith wi' that hatchet?' He says, interrupting his own little melody. 'He wor fair goin' at it.'

'Good for 'im.'

'Seven frames, that's a good crop, George.' He takes up his tune again and Mellor fingers the barrel of the pistol inside his coat. He wonders if Hirst will dare to replace them. He wonders, with some irritation, who shot the dog.

No one is up when they get to Balderstone's. The house is in darkness. They mass in the yard. Mellor puts Schofield out front to keep watch on the road and then he goes to the door, banging hard, over and over, but no one stirs. They'll be hiding upstairs, he thinks. He beckons some of the men forward and lets them take care of the door. They give it a solid pounding with their hammers, and part of the wood splinters before it swings inwards, screeching on the hinge. Inside the blackness of the shop, Mellor looks about at the equipment. Footsteps come at last on the stairs. James Balderstone stands wide-eyed in a crumpled night shirt, his wife just behind with a pale hand on his shoulder.

'Down you come,' says a Luddite called Lodge, who has spotted them first. He takes Balderstone by the arm and pulls him down the wooden steps. John Walker goes for the wife, but she screams and plants her hands across her mouth in fright.

Walker laughs. He shakes his masked head, the calf-skin flapping grotesquely, and waves to Ben O' Bucks to fetch the woman down. Ben goes and gets her. She's backing away but he takes a firm hold of her nightdress at the waist and forces her down the steps.

'We're not goin' to hurt yer,' he says, though his voice is trembling with excitement. 'Just keep tha mouth shut.' He pushes her alongside her husband then pulls out the pistol he is carrying and points it at her. Lodge has a pistol pointed at Balderstone, who stands silent and sullen, his arms folded.

'Where's thi frames, Balderstone?' Mellor asks, while Dean overturns benches at the back of the shop and Thorp pulls pairs of shears down from their hooks on the far wall.

'Tell thi men to stop it,' the shop owner retorts. 'I've got none.'

'That's not the tale I've heard,' says Mellor. 'Now where are they?'

'Oh blummin' ummer,' says the wife, who has gathered her wits and vaguely intuits that the crazy, shaking man who is aiming his gun at her is taking orders from the calmer one doing the talking. 'There's only one. It's out back.'

Jonny Dean has heard and he heads immediately into the unassuming little room, twirling his hatchet in his fist.

Balderstone shakes his head.

'I should fetch thee a crack for that,' he says to his wife.

'Would yer rather 'ave a bullet, yer stupid sod?' she asks.

Mellor leaves them and joins Dean, who is braying merry hell out of the lonely frame that sits in the middle of the back room. It's already twisted, snapping apart, but Mellor has the sense that the thing has, likely as not, never been used. He looks about him.

There's a nelly on the wall, a bench to one side, couple of baskets and buckets. No more frames. He feels angry - unaccountably angry. Surely he should have felt this anger at Hirst's shop, where all those frames were lined up and putting out cloth already. It's a subverted battle fury he feels - like a soldier who has walked into an enemy den with his gun cocked and his blood up only to find the place abandoned. He goes back into the main room.

'Get them shears broke,' he orders the men who are standing about.

'What for? I've just the one frame, and thi big bloody felly's seeing to that. Leave mi shears alone!'

'Nay, I cannot,' says Mellor. 'Tha's done a stupid thing getting thi sen a frame. I've to make sure thi won't make that mistake again. An' if tha's any on order, I suggest yer cancel that order, first thing tomorrow.'

Balderstone grows redder in the face, but he keeps quiet. Mellor can't be certain there were more frames on the way, but he thinks maybe he's right. Otherwise, why would his step-father have heard that Balderstone's was a good place to hit? Still, it troubles him, that one, lonely frame.

When the eight pairs of shears are ruined, Mellor pulls out his men.

'Good night,' he says to the bewildered couple as he leaves and Mrs Balderstone finds herself nodding him a good evening in return before she catches herself.

'Go on all reit?' Wood asks, in the morning.

Mellor is slumped on a buffit, drinking a cup of buttermilk that his mother has saved for him. His eyes

56

are screwed up, his copper hair crazily ruffled, and there is a faint patch of black under his chin that he missed when he was cleaning himself up.

'Reit enough. But thi man, Balderstone, had nobbut one frame.'

'One? I heard he'd more, but tha nivver can tell.' Wood hooks his thumbs on the waistband of his breeches as Mary stirs whey into oats in her big cooking pot that hangs over the fire. 'Tha's late this mornin', lass,' he tells her.

'Aye. Fetch me that treacle pot,' she orders. She could tell them both that she had no sleep for worrying about George, but she'd not make her son feel bad, not the way he's looking this morning. He's had five or six hours sleep, but with it being a Sunday, at least he doesn't have to work. Wood passes her the treacle and sits himself down in the wooden chair.

'Hardly worth it,' says Mellor. 'Walking all't way up, and nobbut one frame.'

'Aye lad, thi said. Mebbe he had others on order.' Wood won't be drawn. Mellor glares at him for a moment, then gives it up. Wood is probably right, but it hasn't escaped Mellor's understanding that a few local cropping shops out of action puts Wood in a good position - fewer competitors means more work for him. Anyway, there was a frame, Mellor thinks, shaking such notions of duplicity from his mind; there was a frame and that makes Balderstone just as guilty as Cartwright, Atkinson or any of the rest; and the tip about Hirst was a fair one. It was a good crop, as Thorp had said.

Mary slops some porridge out into a bowl for Wood and dollops a lump of treacle on top. She gives Mellor the pan and takes the cup from him.

'Mind you eat a good amount o' that,' she instructs her son, listening to Elizabeth and Daniel moving around above. They'll be down in two minutes for their share, and George, she knows, would hand over more than he should to his ever-hungry siblings. A memory strikes her with sudden tearing viciousness - Franny with her little skirts clutched between plump hands, leaning forward for a mouthful of George's oatmeal. She blinks it away and taps the side of the pan to enforce her command.

'Aye mam, thanks,' Mellor says.

'An' no more of all that business,' she warns both men. Mellor nods. He has no wish for his brother and sisters to know any more than can be helped, not because he is ashamed - far from it - but because it's dangerous.

Betty, his big sister, comes in from the yard, hoisting a bucket of water which she dumps with a splash on the scrubbed stone floor. She wipes a damp hand over her forehead, slicking back a loose tendril of greasy hair. Her cheeks are deep red from the chill outside. She looks hard at George, then lifts her underskirt, licks a patch and scrubs with it, stiffly, under his chin. The black comes off on the linen, joining smears of mud from the yard and old cooking stains. Betty is a pretty woman, or should be. She carries, like their mother Mary, too much flesh under her chin and around her jaw, but her hair is rich in colour, like George's own, and she has wide-set eyes and a slim mouth with a firm bow to her upper lip. Betty is coarse though, and she doesn't hold with sentiment. Mellor suffers with good grace her rough attempt to clean him up.

'Watter's there mam, I'll be up an' see to them bedrooms,' Betty announces with a martyred air, before trudging up the stairs to deal with sheets or bedpans or whatever other myriad jobs await.

Mellor eats some more of the porridge, then sets the pan on the side for his siblings. He takes his coat from the hook and draws it on.

'Chapel,' Mary reminds him, unnecessarily, as he leaves.

'Aye mam,' he says, closing the door on her.
He meets Thorp on the bridge, the other man kicking affably at the stone wall and glancing up at the sky, watching for rain as he waits, having walked across the top of town from his home on Cropper's Row.

'What does tha think, Will? A good job overall?'

'It's allus a good job if there's a frame been broke.' Thorp, loyal as always.

'Ready for tonight?'

'Aye. I' sh'll remind the fellys at Chapel today. How's Smith?'

'Sleeping it off.' Mellor has left Tom Smith in the room they share with Hall, snoring deeply in the tiny bed in the corner.

'Why aren't we?' Thorp laughs. They amble over the bridge and down the dirt path to the canal side. The river and canal weave eastwards along the old royd towards Huddersfield. West of here, at Paddock Foot, an aqueduct elevates the canal above the River Colne's flow, the ribbons of water levelling up and running parallel, leaving a narrow band of land between them. Wood's shop sits on the far bank of the river; Fisher's, where Thorp works, is over by the canal. The path the two men take slips between the waterways and joins the towpath on the canal, the newly cleared surface already compacted from the constant tread of horses' hooves. Dark, still water sleeps in the cut, green at the edges where the mossy stone walls glimmer and sometimes sparkle. The river ebbs and flows gaily while the canal forms a narrow, black fissure, slicing west from Huddersfield all the way to the great tunnel at Marsden, where it drives directly into the hillside and eventually comes out in Lancashire. A lot of the cloth pieces that Mellor and Thorp finish are packed into barges and transported under the tail end of the Pennines to be sold at markets in the neighbouring county. The canal has been good for their business, in these hard times.

'I've summat to ask thi,' Mellor says, messing with the brim of his cap and keeping his eyes focused on the mirrored sheen of the cut.

'Na then, what's up?'

'I need to know what tha reckons, what tha thinks of how I'm doing wi' it.'

'Tha's doing grand, George. What's this? Losing faith?'

Mellor bites at his lip. The action pulls the normally square angles of his face into a hollow and worried expression. Thorp waits for his friend to answer. He knows George, even if George doesn't quite know himself at times. He's used to the dips in his energy, and the way that after a good night of drinking, breaking or fighting, Mellor will come over all despondent. His moods don't always fit right with the moment. Thorp himself is happy enough. As far as he is concerned, last night was one step on a long road and he has the patience and the reserves not to worry if a shop turns out to have only one frame - in fact, isn't it more of a success? Shouldn't they be more worried if they were unearthing scores of the damned things all over the place? And as for Mellor being the one to lead it, well Thorp's proud of that, and he doesn't see how his friend could be doing any better.

'They listen to me, the men? They do what I say?'

'O' course they do. Tha's seen it thi sen. Last night, didn't they all foller thi? Didn't they smash when thi said to smash and stop when thi said they'd to stop?'

'That's just for show,' Mellor says. 'I mean, deep down. Will they trust me?'

'I'd say so.'

'Aye, well tha would.'

'Oi, now, this in't abaht us being mates,' Thorp flashes, 'I'm not a gormless cretin, follerin' me friend and not asking why or what for. I sized you up, George, when first we ever played together, when tha were little more'n a kid, an' me an all. How can I put this so's tha'll understand? I'm not follering yer an' trusting yer because I'm yer friend. It's t'other way round - I'm thi friend because I trusted yer, an' I still do trust yer an' I think yer the one that's got his head on reit abaht all this.' Thorp gestures wildly at the canal, the trees, the hard hillside of Outcote, as if the troubles they face are sewn into the landscape of the town. Then, with Mellor still gazing at the cold water, Thorp punches his arm. Mellor poises him back, right in the soft part of Thorp's calf and they grapple for a moment on the towpath, laughing and swearing.

'You'll 'ave us both in, yer bloody idiot,' Mellor shouts, clouting Thorp in the temple.

'I'll 'ave *thee* in, if tha goes on any more.' Thorp settles his cap back on straight and throws a pretend blow back at Mellor. A couple walking on the opposite bank glance fearfully across at them and speed their progress away from the fighting men.

In chapel, they sit nursing bruises. Thorp, pressed up to his sister and her husband, balances his adoring niece, Annie, on one knee while Mary and Abraham Ashton pass the mewling baby back and forth between them. Thorp tries to stretch his aching legs in the cramped space between pews while Annie giggles and pokes his jaw, and occasionally aims a swat at baby sister, Maggie, being cajoled and diddled next to her.

Mellor, sitting on Thorp's other side and subject to some shy prods from Annie, has a headache from lack of sleep, but still they both concentrate on the words of the preacher at the front, and when it's time to sing, they join in with enthusiasm. Mellor would have come along without his mother's pointed reminder, for he does believe in a God and a heaven and it seems to Mellor that the Methodists have got most of it right, with their concern for the poor and the weak. What frustrates him is that most of them won't go far enough. The ministers admit that the poor are abused and they call on God to witness the sufferings of the congregation; that they bring some comfort to bear is without doubt, but then they'll extol the virtues of obedience, subservience and devotion. Just be good, and it will all come right, is about the best sense Mellor can make of the moderate message of the Wesleyans. The Kilhamites, to whose chapel he belongs, are better, but not by much.

His mother sits with Wood and the others - Betty, Daniel and Lizzie - on the pew in front. He wonders if she would come here, to the New Connexion Chapel on Buxton Road, if a Wesleyan one were closer to home - how committed is she to the heightened radicalism of the Kilhamites? Certainly, no matter how close she lived to the parish church, she would not go there. She's a non-conformist through and through, as is Wood. Methodism, not Anglicanism, is their religion of choice, just as it is for most of Huddersfield's belligerent population. But if, when the New Connexion was formed, the Wesleyans had taken control of this building, and sent the Kilhamites off to some place further on the top of town, or down at the bottom of town, would Mary have walked there for the more radical service, or would she have stuck with the Wesleyans? He knows where he would have gone, and John Wood too, most likely. The Kilhamites aren't called Tom Paine Methodists for nothing, although he knows it gets the preachers riled to hear their beliefs likened to those of a Jacobin revolutionary.

There's a lot of confusion, though, in the ranks of the preachers. One week he feels the preacher's eyes scouring the men of the congregation, and he hears words of warning and reprimand, and another week a different preacher will sound a note of encouragement, will hint at the complicity of King and Church in the miseries of the poor, will smile as he tells the tale of Christ breaking the tables in the temple. Then, Mellor feels he is being spoken to directly, by these sympathetic men of God, and he sings loudly, '...while nature shakes, And earth's strong pillars bend, the temple's veil in sunder breaks...!' and he thinks about

63

breaking frames while his voice rises in congregation.

At the end of the service, he slips out of the end of his pew eager to catch up with the men outside. They're huddled around, talking about the new Acts of Parliament that everyone believes will be passed very soon. Ben O' Bucks is quietly decrying the Bill, which will see men hanged for breaking frames.

'It's against t'bible,' he hisses, 'which says an eye for an eye. Hang a murderer, aye, but a frame's not flesh and blood.'

'What they mean by doing this,' says John Walker, in a tone more audible to the curious ears of families squeezing past, 'is to let us all know that they rate t'new machines higher than t'lives of ordinary men. They're saying men, and their families, can die of starvation, and that's all reit, but if them same men go out and smash up a frame that's put them out o' work, then they've committed worse than murder.'

Thorp walks past with a nod, shepherding little Annie round the men. Mary carries the baby while Abe stops at Mellor's side for a moment. Thorp's brother-in-law, Abe Ashton, is a cloth-dresser too, and a paid-up member of the Brief.

'How can it be so? How can parliament say that's reit?' O'Bucks is asking.

'Happen a Tom Painer'd say it's because even the dog of a rich man is considered to be worth more than a poor man. And by ummer, them frames cost more than any dog,' Mellor puts in.

'Thorp says it went well last night,' Abe murmurs privately to him as the others carry on with their indignation. 'I'll be out next time, it were just t'baby were playing up an-'

'It's fine, Abe,' Mellor assures him. He'd never hear the end of it from Thorp if he berated Abe for staying home to help Thorp's sister out. 'How's the little one today?'

'Gripe, Mary thinks. Or wind. Or are they t'same thing? I don't know,' Abe shrugs, bewildered. 'Maggie's harder than Annie ever were. Be easier out breaking frames than trying to get that one to sleep.' John Walker's wife pushes between them. She has been waiting for her husband to finish his conversation, a child weighing heavy in her own arms.

'I've got summat that might work for that. Morning George,' she says, angling Abe away and towards his family as Mellor gives her a smile. Mrs Walker joins Mrs Ashton to discuss the merits of various ointments and medications and Mellor waves goodbye to Thorp who is giving a delighted Annie a ride on his broad shoulders so that she towers at least seven feet in the air.

Mary Wood comes out of chapel and brushes past the group of men, a basket pulling heavy on her arm. Her shoulders tilt to the left, like an old woman gradually bending back to the dark earth, and she turns uphill towards town.

'Mam, where ye going?' Mellor calls after her.

'Bottom o' town,' she calls back. 'I'm taking this to Alice an t'kids.'

'I'll be off,' Mellor calls to all the men still gathered, 'Si thi soon.'

He runs to catch up with his mother, who can walk at a surprisingly swift pace, and as he comes alongside, he scoops the basket from her arm.

'Good lad,' she says, rubbing the inside of her

elbow. 'It were enough, lugging it over here, an' I'd to go past Engine too.'

'Wood din't fancy giving you a hand?'

'Be seen carrying me basket? They'd think he'd gone soft.' She laughs. 'Yer not bothered about that yer sen, George?'

'Nay mam, nowt wrong wi helping an owld lass out now an' again.'

'Give over, I'm still nobbut a young-un,' she retorts, smoothing the sleeves of her dress.

At the brow of Buxton Road, they turn right and saunter downhill along Back Green. The hedgerows are dusted with cobwebs, the dew still fresh upon them. The road goes down through Shorehead and they bear left towards Low Green at the bottom of town where Mary's friend, Alice, lives in two tiny rooms in part of a cluster of houses, facing inwards to a dirty stone yard. Mary leads the way though the little passage into the yard, where three children are playing with an emaciated cat.

'Thi mam inside?' Mary asks a small girl with dirt plastered in a smear up her left cheek and limbs not much thicker than those of her feline playmate.

'Aye, she's mekkin me a coit, Missis Wood.'

'Is she now? Well I'll step in an' 'ave a word.' She first dips her hand into the basket Mellor is carrying and pulls out some greyish oatcakes, cold and plain. 'Ave one o' these, but don't feed 'em to that cat!' The children hurry to her and grab an oatcake each and Mellor's stomach churns to see how they cram the food in. He imagines Sally or Franny, who would be about this age if they'd lived, dressed in rags like these children wear, messing about in a filthy yard covered in human mess, cold and starving - and on the heels of that awful alternate reality comes the nightmare vision of himself hanged for breaking frames, Wood put out of business by the machines, his mother, Betty, Lizzie and Daniel forced to beg, living off pennies from Mary Ann and William's meagre earnings and slowly starving to death. They are all just an inch away from it, no working man in this town is safe; their women and children are hanging by a thread.

'Alice,' Mary calls, stepping through the doorway into a darkish room almost as cold as the yard outside. Mellor follows her in, tapping his boots on the doorstep to shake off any muck. The floor is bare stone, and black with age and dirt. In front of him, a grimy wooden set of steps leads up through the ceiling hatch into the upstairs room. Over to the left, his mother's friend is hunched in one of two chairs, drawing a long needle through old broadcloth.

'Come an' sit thi down, Mary,' she says, glancing up from her stitching. 'Oh, an is this your lad? He's fair grown up since I last had sight of 'im. Sit thi sen on't table if thi like.'

'I'm fine just standing,' he says, taking in the rickety wooden structure, bereft of all but an empty bowl, a flat piece of wood and an old, blunt knife. His mother sits down in the spindle chair opposite Alice. They are either side of the blackened hearth, where some coal and a few pieces of wood are piled.

Alice draws another stitch through and then she stations the needle in the cloth and puts it down on her lap.

'So this is George,' she says again, and she stares straight at him, unafraid to meet his eyes.

'He manages the shop now, Alice.'

'Does he, Mary? Manages more than that, from what I hear. Now tell me - this to-do on Hartshead, were that you? You can tell me, I won't breathe a word.'

Mary gives an impatient snort and snatches the basket from her son.

'Ave brought this for yer, an' I sh'll thank thi for keeping thi nose out o' mi son's business.'

'Oh Mary, now don't be so touchy. All town knows it's 'im.'

'Then they've a sight more sense than to be kallin on it.'

George can't help a slight smile, but his mother catches his eye, and her frown reminds him that this isn't a safe conversation for any of them.

'That's not much of a woodpile,' he says, changing the subject.

'Aye, an' I daren't even light it til we're all half-frozen. It's to see us through the whole evening.'

'I'll find thi something more.' George nods at both women, leaving them to their conversation, and heads back out into the yard, where the children have made short work of their oatcakes and are now playing some kind of jumping game. He walks back out onto the street and sets off towards the old corn market. The children abandon their game, and hop along in his wake. He pretends not to notice them as he strides. At the top side of the corn market are a couple of large stables, and round the back is a little coppice wood, walled off from the old tenter fields alongside. He clambers over the low wall and scours the ground for a few old branches.

'Come here and mek thi selves useful,' he shouts to the children, who are sitting on the stone wall now, watching him. They look sullen and wary, but they come, pushing and shoving at each other. Mellor puts some damp branches into the girl's arms.

'These are all wet,' she complains.

'They'll dry off quick enough. It's just from being laid on't ground. They're not rotten inside, they'll be dry enough to burn.'

He finds a few more pieces and sends the little girl and her young brother home with it all. The third child, another girl, loiters about. He can tell she's not their sister - must be a neighbour - but he won't send her home with empty arms.

'Come on,' he says, taking her out of the woodland and down through the fold of one of the dressing shops. On his left is the snicket through to the Well, the complex of buildings owned by the Horsfall family - a big warehouse, dyehouse and several workshops stand on that site and Mellor avoids it. The girl scurries after him, past dye houses and more stabling into the open square. There's a big cloth warehouse on the corner, and round the back, half hidden under a pile of rubbish, he finds an old, broken down cart. It has loose, rotten boards on the back, and he kicks vigorously at the side, until two of the pieces come away.

'Oi! What's tha doing?' yells a man from the cottages over behind the pub. He starts to stride over, but his pace eases when he recognises Mellor and he shakes his head. 'Might a' knowed.'

'How are thi, Mr Dyson?'

'Not so bad. She's not yours, is she?'

'Nay,' laughs Mellor, 'I'm just seeing her reit for a bit o' firewood.'

'There's easier picking than that. Nip round t'back, they've left t'coal delivery out in t'yard.'

'More fool them,' says Mellor, 'Thanks, Mr Dyson.'

He keeps hold of the wood he has wrenched off the cart and takes the girl round the other side of The Mason's Arms, where, true enough, a pile of coal has been left, huddled in the corner and covered by sacking. He drops the wood, lifts the girl's outer skirt and tucks it up under her chin. Then he makes her take hold of the hem of her filthy petticoat underneath and he quickly fills the pouch with coal. With a bit of faffing, he gets her to keep hold of the petticoat bundle through the top layer of skirt, so that though it's clear she is carrying something, the coal is concealed.

'Go on now, go home, don't stop for anything.'

She nods, a bit frightened now, because this is stealing and she's old enough to know that she could get in serious trouble, but she clutches the bundle determinedly and hurries off. Mellor fills his breeches with coal and then hoists the pieces of wood onto his shoulder to walk the short distance to Alice's yard. He catches up with the little girl as he arrives - she is just smuggling her load into her own home. Alice's two children are back outside, playing their jumping game again.

Mellor takes his illegal load into Alice's house where she and Mary are still sat by the hearth, and they turn in silence as Mellor starts to extract the coal from his breeches. He's laid the big planks of wood on the floor, where the two children have already dumped the branches he gave them. After a few seconds of stillness, Alice jumps up and fetches an old, damaged water bucket. She frets around him, picking up every last piece of coal and cramming it first into the bucket, then directly onto the step by the hearth.

'What am I goin to do wi' them?' She asks, staring at the planks.

'Av thi an axe or summat?'

'Nay, I've just what thi can see.'

Mellor rubs his forehead, leaving a sticky black trail just over the top of his eyebrows. He picks up the wood, branches and all, and hoists it back out into the yard, knocking the walls and door frame as he goes. He'd felt good when he collected this wood, and even when he'd stolen the coal. Now, his mood has switched and he wishes himself up in town, swilling some ale with Thorp or back in his own home, cleaning up his boots or reading an old Mercury.

He props one of the planks against a front step so worn it looks like a slab of grey, melted butter. Then he brings his foot down on the raised plank with all his force and the board bends - but it only splinters just a bit, in the middle. He props it in a better way, and does the same again, and again, increasingly frustrated each time it bends but won't snap. It recoils and hits his ankle and he swears, starting to sweat under his greatcoat. The children stand on the far side of the little yard, watching him. When he rips his greatcoat off and throws it to the cobbles, the eldest girl who carried the coal in her petticoat, comes running forward and picks it up to hold it for him. Her mother hides behind another of the doorways that face into the yard, watching the tall, muscular stranger attacking the plank of wood. The wooden length finally breaks into two pieces, and those pieces are easier to smash now. He gets them into eight sections that will fit in the hearth and bundles them together under his arm, then he strides back into Alice's house, where she is sweeping coal dust off the floor with a sparse broom, and drops them on the stone. He goes back out and breaks the branches up - they break with ease, the insides dry as ancient bone. The girl and boy, Alice's children, run to gather the pieces and take them inside to their mother. The other girl hands him his coat back.

'Ave thi an axe, or summat to chop that up wi?' He asks her, pointing at the remaining plank.

'We'll have summat,' she nods.

'Then tek it over to thi door and give it thi mam. I'm done for today.'

'All reit, cheers mister,' she says, and wastes no time dragging the heavy plank over to where her mother has stepped cautiously outside.

Mellor breathes long and hard. He's out of breath, having exerted himself ridiculously over that bloody plank of wood. He draws on his coat, aware of the girl smiling at him from across the yard, her fear gone now that his ferocious vigour has dissipated and her own act of thieving the coal is safely removed to memory. She must be eleven or twelve. Her hair is a dirty, dark blonde under her cap, and her eyes are sloping, nose pointed and irregular. He imagines bursting back into Alice's house, taking all the wood and coal that he'd got for her and giving it to this nameless little girl who picked up his coat and spared him a smile.

'Mam, time to go,' he calls, not wanting to enter the grimy, dismal house again. The two kids come out onto the doorstep. The little boy has such wide, worried eyes that Mellor loses the bitter, black feeling that had gripped him.

'Tha sh'll have a warm fire tonight,' he assures them, as Mary comes out, Alice in her wake. Mary's basket is empty now, lightened of a load of oats, potatoes and root vegetables, along with some small pieces of good cloth that she was able to spare.

'Get that coit finished quick,' she warns Alice, looking down at the sallow, goose-bumped girl. 'This young-un looks cold 'an we've a way to go afore spring is properly here. Get that fire lit. Don't be stingy with it, while them children are freezing.'

Alice nods with a sigh.

'Thank you, Mary, but even that lot won't last for long. We'd be in us graves if it weren't for a bit of help. Thanks George. We'll si thi again, I hope.'

'Aye. Si thee, Alice.' Mellor sets off at a pace. Mary hurries after him, out of the yard and they fall into a more reasonable step as they skirt the back side of town.

'Well now, son, what were that foul temper about?'

'I don't know mam.'

'Yer threw muck all on her floor, and left a great big mark on t'wall. To say nowt o't tone o' thi! She thought she'd offended yer.'

'Appen she had.'

'How's that, then? I don't understand thi, George.'

'Oh mam, leave it will thi? All as I know is, I went an' carried back a load o' wood an' I stole a load o' coal and all as she can say is, "what'll I do wi this?" Oh, it made me fair mad.'

'Alice in't a lazy woman,' says Mary. 'I know thi

73

might think she can go an' get her own wood and coal, but it's not so easy, when you've to think about everything else an' all. How much wood can she carry? Go out and get a load today, an' it's gone by tomorrow, an' she's to mek coits for both bairns, and she's to find some food from God-knows-where, and she's to cook it on a fire that she's never enough coal for, and that's all afore she's even thought about how to bring some money in.'

Mellor has no answer to that. In fact, he's feeling a touch ashamed, because his mother is right - he had indeed been thinking that Alice was lazy. More than that, he had expected some gratitude from the woman - but how could she be grateful for a few days worth of coal and wood when years and years stretched before her of not having enough food and warmth to raise her children, of never having any peace nor any rest until the grave?

'Tha's to do what tha can. But you've not to ask for owt back, son,' his mother says. 'Look to the Lord if yer want yer soul warmed. Women like Alice have got nowt left to give.'

3
Army of Redressers

He never thought about that girl from the bottom of town again, until the next time he saw her - fox-like eyes aghast, mouth a black cavern as she watched him climb aboard the gaol coach. Her horrified countenance was the last clear image he registered of Huddersfield; Kirkgate's sloping carriageway and the Church of St Peter framing her with a timeless quality. Still so slight, wrapping her coat about her against the autumn chill, a smaller friend at her side wearing an ill-fitting and crazed coat of a hundred different weaves. Had she followed his fortunes and known when they took him up, then come for a glimpse? Or had she simply waited on the street like all the other passers-by, wondering which local men the gaol coach was taking? Without her name, will God know who she is now he prays for her?

He prays anyway, up on the drop, knees aching on the hard wooden boards; he prays that the girl who picked up his coat from the dirty flags will be warm and well-fed and will not sink, like so many from the crammed yards, into prostitution and starvation. He thanks God for John Wood, who will see that his own younger sisters and brothers are kept safe - Daniel, Elizabeth, Mary-Ann, William, he enunciates one by one. He asks God to watch over Betty. Mother, he thinks, you must protect Betty, but he does not voice this aloud. He cannot articulate the painful awareness that Betty has no masculine protector - that Wood is not necessarily to be relied upon by those not of his own blood - because this recognition would entail, by way of explanation, an accusation that Wood has failed him; that Wood has led him here and abandoned him. He cannot name this fear in his prayers - his oath forbids the identification of a brother Luddite, and the Chaplain beside him is all ears. And in any case, hasn't he, Mellor, failed others in the same way? Hasn't he led men to death and destruction by championing the cause and willing them along? Yet, he kneels here upon the boards, does he not? He shares their fate. Where is Wood? (Where, for that matter, is his mother?) I would rather be here, Mellor asserts, facing my fate, than be hidden in the shadows or watching my friends from below, or waiting to hear how badly they have died. And, with a renewed strength, he prays for John Booth to whom these thoughts have naturally taken him: prays that his soul and Booth's will be reunited and that John Booth will forgive him as he must forgive John Wood.

And, like an answer to a question he has not asked, Baines's voice comes back to him, a grandfatherly crackle of careful enunciation, softly sing-song in his ear, carried on pipe smoke and ether.

Baines is reading: ' "All hereditary government is in its nature tyranny. An inheritable crown or an inheritable throne, or by what other fanciful name such things may be called, have no other significant explanation than that mankind are inheritable property. To inherit a government is to inherit the people, as if they were flocks and herds." '

They are in a room of high morals and free thinking, budding socialists and wizened Jacobins; Booth's haunted pale face is a comfortable fit. Baines

76

reads on, his voice filling The Crispin's private meeting.

' "Hereditary succession is a burlesque upon monarchy. It puts it in the most ridiculous light, by presenting it as an office which any child or idiot may fill." Have yer ever heard a bigger truth? What is that Regent if not a child and an idiot?'

'What's a burlesque?' Mellor asks Booth, his voice a low undercurrent.

'I don't know; a trick, a joke?' replies Booth impatiently.

The lad resonates with natural anger and spirit, here in Halifax, with seasoned thinkers who talk his language and share his motivation, but what, Mellor asks himself as he tries to keep up with their high-minded reasoning, comes at the end of all this? At the end of Mellor's fight, the frames are gone, the sprawling mills have their place but are contained and the hills are alive with cloth-making again. At the end of Booth's argument, the men of King and Church are lined up at the gibbet and their women and children follow. Will Booth pull the noose tight and drop the floor beneath their feet?

It chills him, to think that John Booth's heart may be crystallising - that inside a young man of such frail dimensions lurks a will of resolute clarity and an appetite for such terrifying change - because, beyond the drop and the twitching for which the Republicans clamour, there lies a shadowy mass of people like Baines who must, perforce, institute a new order and Mellor can barely envisage what this would be, far less whether he would choose it. His instinct is to protect this boy, and he never leaves John Booth alone in The Crispin. Booth has all the enthusiasm but none of the caution needed for this game. The Crispin is nothing like The Shears. While you feel the warm throb of anger and physical prowess in The Shears, The Crispin is alive with passion of a different sort - the kind that comes from reading a lot of books and having grand notions of what the poor can achieve. Inside this unassuming public house, a stone's throw from the parish church of Halifax, croppers mingle with weavers, saddlers, shoemakers, hat makers and there are young men and old men, the weak and the strong. The pub brims with reactionary types, some with lofty aims of overthrowing the government and others with more earthy aims of pulling down a few mills. John Booth fits in well here, finding his feet, and his voice, in this mixed and talkative crowd. He whips on his greatcoat and scampers along with Mellor whenever the latter goes there, but Mellor feels always a shade out of place.

Sitting next to the esteemed John Baines is his son, Zach - flushed, eager, very young; Mellor guesses thirteen, maybe fourteen at a push. The boy fetches and carries; Mellor watches him bring fresh pints for his father and older brother, now the reading has ceased for a while and individuals can debate and argue and vent their spleen in the shared belief that a true revolution is coming. Booth remonstrates with the rest of them about all the wealth that exists in the West Riding, about how people are starving to death while mill owners inflate their profits - and about how the new finishing frames are the apparatus the higher classes are using to squeeze the last drop of wealth from the destitute.

'Aye,' Mellor interrupts, 'An' that's where we should be taking action. We should be out breaking. Now who's for doing some real damage?'

Eyes turn in his direction. Job Hey raises a pint to Mellor in agreement and Baines retakes the floor.

'What are yer thinking, lad?'

'I'm getting tired o' hitting all't little cropping shops. It in't mekkin enough difference. What we need is a big victory - summat that'll scare all t'others into getting rid o't frames an' cancelling their orders.'

Mellor is speaking from recent experience - two nights previous, shops were ambushed in Linthwaite, Slaithwaite, Lockwood, Honley and South Crosland - their busiest night so far, a frantic burst of effort, but with maybe only a score of frames destroyed. Mellor must make the Halifax men see the necessity of scaling up their endeavours.

'We're planning on Vickerman's soon enough,' he says, 'and that'll give 'em a fright, but we want to keep it up - get bigger and better.'

'We'll need more guns,' Hey chips in. 'They've committees set up an' troops moving in. T'in't going to be so easy any more.'

'We're going after Vickerman,' repeats Mellor, wanting the focus off the troops and back on their run of success. 'An' after that, we'll tek us pick - Ottiwells, Bradleys- The Liversedge lot want us to wreck Rawfolds. We've a choice to mek.'

'See how Vickerman's goes,' says Baines. 'You keep doing what yer doin, Mellor, an' yer can count on our lot from Halifax to help out.'

The promise made, Mellor can relax. He had one aim tonight - securing the cooperation of all the men who answer to Baines, and with those openly spoken words, Baines has delivered. John Wood said Baines could secure the agreement, but Mellor had not been so sure.

'Action, lad, action,' his step-father had insisted, as Mellor stepped out that evening. 'You've to keep 'em moving forrard.'

'They'll none be moved by me alone,' Mellor had complained, but Wood had rebuked him.

'Aye, an' that they will! Has tha seen anybody not moved bi thee? Yer shall 'ave 'em dancing to yer tune, son.'

But his stepfather hasn't sat in the smoky, beer-swilling room of Jacobin-flavoured idealists, listening to lectures on how the evils of monarchy and church have paved such an unjust society. He hasn't had to bite his tongue and inhale useless rhetoric, nor dig his fists into his thighs while thinking about how many frames he could have broken instead of wasting time discussing a mad king and his rascal of a son. How long, Mellor asks himself, before he can truly command the numbers he needs in order to inflict the critical level of damage on the industrialists? He must effect that phenomenon which the Brief Institution conjured against Gott in Leeds almost a decade since - he must achieve the tipping point in the balance of power, where the wealthy mill owners will throw up their hands and say, 'enough, it isn't worth all this trouble. No more frames!' And he'll do it by making their businesses suffer, by breaking their frames - not by arming villagers with pickaxes and hauling the wealthy out onto the streets to have their heads lopped off.

This is the night when he realises something about himself. Sitting there in The Crispin, ale in hand, listening to old white-haired Baines lecturing about the rights people have to own the produce and the property of their physical labour, he realises that he is frightened of revolution. When anyone makes a fleeting, light-hearted reference to France, to that horrendous, blood-soaked spectacle that was the Gaulish new beginning, his gut twists. Not in the West Riding, he thinks, not here in our hills and valleys; the only ones to suffer here should be the men that commission the frames, and even then, it's their frames I'd break, not the men themselves.

It is essential to Mellor that he clarifies internal dilemmas such as these - March has seen him on his mettle and he must be proactive and sure of himself in order to maintain the Luddite gains. His first pricking of concern is that the army has started to move about in that imperious and clownish manner that armies can't help but display and yet seem so self-importantly unaware of. A troop of Scots Greys has arrived in Huddersfield, sent down from Leeds. This tells Mellor that Huddersfield is now considered the more volatile of the two places, and he applauds his own industry in making it so. The second occurrence, which like the army's grandiose deployment, also has the hallmarks of pomposity and posturing, is the instituting of a new committee hosted, unsurprisingly, within the premises of The George public house. The members of the Merchants and Manufacturers Committee are the regular crowd in The George in any case and their bristling, whining complaints are nothing new, but it interests Mellor that his enemy has finally begun to organise. He expected it - the township is well past calling the breakings a 'bit of trouble,' and the population is hunkering down, either openly choosing sides or steadfastly keeping out of it. The troop movements and the new committee are signs to Mellor that this is becoming a war - that the aggression he is leading is at last posing a serious threat to men like Horsfall, Atkinson and the rest, that each action will bring a countermeasure, that both sides much be prepared for an escalation, and that both sides must be clear upon the principles and objectives of their engagement. A clear focus, for Mellor, is crucial

From the impassioned, urging tones of Baines, Mellor submits to the strident, gritted anger of John Wood a few days later - the latter reads from the paper to a rapt and bewildered audience in the dressing shop at Longroyd Bridge. Mellor wipes a thoughtful hand over his chin while Hall, Smith and O 'Bucks pause in their own work and look at each other.

'They've gone and done it then,' Wood comments, as he folds the Leeds Mercury into a tidy rectangle and lays it aside.

'How can laws change, just like that?' Ben snaps his fingers to illustrate. 'How can they level up breaking a frame wi' taking life?'

'They do what they want,' shrugs Wood, 'especially when they're worried.'

Mellor doesn't speak. He picks up his huge shears again and continues cutting.

'Has tha nowt to say, George?' asks Hall.

'Meks no difference,' he sighs, 'Like John says, they're worried, an' they're panicking. It means that what we're doing is working.'

'How's it working if they're going to start hanging folk,' persists William Hall. 'How's that good for us?'

'It were never goin' to be easy. We allus guessed they'd come down hard, when they got flaid of all't breaking.'

'It's wrong what they're doing,' says Ben O' Bucks.

'All the better,' Wood replies, 'If it's wrong, then we'll have more people on our side.'

'Except for them as join the Manufacturers and Merchants committee,' complains Will.

Mellor keeps shearing his cloth, He's not happy with the mood in the shop today. Truth be told, he's getting tired of hearing everyone moan and chelp. He wishes they'd all quiet down and get on with the work. The heavy shears open and close silently at his waist, slicing the tiny tongues of thread on his piece. As he concentrates on the smooth flow of his trunk-like arms, the wide inverted triangle of his back presents a wall of apparent indifference to the other. Will inhales and exhales sharply through his nose. Ben is frustrated and tense. Tom Smith is subdued, raising the nap of a piece over at the nelly and following Mellor's example by keeping his back to the others. No doubt he's just as frightened by this new piece of legislation, but he's cottoned on, like Mellor has, that to panic and fret only makes the fear worse.

From what little Mellor understands of how these things work, parliament has met more than once to talk about changing the law, so that men can be hanged for breaking machinery, and now, finally, they've done it and the law is changed and men will die for striking metal and wood. It's a nonsense to him, that a group of rich men down in London can sit together and decide the fate of working people hundreds of miles north - a nonsense, but not a surprise. After all, it's only three years since the government decided that the workers in the woollen trade, the very backbone of the country, would not be protected.

The Brief Institution, with others, had worked so hard in 1806 to argue the case that old legislation should be invoked. They spent thousands of pounds on lawyers and statements, papers and figures, to show that enforcing the existing protections would mean maintenance of a basic living for entire communities. And yet - instead of dusting down the old laws, the government wiped the board clean and took away what tiny fragments of security the trade had left. They weren't impressed by the presentations of the Brief Institution - far from it. They were, in fact, frightened that a group of workers could afford to represent themselves so well.

Mellor won't ever forget that in 1809, the same year his apprenticeship of blood and sweat ended and the callus on his wrist was fixed forever, the government struck the cropping trade with what might yet prove to be the death blow. Limits on number of looms - gone. Fixed-length apprenticeship rules - gone. Gig-mills? The more the merrier. And who does it benefit, all this new freedom within the trade? Oh yes, there is more money to be made and the mills grow bigger by the day, but normal people grow poorer. They starve in hovels while the mill owners build pretty new wings on their mansions. All the money rises to the top, a viscous oil floating on a broth of broken, screaming bones, while rich, unseen hands add fuel to the fire under the pot.

Mellor feels a hand grip his shoulder and he jerks, startled, resting his shears.

'Go easy on that cloth,' says Wood, 'It's done nowt to thee.'

'Aye.' Mellor wipes his forehead with the back of his hand and is shocked to find it wet with sweat.

'Anyway lads, thi mustn't be mithered. Might as well hang for a sheep as a lamb now,' Wood laughs.

Might as well? Mellor thinks. Is that where we're headed? He glances round the shop and sees that Wood's humour has had the same deathly effect on the others as it's had on him. Wood senses it too.

'It won't come to it,' Wood says quickly. 'They'll never find us out. We're too tight up here, too twissed. Nobody's ever controlled these valleys but the people in 'em. I'm telling all o' thee, there's nowt to be flaid of.'

Wood talks a bit more, until Ben and Will are chiming in agreement with him, talking about how the West Riding is different from anywhere in the world, and how laws made in London don't matter a bit up here. They ease up and start recounting some of the recent breakings, even laughing about how Joseph Radcliffe, the magistrate up at Milnsbridge, has been seen riding out on his horse with his special constables, trying to make his fat presence felt, now the weather is a little warmer.

What's wrong with Mellor? He can't join in, remains averted, clinging to the shears, but the work comes hard to him and his limbs tremble with weakness. Usually, the anger he feels is what drives him and makes him strong - on his nights out he depends upon it - but the anger he has just experienced is directed at something so enormous and unshakeable that he has allowed it to rebound into his own spirit, and now the fragments of despair and helplessness are lodged there and he can't shake them out. He's in a clammy sweat all over and he feels he might faint. He grips his shears intently, the iron handles slick in his fingers, and refuses his own desire to sit down or go outside for air. He feels if he can't get past this, it's all over. All those nights leading men, giving orders, wielding a pistol, risking being taken up, and yet here in this room is the real test - can he finish this piece of cloth without falling, white-faced to the floor? Can he stand up against this terror within him?

His mind rails against Wood and his stupid newspaper, against the men around him who have been so easily levered from their own little pits of fear by a few superficially soothing words, against his own muscles that have betrayed him and now quiver under the weight of the shears. If anyone speaks to him, he'll collapse. He prays that they leave him alone. Bile rises in his throat and he forces it back. Just finish the piece, he tells himself, over and over, and he focuses on the nap drifting to the floor, on the cloth spooling as he repositions it across the table, on the weak rays of sun catching the metal and making the shears glow as if they were some guiding light. He catches this idea - a thousand Sundays in chapel and a good mother have imprinted their message upon him to depths he has not before understood and he repeats it to himself - A guiding light; a protecting light; God's light. And there, with that repeated mantra - God's light, God's light - the words circling, spinning until no other thoughts can enter their orbit, he feels the tension in his shoulders begin to ease. He has found something bigger than the thing he fears. What does he fear? The government? King and Country? The law, the rope-but God is bigger than all of that, and Mellor is protected, by God's blessing. This new law matters as little as the old one, it can't touch him. The enemy he sighted, huge and immovable, is tiny and helpless in God's sight. He stands protected; in God's light, it is he who becomes the huge immovable force. Each breath he takes confirms it now. The clamminess is gone, the dizziness lifted, that terrible despondency evaporated. He probes for the fear in the socket where it so recently sprouted, but he can't find it. That catastrophic despair is gone. God's light has melted it away. And the anger? Is that still there? Please God, that it is, because he needs it. What is God, asks Mellor, but love, and vengeance? And he finds that yes, the fear is gone, but the fury, by God's blessing, remains.

Sunset over the town is one of the sights Mellor most loves. As the golden disc settles beyond the high hills, immense shadows sweep the crofts and tenterfields, and the grand public houses turn dark faces into dusky streets where mucky panes of glass catch the final reach of the sun's dying rays before being firelit from within. Up on the valley sides, green grass melts into blackness and the pale squares of cloth stretched on their tenterhooks glow in the dark like an after-image on a darkened retina, before surrendering their fading impressions to nightfall. Huddersfield, with pubs and houses dimly lit, nestles jewel-like and opaque in the heart of the terraced hillsides of shale and sandstone and grit, ringed by moors of peat and clay whose black peaks glower silently as the sky dances colour behind them - pale kersey blues and greys, with a glorious outburst of violent pink, then the silky, viscous flourish of royal blue bowing out to the blackness of night.

If he were asked to summon an image of his town, he would see it like this - at sunset, with the buildings only half in focus, and the far moors encroaching and the dark fields spotted with the squares of cloth, a murmuration of starlings expanding and contracting high above in perfect aerial display. This town is special. Not for nothing does it have the outstanding reputation for woollen cloth. Mellor could not describe exactly why it should be so, but he knows, as do all the cloth-workers here in the Colne Valley and the other valleys that converge on the town, that the water from the hills brings some kind of magic.

He thinks it is the purity of the moors, maybe something to do with the grasses there, or the peat through which the water passes. It hasn't occurred to him that the underlying rocks themselves are the key - that within the millstone grit are grains of felspar and that when these decompose they do perform a kind of magic, mixing with lime and magnesia, exchanging acids and giving the water a resulting combination of insoluble silicates and carbonates and sulphates of soda and potash, making the water into liquid silk. What Mellor *could* tell you is that the water is so soft, you'd likely find none better, anywhere in the world, for cloth-making. It lathers with the tiniest quantity of soap, leaving wool that is free of crusts and residues -

wool that dyes easily and evenly. The water drains from the moorland down towards the town, a never-ending bounty and the font of all the local wealth.

But a font of wealth draws the greedy, the selfish and the arrogant. Where money rises up, the determined and self-interested will follow. Where once Huddersfield was a wild place, barely known, with Almondbury drawing small crowds to its market just a few miles away and local folk making a decent living from their high quality cloth, now Huddersfield is the magnet, drawing businessmen and self-publicists into its environs, and expanding ever outwards as the turnpikes and canals are built, and the old tenterfields are developed into yards and buildings for the growing population. People like Cartwright over at Millbridge are flocking in, taking over the old fulling and scribbling mills, turning them into factories. People like Joseph Radcliffe at Milnsbridge are making their names as lawgivers, raising themselves above the locals in a way that the town has never seen before. Here, in Huddersfield, no one doffs his cap, but for how long will that be the case?

Mellor swings down from the tree, brushing bark and dirt from his hands and breeches and setting his cap straight. He's one of the first here, at Pricking Wood. Others are walking up from town. Thorp is sat with Tom Smith and Mellor rejoins them. O'Bucks isn't here yet, but he will be, as will Hall and all the other stalwarts. Mellor has few doubts about the turnout tonight. The more hated the target, the easier it is to guarantee a crowd - and there's none so hated as Francis Vickerman. What Mellor fears is that the execution of the plan will let them down. With an ambitious hit comes the logistics, the reliance on others playing their part. It's not so simple as turning up, breaking frames and marching off again. To breach a shop like Vickerman's, Mellor needs more on his side than raw enthusiasm - he needs time, and he needs forewarning. His greatest threats on this fifteenth night of March are the two troops of dragoons stationed in town, who during the evening will themselves march out with the opposite and determined intention to secure and fortify Vickerman's buildings at Taylor Hill. If Mellor allows just one Luddite to be harmed or taken up then tonight will be a failure.

'Jem's a good lad, in't he?' Mellor says.

'Oh aye, don't worry George,' Thorp assures him. 'Them kids love all this. It were all I could do to talk him out o' comin' up here his sen. Little bugger,' he adds, affectionately. Thorp's young cousin, Jem, is a bell ringer at the parish church, and his signal is one on which Mellor is relying. They'd been to see Jem a few days ago, after he and Thorp came up with the idea. Let's not get his mam and dad involved, Thorp had cautioned, so they waylaid Jem while he was walking home from church and put the idea straight to the boy.

'Ring t'bells when t'soldiers ride out?' Jem had repeated. 'Aye, I can keep watch and tell Jonas to mek t'others wait for me afore they start ringing.'

'What about t'vicar, won't he notice what tha's up to?' Thorp had asked, concerned to be causing trouble for the boy.

'He might if all of us came running in an' starting pulling hell for leather, but no, he won't spot if I come in a bit puffed, like I've been held up, and then we all set to, ringing as usual. Jonas'll mek sure they don't start wi'out mi. What's doing, then? Is it Taylor Hill? That's where t'soldiers go, in't it?'

'Happen best thi don't know, Jem,' Mellor had said. 'Just do thi part, that's how it works for all of us. But if yer do this reit, yer can be sure, it'll keep a lot o' good men safe.' He had given the boy some coins then - enough for himself and for his friend, Jonas and for whoever else Jem must involve. Jem had fingered the money with contemplative, pursed lips and then wrapped it in his hanky and tucked it in his woollen sock.

If and when Mellor hears those church bells pealing tonight, it means the dragoons have set out from Huddersfield, on the road to Taylor Hill. Should Jem's plan go awry, Mellor has back-up. He's asked John Walker to keep look-out at Brooks Corner and fire a pistol when he sees Vickerman's guard assembling. Walker was frustrated not to be at the main event, but he'd seen sense soon enough. As Mellor pointed out, he'd have hands-a-plenty ready to do some damage at Vickerman's, but there were few he'd put his trust in to keep the whole lot of them safe. He needed someone like John Walker out on the road - a man who was fearless but sensible. Walker would need to keep alert for a good few hours, and he'd need to fire his pistol and be off before anyone, including the soldiers on horseback, could find him and take him up.

'I'll have a word wi' Bradley,' Walker had said, and Mellor agreed - better that a pair of them held watch. It wouldn't do for the troops to pass by while Walker was busy having a piss.

The final part of the planning was to have everyone arrive here, discreetly, at Pricking Wood, but they've all had a lot of practice by now in making themselves invisible. They know to walk in pairs, threes at most, since bigger groups draw attention. They know to keep their caps low but not to hide their faces, and to walk easily, not giving any sense of urgency. They know that if they see more Ludds ahead on the road, they should hop over a wall and take a different path, so no snaking line of dark-coated men can give the game away prematurely. They know also to be polite and have a ready answer for any constable or busy-body who draws alongside on horseback and enquires as to their business on the road at this hour.

Mellor prays that Radcliffe is not abroad this evening - or that if he is, he has chosen the wrong end of the valley to patrol. So far, Mellor is hopeful. Men are arriving and clustering together within the protection of the trees, and none has reported any run-ins with the authorities on the way. O'Bucks makes his way to them, and the Brook brothers are here. Jonathan Dean is tying a piece of cloth around his face. Booth, also, has turned out.

'Ready for this, John?' Mellor asks him.

'Aye,' the lad answers, but his hands shake as he smears coal dust over his face, and Mellor helps him, running his hardened fingertips over Booth's cheekbones and spreading the black soot down to his jawline.

'It's gone eight,' Thomas Brook calls out, tapping his timepiece.

'Reit,' says Thorp, getting up. 'Time to be gone?'

'It's time,' confirms Mellor, and the men shuffle into

order, lining up just as they do when they train. Mellor feels instinctively for the hard shaft of the pistol strapped against his side. He pats it and then strokes the grip of the scythe sword tied to his other hip. The blade rocks reassuringly over his outer thigh muscle. Mellor sets it steady and wraps his greatcoat tight around him. The night is cold, despite the approach of spring.

They take off down through the woods into Lockwood, stumbling over protruding tree roots that break the ground like dragon spines and trying to avoid the thickets and tangles of bramble, until they catch on to the thin track that leads them into the open. Mellor marches them up, out of Lockwood and towards Taylor Hill in silence. The steep incline forces them to concentrate on breathing. The houses they pass along the way shroud themselves in darkness, and yet the occupants cannot but be aware of this marching column of men, and they cannot doubt the destination. Francis Vickerman has been vocal and active in his founding of and support for the new merchants and manufacturers committee, and he has spoken witheringly of the Luddites and especially of the croppers. He is not a man well-liked, even in his own social circle. No wonder he has pressed for troops for his protection. He knows he is vulnerable, but not even he has guessed that the determination of George Mellor is such that a raid would be planned for the tiny sliver of time between sunset and the arrival of the guard. Vickerman has taken precautions against the mob, but he has not prepared for an army, and that is what Mellor's small group of men now truly resembles.

They come to Taylor Hill barely out of breath, though it's been such a climb out of Lockwood and they're weighed down with weapons, some of them heavy. These men are fit, used to hard work and strenuous walking. Mellor commands axe and hatchet men, hammer men, pistol men. Their unnerving silhouettes surround the house, trapping those within.

Mellor goes to the door and gives three loud knocks. The knocks meet with unnatural silence and Mellor calls out, 'Open t'door and nobody will be harmed,' but still there is silence and Mellor nods to Ben, who fetches a hard crack to the door with his hammer. Part of the timber splinters but Ben has to hit it twice more before the catch gives way and the abused door swings wildly inwards. Mellor steps inside with his pistol in his hand, and his Ludds flock in around him, swarming through the workshop.

Mellor, Thorp and several others find the entry point to the dimly lit dwelling house where they must secure Vickerman. They find the man with his wife in the kitchen, silhouetted by the rich orange glow of a beeswax candle, half-eaten food still on the table.

'Yer were warned,' Mellor accuses, jabbing the air with his finger, 'and yer would not listen! Well, si thi now, thi frames are being smashed to pieces so happen you'll think on yer ways and stop trying to do honest men o' work.'

'The Committee will hear of this, and the magistrate will find you, all of you. You'll hang for this, you coward. Clean thi face, take thi handkerchief from thi foul countenance! Or are thi flaid?' Vickerman flails his arms as he speaks, evidently furious but entirely helpless without any weapon to hand. His wife grasps at his sleeve, petrified. A small boy runs into the room, tears streaking his white face.

'Go back, Joseph,' she screams, 'Go back to bed.' More tiny faces peer round a doorway and Vickerman's wife breaks ranks to run to them, ushering them backwards. She spares a look back at Mellor as she goes and he nods and waves her onwards. He doesn't want the children present any more than she does.

'I want you out of my house,' Vickerman rages, 'I insist you get out now and leave my family in peace.' He is balling his fists, punching at his own thighs, dark strands of hair slipping from their carefully coiffed position and whipping about his broad forehead. His eyes are dark slits in the rectangle of his face, lips wet with his own spittle. He wipes his hair back impatiently and rocks on his heels.

'There'll only be peace when thi an' thi friends stop using the blasted shearing frames,' Mellor says, in parting. It's tempting to stay and argue with the man, to force him into some kind of submission, but it would be a waste of valuable time. He could never persuade a man as saturated in personal ambition as Vickerman that there are greater things on earth than what profits an individual man can make. He checks the guard around him - James Brook has his musket pointed at Vickerman and on Mellor's other side, with loaded pistol fixed on the same target, is Booth, his slim face transformed into a sleek canine appearance by the blacking that picks out the whites of his eyes and teeth. They are braced by three or four others with mattocks and axes.

'Keep him here,' he tells them. 'Try not to shoot

him.'

Mellor leaves the discomforting surroundings of the home and goes back into the shop, where the beating clang of hammers descending upon frames is deafening. He is dimly aware of Francis Vickerman shouting in the back, arguing with his captors that they are only bringing themselves closer to the noose, and the sound of the man's voice - so smug, so full of unjustified authority - makes him lose control. He has no hammer, so instead he pulls out his sword and drives it full force into one of the windows, spilling shards of glass over the dusty floor and out into the yard. Then he puts through a second pane, and a third, and he keeps on going until there isn't a window left intact in the shop.

The cold air floods inside, a refreshing breeze for the men who are sweating as they take apart the contraptions of wood and iron. Mellor begins to pull shears from the walls, laying them ready for the great hammers to land upon. One of the shearing frames has cloth left on it, and perhaps this is why his men have so far left it alone. Mellor snatches up the fine piece and strides through to the kitchen where he chucks it on top of the stove to scorch, despite Vickerman's howls of protest. The manufacturer jerks forward but Drake bars his way. Mellor leaves the cloth on the heat, not caring whether it burns nor what it takes with it.

There is a clock on the mantel. It tells him the time is twenty minutes shy of nine o'clock. He picks up the heavy timepiece and slams it to the floor, crunching the wooden casing and shattering the internal mechanisms. Vickerman's wife, who has re-entered the room, gives a pathetic cry, but Mellor is in no mood for compromise. In the worst of Huddersfield's many yards, he's seen children so damaged by hunger and poverty that they put him in mind of feral animals, bony and rag-wrapped, carrying only the faintest memories of dead fathers and bitter love for their starving, struggling mothers. Vickerman's mantel and table hold beeswax candles - the type that even Wood cannot usually afford for Mary. There is a great ark full of oats, more butter in the dish than Mellor has seen in any home, and that princely clock was just one of the ornamental extravagances that litter the house. Now it lies, crushed and irrelevant, on the flagstones.

John Booth stares at the cogs and springs and the shattered wooden casing. It's difficult to read his eyes, framed in hellish coal dust and rimmed with redness from the consequent irritation. Easier to see is the impotent fury on Mrs Vickerman's features as the twist of her mouth catches the glow from the large candle. Mellor supposes that the clock cost a lot of money. He wonders if she will mourn the loss of the handsome decoration and whether they will buy a replacement. When the Ludds have left, will Vickerman have the place swept clean, new windows fitted and a host of new frames delivered? Will he order in a new clock, bigger, more egregiously expensive than the first, to please his outraged wife? Will he continue to tell his friends that, Luddites be damned, he'll have what machinery he sees fit to employ, and beggar the bloody poor? Mellor stamps on the clock and kicks the remnants across the floor.

As the pieces skid under the table and smash into the wall, the hammer blows from the adjoining shop are met in harmony by the distant pealing of church bells. Mellor runs back into the shop.

'Two minutes,' he yells, looking about him at the strewn, ruptured equipment. Men are falling about as they trip on broken iron in the near darkness, and Mellor kicks buckled shears to one side of the room, clearing the path out. The troops have left the town and must now be on the march here. It's possible they will come at speed if word of the attack has already been carried out to meet them. There is a final spurt of energy from the breakers, then a shot fires - not outside, but much further away.

'That's it, everyone out,' he orders, pushing the men past him and counting them out, and silently thanking young Jem and John Walker for the warnings. The shop is clear, the men are rushing outside, and Mellor goes back through the kitchen and relieves Booth, Brook and the other men holding Vickerman.

'That's our business finished, Mr Vickerman,' Mellor shouts from the doorway, 'If tha gets more frames, same'll 'appen.'

There is an answering volley of abuse from the manufacturer but Mellor does not stay to listen. He bolts out, and shouts 'Company one,' then waits for the answering tide of numbers that tell him the men are all there. Company two gives the same retort, scaling through their identifying numbers as fast as they can. Mellor is satisfied. 'Dismissed,' he yells, and his army dissolves into the shadows. Mellor himself bolts for a cut-through he knows towards Newsome, and Thorp joins him. They make for Newsome Cross, then down to a scrubby, bramble-thicketed bank of the River Holme, where they can wash off all the blacking from their faces and listen to the unmistakeable sounds of troops on the road above them, riding in the direction of Taylor Hill.

4

The Sanguinary Contest

In 1811, a comet appeared in the skies over England. Through late summer and autumn it charted a spectacular course, the streak of white becoming clearer and brighter, hanging overhead like the sword of Damocles. The Year of the Comet - that's how 1811 would be described by anyone who was alive to witness that flaming, angelic blade thrusting through the heavens.

People gazed upwards night after night in fascination, awe, and eventually in concern, fear, weariness. Signs of such magnitude are hard to dismiss. It must mean something, this oppressive, evaporating tail of a distant celestial body. To whom was it signalling doom? The mad King? His errant son? Russia, under threat from Napoleon? Or the people of England, who had already suffered such horrendous harvests that they were starving and dying? The people needed no portent of doom - doom was already upon them - so they contented themselves with the knowledge that the sword of Damocles hangs only over those in power; the King, surely the King.

Mellor had looked upwards, like everyone else. He saw, not a sword, but a path of starlight. It made him smile. Now, on the drop, he thinks about that comet and wonders if it was a sword after all. A sword hanging over a different kind of King - a King Ludd.

He doesn't like that title, though some of the men laughingly call him that - in one of the letters he helped to write to Justice Radcliffe, he remembers berating the magistrate with the insistence that the

Luddites were governed not by sovereigns but by equity. Mellor is no King; he has never even desired that kind of unaccountable power. Perhaps, then, it was not a Damoclean blade hanging overhead in warning, but the righteous, blazing sword of Michael, glowing bright against all the evil rising up from the earth; a sword to show them the way; a path, after all, just as he had first perceived it.

Mellor's actual voice has dipped to a whisper, his thoughts outpacing the method of his prayers. He is barely aware, now, of the Ordinary at his side. Absorbed in his communion, he follows the strand of memories, trusting that God is attending to it all, spoken and unspoken, and that He will knit it into form.

Such faith as Mellor possesses is impossible to manufacture or summon at will; it must be encouraged and nurtured, and protected when the winds of fate blow hard against the immature stems. When his father died, Mellor had suffered the painful bewilderment of the faithful, comprehending only that his father had been taken from him by a God who must not care about his distress. Mellor's mother educated him otherwise, pointing out the great suffering that God had endured, watching his son on the cross. Suffering, he had learned, must be borne. The greater the suffering, the more ready the ascent to heaven.

Little George had accepted his mother's words and found them comforting. He prayed regularly and did not complain overmuch about going to chapel. Faith became a given, and something he drew on in those miserable nights through his long apprenticeship when his arms ached and his wrist hurt so much that he couldn't sleep - a quiet communion with his own personal God; childish imaginings maturing into a deeper understanding of scripture. Time and again this past year, his faith has reared up more than equal to his fears, dousing them with an opalescent blast of heavenly clarity.

It must be meaningful, the ease with which he visualizes rays of brilliance, streaming upon him. They appear immediately he attempts to imagine them, as if they were there all along and he has somehow tuned his brain into an upper, unseen part of the spectrum where God's message shines in permanence. Time passes differently, under these great, supporting beams of light. An hour, a minute - meaningless; the most complex dream, a whole universe of parallel reality - conceived, born and aged in a single rapid eye movement; a single second of revelation lasting the thick blackness of an earthly night; a prayer measured in minutes that bridges a millennia. The march of time is a fallacy - Mellor has felt the world pause before, just as he feels it now, when the next beat is breathlessly held, the cog shifted into reverse-

A spinning shilling, up, up and through the air, heads and tails flashing, falling, flashing, falling, into his palm. A reverie so strong, the gathered crowd are in thrall, spellbound in the stillness of the seconds. Then- palm, slap! - onto the back of his other hand, and the illusion of time resumes.

'Tails,' he announces to the silent crowd in The Crispin, taking only a brief glance at the irrelevant coin. 'Rawfolds.'

And so, at an April meeting in Halifax, it is decided. How he hates Horsfall, that cruel tyrant of Ottiwells Mill who would rather see Luddites dead at the hooves of his horse than let decent men work a proper living. But Cartwright's quiet defiance - ordering more frames after the Hartshead job - has angered Mellor, and Rawfolds is perfectly placed for a raid, well away from the judicious Magistrate Radcliffe of Milnsbridge.

A coin toss for such a decision is an absurdity, but let the brethren have it if it stops their arguments. Baines isn't fooled; he's old enough to know how easily confidence can be tricked, and wise enough to know that Mellor's decisive discretion will end hours of circular debate. The Halifax men prefer Ottiwells Mill as their quarry - Marsden is closer, easier to approach, and Mr Horsfall has been so very provocative. The deputation from Huddersfield could go either way but the delegates from Leeds and Liversedge are adamant that Rawfolds makes the best target. The decision is a military one - maximum damage for minimum risk. With so many Luddite units committed to the operation and only a tiny guard presence at Rawfolds, success seems assured.

Saturday 11 April dawns, overcast and cool with the threat of rain lingering on the peripheral hills. Joshua Dickenson calmly unloads gunpowder and ball-cartridge onto a table in the shop, making sure Mellor, Ben O'Bucks, William Hall and Tom Smith have what they need.

'Been to Fishers?' Mellor checks, wanting to be sure Thorp has received the ammunition he needs.

'Aye,' answers Dickenson. 'And John Walker's passing a few pistols around his place and next door. Now, this message I'm passing on to t'boys at Jackson's - it's all of us, Hirst an' Hartley especially, to meet you at Dumb Steeple by ten o'clock, eleven at latest. All of us at Rawfolds by twelve.'

'Perfect. Make sure they stick to it at that end.'

'Will do. Any word from Halifax?'

'They're on,' confirms Mellor, having been assured the previous day that Baines's men know where they're going. 'We'll have plenty from Elland thief hoil too, and from Rastrick way.'

'Owt else tha needs?'

'Nay, that's it.'

'Good luck then,' says Dickenson, departing the shop with his cap pulled low and his bag hoisted onto his back. The men left inside silently clean their weapons and pack their ammunition before stowing it all in the back room. The atmosphere is tense, the men unwilling this morning to engage in the kind of banter that might precede the usual, small scale operations. Wood comes in and has a quiet word with them all before hurrying off into town to confirm to his associates that Rawfolds is definitely on. When he leaves, Mellor feels some relief. He can't stay on edge all day. He needs to unwind, and focus on the cropping. Thankfully he is left alone for some hours, until Betty corners him in the yard during the morning and demands to know what he's planning. When he stays quiet, she shouts, enraged, 'I sharn't find a man, George, because o' thee! They're either against what you're doing, or they don't want to be caught up in it, an' my Jack were both and now he's finished it wi' mi.'

The reason for her sudden anger clear, he reacts defensively.

'I could point to three score o' good men who foller me wi'out question, an' scores more who secretly catch my eye or give a nod. Pick one o' them.'

'Oh aye, stupid bloody fools wi' no sense, running around wi' their faces blacked up an' more chance of ending up in York than coming home at neet.' She slaps the outhouse wall, curses at the gritty pain and rubs the reddened palm on her skirts, sucking in a ragged sob. They both pause. 'Bloody hell, I'm sorry George. Tha knows I din't mean it.'

'Aye lass, I know'd thee were on my side all along.' He meant it playfully, but a heavy sadness descends over her, binding and softening her, making her look more like the young girl she once was. He feels as if he'd just forced his big sister to accept the Oath. Poor Betty, he thinks, she's already as twissed as any Ludd. 'I'm sorry too, about Jack an' that.'

'He wor an arse. The things he said... bloody coward. I told him, if he went telling tales, he'd wekken to find his legs smashed.'

'Betty Mellor! Tha's worse ner me.'

'Happen tha should swear in some lasses,' she snaps back.

'It's Rawfolds Mill tonight,' he says, exchanging, at last, a secret for her sacrifice. 'I've well over a hundred men, more from Leeds. There's no need to worry.'

'Oh George. There's allus a need to worry. Just, keep thi sen reit and get thi sen home in one piece.'

The weather gets no better during the day. In fact, it drops colder than you'd expect for an April afternoon. This will make the march uncomfortable, but it might clear the roads of itinerant traffic. Mellor looks out of the windows every so often, watching the knotted thread of people passing through Longroyd Bridge. The hours fall away heavily. When, finally, it's time to eat, Mellor, Hall and Smith manage a good feed, and Betty makes sure they have plenty to go at. Mary bites at her thumb nail, the air around mother and two eldest children oppressive and expectant; the two live-in croppers sup nervously, on edge, and retire to the shop after the meal.

Daniel is abed by nine o'clock, exhausted by a day of fetching and carrying for his father. Elizabeth sits mending with Betty, working swiftly on two frayed girls' shifts and a man's torn shirt in the twenty minutes of good light that the rush candle will give them before smoking out and leaving them with the low glow of the fire - the only light permissible by the watch-and-ward after ten o'clock. When Mellor finally leaves the house, Elizabeth is yawning and drowsy, and only Betty and his mother pay silent attention, as he steps into the icy air and closes the door carefully behind him. He meets William Hall, Ben O' Bucks and Tom Smith out in the shop. Ben has been home to his mother's place for supper but has returned for his gun.

'You three set off, head up Outcote. I'm meeting Thorp on t'cut.'

'Reit, si thi at Dumb Steeple,' says Ben with a mock salute. Mellor gives them a few minutes head-start, waiting alone in the empty shop, surrounded by the tools of his endangered trade. He spends the slow seconds looking at his shears, and lifting and tossing the heart-shaped weights that are used to press the blade down. He settles them, like pets, on the bench.

When enough time has passed, he heads out, taking the path down to the canal. It's bitterly cold. There is the sting of thin, freezing rain in the breeze and the night is very dark, barely a star visible in the sky, the tow-path only a slightly paler shade of black than the inky ribbon of the cut. Thorp's outline is an unnatural void against the charcoal shrubbery.

The canal skirts the south of town and they march apace, taking advantage of the easy ground, mindful of the watch-and-ward. At Aspley they switch to the River Colne, which will take them right along to the meeting place.

'We've time enough,' Mellor says, slowing, 'Let's not wear ourselves out on this stretch.'

'Aye, we've another long walk after we've all met up,' agrees Thorp. 'What is it, about two or three miles?'

'Mebbe a touch more, an' that's hoping we don't get lost.'

'We'll be reit, it's only up t'Shears and then a bit further out. We'd find it, even wi'out the Liversedge fellys.'

The river walk takes them within a quarter of a mile of Bradley's Mill, which is operated by the Atkinson brothers. Lights are still burning and Mellor expects there are soldiers in the yard there. The Atkinsons drove off a gang of Ludds earlier in the month - another reason why Mellor is convinced that Rawfolds is the place to hit. He expects it to be relatively undefended. Cartwright has been holed up inside every night, according to reports, with a few men for security, but no troops on site and no billets of soldiers nearby. Rawfolds is a lonely, quiet place.

Up ahead, the river twists and turns. They switch from riverbank to track and back again as needed, avoiding boggy ground and finding the most direct route whilst avoiding the other small groups of men coming this way on parallel paths. The walk is interminable, the darkness never-ending to Mellor. A part of him enjoys it, the safety of anticipation prior to irreversible commitment, and a part of him strains to arrive and take charge before any element of his plan can go awry. Perhaps we should have come separately, he thinks, since he and Thorp are in joint command - if they were picked up, who else would take over? But he is pleased, as always, to be walking with his best mate, whose cheerfulness, lacking at times during the planning of this event, has returned in force with the pregnant menace of nightfall and is evident in occasional whistling and inconsequential remarks.

They eventually reach a point where different tracks intersect, and just back from this natural passing place is the obelisk that marks their temporary pause. The Dumb Steeple is set just inside fields belonging to Kirklees Priory, and behind it, the land undulates away to the north, fading into the moorland of Hartshead. The field is already filling with men. Joseph Drake, John Walker and Jonathan Dean are there, having met at Dean's house and walked together. Mellor and Thorp join them. There are muted greetings, quiet acknowledgements. It's difficult to make out all the men, in the darkness, with faces disguised and many wearing carter's smocks or even women's petticoats. A steady trickle of men flows into the field, swelling the gathering over the next half an hour or so. Mellor watches them come, greeting nearly all, making some

108

of them take off their distinctive greatcoats and turn them inside out.

'I'd know thee a mile off, Ogden, in that fancy coit,' he says, to the lad from Cowcliffe who's come with one of his friends. Jeremiah Ogden has a big brother, John, and the pair are often confused, but John's not twisted-in - sympathetic but not a Ludd - unlike Jem, who is eagerly pulling his coat back on inside-out. There are others, with faces clearly visible under their caps, or making too much noise. Mellor intervenes, getting them to black-up, calm down, forcing order on the group, but they are restless under his yoke, fidgeting and shuffling in the muddy grass.

When a couple of men arrive with bottles of rum, it's not a minute too soon, and Mellor, who ordered this alcohol yesterday, makes sure the bottles are passed around, with every man getting a good drink to stiffen him up. It's money well spent; there is a collective relaxation, a sigh passing softly through the cold night. He takes a long drink himself, feeling his throat burn and eyes water. Black, capped shadows fill the enclosure, shifting and flowing in groups, as if they were merely a dream of an army, their wispy exhalations puffing and disappearing.

Mellor calls out for those without arms to come forwards, then for his different companies to form up. Pistol men move out to the west, muskets to the middle, hammers and axes to the east. Mellor surveys the empty-handed recruits before him. He gives the bulkiest ones the few hammers and axes he has, then doles out some old muskets, pistols and a load of pikes and mauls.

There are so many pistol men that he splits them

into two companies. This is easier said than done, in the dark, with discretion the crucial factor. Mellor gesticulates with his arms, Thorp runs through the group, pushing men to one side or the other. Eventually the companies are formed and Mellor leaves Thorp to number up his men. Both pistol companies will be under Thorp's control. Mellor goes to his musket company, where the men have got themselves into two lines, and he numbers them up with relative ease, before moving on and doing the same with the hammers. Then he steps back, in front of this great assembly of men.

Missing from the ranks are some of the Halifax men and this is galling, given Baines's promise of support, but even so, he has about three hundred men here - twice what he has calculated that he needs. He also has his guides, John Hirst and Samuel Hartley, who are part of a strong Liversedge turnout. This pair will walk up in front with Mellor, making sure they don't take a wrong turn on the dark moorland. He has another pair - his own workmate, William Hall, and George Rigg, to walk at the very back and stop the procession straggling.

Mellor knows there are men here tonight who have thought twice about this venture, who would possibly not have turned out except for the contemptuous reprisals they would suffer if they stayed away. These are the men who look unhappily about them as if trying to fathom a way out. Mellor cannot allow any of them to scarper. Hall and Rigg must be on the lookout for escapees. Any hint of fear or even uncertainty might spread like a contagion through this little militia and Mellor will not have all his hard work

110

spilt and scattered over moorland walls by men running for home. He needs to get them to Rawfolds before doubt sets in, and, with this in mind, he checks the time with Thomas Brook and then begins the orderly exit from the Dumb Steeple field and up towards the packhorse tracks that criss-cross the moor. All the men are paired up for this march, the only sensible approach to squeezing several hundred men through paths, tracks and stiles. Pairing off limits the noise, keeps them from coalescing on the wider stretches.

They pass cottages and farms and the pounding of boots must alarm the occupants, but no one troubles them, or so much as steps outside for a look. No one could live in this part of the world and be unaware of what forces are at work in these awful times. Whether people are in favour of or against the Luddites, they stay hidden inside and pray for the safety of their own families.

The march to the Spen Valley is, for the men themselves, an oddly peaceful time. They walk without speaking, which gives time for reflection. Jonathan Dean, carrying his heavy hammer, is focussing on keeping up his pace, despite the weighty tool which painfully indents his shoulder. He wants to get there and do some damage, and he is picturing the way his hammer will swing at the reportedly reinforced doors of Rawfolds. At the back of his mind, he holds a picture of getting home safe and sound to his five sleeping children. John Walker is grimly satisfied to be at the heart of this raid, having been a glorified lookout for the Vickerman's job. John Booth is nervous and excited, but as he grips his musket he fears for what is to come and whether he will stomach the violence that may occur. Booth does not know what he will do if he comes face to face with Cartwright. Could he shoot him? Stab him? And how will he feel about himself if he cannot? These concerns flit around, landing only briefly in the young man's consciousness as he is carried along in the shadowy caterpillar of men. Ben O'Bucks is flying high, feeling at his best in this brotherly gang of men. It unnerves him that he gets such a kick from the raids they carry out. Daily life has none of the thrills he experiences on these dangerous nights and he is aware that his thorough enjoyment of the action puts him at grave risk of errors in judgement. He thinks briefly of his mother and reminds himself to be careful tonight, but still his chest fizzes with anticipation.

Towards the rear of the procession, a man named Rayner has already leapt a wall and begun a dizzyingly speedy race home. If he is caught by the constables, he'll be arrested. If he is caught by the Ludds, he believes they'll kill him. This run home could prove more dangerous than simply carrying on to Rawfolds and letting fate take its course, but Rayner has had enough. He wants to go home, sleep soundly and stay in one bodily piece. He streaks across the moor before anyone even notices his absence from the line. It helps that he is the running champion of his village. His partner, realising after dismounting a stile that Rayner has gone, will keep quiet about it. He doesn't want to be responsible for whatever form of Luddite justice Mellor might consider necessary. Besides, he reckons there are enough men here, and if Rayner hasn't the heart, let him go. Rayner isn't the only one. A man named Naylor is wavering too, and when he finds a chance to slip away, he takes it. He gets all the way home and then, indecisive by nature, wonders if he should go back.

For most of the men, there is no question about continuing. They've taken a binding oath for good reason, and if this is the way forward then so be it. By removing choice from the equation, they make the journey easier on themselves. Putting one foot in front of the other becomes as inevitable and necessary as breathing. Some, like Tom Smith, do it with heavy heart. He's thinking of his sweetheart at the Brown Cow, desperate to be back with her, wondering who will warm her if he never returns. Others, like James Haigh, are eager to inflict a blow and by so doing, extract and redirect some of the righteous anger within themselves before it turns to poison.

How does Mellor feel now? He can't afford to ask himself this question. It's not about how he feels, but about the job he must do. He has a duty to these men marching on behind him, and if he can allow one thought to permeate his concentration, it is that he must not fail them. He won't consider what failure might look like, and blindly shuts his mind to the hints he has received about Cartwright's determined hold on his mill. He knows the man has been sleeping in there for days, if not weeks. A man doesn't hold a mill alone. Cartwright has soldiers with him. Mellor knows this too, but Abraham Pule, one of Cartwright's previous employees, has insisted to the Brief Institution that it's four or five at most, with maybe a couple more patrolling in the yard. Once they are inside the mill, it won't matter. A few soldiers can't hold back three hundred men. Cartwright's grip on his mill, his nightly occupation of the huge building, doesn't matter, not against so many Luddites.

The procession passes through Hightown and then begins the descent into the Spen Valley. Partway down they halt, assembling on the hillside at Mellor's order. Down at the bottom, the beck winds indifferently along the valley floor, passing right alongside Rawfolds where the dam powers the great wheel. Marshland and grasses surround the stream and further back, woods colonise the slopes. All of this, shrouded in darkness, is barely visible to the men from Huddersfield, Liversedge, Elland and Rastrick who sit waiting for news of their reinforcements. Mellor has been promised that the Leeds men will meet him here, converging on the north of the beck. Someone should be here, now, to speak with him, but the hillside is empty. The northern bank is in blackness, no signal lights. If there are men out there, Mellor can't see them, and they are not responding to Mellor's own signal lights. He cannot risk calling out. Rawfolds is close now. Any hint of shouting in the valley will put Cartwright on his guard.

'Take a rest,' he says to the men, who gladly drop their heavy tools to the ground. He tots up the figures dotted around him and finds the total in broad agreement with the original tally. Clasping and writhing his hands, he nods. This is good. And the Leeds men will turn up. One side just needs to make a start and the other will hear and join in. Mellor will lead the initial assault - he has more than enough men - and then the Leeds contingent will hear the clamour and race down the hillside to provide reinforcement. Just - not too soon. Though it agonises him to wait, he knows he must catch Cartwright when the mill owner least expects it. He wants them all fast asleep. The later he can attack, the better. Mellor also wants his men to gather their strength. Three miles may not be such a long way, but nearly all the men here have walked many more miles just to get to the Dumb Steeple in the first place. And walking in the dark and the rain is exhausting. You can't see to step safely - you turn your ankles, sink into puddles, slip back with each muddy uphill step, struggle over stiles catching splinters in your hands and it's so cold and wet. The distance feels tenfold what it really is. They are all tough, hardened men, but men they are, not machines. There's no shame in taking some time to recuperate. Mellor takes the opportunity to talk with Thorp and Dean.

'If there's more men in t'yard, Jonny, keep yer company well back. Let me an' Thorp handle them, and you wait for yer chance to get to that door. That's the most important thing. Quicker an' cleaner we can get in, easier it'll be.'

'Don't worry about that, we'll get straight to it,' Dean assures him. 'Just keep them soldiers off us and we'll get you into that mill.'

'We'll be in an' out afore any real soldiers turn up,' says Thorp, confidently. 'Just so long as they don't hear us up here now an' call for troops early.'

'Listen,' says Mellor with a smile, 'Hear that?' They all tip attentive heads and slowly pick up the rushing sound of water through the mill race echoing up the valley. 'They'll not hear us, as long as we keep quiet and that beck keeps flowing.'

'This mill door,' hesitates Dean, 'We've heard it's been toughened. Know any more about it?'

'Nay,' Mellor admits. 'Just something about metal studs. They're all doing it, finding ways to make it harder for us to get into t'mills. But a door's a door. It'll come loose.'

Dean nods, pensive but not over-worried, and rejoins his company.

The rain sprinkles a soft pattering refrain over the hushed banks of the valley. Sporadic gusts blow an icy spray at the men who sit and wait on the exposed hillside. They pull their coats tighter against the chill and ignore the spreading damp over the seat of their breeches. James Haigh reties the laces of his sodden boots and Jem Ogden chews on a tough stem of grass. John Walker paces about, watchful and alert. Tom Smith is actually asleep, curled up on his side, head buried in his collar. Leaving Thorp to return to his company, Mellor wanders a short distance away, in the direction of Rawfolds Mill. There are no lights in the valley, nothing to cast a gleam on the obscured mill waiting for them in the valley bottom, not even a sliver of moon in the sky. The time is reaching midnight. Mellor has been stood awhile, looking down into the darkness, when Thomas Brook strides over to him.

'See anything?'

'Nowt. No lights. I reckon they're asleep.'

'We should go now, afore we all catch us death o' cold.'

'Aye,' says Mellor. Reassembly begins; a low hum of answering numbers and slow shuffle into line; the lead company departs downhill, gathering pace as the mass behind filters down the narrow path. At the army's head, Mellor is almost running, keeping slightly ahead of his men, and watching all the time for light or movement ahead. All is clear. The only disturbance to the slumbering night is the trample of footsteps behind him and as they swoop down towards the beck, Mellor thinks how well the evening has progressed, and how the battle is at least half-won.

The three storey building looms into visibility as the path widens. Underfoot, the ground is stony and rough. He knows that there must be men patrolling inside the mill yard, men who might hear the scrabbling, shifting sounds of boots on the gritty track. How close can he get before the alarm is raised?

He presses his musket men up to the dry stone walling to creep on towards the gate. Hartley is nodding him on, pointing and grinning, equally aware that they are on the cusp of a great victory, and he runs ahead a small distance to scope out the situation inside the yard. Looking back to Mellor, he raises a hand with two fingers splayed - two guards. Mellor gives a thumbs-up, and hastens his men on until they are at the gate itself.

Hall and Hirst are at Mellor's side, and he waves them in. Hirst unlatches the gate as carefully as he can, easing it open with barely a squeak, and the pair rush in, straight upon the unlucky guards. The guards carry blunderbusses, so this could go terribly wrong for William Hall and John Hirst, but they don't hesitate or pull their punches, falling on the men with vigorous poising and and blows that bring the hapless pair to the ground. More of Mellor's men swarm in and fall on the men, taking a firm grip on arms and legs, and the guards are half-carried, half-dragged from the yard onto the track outside. Apart from some scuffling, gasping and hard breathing they achieve this without any noise. The guards are stunned and semi-conscious - easy to tie and gag. Then they are carried away into the fields, deposited in a hedgerow and watched over by a pistol-wielding pair of Ludds who will remain until the action at the mill is properly underway and they are needed in the yard.

The yard lays open, inviting the the musket men in. They run through the gates, lining up to face the ground floor windows, Thorp's company close on their heels. At the trailing end of the procession, someone fires a signal shot for the benefit of the Leeds company. Mellor waves Jonathan Dean forward with a small unit of hammer-men. Deep within the mill, a loud bark ricochets, first once, then in a volley of canine warning, and with the collective fear of impending discovery and retaliation, the musket men begin to fire, straight into the mill windows.

The tall panes of glass shatter and fall just as Dean begins to crash his enormous hammer into the great wooden door. With terrifying swiftness, the midnight silence is rent apart in a cacophony of attack. Smashing and pounding fills the air. Hartley shouts to Mellor, 'The other door!' and Mellor immediately runs to the back of the yard, directing more men with hammers and axes round the side. All the ground floor windows are smashed and Mellor can see into the mill, can hear the sound of the dog barking furiously, but there are no men in there. He wonders for a full second where the soldiers are, and then the onslaught starts.

Like a counterpart harmony to the Luddite fire, a rain of shot hollers out from above, spewing from the first floor windows like a killing rain, driving into the exposed men below. Glass, blown out from the firing within, falls down onto them in long sharp splinters. Mellor runs to the minimal shelter of the mill wall, aims his musket upwards at a sharp angle and fires towards the window holes.

Dean takes a horrified pause as he looks behind him. Smoke from the musket fire is filling the yard, making it even harder to see what's happening, but he can see blood on faces, a figure on the floor and there is yelping and screaming too. Merciless now, Dean swings his hammer hard into the door, desperate to force entry and get the men out of the yard and into the ground floor of the mill where it will be harder for the soldiers above to shoot them, but the door in front of him will not give. He should be through it by now - he can hear Mellor shouting that they have to get in - and he strikes blow after blow, but it's like hitting solid iron, with no discernible weak part.

The more he hits, the more he understands that this door is more iron than wood. Cartwright has had it studded with so much metal that it's almost impregnable, but Jonny Dean, a cloth dresser through and through, has muscles like an ox, and the will of a beast too, and he keeps on at it, knowing that even iron will give in the end. Besides, he has nowhere else to go. The yard is being sprayed with a never-ending stream of gunfire and anyone attempting to run across to the gate will likely get shot. Each time a Luddite fires, the bright flash of his weapon draws an instant reply from the marksmen above.

Alongside the length of the building, men are scrambling at the walls, firing madly at the hundreds of windows and even piling round the side of the building to the beck, where they come perilously close to knocking each other into the water. The open, undefended mill yard, previously so vulnerable and inviting, has shed its disguise and turned into a trap - an open, hungry mouth from which the Luddites have no escape, and no safe space in which to regroup and reorganise. Worse still, the bell overhead is clanging violently, pealing out across the whole valley a message that troops are needed at Cartwright's mill.

Mellor registers the bell in horror - if the cavalry come, they have no chance of escape. For the space of three or four loud clangs, his blood runs cold, then abruptly the noise ends. It doesn't resume, and Mellor guesses that the over-excited bell-ringer has broken the rope. He thanks God for this small mercy and keeps firing his weapon at the windows above. John Walker is trying to scale the wall of the building, firing upwards with one hand as he clings on, unafraid despite the unrelenting threat of fire from above.

The noise of musket shot keeps on and on, and with it the moans and screams within the yard. Mellor can't see who is injured, but he knows when Dean gets hit because the vicious pounding at the door, the heartbeat to their offensive, slows up for half a minute. Dean slumps to his backside, clutching his wrist and gazing in disbelief at his hand, shredded where musket fire has ripped it apart. The shot has flown through the splintered port-hole Dean has made in the door, disabling the man's hand with vicious precision. Other men take his place, chipping away at the ragged circumference of the hard-won gouge, slivers of wood and shards of iron flying like sparks in the smoke-filled air while beyond the resisting portal, the mill floor stands empty and still, a world away from the crashing terror of the yard.

When the bell begins to ring again, it's too much for many of the Ludds. Mellor shouts to them all that the door is breached - 'It's open, keep firing, we'll be in anytime,' he yells.

'Fire at the bell, stop that bloody ringing,' Thorp screams, and though some men respond, aiming upwards with their muskets, others are rushing blindly in the choking mist, dodging for non-existent cover, tripping over injured comrades and discarded brick bats and powder horns. Thomas Brook finds himself pushed backwards into the zone of fire and for a dizzying moment feels shot passing all around him. He darts in terror round the side of the mill, misses his footing, and falls headlong into black, freezing water. The heart-stopping cold of the beck shocks him back into his senses. The dam is shallow, and he gropes his way out, oblivious to the loss of his hat, bobbing steadily away from him on the water's surface.

Mellor can't bear it - they are so close to a breakthrough. Even with all the firing and screaming here at Rawfolds, the rest of the valley is still quiet - there is no sound of approaching cavalry. A few more minutes and they could be inside. Where the hell are the Leeds men? Surely if they are near, they should hear the commotion and rush to assist? Mellor looks in dismay at the emptying yard. He has less than half the men he came in here with. Blood stains the ground, and Mellor doesn't know who is injured, who may be dying. Thomas Brook comes at him with a frozen, white face. He drips with water and his bare head is plastered with wetted hair.

'We've got to go,' he says, 'Come on lad, it's over.'

Mellor grits his teeth and tears himself from the sight of the studded door, battered but still holding, and free now of all attackers. Dean, dripping blood in his wake, is leaving, and his men with him. Flitting shadows skirt the perimeters, ducking and running from the incessant musket fire. James Haigh is sunk to his knees halfway to the gate, and Mellor yanks him up on his way past.

'Mind mi bloody shoulder!' the panicked man wails and Mellor smells blood and gunpowder from a musket-ball lodged deep in Haigh's upper body. They stagger from the yard, surrounded still by the manic firing from the upper windows, each shot lighting up the upper level of the mill, and Mellor sees the human outlines with their weapons, tucked behind some kind of shielding. Flagstones, he realises. They've pulled up the mill's own flagstones as makeshift embrasures. Not one Luddite shot has had any real effect at all. He curses Cartwright, dragging Haigh and following Brook across a footbridge over the beck to the south bank, away from the route any troops will take.

Joseph Drake and Ben O'Bucks fall in with them, and Ben catches Mellor by the arm.

'We've left some,' he panics, 'I heard screaming when I came out o' t'yard, but I couldn't see for all t'smoke.'

Mellor can hear it now; a desperate, thin keening, ebbing and flowing on the wind.

'Jesus,' he whispers. 'We cannot go back.'

'Nay, we cannot,' Brook agrees, running a hand over his damp head.

'Where's yer hat?' Mellor asks.

'In t'watter,' Brook admits, embarrassed. He knows this is a problem for their return home. How can he possibly make it all those miles to Huddersfield? Any soldier or constable out patrolling will take him up just for being hatless. No one is without a hat, not ever, not without some nefarious reason. Brook looks around helplessly, as if he might find a cap growing in the marsh grasses.

'Come on,' says Mellor, striking out in sudden anger on the packhorse trail. 'I'll find thee a bloody cap.'

Circling back towards Hightown, forcing tired legs to cooperate, on and on through the fields and lanes, Brook's feet are sore and blistering in his wet boots and Haigh is trying his best not to whimper but the pain in his shoulder is excruciating and every step sends spasms of sharper agony through the open wound. Mellor can still hear faint screaming - his mind's doing; even the wind couldn't carry the noise this far. Ben O'Bucks is traumatised and light-headed. He's been a lucky boy, averting disaster and misfortune for most of his life, and this setback has been a great shock, presenting him with the truth of his own mortality. He wants to get home and forget this whole night, and never mind Brook's sodding hat. But Mellor is insistent, and brays on the door of the first solitary homestead they encounter.

'What's tha doing?' exclaims Drake, nervously stepping from one foot to another, but Mellor ignores him and knocks until a woman comes to the door. She peeks out, wide-eyed and fearful.

'Evening missus, I need to trouble thi for the loan of a hat. Has thi husband got one we can borrow?' He doesn't bother to smile, and neither does she, as she looks past him and takes in the sight of dripping wet Brook, bloodied Haigh, fidgeting Drake and gaunt-faced O'Bucks.

'I've got one,' she nods, disappearing for half a minute into the unlit cottage and leaving them like errant children shuffling at a schoolmaster's door. When she returns, she passes the cap over promptly, says 'Now be off quick, mind,' and closes the wood in their faces. Mellor hands the cap to Brook who pulls it on and sets it straight with great care, as if it were a talisman.

Mellor curses himself for not asking for some food. He reckons he'd have got something out of her, unfriendly though she was, and they need it badly. Brook is depleted from his drenching in the freezing mill dam and O'Bucks needs something to revive him from the dumb stupor that has taken hold of him. Whether Haigh can manage to eat is questionable, but he's the weakest and if they can get food into him, so much the better. The blackness of the path ahead gives few clues, but Mellor thinks Clifton is not too far away and he marches the men on, promising them food and drink if they just keep moving forward. Twenty minutes later, Mellor is knocking on the door of another cottage, while Haigh lies down to rest his shoulder. The blood is clotting and the other men think he will live - at least until any infection sets in - but the pain is no better and his low moaning through a rictus of bared teeth unnerves them all.

Mellor's persistence at this cottage is rewarded when a concerned face appears at the window. Again, a woman. The men are too scared to come to the doors themselves - expecting to be pressed into the service of the Luddites, or perhaps afraid of being discovered avoiding duty.

'We need food,' Mellor says. 'Got any thi can spare?' He jangles some money in his hand and her eyes fixate upon it.

'I've some bread, that's all, lad.'

'That'll do, and watter?'

'Aye.'

She busies about inside, and within seconds, passes out to Mellor a large jug of water. He holds his hands out for the bread, but she insists on taking his money first.

'It's not that I'm suspicious by nature,' she says, once the trade is safely done, 'but tha's picked a funny time to come troublin' folk.'

'Thanks,' Mellor nods, 'Reit grateful to yer.'

'Is that felly alright?' she calls after him, looking towards Haigh on the ground.

'Drunk,' replies Mellor. He tears the bread apart so they can each have some. Drake wolfs his down. O'Bucks and Brook eat more steadily. Haigh only manages a bit, but drinks lots of water which Mellor takes as a good sign. After five minutes, they deposit the pitcher in the lee of a wall and leave, watched with curiosity by the woman in the cottage whose natural inclination to offer some linen bandaging to the clearly injured man wisdom had suppressed. She expects she'll learn what that strange visit was all about when morning rolls around.

But dawn is still a long way off for Mellor and his exhausted gang. They navigate the tracks back in the rough direction of Huddersfield, too tired to be cautious and protected only by the black night and the steady wind and drizzle that camouflage their slow, scraping progress. Somehow they come to the relative safety of Bradley Woods where they rest for a short time.

Thomas Brook is coughing and shivering, desperate to get home, and he sets off before the rest, confident, now they're on the outskirts of Huddersfield, about finding his way alone. Drake offers to go with Haigh and get him safely over to Dalton, so here these two depart also, leaving Mellor and Ben O' Bucks to follow a different trail onwards towards Longroyd Bridge. Ben is still silent, which leaves Mellor free to begin the torturous review of the night's events.

They walk along the riverside, but Mellor is oblivious to the harsh rush of water over stones. One by one, faces parade through his mind as he checks off who he saw in action, who was wounded, who might have been left behind. Images blur and he cannot be sure of his own memory. He knows Jonny Dean's injury was not a fatal one, though it was painful enough to send the big man running into the night. But John Walker? Mellor's last memory of him is seeing him hanging by one hand from a first floor window while he tried to shoot his pistol inside with the other. John Booth was in the fray; Mellor saw his face in the yard, stricken with panic. And what about Tom Smith? What about Thorp?

Does it even matter who has escaped and who has fallen? Someone - a brother - has surely died there at Rawfolds and Mellor's gut is twisting and heaving at what has already slipped from the present and into memory. How can it be that the magnificent attack is over already, and how can it have gone so wrong? Everything was perfect, damn it. This is not the way it should be, it's not what was supposed to happen. He plays it over in his head, as if by looping the action through his consciousness, he can hold that terrible carnage in the present, instead of resigning it to the past where he no longer has any control over it. If he was still in the yard he could carry that man out, the man who was screaming. Why did he leave? Surely there was time to go back. Why didn't he go back?

'I think we left a few,' whispers Ben Walker, driven, presumably, by similar mental anguish.

'A few?'

'I heard more than one, George, in that yard. And did thi see t' blood on t'ground? Going off in all directions, like a lot had been wounded.'

No, Mellor had not seen all the blood. He tries hard to remember the scene as he ran from the yard, but all that sticks in his mind is Thomas Brook, sopping, hatless, and the overriding need to find a cap.

'Who did we leave?' Mellor asks.

'I don't know. I could guess-'

'Nay, don't guess.' Mellor shakes his head. 'We'll find out tomorrow.'

'Where were t'Leeds lads?' O'Bucks bleats. 'That's what I don't understand.'

'Late, I'd say. And bi' time they'd got there and heard all t'commotion, they'll have turned tail home again. Would you ha' come down out o' t'hills if you heard all that racket? Must've sounded like he'd a full company defending his bleeding mill.'

'He did a good job o' keeping us out. We'd no chance there, George. That felly knew what he wor doing.'

Mellor doesn't respond. What response can he give? It doesn't lessen his sense of responsibility to know that he has come up against his equal. It only reaffirms that he took several hundred men into a trap and that some will die - or have already died - because of it.

They take a wide route over towards Red Doles, rather than heading too close to Bradley Mills or the lanes in that vicinity. It's possible that word of the fight for Rawfolds has reached the Huddersfield magistrates - a few soldiers on horseback might well have been dispatched to alert the main authorities and constables could already be abroad, watching the roads and tracks for returning stragglers.

Ben looks at Mellor once or twice - Mellor feels the other straining for some words or some sentiment - but neither speaks. It annoys Mellor, that he is the one being peered at. Why should he not take surreptitious glances at Ben? Aren't they all in this together, equally sworn? No, of course not, Mellor chides himself - that men should look to him for direction was precisely what he encouraged. But what should Mellor do now? He has tried a large-scale attack on a mill and failed. Must he fall back to the pathetic campaign of searching out shearing frames in the cropping shops, one at a time? The weight of it presses upon him and though he walks ever quicker, he can't shed the sickening pressure. When they intersect with the broad canal, the ground is at least firmer underfoot and the black line of water provides some guiding comfort, a visceral tether to home.

Nearer town the canal passes several dye works, the smell of chemicals competing with the stink of the neighbouring pinfold where the stray beasts are kept, and just as Mellor contemplates whether to keep to the canal or risk cutting the corner off their journey by turning over Seed Hill and Back Green, a figure looms out of the scrub on their right. Ben starts, but Mellor puts a hand on his arm.

'It's Thorp,' he says, recognising in a heartbeat the shape of his friend.

'Christ! I'm glad to si thee,' Thorp splutters, coming towards them, 'I thought thi might ha' been taken up.'

'An' me thee, I didn't know if thi got out or if thi were t'one that-' Mellor is overwhelmed and Thorp grips his upper arm and holds him steady with a strength bordering on violence.

While Buck's presence has sucked life from his shattered spirit, Thorp's revitalises Mellor immediately. William Thorp won't take covert glances to see how he is holding up. He won't complain or whine about the Leeds contingent. William Thorp, whose home on Cropper's Row is just a few minutes' walk away, could be wrapped up in bed by now, but instead he has stayed out, surreptitiously patrolling the canal route in the small chance of being of help to whomever might be returning this way stunned and bleeding. Thorp has an inner pool of strength that never drains away and Mellor can feel it filling him up, soaking into his biceps under Thorp's crushing

129

grasp.

'Nay, it were Booth,' Thorp says, 'Booth an' that felly who took us down there - Sam?'

'John Booth and Sam Hartley?' Mellor echoes faintly.

'That's them. I didn't see Sam Hartley mi sen - one o' t'other men told me. But I saw Booth go down. I couldn't get to him, wi all t'shot being fired. I were too far away, an' he'd ha' never made it back. Took it badly in t'leg, I think.'

'Nay, not Booth,' cries Mellor, pulling away from Thorp.

O'Bucks is startled. He steps away from Mellor, who is letting out a deep growl as if in awful pain. Thorp looks at O'Bucks and jerks his head, his meaning clear.

'Bad news, poor lad,' O'Bucks nods, 'Well I'd best be off. I'll see thi both in t'morning,' He slips gladly into the night on this current of meaningless words, leaving Thorp and Mellor stood together, the latter with his head bowed into his clenched hands.

'He were just a bloody bairn, he were supposed to stay well back,' Mellor howls.

'I think he got a bit eager,' says Thorp. 'But it could ha' been anyone. Just bad luck it were him.'

Mellor rubs his eyes harshly with his knuckles and gives a raw sigh, straightening up. Thorp bites a finger nail and waits, watches the water and the black sky within it.

'James Haigh's been hit,' Mellor says, at last. 'And Jonny Dean.'

'Aye, I saw Dean coming home. Big bloody hole in his hand. There wor a lot o' blood all over on't way back. But short o' summoning 'em all up and checking' t'numbers, we'll not find out. If there's dead 'uns, family'll bury 'em wi'out fuss. Them that's injured'll go to ground.'

'Booth's a real loss. He were a lad wi' some good ideas.'

They stand reverently for a while, thinking about the nineteen-year-old and his Republican ambitions. There is still a chance, they know, that Booth might live - if Cartwright gets a surgeon in and takes care of him, and if it's a clean wound. But if he survives, he'll go to York, and if he goes to York, he'll hang. He shouldn't - not for standing in a yard shouting threats, nor for breaking a few windows - but the law of the land protects mill windows and the equipment inside with lethal force now.

'You know, Will, we've done all these breakings, we've carried weapons an' we've pushed a few doors in, but we've never harmed a person, not once, not even when they were swearing an' flailing. They've shot first, probably killed first. Their side, not ours. What we do now, it's self defence.'

'Tha's reit, but t'magistrates won't see it that way.'

'I don't care. I'm going after the mill owners. They've taken ours, we'll take them.'

'Reit,' nods Thorp. 'Reit.'

Somewhere in Roberttown, Booth and Hartley are still screaming as a surgeon and several over-eager inquisitors go to work under candlelight in the dark of the moon, but the black, still canal where Mellor and Thorp stand in terrible contemplation is blessedly peaceful.

5
Each Haughty Tyrant

In the gloomy light cast by lamps suspended overhead, the Crown court wore an ethereal cast, like an oil painting spectrally animated. On the right, as viewed from the entrance, were the great chairs in which the judges were stationed, the Royal coat of arms adorning the wall above, offering its validation to the stout chests and righteous faces gathered beneath. The dock, where he sat and received their contemptuous scowls, was to the left.

He made a game of their scorn, turned the prosecutor's words inside out, so that they became the accused, and he the judge, able to point to one after the other - guilty, guilty guilty, the term overlaying them with golden glint, their statuesque presence a testament to their inhumanity.

Whispering to each other, pointing at him when they felt his expression gave something away - these petty assaults he redirected, imagining their fascination to be the morbid desperation of the accused, their existence dependent upon *his* interpretation of justice, *his* exercise of mercy. His inversion of reality was so assiduously maintained, that his countenance betrayed only a wan kind of benevolence. Whatever betrayal they sought or imagined in his features was never exposed and they averted their eyes more than once when his unexpected demeanour disturbed them. It was a kind of power. It was something.

Here he is with nothing: only breeches, a shirt, leather boots; chains on loan - jewellery of the condemned, to be unlocked from his stiffening corpse and made over to another; body, appropriated by the state, to be hanged by the neck until dead. All he owns is the truth, tucked deep inside - a winged nugget of honesty, the essence of his soul, ready to take flight when this mortal sheath is shed.

Unjust judges watch - Radcliffe, of course, is present. This is the Milnsbridge magistrate's big day, his princely gut and twiggy legs staking out position; fellow magistrate, Joseph Scott is stationed nearby. Cartwright (lodging in York until the Commission tries those accused of attacking his mill) is surely in attendance. The Atkinsons, Vickerman, William Milnes, George Whitehead, and on and on- the procession of those whose frames he has destroyed, whose lives he has threatened, suddenly so unimportant, so diminished. Forgiveness soaks his marrow, a genuine and free allowance of all the harm they have done him, and a wish for all the harm he has done to be forgiven also. Harm was never the real point, after all. Such hatred came later.

In the beginning, there was hope; and here, at the end, with nothing other than truth in his heart, he finds hope again - for them, for himself. The extreme of terror places him in the eye of the storm - long, dying moments of lucid contemplation. Odd - to think he is dying, even now - that in his physical wholeness, he is irretrievable, moving swiftly towards his death. He thanks God for the current luxury of painlessness, for the beautiful health of his body, for the feel of cold air on his youthful skin, for the pressure of the wooden boards beneath his sturdy legs and for the gratification of each rhythmic filling of his lungs. He thanks God for the health of the people before him, that they too have the wonder of breath and beat in their chests and he wishes it, so fiercely, for all, a great and unexpected love of life amassing and washing over him. Submerged for precious seconds in this heavenly splendour, he grasps at receding rivulets, pearls of ecstasy draining from his clutch, tiny promises of what lies beyond the horror, the emptiness, of the solitary, ghastly drop.

'Word's come from Roberttown that John Booth is dead. So is Samuel Hartley. There's going to be inquests, I expect.' Thomas Brook lights up his pipe and sits down to rest on a stool. Mellor sits on the floor and rests his elbows on his knees, hands steepled under his chin, gaze steady. Smith, Hall and Bucks gather round. The apprentices, Bower and Sowden come to a halt in their work.

'Does tha know any more abaht it?' Mellor asks

'Well,' Brook draws on his pipe and pulls a long face that says he has nothing good to tell, 'quite a bit, as it happens. I sh'll try to tell it as I heard it. Start's wi' Booth getting shot in t'leg. Reit bad, it were, a proper big hit that more or less smashed his whole leg off. An' Hartley got it in t'chest, so's they say, but fired on from above like that, it went reit through, probably into his belly. Made a reit mess of him. I can understand Booth living on wi' a wrecked leg, but I sh'll nivver understand how Hartley lasted like he did., nivver.

'When t'smoke cleared, some o' t'local manufacturers come running up an' got Cartwright to come out. He were still inside, hiding behind his flagstones like a great coward. It's a wonder he didn't fire on them as was coming to help! So out he comes and looks at all his smashed windows an' then someone says to him, what are thi goin' to do abaht these lads? An' by all accounts, Cartwright says, I'm not goin' to do a bleedin' thing 'til they tell me who's behind this. An' Hartley an' Booth are still screaming an' begging Cartwright to shoot 'em and put 'em out o' their misery. But they don't say owt about the Ludds, even when he kicks at 'em. But some o' t'other's that's there say: nay, Mr Cartwright, thi can't be kicking at 'em like that - and so a gang of 'em makes stretchers out o' some gates to carry 'em up road.

'There's an inn, The Star, up at Roberttown, but listen to this - it's two bloody miles away. But Cartwright won't let 'em in his mill, so they have to be took away, even though they're screaming, and t'surgeon could be brought to them. But, see, there's a crowd now, an' some of 'ems laughing at Cartwright, even jeering a bit, an' he doesn't want a scene in his mill, an' he doesn't want any Ludds getting in if they open t'doors for t'wounded, so up to t'Star they go, bounced around all t'way, and still they're alive. Can thi believe that? I should have thought God in his mercy would ha' took 'em off by then.

'So then, they're in t'pub, an' Parson Roberson, that angry felly from up that way, comes shoving his nose in, and then t'surgeon's there as well, an' Cartwright - all of 'em crowded into t'room. Now, this next bit is what they're saying, but no one rightly knows: the lass at The Star told folk they were using aqua fortis on 'em, torturing 'em and asking 'em questions, 'an that the surgeon was trying to work, but the others were just interested in getting answers, by any means. They tried to take Booth's leg off properly but it killed 'im, an maybe they scooped a bit of shot out of Hartley, but they were nivver goin' to get all that musket ball out. So he died too. Hartley's being taken back over to Halifax, funeral on Wednesday. Booth's funeral looks set for Thursday, here in Huddersfield.'

Brook crosses his leg, free hand steadying himself on the stool while the other hand grasps at his smoking pipe. The noise of his lips pah-pahing on the stem is the only sound in the shop. Even Wood is lost for words, supporting himself against one of the trestles, trying to comprehend this grisly news.

Perversely for Mellor, this is exactly the kind of thing he had needed to hear. Now he knows that it was as bad as it could be, that both men suffered terribly, and that Cartwright is truly the vicious type of coward who will maintain his own supposed rights directly in the face of consequent human suffering.

Rawfolds, he is coming to realise, has been the complex type of event that represents both a failure and a success. The Ludds have lost the battle, but the swing of mood is now bound to be in their favour. Brooks has just described onlookers jeering at Cartwright, and evidently tales are now circulating that Luddites have been tortured by the malicious manufacturing community. The public are ripe with indignation at the mill owner.

Mellor can do nothing about Booth's death, nor about the pain that was inflicted on him - but, by God, he intends to liberally wax the boy's memory into martyrdom.

'Thanks Thomas, for coming an' letting us know.

It's been hard waiting for news,' Mellor says. (Sunday and Monday for all of them, interminable, lost to baited breath, tense limbs, silent pacing and children being ordered out of doors to play; the visit to chapel, as if nothing had happened, sitting, singing, overly straight and attentive, men all around him pretending no injuries, affecting to be perfectly well-rested, a million miles away from having been up half the night being shot at. By God if it wasn't all so horrendous, it would have been funny - Thorp singing at extra volume to conceal a subdued Mellor; Ben somewhere near the back, recovered but altered by Mellor's unpleasantly human reaction to being told about Booth. He'll get over it - he's almost normal with Mellor again - but he'll never regain that innocent ability to hero-worship another man, pushed now onto the hard, lonely road of trusting his own judgement.)

'Least I could do. I'd suggest a bit o' something from t'Brief fund for Booth's funeral, but I'm none too sure his father'd take it, being a preacher an' all.'

'Aye, that's true, but I'll offer it. I sh'll go see him mi sen.'

'Nay, don't do that son,' interjects Wood, holding a hand up at Mellor. 'Yer need to keep yer head down for a bit.'

'That's reit,' agrees Brook, 'I'll arrange it, George, don't fret. There's men who weren't there, cast-iron alibis. I'll send one o' them. John's father were a cropper afore he were a preacher. He might take it, tha nivver knows. And the Halifax lot can sort out Hartley's.' Brook is pleased to do something for Mellor - he knows he owes the lad for keeping a clear head and getting him that hat when Thomas himself

137

could barely think straight.

'We'll see you a' Thursday then?'

'Aye, a grim day it'll be,' says Brook.

On Thursday at just past 6am he blinks from a troubled sleep into startled, glassy consciousness. The events of Rawfolds are dropping away behind him and he doesn't relish the thought of reliving all that trauma today. Equally, though, he is eager to give Booth the kind of send-off that he heard Hartley received in Halifax yesterday. There had been an unseemly argument at the parish church because the expected minister slipped away to Huddersfield and the other - Jabez Bunting - is openly hostile to Luddism and refused to conduct the service while Painites were demonstrating outside. But apparently none of this shoddy behaviour on the part of the clergy had diminished the impact of crowds in their hundreds, decked in armbands of white crepe to show their solidarity in mourning with Hartley's grieving family.

From the Parish church, the body had been taken to the Wesleyan Chapel on the South Parade for burial, giving the assembled masses another chance to participate and protest. Slogans were slashed on walls - sharp reminders about innocence and vengeance and the wrath of General Ludd; something for the assembled military presence to ruminate upon.

Mellor is anxious, having had all this detail relayed to him in the shop last night, to see the same wave of support, and appetite for retribution, on display for Booth. He kept a low profile yesterday - like many Huddersfield men he guessed that walking over to Halifax for the funeral would fetch them into the clear sights of Justice Radcliffe at a time when the eager magistrate is looking for any and all clues as to who might have been at Rawfolds. Today is different - today he will take the risk of coming to Radcliffe's attention.

He dresses and leaves the bedroom. Smith and Hall are still abed snoring. He doesn't feel like eating, despite Mary's insistence, and he refuses her oatcakes. She watches him wandering about in the yard, and feels her son slipping from her, a veil dropping between them. She can do nothing to make this day easier for him.

At 8am, he walks up to town. There are soldiers everywhere; soldiers patrolling up Outcote Bank on horseback, soldiers gathered on the edge of town, soldiers spilling from the public houses that serve as temporary barracks. In Halifax, had Mellor only been able to witness it, the affronted public had outnumbered troops, but here in Huddersfield, the once discreet military presence has steadily swollen, and martial law oozes onto the streets, inns filled to bursting with uniformed men. Uneasy under their stares, he makes his solitary way along the top of town, dropping down towards the square, and here are yet more troops, massing near the pubs that fill this part of town, their horses wedged into the yards and stables. A few townsmen hang about near The Brown Cow and he ventures over. Joseph Drake is there; he doesn't know the others by name.

'It's already happened,' bellows Drake in disgust, as Mellor approaches. 'They've buried him.'

'They can't have,' Mellor says. 'They can't have done that.'

'Well they 'ave, first thing this morning,' Drake spits on the floor, slitted eyes directed at the blossom of soldiers outside the George Inn. The pub stands next to a field of thirty acres that wraps the northern edge of town, and soldiers litter the coarse blanket of green as though washed there by a tide.

Mellor turns his furious gaze on them, his fists clenching involuntarily. He takes a few steps forward, but Drake and his friends drag him back. The soldiers glance and shrug, blank, invulnerable, disinterested.

'Not now, come on lad,' pats Drake, but Mellor shakes him off and breaks away in the direction of the Parish Church. He has to stop short. There are even more troops here, blocking the road, ready to divert onlookers and stop any groups forming. The day is a waste, an anti-climax. Mellor feels as if he has taken an enormous breath in and now cannot expel it. He can't contain his fury, but there is nowhere in which to release it. His heart is beating too hard. If he'd eaten any breakfast, he would surely now be retching it onto the cobblestones.

He veers into the shadows of the Packhorse yard, striding blindly, tripping over beggar children with their grimy hands out-stretched, oblivious to the ostler moving between stalls with his sloshing pail of water, the steamy snorts and dreamy snuffling of dozens of horses softening the clank and clatter of the waking day. Past two hundred yards of stabling and granaries he barrels, and back out into the open, but when he turns north again - more soldiers. He pivots towards the less developed part of town, where rough patches of old Broadtenter have run wild. A dirt path lined with thistles and nettles leads him out onto Back

Green, but he doesn't follow the road. He crosses it and heads over into the intake, almost running now, in damp, dew-covered, blessedly empty fields. When he gets to the river at King's Mill, he crosses the footbridge and keeps going, all the way to Longley, sticking to fields and paths, gulping clean air. Where the ground takes a sharp uphill aspect, he welcomes the increased effort and the strain in his thighs, picking his way through snickets of gorse and bramble.

Emerging onto a well-worn track, he recognises his location and ploughs on, still heading uphill and ignoring two people on their way down who begin to greet him and are left fish-mouthed. As he crests a final hillock on the crown of Almondbury, the ground ahead fans out in a grassy plateau, devoid of people but dotted with several rabbits who dart headlong over the edge and down the hillside as he approaches. He walks over the flat summit, a gentle south-westerly buffeting his face, and negotiates the pathway to the very tip of Castle Hill, where it rises to its highest point, in a last, lumpy plateau.

The wind presses harder on the tops, but not enough today to be uncomfortable, and he brakes to a gasping halt, doubled over, starry specks nettling his vision. Before him, when he sits heavily on the grass and raises his head, lay the valleys; the dark, furry mass of Honley Wood; Meltham nestling way down inside the ridge-backed dragon's curve of West Nab and Deer Hill; Berry Brow, Taylor Hill and Farnley Tyas slumbering peacefully at his feet. Birdsong rises from the undergrowth on the sloping sides of the hill. The people in the villages might as well not exist;

their problems, their poverty, can be forgotten. The happy valley of Huddersfield, carved and anchored on the bed of the Vale of York glacier, is eternal. No famine or pestilence can touch it.

It would be unclear to even a close passer-by whether Mellor is actually crying . Certainly, he would deny tears and he may not, even now, be aware that his body is working hard to push the collective toxins of months of strain out through his eye sockets. If such helpful tears are falling, then the wind is drying his face too fast to tell. There are no shuddering bodily convulsions, no defensive wipes of the cheeks, no throat-clearing coughs to clarify his state. He might just be a man taking a few precious minutes to admire the view. The far hills hold his gaze, though the hills are not what he is seeing.

He is remembering Booth - young, naive John Woodhead Booth, whose apparent timidity disguised his firm adherence to Luddism, whose physical limitations precluded the occupation, but not the spirit, of cropping. Mellor is recalling the times he took Booth to Halifax, tangling him deeper and deeper within the Luddite network and raising his passion for the fight. Their walks to and from Halifax, long miles of quiet tracks, held conversations that opened the door for a real friendship - one not based unequally on Booth's initial admiration of Mellor, but on a joint understanding and appreciation of the values for which they both were fighting. One thing Mellor is sure of is that Booth came naturally to the Luddite cause, following beliefs that were all his own. Mellor did not drag the boy in - there was never any question of banging on his door and dragging him from bed to do drills, as was required with some recruits, and Mellor never pushed Booth into taking part in breakings. Booth would have been at Rawfolds whether Mellor told him to come or not. The fault for what happened to John Booth lies entirely in the hands of William Cartwright, with his blazing muskets and bitter intransigence. Of that, Mellor has no doubt.

The premature funeral is a slightly different matter - a result not of one man's greed but of a rigged system. Mellor is furious at the authorities who have purposefully denied a whole town the chance to grieve. For this, he blames the Manufacturers and Merchants Committee, who have been begging parliament for military aid and denouncing the lawlessness created by the inconvenient inevitability of starvation and poverty.

This wretched committee is the perfect illustration of the problem Mellor is fighting against - the magistrates, the manufacturers and the church have it all stitched up between them. They create and enforce the laws that govern their own interests, but their interests do not coincide with the interests of the majority. The committee members have decided that a mass funeral for Booth will run the risk of inviting demonstration and protest, so they have prevented the possibility. If desperate parents laid their starving children outside Woodsome Hall or Milnsbridge House for assistance, the magistrates there would most likely respond by throwing children and parents alike into gaol on the basis of some legal perversion concerned with protecting the rich from the horrible truth of inequity.

Mellor stands and brushes grass seed from the seat

of his breeches. He has to get back to the shop. If there's to be no funeral, then he's no excuse for not working, and it's getting on towards the middle of the morning. Also, Mellor now has a new plan in mind. He has unfinished business in Liversedge; he and Thorp have arrangements to make.

Amidst the commotion of the past week, news has filtered through that one of the men from Rawfolds is to be sent to court-martial. Holding a romantic appeal to both Luddites and the general public alike, this man was inside the mill with Cartwright, but refused at the last moment to operate the guns which were intended to decimate the Luddites. As a militiaman, he can be tried for this failure to follow orders, but the only appetite for his persecution comes from Cartwright, who has pressed hard for the trial but has absolutely insisted it should not be held anywhere near his mill.

The whole situation both amuses and angers Mellor. Many militia regiments have now been drafted in from different parts of the country, but most of the individuals within these units are working men with complicated sympathies. It would suit Mellor to harness these sympathies, but the Generals are no doubt wise to this danger and never keep their troops in one place long enough for their soldiers to form any subversive links. Yet evidently this one soldier has acted in a decisively subversive way. Maybe it didn't feel subversive at the time - maybe firing down upon the heads of men whose only threat was towards shearing frames felt like the greater wrong - but for this compassionate response, the soldier finds himself in hot water. His court martial is set for Saturday, the judiciary conceding it may be held in Huddersfield and not near Rawfolds, and Mellor guesses that William Cartwright, chief accuser, will be present at the proceedings, his testimony being crucial to the case. This also means that Cartwright has to return home from town at a time that can be reasonably predicted.

'So I say we wait for 'im in Bradley Woods, and shoot 'im as he passes by,' explains Mellor to Thorp.

'Agreed,' says Thorp. 'Just us, or any o' t'others?'

'Just us. We'll be going over there in daylight so we don't want a lot o' men arousing suspicions.'

'What if he's not by his sen?'

'Then we leave it, just walk home.'

'Ben's had a crack at a live target, sure thi don't want him along, now he's shown what he can do?'

'Ben O' Bucks took a lucky shot at a man in his house - an' missed. Nay, we don't need Ben,' says Mellor. Truthfully, Mellor is no more confident of his own aim than he is of O'Bucks's, but a slight distrust of his work colleague is festering within him, prompted by an increasing level of impudence from the other. The fiasco of Rawfolds has left a lot of men reeling and has disrupted the normal order of Luddite business, with drills and breakings on hold and a pervasive funereal atmosphere in the shops. It would be easy for Mellor to lose confidence now, as his hold on the delicate framework of Luddism in Huddersfield is put to the test, and he knows enough about self-preservation to recognise that it is the influence of men like Thorp that he needs - not that of Ben Walker, much as he usually gets on with the felly, and much as he appreciates Ben's independent efforts - on the night of Hartley's funeral, O'Bucks fired a pistol into the home of Constable Whitehead and nearly killed him. Yet Ben's very eagerness is what unnerves Mellor. Spontaneity can pay off, but it carries such risk. Mellor wants someone he can trust to stick to the plan. He wants someone who will follow his command, not jump the gun.

So that is how the pair of old friends find themselves waiting discreetly, tucked into the hedgerow of a slim track, on the late afternoon of Saturday 18 April. It's one week exactly since Rawfolds. Cartwright's horse will soon carry him by and Mellor will fire at the mill owner and hopefully the shot will be fatal. The world around Mellor has taken on the qualities of primary colours - simple, well-defined and arranged according to some purposeful pattern. With Rawfolds now seven days distant, it feels to Mellor that defeat in the mill yard was not just inevitable, but a matter of fate, and part of a wider plan. More men have been twisted-in this last week than at any time for months, and this is directly attributable to the disgust raised by Cartwright's vicious response. Booth and Hartley's ultimate sacrifice has invigorated the Luddite campaign in a uniquely powerful manner. Yet if their deaths were meant to be, then so is the vengeance that must follow. Not to shoot Cartwright would be, for Mellor, the immoral path.

Mellor has not arrived at this understanding easily. In sermon after sermon, he has listened to the standard Methodist fare which tells him to turn the other cheek when the first has been assaulted, and to accept meekly his place in this world, safe in the knowledge that a greater inheritance awaits. The actual killing of another human being, in cold blood, is a pursuit in which he never anticipated nor sought involvement. He has no reckless urge for violence, no sadistic taste for infliction of suffering - indeed, Mellor's cause is directly opposed to human suffering - but in the absence of true justice and fairness, he cannot accept a sentence of passivity, and all other levels of action have failed. It's all right for the ministers to talk about turning the other cheek, but must the women and children turn theirs too, to be ground underfoot into the dirt? Where does it all end? With a slave-class that will trudge into gigantic manufactories every dawn to be chewed up and spat out, their progeny filling their prematurely vacated places?

Mellor has at times begun to question his religion based on this observation of what he considers the logical failure of passivity. He has certainly lost faith in various preachers over the years, but his faith in God Himself has never diminished, and this fundamental grip on his own spiritual world allows him to see past the corruptions which King and Church place on the divine message. He trusts only the preachers whose clothes are tattered, only those who are unafraid to vent their anger. He trusts the stony messages of the old testament, and if he needs reassurance, these ancient, blood-spattered laws are the ones to which he turns. A church which encourages its congregation to sacrifice their children into poverty and starvation is an aberration. Jesus, Mellor notes, died to save us, not to watch us destroy ourselves, and where He saw injustice, He railed against it in anger.

Mellor believes the natural and energetic desires of the human spirit for peace and compassion are abused by the nurturing of pure meekness and submission. The physical manifestation of a healthy spirit is a body which is able to be active and healthy also. Where an imbalance occurs - where some part of life is suppressed and suffocated - humanity must balance rights and wrongs not through the neutralising process of spiritual apathy, but in blood and bones, the medium of its true existence. A sacrifice is only worthy if it has real meaning, if it shows the true spirit of the person. The hundreds of helpless, subjugated people dying - meekly, submissively - throughout Huddersfield for lack of food and warmth will make no dent on the consciousness of the country, but the tortured expirations of two young, healthy men fighting inequity has caused a ripple across the entire north of the country.

The execution of Cartwright will balance the books between Luddites and manufacturers. It will restore the imbalance of justice that occurred when two men died because they posed a risk, not to human life, but to cast iron machines. Mellor knows without doubt that here, under the canopy of heaven, a soul is worth more than a machine. Cartwright's violation of this most fundamental truth is his own undoing. Mellor's pistol is merely the apparatus of the necessary reckoning.

The clattering of hooves approaches and Thorp and Mellor press themselves back into the springy hedge. Their faces, as always, are blackened, hats pulled low, and they both wear handkerchiefs tied round nose and mouth

'Is it him?' Mellor asks, bobbing his head forward to look, but Thorp lifts his shoulders uncertainly. They have to wait until the rider comes nearer, and even then, his hat shields his face, but at the last feasible moment for the would-be assassins who are now within the rider's clear view, he lifts his head and looks directly at Mellor for a long second. Then Thorp and Mellor lift and point their pistols. Cartwright's face pales with understanding, fear and finally a bitter determination. He kicks his horse hard in the side and sends the beast rearing up as the shots blast harmlessly past him, leaving each raised pistol with a spectral halo of smoke. Thorp staggers, reaching out, but misses the bridle, still an arm's length away, and the horse drops back onto four legs and bolts, head-down into a gallop, with Cartwright braced and clinging on to rein and mane. Mellor gropes for another paper cartridge, but the moment is lost and the mill owner is out of sight, a dusty void left in his wake.

'Damn!' Mellor throws the gun on the ground. 'Damn him!'

Thorp stands with his head bowed, hands on hips.

'I thought I'd got 'im, I'm sorry George.'

'Nay, I missed an' all. He were reit there. How the hell did we miss 'im?'

'He were moving, George, don't be hard on thi sen. It's not easy to hit a man on a moving horse. An' that all happened reit bloody fast.'

'Aye,' says Mellor, pulling the concealing face-cloth loose and using it to wipe coal dust from his eyes.

'If we'd ha' been in luck, he'd ha' come off that horse when it reared and bolted. Just bad luck for us.'

Thorp is right, but it's a frustrating failure all the

same. Mellor picks up his gun from the stony clay track and tucks it back in his breeches. They walk into the woods, find a muddy little stream and use their wetted face rags to clean off the blacking, conscious that they need to be off, as Cartwright will undoubtedly alert the magistrates and have troops sent out to track them down.

'I don't think we'll get another chance with that felly, George, not now he's had that shock,' Thorp says, washing his hands in the shallow flow of water and shaking them dry. He's put his cap on a rock while getting his face clean, and now he rakes his fingers through his damp blonde hairline and fits the cap snugly back on. He traces his fingers around his face, checking for black residue, satisfied when they come away still clean.

Mellor, crouched by the stream, cups more water and rubs his eyes, reddened from the soot. Then he gives his face a vigorous scrub dry with the inside of his coat.

'He'll not travel now, unless he has to, an' then it'll be wi' soldiers,' agrees Mellor. Cartwright hasn't the bullish, invincible nature of some of the other mill owners, which perhaps explains why his preparations at Rawfolds were so effective - unlike them, he accepted his own vulnerability and took serious measures to correct it. They can be sure, therefore, that Cartwright will not allow another such easy attempt on his life. On the hike back to Huddersfield, Mellor and Thorp chat about who they should target instead.

A copy of Saturday's edition of the Leeds Mercury

150

finally makes its way into Mellor's hands on Monday 20 April and the whole shop downs tools to listen to the report on Rawfolds. Friends from neighbouring dressing shops are sent for - John Walker, William Thorp and others slip inside and stand in silence to hear Mellor read what Edward Baines, an editor with a slightly more sympathetic outlook than most, has to say about the pitched battle and its aftermath.

Mellor begins, 'We have made it our business to collect a faithful narrative...' and then, incredulously at times, he proceeds to read the long article in which the Leeds Mercury tries to describe events. Where Baines has written of the previous destruction of 'obnoxious machines' there is a muted cheer. But then the intrepid editor ventures into the dark unfolding of the previous Saturday night and they all go quiet again, trying to match the newspaper-man's calm and not entirely correct analysis with their patchy, distorted memories.

Such facts as were not available to them that night are reported with unnerving detachment, and thus they hear that no less than one hundred and forty musket balls rained down upon them that night, and that had they been successful in breaching the mill, a barrel of vitriol was poised to drench them in burning agony on the staircase.

They hear with contempt the fictional words attributed to Booth and Hartley, who supposedly cried that they would tell all their secrets in return for aid - that they refused to divulge any information at all during their later tortures is proof enough that this is complete fabrication, but Baines's account of their injuries and suffering is, at least, undiluted, and he hints at massive casualties - 'traces of gore' leading from the scene in all directions.

When he comes towards the end, Mellor hesitates and regards the men around him. Continuing in a slow, careful tone, he reads:

' "We have of late frequently deemed it our duty, from the regard we feel to the labouring classes, and to the laws of our country, to warn those that are engaged in those violent proceedings, of the fatal consequences that await them in the unequal contest which they are now waging with the civil and military power of the country. Let them reflect deeply on the fate of Hartley and Booth. Let them recollect that they themselves may be the next victims, and let them stop in this desperate career before it is too late." '

Mellor lowers the paper.

'Baines is speaking the truth,' he says. 'But we've all taken the oath. When we were twissed, we knew what it'd come down to. An' listen to what he says about his regard for the labouring classes, about our desperation, about it being an unequal contest - he's no lover of King and Church, whatever else he has to say to keep his paper being published. He knows we've got a fair case, and that we're getting the sharp end o' the stick. Why else would he set so much store by what happened to Booth an' Hartley? He'd no need to do more 'na mention 'em in this article, but he told all about it, how they were injured, how they suffered. What will his readers think o' that? They'll think we've sacrificed two good lads to an honest cause, that's what. They'll wonder why Cartwright wants shearing frames so much he'd boil us in vitriol to keep 'em.'

The men around him agree, nodding and echoing Mellor's sentiments. One or two want him to read a few of the paragraphs again, and Mellor willingly obliges. Literacy attracts a duty, where it graces the working classes - knowledge is a power that must be deciphered and distributed to the many by the few who are lucky enough to know how to read. He reads several other articles and then conversation turns to the flogging which will take place the next day, for the regimental court martial which took place on Saturday has passed a harsh sentence, surprising everyone, not least William Cartwright himself; despite the manufacturer's outrage at the man's refusal to defend Rawfolds, he nevertheless balks at the thought of the soldier receiving three hundred lashes.

It is a severe penalty - survivable, but cruelly dangerous. It means scores of lacerations, open to the bone. The pain will be excruciating, and few men retain consciousness throughout such a punishment. If traumatic shock doesn't carry him off, a slow, agonising infection is highly likely to do so. Recovering from the flogging, if it is possible for him to do so, will possibly be worse than the flogging itself. Imagine the rough alcoholic bathing of such deep cuts, and the abrasive dressings, if he is lucky enough that someone even attends to him in this way.

'Best of it is,' chuckles John Wood, 'Cartwright himself begged the court not to do it. He pleaded with 'em to reduce it a bit. But they don't want other soldiers doing what that one did, so they want to make a real example of him.'

'All they'll do is make people angry. Most o' t'people watching will have had husbands, sons, brothers at Rawfolds that night, an' then they've to watch this man who wouldn't fire at 'em being ripped to pieces,' rants John Walker, throwing up his hands.

'Calm down, lad,' Wood says. 'This man in't our concern. It helps us, that's what I'm saying, if the courts look like they're in t'wrong.'

'Where are they doing it?' Mellor asks, in case anyone's heard, but no one seems quite sure if it will happen in Huddersfield or Liversedge, though the soldier is being held in Huddersfield's gaol, the filthy, freezing Towser.

It's a curious fact that despite Huddersfield being the epicentre of current Luddite activism, the number of overt demonstrations against the authorities has been nigh on nil. Throughout the north of England this past week, large mobs have been erupting, empowered and embittered by what has happened at Rawfolds. In neighbouring Sheffield, crowds bereft of other ammunition have taken to potato-throwing instead, and continued with their tuberical assault despite ineffectual magistrates reading the riot act. In Skipton, and Carlisle too, crowds have besieged officials with a similarly starchy onslaught, but most alarmingly for the authorities, workers in Birmingham - a place with no significant links to the cloth trade whatsoever - have risen up too. In Stockport, Luddites have embarked upon a ruthless campaign of breakings, beatings, burnings and sackings. For Stockport, as for Manchester's other satellite towns - Bolton, Macclesfield and others - no help is forthcoming from the provincial centre, where the garrison commander is overrun, though Colonel Clay has managed to send help to Burton's Mill at Middleton, a place under siege by Saddleworth croppers and colliers. Something of

154

the nature of Rawfolds has happened there at Burton's - workers shot and killed - though news is only just seeping through to the men sat talking over the paper in Wood's cropping shop. These places are just the tip of the iceberg - countless other towns and villages are turning snarling faces towards their petty administrators. Yet whilst so many communities are openly demonstrating their resentment at the government's appalling indifference to poverty and starvation in the north, the lidded cauldron of Huddersfield simmers, the Luddite network safely blanketed by nightfall, blacking and closed lips.

Even if the general populace decided to throw caution to the wind and show their support by taking to the streets and lobbing stones (or potatoes) at Milnsbridge House, their attempts would meet with absolute disaster for one simple reason: the government has flooded Huddersfield with troops; The town is under military control, and no one can doubt it. Wherever a man goes or whatever he does, he can be picked up, carted off to Milnsbridge House, interrogated and thrown back out on the street whenever Joseph Radcliffe likes; or worse, he can be sent to York Castle on the flimsiest platform of legal spite.

Though Mellor and his friends don't know it, even the judiciary in York are becoming exhausted with the flow of prisoners from Radcliffe's auspices, and they fear a dilution of the courts effectiveness if too many prisoners are held on exaggerated and badly evidenced charges. Undeterred in his intransigence, Radcliffe has besieged the Lord Lieutenant, not to mention parliament directly, with continual requests for extra resources, to combat what must be admitted as a serious challenge to law and order not just in Huddersfield but evidently the whole of the country. It is probably safe to say that Radcliffe feels himself as smugly vindicated by the present riotous state of the north, as the Luddites feel their cause validated by these same uprisings. The rioting proves to a disconcerted government that very fact which both partners in this dance have known for months - that there is terrible storm brewing, and that the dark figures parading on moors were real all along.

In a town so thoroughly under daytime control, with so few open opportunities to gather together, gossip and share strength - where even the rightful expectation of a dignified funeral has been subverted by military force - the flogging of the Rawfolds soldier is a rare chance for crowds to form.

In the eyes of the law, the very benefit of applying this punishment is that it might be witnessed by those in need of a good scare. The flogging as a deterrent becomes rather redundant if no one is allowed to watch. So, for once, on the morning of Tuesday 21 April, Mellor leaves his abode with O'Bucks, John Walker and Thorp and they walk into town with an uncharacteristically minimal expectation of being stopped and questioned. Others are going the same way - not a great many, but enough to mean that from Towser, the grim little gaol in the town centre, there is a gathering strong enough to form a proper procession as the guards bring the soldier out.

'They're taking him to Liversedge,' comes a shout through the crowd, as the dragoons mount up holding chains to drag the disgraced militiaman along. An excited ripple passes through the ranks of people - the anticipation will be drawn out over a two hour walk, the climax to occur near the actual mill, the scene of the crime. Even Mellor is stirred into an uneasy kind of thrill, despite a simultaneous loathing of the feast-day atmosphere. As they leave the town, more and more people join onto the tail ends of the crowds, shifting along noisily in a happy parody of the captive's reluctant and forced march.

In the white spring light, Mellor breathes in the scents of the hedgerows, and of the river, free to simply be, because for today he has no calculated intent, no illegal plan and he leads no army, commands no muskets; his only duty is to bear witness to the brutality of the state. The sympathy and regard in which he holds the soldier at the front of this peculiar parade is the only burden he bears. One of a crowd, carried in the multitude, his anonymity is a liberation.

They've already passed the Dumb Steeple by the time Mellor glimpses Betty among the procession. Her female companions are busy clutching their long skirts out of the mud. One of them carries a basket, probably with food for the three of them, and Betty sails along serenely with a thick lock of auburn hair whipping free from under her white cap. Outside of the kitchen, away from the yard, she looks entirely different yet intensely more familiar. The set of her nose, the fierce burning eyes contrasting with her placid mouth - if she were dressed in breeches with hair cut short, she'd almost be his twin. She catches his gaze and gives him a girlish wave as she wraps her shawl tighter about her shoulders. He returns the gesture awkwardly, losing sight of her as the people around him press and jostle. Someone shoves past and he poises the offender at the back of the knee, sending him onto the floor. Loud curses follow from the trampled man, but Mellor is swept onwards before he can respond. He doubts it would have ended in a fight. There are few men that would challenge George Mellor these days, even if they were unaware of his status within the Luddite ranks. His muscular frame towers over most of his contemporaries.

In the fields, cows guard fragile calves and the sour tang of fresh pats drifts in the air. Inscrutable bovine eyes, darkly fixated, follow the merry cortège up and over the tops into the Spen Valley that lays beyond Hartshead. William Cartwright is unsuspecting, working within his fortified mill, surrounded by the troops he has succeeded in demanding from the nearest garrison. Mellor has the supreme delight of witnessing the man himself come unstuck; flailing through the yard and up the track, arms waving in horrified refusal at the mounted dragoons.

'No, sirs, no; away with this crowd! What do you wish to do? Set a mob upon my mill? Take the prisoner elsewhere. The punishment should have been conducted in Huddersfield!'

'The flogging is to take place here, Mr Cartwright. That's our orders.' The Captain slips from his horse and begins walking about on the grassy land, surveying the area and looking up the hillside at the winding streams of people still making their way down.

'This is preposterous,' cries Cartwright. 'You've brought Luddites right to my door, you fools.'

The crowd is sniggering at him whilst the dragoons poke a halberd into the ground, trying several places until they find a soft enough spot to drive it down by a couple of feet. Cartwright looks on, struck dumb. He raises nervous eyes to the mass of people and flinches under their alien gaze. A blush spreads on his richly tanned skin and he fumes as he hears mocking voices - 'Thees is preepohsterous!' - mimicking the odd inflections of his accent. Mellor watches his tall, slim nemesis, takes in the clenched fists and the lined forehead, the way that Cartwright steps back slowly, into the folds of his guards who have belatedly marched up from the mill yard and now stand flanking the beleaguered manufacturer.

How slender and vulnerable William Cartwright appears when one is looking down upon him from this hillside, Mellor thinks; how utterly ineffectual. Around him, on the grass and perched on stones, people are unwrapping cloth packages of bread and cheese.

The dragoons push the militiaman to his knees and tie him to the halberd, holding his arms up the shaft and wrapping rope around them to keep him securely upright when the cat o' nine tails begins its work. His fingers almost touch the great metal hook, and the axe end rises up above his head like some grotesque crown.

The commanding officer begins shouting at the other soldiers and they line up, ready to take turns with the whip, which is now produced and handed to the first soldier. Mellor searches the faces of these men for signs of compassion, but finds only a confused bitterness - whether towards the criminal

159

before them or to the authorities who oblige them to flog him, Mellor could not guess, but he is certain all these dragoons find amusement in irritating Cartwright. The peculiarities of civil, industrial conflict include an expectation on the part of the manufacturing classes that the army should respond directly to their needs. Yet the army, filled with men of the working classes, feels the pin prick of class consciousness on its collective soul; and the whole structure bristles at the effrontery of non-military persons wedging themselves into the hierarchy of military command.

The Generals and Commanders resent it also, this presumption that their skill and courage should be subjugated to the will of these petty industrialists - men of no genuine social rank or power. The armed forces, crammed into the hostelries of the West Riding, must wonder what it would be like to be serving alongside Lord Wellesley - facing real enemies on foreign soil, instead of hunting down Englishmen in the northern shires.

The commander announces the crime - neglect of duty - and the sentence - 300 lashes - while the gossiping crowd goes silent. Only the soft sound of steady respiration fills the air, hundreds of onlookers breathing in harmony. They can hear the shuffle of the commander's boots as he moves out of the way and the intake of air from the soldier who raises the cat o' nine tails high before splicing the air with the savage weapon. It makes a whooshing slap, sending a gasp rippling outwards through the body of people watching. The victim's fingers are white as they grip the halberd. The blood springs out in lines across his skin. A call of 'one' is given and the whip goes up again, and so it goes on, the weapon repeating its dizzying descent over and over, while the prisoner howls at each stinging crack. Most of the audience have never seen a flogging before - it's a military punishment, not a marketplace shaming - and the barbarism of the punishment shocks them all. They'll read - those of them that can read, at least - in the papers in the coming week about how Sir Francis Burdett has just condemned the use of flogging and how he has spoken at length to an engrossed parliament about the terrible infliction of injury that the cat o' nine tails is designed to achieve. He has, perhaps, exaggerated the likely consequences of a good flogging - not everyone dies from it, after all - but it's true enough that the whip is designed to tear flesh and draw blood with just one hit, and that grossly inflated sentences of two or three hundred lashes will almost certainly produce life-threatening damage.

As the cords of the whip strike, they take each cut deeper towards bone. The men, women and children of Huddersfield and Liversedge observe as blood begins to stream from his back, soaking the waistband of his breeches. Cartwright has had enough - he presses forward and pleads with the commander to stop the flogging - enough is enough - but the commander refuses to listen. The whip is passed to the next soldier in line and the thrashing goes on.

At each terrible moment of contact, the prisoner gives a mangled wail and he continues to sob between strokes. The count has reached fifteen. The result of three hundred lashes is unimaginable. This man is no hardy naval recruit, toughened by years of service under threat of mortal peril, bearing salt-hardened skin and callused senses. This is an ordinary man, who has offered his services to his local militia in order to keep the peace - not to fight a war. His skin splits like barley pulp under the onslaught.

Some of the people in the crowd are calling out for it to stop. Cartwright rubs a claw-like hand over his now grey face. He tries again - shouting at the officer that they must stop, even grasping the man's elbow. Mellor isn't moved to see the mill owner intercede so passionately. He knows it's because of Cartwright that the whip is falling in the first place. He could have kept quiet; no one but the men in that first floor of the mill needed to know what had happened. The mill survived despite this one man's refusal to fire. Cartwright could have respected the militiaman's conscience. Who was he to give orders in the first place anyway? Cartwright didn't have the right to order one man to kill another.

The army surgeon bends down and takes a disparaging look at the prisoner, slumped against the pole. He motions to carry on and Cartwright groans in despair, begging for an end to it. The crowd has joined in with more vigour, rising determinedly now from the apathetic shock induced by the gruesome spectacle. With the crowd turning, the commander finally calls a halt. The score stands at 25. The militiaman is insensible. The army surgeon releases his wrists, burned bright red and blistering where the rope has dug into them and the prisoner slumps to the ground, falling on his side. The crowds press forward a little. The reddened cat o' nine tails is discreetly put away.

From the track, near the front of the crowd, a man in upmarket clothing steps forward. He glares at Cartwright with distaste and doesn't bother to acknowledge the commanding officer, but stoops to the fallen militiaman and puts a glittering coin into his hand.

The victim can barely look up, just fingers the coin without a word, but onlookers see that it is a whole golden guinea that he holds. When the benefactor turns, Mellor recognises Abraham Jackson, the currier who lives just on from The Shears at Liversedge. He's a manufacturer sympathetic to the cause, proof that profit and trade do not depend on replacing men's work with wretched machines. A path parts for Jackson as he walks away, and his movement is the signal for many to drift on in his wake. Mellor watches as some rudimentary bandages are applied to the wincing militiaman's back and a drink of wine is pushed to his mouth, no doubt to fortify him for the march back to Huddersfield, where he will spend some hours on display for the benefit of those who couldn't make the journey over to Rawfolds. But Mellor has no desire to see this injured comrade struggle the seven miles or so back over the hills. Neither do his friends - they're all ready for home. It's made them sick to their stomachs to watch that. At least if they come for us, thinks Thorp, who has possibly the strongest stomach of them all, the rope will be quicker.

Emboldened by the support Mellor witnessed in the crowd on Tuesday, he plans another shooting on Thursday. He has no intention of going back over to

Liversedge - let Cartwright stew in his own mess for a while. Instead, Mellor intends to target Joseph Radcliffe.

The man is gaining the ear of government, petitioning for extra troops and taking up men and women on petty accusations so he can hold them for interrogation at Milnsbridge house. He has a prior history of intolerance towards the public, having interfered over and above the call of duty some years since to subdue women protesting the price of flour.

For those with long memories, a pattern has emerged concerning the behaviour of Joe Pickford - for Pickford was his name before his dying uncle made him sole benefactor of his estate - and this pattern shows that the portly magistrate with his long nose and white-whiskered chops likes to put the boot into the poorest people who dare to make a fuss. Perhaps he is scared that sympathising with those in need will somehow drag him back down into the lower orders he so serendipitously escaped. Perhaps he is simply indifferent to suffering, but whatever his personal motives, the ruthlessness with which the plump, little-legged man now pursues his own townsmen has become a thorn in the side of the Luddites, his character possessing an unnatural talent and fervour for rooting out suspects.

Joseph Scott of Woodsome, by contrast, manifests a far more appeasing and practical tone, his appetite for the letter of the law tempered by a native empathy. It has long been a bandied sentiment within the ranks of the twisted-in, that the whole business would be more productively concluded with Radcliffe out of the way; that perhaps, if they exerted enough pressure, Scott would even be amenable to some negotiations and representations on their behalf. It's a long shot, but there is more chance with Scott than with Radcliffe.

He should have been a gonner last Wednesday - O'Bucks was after Radcliffe the night of Hartley's funeral, but ended up stomping - frustrated and unsatisfied at having failed to catch the magistrate out of doors - back through Paddock where firing into Constable Whitehead's home provided some relief.

This time, Mellor has been told exactly where Radcliffe will be, and he feels he cannot fail. Yet, for all his enthusiastic planning, this attempt goes the way of the previous one. Mellor and his few accomplices, having met by Radcliffe's plantation on information that he is there, cannot actually identify him in the field. They spend a while watching a group of men chatting, then fire wide of the group just to give them a scare.

Running away from the scene, they can at least hope that it puts men off working for Radcliffe. Anything that makes his life difficult, or takes his attention from the rounding up of suspects is a good thing. But catching the man himself out and about has become almost impossible. Knowing that he is under constant threat, the shrewd magistrate - having only a few weeks before made himself a very visible presence on the byways - is now keeping indoors.

Mellor goes into town that night, frustrated and tense, to drink at the Queen's head, meeting Jeremiah Ogden who comes along to most of the breakings and Joseph Drake who is palling about with Mark Hill. Pint after pint slides down his dry throat but his shoulders prickle inside, filled with an itch he can't scratch, though he stretches and laughs along and tries to unwind.

Late in the evening, when Hill has gone home, and Drake has set off alone back to Longroyd with a 'suit thi sen' at Mellor, and Ogden too has gone in search of a bed, a woman sits on Mellor's lap and whispers in his ear and he follows her outside, into a dark corner of the yard beyond some stabled horses. While she asks him in awestruck tones whether the rumours about him being King Ludd are really true, he pulls the kerchief at her neck aside, and slides his hand into the top of her shift, finding a small soft breast. She squeals at his cold palm, but lets him carry on and makes no objection when he starts the arduous task of lifting up her long skirt and petticoat, overcome with unexpected urgency, frustrated by the folds.

She stumbles, laughing, all plump thighs and liquor breath, and he presses his face into the scented cotton kerchief at her collarbone while he holds her against the wall. Later, her face and words a blur, he recalls instead the harsh fragrance of rosemary and fingernails in the back of his neck. Sex is a fractured experience for Mellor - something always missing. His mother advocates settling down, as mothers always do, but that's not what Mellor craves, and it's not what he deserves. He needs someone who will set his heart pounding, raise the hairs on his arms, believe in him, cradle him - a love affair that will sweep away his emotional indifference, a romance both feral and pure. The future - ephemeral smirking goddess - lays an open invite before him; all the time and all the people in the world. He's in no rush. Ludding takes a lot of energy; love can wait.

It's different for women, though. Poor Betty. Before she knows it, she'll be an old maid, left behind as her half-sisters marry off. He's glad, in a way, that he hasn't found the right woman yet. It would feel wrong to surge forward into his own separate future, leaving her to fatten then wilt. He'd like to see her married and happy and still feels the niggling, thorny responsibility for her latest heartbreak. If she found a good, solid man, with no links to Luddism, just a nice steady job in hand, that would suit Mellor fine. He didn't like that last bloke she took up with, but just imagine if it was her lover left bleeding in the mill yard at Rawfolds, or being hunted by that infernal Radcliffe. She could have ended up with a man like James Haigh, and the heartbreak then would surely have been far worse. Haigh's got a wife, left alone at home; a wife who patiently gritted her teeth while he made his desperate escape from Huddersfield with the open wound in his shoulder causing him agony, and who now sees that her patience has been in vain and that however long she waits, he won't be coming back to her. Poor Haigh, he's probably in the sweating room right now, with old Pickford breathing down his neck. There's no way out for him, except by special transport to York, and that will be a one way journey. The news that Haigh has been taken up by the magistrate has bothered Mellor a great deal.

He doesn't want to think about it, as he tosses and turns in his own meagre bed in the night. William Hall grunts in his sleep and Mellor tries to get comfortable without shaking the shared wooden frame. He sinks in and out of patchwork dreams, where the woman from the pub threads a rosemary crown into his hair, and a friend whispers in hot, beery breath, close to his ear, that Haigh is caught, brought in from Methley, blood caked on his shirt. Brook says, it's the hat, George, it's that bloody hat, we're done for now. Mellor tries to remind Thomas that they got a new hat, but his mouth doesn't work properly - all that comes out is a submerged gurgle, and a hat like a bright lure floats round and round the mill dam. Haigh is disappearing behind a big set of wooden doors but Mellor is too far away now and he can't pull the brother back. Joseph Ardron stands in the shadows and shakes his head slowly. He mouths to Mellor, and Mellor lip-reads the words - let him go, we've done all we can. But then Ardron starts to laugh and Mellor is as frightened as an infant while he watches the gaping, silent mouth of Haigh's master contorted in paroxysms of hysteria.

The dream clings to him the next day, nipping at his brain. As he waits for news of Haigh - for surely someone will bring them news soon - those unconscious phantasms linger though he tries to dispel them. Joseph Ardron is no nightmarish fiend - he is a master cropper, Haigh's boss, and a friend to the Luddites. No, not just a friend; Ardron and other men like him are crucial to Luddism. Who is it that nurtures the young croppers and introduces them to the oath-takers? Who allows the apprentices in their household to come and go at unearthly hours, and never asks for a word of explanation? Who takes in the weapons, delivered by moonlight, and hides them under the fleece? The master croppers, of course.

These well-off men, who run the shops all over town and cosy up to the big manufacturers in The George over the market day dinner, will lose all they have if the mills continue to grow out of proportion, swelling their floors with shearing machines and gig mills. Most of them, like John Wood, are too old, too well-known, to play a direct hand in the murky business of insurrection. Yet for all George Mellor's leadership in the fields and on the moors, as he takes men to the places where the frames are hidden, the true leaders are people like Ardron, like Wood, who feed him the information and mop up the mess afterwards. Ardron shifted Haigh from place to place - through the homes even of his own family, at great risk to them all - trying to hide the injured cropper from Joseph Radcliffe. That the constabulary found Haigh was due not to Ardron's neglect, but to the tales told by a local surgeon who treated Haigh while he was still in the town.

What Mellor and Ardron and countless other men throughout the West Riding must now hope is that Haigh keeps his own mouth shut. The wounded twenty-one year-old cropper could tell tales aplenty and maybe even talk himself out of a charge if he drops enough Luddites into Radcliffe's lap. Only the oath binds him. So far, in the cat and mouse game of breaking machinery, the oath has barely been tested - Radcliffe has failed, despite all the men he has interrogated, to press his finger to the throbbing pulse - but now he's got a bona fide Luddite, alive and with a musket wound. How deep and how hard will he probe to dredge from Haigh the delectable secrets within? How resolute is Haigh's faith, in the cause and in himself?

'Tom says tha's not sleeping well.' Betty folds a beautifully finished piece, due to be picked up in the late afternoon. Mellor regards her from behind his work table then turns away with a water can in his hands.

'How would he know?'

'Don't be like that, George. He's just a bit worried.'

'We're all worried, Betty.'

'It's this James Haigh, in't it? Well I don't know all o' t'ins an' outs, but I can tell thee this: tha mustn't worry.'

'Oh that's grand Betty,' he laughs, 'I sh'll make a note o' that.'

Betty slaps the heavy piece over an empty trestle and rounds on him, arm muscles still tensed from handling the heavy fabric.

'If he'd said owt, they'd ha' been here by now.'

'There's time yet.' Mellor lecks a piece spread out on the floor. Smith and Hall are out in the yard enjoying a bite of muffin bread in the rare April sunshine. Bucks is in the little room at the end of the shop, cleaning cards with Sowden.

'Have some faith, George. He's twissed, an' I know what that means.'

'He's been shot, Betty. He's got a dirty great hole in his shoulder and God alone knows what Radcliffe and his men will do to 'im, to get 'im talking, an' he's a wife to go back to.'

'Why don't yer look at me, George?' Betty enquires, softly. She waits until he faces her, so that she can speak even more quietly, lessening the chance that Bucks and Sowden should overhear. 'Have some faith, George. Tha looks haunted. But it won't be thee they come for. If they make Haigh talk, if they hurt 'im an' drag it out of 'im, it won't be your name he gives. He'll

170

give 'em summat an' nowt. He'll name one o' t'others that were there, whose name makes no difference. He'll give 'em the slightest nugget o' gold, not the biggest. Thi can rest easy lad, on Haigh at least. There's no reason for 'im to name thee. An' I'll bet Haigh can keep quiet any road. If Booth an' Hartley didn't talk, what makes thi think Haigh will?'

Mellor nods. She's right, of course.

'That's not all that's bothering thi, though, is it?' She peers into his eyes. 'Yer feeling bad for Haigh? Is that it?'

'Aye, I suppose so,' he concedes.

'These lads, they all took the oath, George. They knew, oh aye, they knew what it could come to. Tha mustn't feel bad.'

'I've a responsibility, all t'same,' he argues.

'People die, George. Whether it's from illness, or violence, or even the law, people die. Tha cannot do anything abaht it, so give over pitying thi sen. Best thee can do is to get on wi' things. I know, George, I've had it to do, what wi' feyther and wi' Hannah, not to mention Sally an' Frances. An' that were family - Haigh in't family, so just be glad it's 'im and not thi sen up at Radcliffe's.' She sighs. 'I'll bet thi can't remember Hannah at all, can thee?'

He shakes his head. There's no shame in that - he wasn't much more than a year old when she died. Her grave is a tiny plot, covered over with wild primroses that their mother seeded long ago.

'She had darker hair than us, long and brown. I used to brush it, an' she used to brush mine. When she died, she were six - old enough to know she were sick, and where she were headed. I thought she were almost grown up, mi big sister. I were half her age. An' yet she were just a tiny lass.' Betty's lips close up tight. Mellor looks at the grey stone floor, partially covered by the wetted length of cloth. If Betty's original purpose was to cheer him up, then she's lost her way. He's not sure what to say to her - hasn't he suffered the same, with baby Sally and young Franny, little sisters he remembers all too clearly? - but she remains standing before him, as if some answer is due.

'I'm sorry, Betty,' he says at last. Sorry for what? For not adequately acknowledging a grief she has held for over twenty years? For worrying about his friends more than an ancient bereavement? It doesn't matter - her grim-faced nod confirms that it was the correct thing to say. She exits the shop, leaving him confused and frustrated.

The limitation of Betty's counsel is that she just cannot comprehend the scale of his activities, nor the pressure on his young shoulders. A few nightmares such as he is suffering are the logical outcrop of an exhausted mind, that's all. Through February and March he was so busy with breakings, he allowed himself to miss night after night of sleep. Now, approaching the end of April, he is consumed with assassination attempts. He has to anticipate and retaliate against the political machinations of the manufacturer and merchants committee, and liaise with the dense underground network of Luddites, many of whom differ significantly in ideology and education.

It's all very well for master croppers like Beaumont and Hargreaves to give the order to attack such-and-such a shop but not take any money, yet what can

Mellor do if he isn't there and the Ludds involved get greedy or threatening? In the background of the planning and the organising, always that screaming from the mill yard - he can't ever fully shut it out - and now Haigh imprisoned, and Jonny Dean with his hand all ruined, and O' Bucks looking at him with stealthy eyes that say, I don't trust you any more.

Mellor rubs his temples. The fine weave of the cloth on the floor is making his head ache. He lifts it up onto the nelly, hooking it into place, closing his eyes for a moment against the intricate pattern.

Haigh is escorted to York in a sealed carriage surrounded by armed dragoons. Mellor watches it rumble past on the cobbles, one of hundreds of people who will mark meaningfully the bleak vehicle's passage. Inside, Haigh is alone, having said not one useful word to Justice Radcliffe, despite heavy provocation.

Only two weeks have passed since Rawfolds, but those events belong now to a different life. Haigh's existence has changed immeasurably; he has lost his health, his liberty and his happiness. The carriage rattles a battle cry to all the Luddites it passes. To everyone else, the clatter is a stark warning. Loathing for the authorities fills Mellor. When, that very evening, he meets with some of the most influential men now within his orbit, his message to them is unequivocal - campaigning hasn't worked, breakings haven't worked, attacks on mills haven't worked; it's time to go after the manufacturers and Mellor wants their agreement. There is some opposition to this. Wood, Beaumont, Hargreaves, Ardron, even Brook have all, at one time or another, eaten, chatted or otherwise dealt with the men whose lives they are now planning to take, but Mellor's voice, along with those of Thorp and John Walker and other stalwarts of the previous month's action, win out. In the gloomy candlelight in the back room of a Lockwood cropping shop, Mellor chips in with phrases and ideas as the more learned men put pen to paper in the form of another warning letter, this time to Justice Radcliffe.

'Appeal to his vanity,' advises Wood. 'Tell him we're writing to him because he's the only man around here who can sort this out. No one wants a civil war, tell him that. He must look to his tenants, listen to their pleas.'

'How about "They look to you for salvation from this injustice",' suggests Brook.

'Or, "They look to you, and only you, for some redress." That sounds better.' says Wood. 'Language is important. We must use the words that put fear in their hearts, words that remind them who we are. We are an army o' redressers, let him remember that. God can deal wi' salvation.'

There is more scribbling, more interjection.

'Who are we naming?' Beaumont wants to know.

Horsfall, Atkinson, Cartwright, Vickerman; all are tossed around as potential targets.

'Not Cartwright, that just draws attention to t'failed attempt,' Mellor says, without any self-consciousness. 'An' if we go after The Bishop, it looks malicious, not political.' Vickerman, his nickname deriving from his self-aggrandising involvement in Methodism, is detested by the Luddites, but they have already successfully ransacked his shop and his home.

174

'Just Thomas Atkinson and William Horsfall then?'

'Aye, just them for now.'

It goes down on paper that this pair will soon be numbered with the dead. The scribe waits for his instructions, as the men try out different phrases, some preferring military terminology, others a fire and brimstone rhetoric, eventually settling on a final conciliatory line - 'And Jesus knew their thoughts and said unto them, every Kingdom divided against itself is brought to desolation; and every city or house divided against itself, shall not stand.'

'There, that's done,' says Hargreaves. He's a shortish man with a dark green jacket that strains at the waist when he is sitting. He blots the letter and shows it around the table. Wood nods, resigned to the biblical tone. Mellor, too, is satisfied. Religiously loaded, the missive has a dignified bearing, whilst retaining the threat of violence that underscores their unswerving purpose. 'How go things in Halifax?' Hargreaves adjusts his rumpled jacket.

'People are nervous,' admits Mellor. 'Old John Baines doesn't like t'idea o' shooting individuals. But I should take him wi' a pinch o' salt. He talks about revolution, overthrowing the rich; there'd be more blood on t'streets wi' what he's trying to sell.'

'I'm not for that,' says Beaumont. 'Are any of us? I don't think we are. All we want is a bit o' fairness back. I'd not see us go down t'French road.'

'There's more 'na one road to get where tha's going,' Ardron cuts in. 'Things were never that fair afore - they've got worse, that's true, but just going back to what we had, I don't think that'll ever be enough.'

'Quite right, Joseph lad,' Wood agrees. 'Never a

truer word spoken. Does tha remember hearing the Ingham brothers speak, just a few years back? They had it spot on - parliamentary reform is needed, an' the Tory hatred o' t'working classes o' this country cannot be tolerated any longer. We're all men, we all have a voice, and what's more, the bulk o' this country sits on t'back of our cloth trade. Yet, we've got no say and we're under t'thumb o' men wi' more money than sense. Men who can drag us off to York, lock us up wi'out trial, just for singing a ditty about t'Prince Regent. Nay, it will not do just to go back. How far back would we go? I've been fighting this same fight all my life, an' I tell thee, I'm bloody tired of it.'

'Even so, the Tom Painers are a bit too far over for my liking.'

'That's as maybe, I'm not saying as I want revolution either. Far from it. I just want people like Burdett to have more of a say, and people like Perceval to rot.'

There is as much hatred in the country for the Prime Minister as there is for the King and his son. Burdett, though, is the people's hero - a slim forty-something man never seen in the West Riding, but most popular in London and as such, reported on at length by the newspapers. Sir Francis Burdett is famous for his devotion to parliamentary reform, and he's even been imprisoned in the Tower for some weeks after supporting an activist who campaigned for public access to the House of Commons. This is the kind of leader they want - an erudite and articulate representative of the masses, who has a visceral understanding of the suffocating injustice that results from being permanently held at arms length from the political system - but Burdett is a southerner, a landowner. Is it truly possible that he feels passionately enough about parliamentary reform to see it through? After all, Lord Byron recently made a big splash in the papers after his furious attack on the proposed use of capital punishment against frame-breakers, but that didn't stop the bill passing through parliament, unchanged, in March, and now where is Byron? On some country estate, soaking up his rum?

Mellor is sceptical. He doesn't believe parliament will ever change. There's no way in - physically or intellectually. They've written letters - and don't forget the big inquiry into the wool trade - but any apparent effort by the Tories to engage with the public is a sham, a teeth-filled facade. This pretence keeps the masses quiet, makes them think their views are being taken into account, their needs represented, when in fact the very opposite is true. Patronised and belittled, the working classes carry on, terrorised by the government's apparent ability to rewrite or overturn any laws as befits their requirements. The civilised veneer of the true politician hides a land-owning, title-bearing autocrat, intent only on self-aggrandisement and acquisition. When the veil slips, the claws come out; suspension of habeas corpus, criminalisation of worker's associations, capital punishment for militant activism. Imprison the impudent workers, transport them, kill them!

When the bones of all the poor men, women and children are used up and no one is left to work the earth and weave the cloth and generate the wealth on which the upper classes depend, what will the honourable ministers do then? Eat their own children?

Mellor can have no truck with these men and their weighted, devious systems. It is his belief that even more radical men like Burdett will fail because their hearts are not really in it. You have to be ready to get your hands dirty - bloody, even - and these soft men, who lift only paper and quill, will never soil their pale skin nor truly risk their own fortunes for the desperate.

Perhaps Mellor is a Republican after all. But why, if Jacobinism is the more extreme view, is ardent Republican Baines so unsupportive of the new plan? He positively flinched at the idea of shooting Cartwright. Is it easier for Baines to contemplate row upon row of aristocrats for the chop, than to tolerate one man falling from a musket ball wound? Mellor tried and failed to understand Baines' logic when last they met, and now he is more comfortable in the realm of his kith and kin - here in the Lockwood shop with men who are cloth dressers like himself and who share his flesh-and-blood intuition for the fight.

'It's four years since we signed the peace petition, an' where did it get us?' Wood turns specifically to the younger men in the room, 'There were twenty thousand signed that petition, in Huddersfield alone. The Inghams, and Tom Haigh o' course, they made people understand what the war was doing to us all. You'd feel unpatriotic for saying owt against it afore, but Haigh got everyone talking about t'Orders in Council, and how they were stopping all t'cloth sales, and how that was forcing half o' t'country into poverty and starvation.'

'I signed it mi sen,' says Thorp, 'I just couldn't get off work for t'meetings. Never heard 'em speak.'

Mellor had. He was eighteen or so when he went

178

with his step-father to a get-together out at Meltham, and to the big rally in town. The logical simplicity of the argument startled him out of his youthful stupor. Who was the war against Napoleon actually benefiting? Only the rich. The poor were dying because of it. The ridiculous Orders in Council - a response to Napoleon's trade blockades against Britain - had escalated the infernal spiral, infuriating the United States of America who now wouldn't deal with either of them. If an eighteen year old apprentice cropper from the West Riding had begun to see this childish temper tantrum for what it was, then why on earth couldn't the government? Must they in all seriousness dig their heels into their precious corner of land and hold all their toys aloft?

'There's business still to conclude,' Hargreaves cuts in. 'We've no time for reminiscing tonight. I sh'll get this letter delivered tomorrow morning. Who's up first, Horsfall or Atkinson? We've plans to make.'

'Leave it to me,' answers Mellor, bristling at the intrusion both into his pensive state and his domain as front-line decision-maker. He didn't ask permission to shoot Cartwright; he's damned if he'll accept interference when it's his body that will be doing the merry jig if it all goes wrong.

'You, my lad, will need help, so don't be so ungrateful.'

'What help can tha be to me?'

'Well, for a start, tha shall want alibis. As many as possible! A court never convicts if you've got a good alibi. Never thought about that when thi were firing thi gun up at Hartshead, did thi?'

'I've friends aplenty for alibis,' Mellor retorts.

'Ey now, give up and listen,' Wood says, 'Friends are fine, but not if they're all saying different things. Listen to William, he's not daft.'

'So when will thi do it?' Hargreaves persists.

'Tuesday,' says Mellor, without any hesitation. 'Market day. Horsfall rides back up Crosland Moor every Tuesday night wi'out fail. He'll maybe call at t'Warren House for a drink. Further up, it's all plantation, perfect to get to an' hide in wi'out being seen.'

'Good,' says Hargreaves. Ardron looks approvingly at Mellor; Wood allows himself a private smile at his step-son's ability to put a master cloth dresser back in his place. 'Busy time, Tuesday night. No one will remember whether thi were in town or not. I can get a good load to say thi were, if it comes to it.'

'Reit. Ta, William.'

'An what about pistols? We'll get something sent round to thi shop, shall we?'

'Nay,' says Mellor. 'I've got a horse pistol that'll do t'job. Just got to get it back from a mate o' mine.'

'Grand, grand. And what'll thi do after?'

'Go for a drink,' says Thorp, laughing.

'Aye, we'll have one an' all,' says Ardron, joining in the mirth. He's had precious little to be happy about these past few weeks, carting James Haigh from pillar to post, listening to the injured man's gasps of pain and putting up with the sickly-sweet stench oozing from his wound and, after all that, watching him taken up by the constables. He's more than ready to toast the shooting of an avowed enemy of all Luddites. The whole town has heard of Horsfall's audacious threat to ride up to his saddle girths in Luddite blood, and more than a few find the sentiment distastefully vicious.

'I'm being serious,' Hargreaves persists. 'Tha wants to get home and get to bed, an' try an' be sure no one sees which way thi went. Then no one can argue wi' yer alibis.'

'I'm very well practised in getting home after jobs like this,' yawns Mellor, checking the time on his pocket watch. 'I've been doing it for months.'

'Aye, tha's done a good job. Just don't get cocky.'

Hargreaves knows when to quit, and he can see that Mellor knows his game. This is why they've chosen him, steered him, protected him. Now they'll fade into the background again and let him ride the crest of the wave.

On Monday, mid-morning, Justice Radcliffe takes possession of a letter that has been hand-delivered to his Milnsbridge home.

'Did you see who it was? Did you see their face?' he demands of his staff, but everyone shakes their heads; no one noticed anything. Radcliffe stomps off to his reading room with the letter gripped in his white fist - another letter, from a supposed friend, giving no useful information, just evil threats. This tactic of introducing oneself to the recipient as a concerned and helpful neighbour, and then issuing dire warnings and Methodist rantings as if merely passing on the mood of the county, is an elaborate style constructed to offer some legal protection to the anonymous writer from a capital felony charge under the Black Act statutes, should their identity be discovered. It has other purposes also, not least to allow the writer to exercise wit and wisdom, but the effect on Radcliffe is measurably consistent. His flaccid, oval face becomes inflamed, he arches his back and he paces about with his small dogs at his feet until his shallow breathing has slowed down. His wife and daughters know to stay out of his way when he's in this mood. It's worse, even, than when he gets news of another mill attack, or attempted shooting, because in those instances his anger transmutes into gay resolve at the opportunity to investigate, interrogate and put himself at the very centre of the action. He's always happier, these days, when a suspect is brought into his specially prepared and empty little room, there to stand until Radcliffe himself deigns to enter and begin his questioning. But when these letters arrive, direct to his doorstep, they strike the magistrate with a helplessness and a weakening of the spirit because he is forced to wait for whatever terrible event has been hinted at within the missive, powerless to proceed in any direction.

If the Luddites knew how troublesome the letters are to Joseph Radcliffe's peace of mind, they would doubtless send more.

On the evening of the letter's arrival, the Huddersfield skyline is lit up beautifully by the spectacle of a stable on fire. It's not Mellor's doing directly, but one or more of the lads has evidently decided to burn down some property belonging to Constable Allen Edwards. Mellor, who has been drinking in The Horse and Jockey with John Walker and Tom Smith, makes his way out to watch, as some helpful people attempt to put out the flames. Constable Edwards has made a real nuisance of himself. Perhaps now he will reassess his loyalties and keep his head down. They enjoy the amber glow and smell of woodsmoke for a short while, but Smith wants to get on and see his girl at The Brown Cow.

'Don't be in such a rush, lad,' cautions Walker. 'Afore yer know it, ye'll be like me wi' nippers all over t'shop.'

'She's a good lass, your Mrs,' says Tom. 'She got another on t'way too?'

'Oh aye, be here midsummer, I should think. Then I might have a struggle, getting out wi' thi, George. Missus won't like it, if she's to cope wi' all t'kids on her own. I don't like to take advantage, tha sees, because she really is very good. Never complains when I go out for a drink or owt else. But wi' a new baby coming, I've got to be decent wi' her, does tha see?'

'Aye, lad, aye. Think no more on it.' Mellor rests easy with his decision not to invite John Walker along tomorrow night. The man has a wife, two children and a baby on the way - but Mellor, Smith, Thorp and Bucks are unmarried. Between them, they'll do the shooting. John Walker, who climbed to the first floor of Rawfolds under heavy fire, and shot his pistol through the windows even though he could have lost a hand or worse doing so, has already proved himself beyond doubt.

Mellor doesn't know what it's like to have a wife, or a child, but he imagines it's a more concentrated form of what he feels for his siblings - that same anxious love, but focussed to a pure beam of feral protectiveness. He has a soft spot for decent kids - like the girl in Alice's filthy yard. There's something not altogether there with a child; their half-formed eyes peer out at an alien world which they decode as best

183

they can. Animal-like in their simplicity, they have a vulnerability which Mellor at times finds excruciating. He heard that Mr Horsfall recently caught a boy with his long horse whip, putting a slash across the child's scalp.

Apparently gangs of children find it most amusing to startle Horsfall's enormous cavalry mount with shrieks and cheers of 'I'm General Ludd!' as they scamper across his path. Horsfall, damn him, has no sense of humour and maybe the little boys and girls on Crosland Hill will maintain a greater distance now they've seen blood pour from their compatriot's small head. You can kill a small child, with a blow like that. Their over-sized heads, thin hands, bony rib cages, are all so fragile and newly formed. He watched his mother wash Franny after she died, five years of life having been so easily extinguished from the lithe, giggling body, leaving a shell of soft white skin and bone, slim and delicate in the bed, a shocking testament to the vulnerability of childhood. It's a miracle that any of them survive infancy at all. Mellor has been sorely tested by his siblings at times, and yes, he has smacked them when necessary - though his mother had usually been in charge of that - but he never lashed out harder than their little bodies could cope with.

You don't grow an oak by bruising the sapling; it just needs to feel a stiff wind to grow strong. Did his father say that? He's heard it somewhere. How a grown man can bring down a horse whip on a child's head defeats Mellor entirely. Is it because these starving urchins are, to Horsfall, less than human? Where does such contempt spring from, that Horsfall can be so easily goaded by high-spirited kids into such bestial action? If these same children had rushed on Mellor screeching that they were constables taking him to York, it's unthinkable that he would have reacted with anger, even if he found the joke unsettling. Horsfall is himself a father; he should know better, should feel at the very least some pull of compassion, some instinct of protection for the weak and the vulnerable; even the condescending paternalism of the rich for the poor might be for a moment tolerated if, in the instance of infantile provocation, it had stayed Horsfall's whip.

The civilising rules that govern human conduct are drowning in the West Riding.

6
A Leaden Medallion

'I hope,' murmurs Reverend Brown, the disconcerted Ordinary on the scaffold, 'that you acknowledge the justness of your sentence.'

'I desire you will not ask me any questions on the subject,' Mellor answers.

When dawn breaks on the morning of Tuesday 28 April, Mellor lies abed staring at the wooden beams above his head. Cobwebs droop from the aged wood and a couple of nine inch nails jut out at right angles, catching the light, shining a rusted orange. It's cold - not unpleasantly so, but enough that he wants to lay pressed under his blankets in the depression of warmth his body has created.

William Hall is lying next to him as usual, the blankets rising and falling with his broad shoulders. No parts of their body are touching, but it wouldn't matter if they were. Sometimes they wake with a leg pressed into the other, or an arm flung out backwards over a chest. If one man is aggravated by the invasion of space, he throws the arm back, or kicks the leg, and the other automatically shifts, repositioning indifferently on his own side of the bed. In the depths of the winter months, they are grateful to share bodily heat.

In daylight hours, Mellor and Hall are friends and workmates, but they aren't especially close. Hall hasn't been here long enough for them to build the wordless understanding that comes with deeper friendship. Smith, too, though having worked his apprenticeship under Wood, comes from Sutcliffe, near Hipperholme to the north of Huddersfield. In the four or five years they've known each other, they've become good mates. Perhaps in a few more years, Mellor will trust him almost as much as he trusts Thorp, though Smith is set to move on in a few months, when his apprenticeship is over.

Ben, a local lad through and through, is right at home at Wood's. His father, a great dandy, is known all over town as Buck because of the gaudy clothes in which he adorns himself. All of Longroyd Bridge was calling his son by the eponymous nickname Ben O' Bucks before the little boy had even learned his real surname. Mellor remembers them coming over the Bridge, time and again, on their way into town; Ben wrinkling up his eyes and freckled nose while squinting over at Mellor, Buck the elder shouting 'How are thee, little George? Say hello to thi mam from me!' Mellor waving back, just a reedy five year old splattered in mud and clutching sticks and stones from his messy adventures in the rough land around the cropping shop.

Ben played with him sometimes, but not often, and increasingly Mellor was indoors practising his reading and writing. On Sundays they might see each other on the way to chapel, Mary talking to Mrs Walker while the boys ran on ahead. As they grew older, and Ben's mother let him wander further afield, they'd gang together every so often, out for a ramble after the preacher had finished his service, laiking with other boys their age, but they were never especially close and Ben laughed at Mellor's book-learning; jealousy, clumsily cloaked. Two years now, they've worked, laughed, drunk together, but there is a fault line in their foundation, an incompatibility of need, a distance reflective of that past age when they waved at each other across the Bridge, travelling the same road but standing on opposite sides. Ben Walker wants security, comfort, certainty. Mellor wants liberty, fairness, change. They've ambled along together fairly well so far, but each has now sensed what he regards as weakness in the other: in Walker, nervousness, dependence: in Mellor, fallibility, diffidence.

Lying in the warm bed, Mellor drifts drowsily. Downstairs, his mother is scraping ash from the fireplace, and the thin grate of metal on stone cuts through the cool, quiet air. The tramping of horse hooves reverberates as some eager merchant approaches on the road into town. Beds and boards creak as his siblings and the lodger, William Hirst, wake and begin to rise. Smith issues forth a couple of pig-swilling snores as he resurfaces from the depths of an alcohol-fuelled unconsciousness. Noise floods the morning. Each minute brings another addition - the clanging from one of the foundries, voices in nearby yards, dogs barking, someone shovelling.

Mellor swings his legs reluctantly out onto the bare floorboards and reaches for his stockings, shirt, waistcoat and breeches, folded on a stool beside the bed. He takes off his nightshirt and the soft, pale white skin of his torso gleams under a patchy covering of dark gold chest hair. Goosebumps raise up under the hair on his forearms before he pulls his work shirt over rippling shoulders, smooth and malleable in the hazy light. The stockings go on, and breeches next, which he fastens below the knee, but he leaves his waistcoat unbuttoned and climbs down the little wooden staircase, greeting his mother with a brief word. She barely looks up from sweeping the hearth. Her hands are filthy from filling the coal scuttle and now she is deftly building a new fire on which to cook breakfast. Betty is in the tiny pantry, digging oats from a barrel and the maid, Mary Thorpe is on her way out to the privy with a bucket, a scrubbing rag, and a face full of justifiably miserable apprehension. Some of yesterday's washing still waits in a pile, faintly damp, for the ministrations of the flat iron.

Mellor goes into the yard, to the big water bucket. He takes off his shirt and waistcoat again, hanging them on a wooden peg, and then he splashes cold water under his arms and over his face, shocking his body with the icy assault. He rubs himself with flattened palms in his armpits, finds the gristly lump of soap and effects a reasonable lather over his upper body. A large rag is draped on the bench and he uses this to sluice himself off, rinsing and wringing it out, before using it to scrub his skin dry. Daniel comes out into the yard, hands shoved into the waistband of his breeches and appraises Mellor drying off in the cold, having studiously avoided the wash bucket himself this morning. Lizzie slips past her younger brother and throws a dry cloth at Mellor.

'Get thi sen decent George,' she giggles. It's a curious thing, being half-siblings, with seven years between them. Sometimes Lizzie is childishly intimate with him; at other times she slips, increasingly as she ages, into an immature kind of flirting. He lifts the rag and bows his head in chivalrous acceptance of her command, then gives himself a vigorous rub all over.

189

In the kitchen, they squash around the rectangular wooden table, gobbling up a thin porridge and waiting for oatcakes from the griddle pan over the fire.

'I'm going to see Mary Ann today,' Lizzie says. 'Does tha want me to take owt, mam?'

Mary thinks for a moment, looks around her at the kitchen contents, then starts putting items into an old piece of flannel - a lump of butter in paper, a slice of dry beef, some hard biscuits, a twist of sugar, a pretty ribbon she's been saving for the seventeen year old daughter who lives away in the home of her employer.

'Don't be coming back late,' Mary cautions. 'I don't want thee abroad after dark, not wi all t'soldiers abaht.'

'I'll be fine, mam.'

'Nay, mam's reit, get thi sen home in good time,' says Mellor. It's alarming, the way these soldiers behave - it's bad enough for any man out wandering past dusk who might get taken up for no good reason, but for the women, these patrolling militiamen are a menace. They prowl the streets, on and off duty, drunk and pumped up on their own importance, grasping and groping at any unfortunate female along their path. They're not much better in daylight, but common decency usually stops the worst excesses. At night time it's different and he's sure that rumours of assaults and rapes have some truth behind them. Lizzie gets up with an impatient sigh, re-tying her cap which has come loose, and throwing a woollen shawl around her shoulders. She grabs the parcel intended for Mary Ann and flounces out with it under her arm. Daniel rolls his eyes at Mellor, man to man across the table.

'Go catch her up,' motions Mellor, with a flick of

his hand. 'Thi may as well walk her into town.'

'Aye, si thi later,' the younger boy sighs, stuffing a final piece of oatcake in his mouth and taking a gulp of weak ale to wash it down before he heads off to his new job at the corn market. The kitchen drops silent, except for the industrious sounds of housework - Mary lining up three flat irons in front of the fire and Betty washing the breakfast pots. Mellor looks out of the small window into the yard. If Frances and Sarah had survived they'd be, what? ten and eight by now; laughing and poising one another under the kitchen table; looking up to their big brother with smiling, pretty faces.

Wood returns from the tiny outhouse where he has been conducting his necessary morning business.

'I shouldn't visit that for a moment or two,' he jokes, seeing Mellor rise to make a move in that direction.

'John!' Betty squeals in prudish horror and Wood chuckles as he sits down and helps himself to the last of the porridge. It occurs to Mellor that his mother has probably not yet eaten and he moves the rough platter of oatcakes, on which one and a half rubbery discs still remain, from Wood's reach.

'Mam, eat something,' he says, holding them out towards her. She pauses, draws a weary hand across her forehead and then takes the half oatcake. He knows Betty will have had her share of porridge as soon as she cooked it. She's no martyr, she takes what she needs, but Mary is like most mothers and makes sure everyone else is fed first. When there's not enough food, she says she's not hungry, even if her stomach is rumbling loud enough to give lie to her claims. Fortunately, it's been a very long time since he's had to watch his mother repeatedly go without. One thing Wood does well is to keep oats in the ark and cloth on their backs. He's just not very good with the little details. He doesn't notice the proliferation of lines on Mary's face or the shaking in her hands when she works the mangle. She sits down as she eats the oatcake, easing herself slowly onto a stool and leaning heavily against the table.

They eat in silence, the three of them. Betty works around them, wiping the table top and poking the fire to keep it nicely ablaze. Wood cleans his mouth on the hem of his shirt when his porridge is done, then tucks it into his breeches. He stands and stretches, knee joints cracking, and sighs as he gazes out of the window. Mary pretends not to notice his pensive behaviour. She doesn't know exactly what they've got planned, but gossip abounds regarding Mr Cartwright's encounter at Hartshead, and the Paddock Constable's house being shot into. She knows her husband and son have pistols stashed in the house and in the shop.

One night, chasing away two brawling cats and losing her footing in the dark, she tripped over three weapons covered by sacking and stuffing in the yard. Frayed grey fabric peeled back by her clumsy stagger, she allowed intuition to guide her hand into flock and straw where she laid her palm on the lifeless metal shafts buried beneath the shroud and felt in the relic at her fingertips the dreadful tremble of rapture, the divine mystery revealed. The touch of the musket tightened her with a cloying desire for normality - a variant of homesickness impossible to remedy, for what she mourns is the past. She hates the retort of rockets being fired up on the moors, the signal shots and the bells clanging as dragoons are called out on the hunt.

The night should be blue-black and starlit, cloud-strewn, moon-dappled, the province of bats and barn owls, a sanctuary from work and ache, a place of dreams, rest, prayer - not punctuated by blasts and shouts and cavalry hooves, running footsteps, closing doors. She carried children into a world she loved, but it sours around her, the colours bleaching day upon day, a tearful wash over the dazzling spectrum of her prime; startling green meadows, haunting ash-gold sunsets, the blaze of violet heather, all now clouded to a miserable hue, impossible to restore.

Mary's world has been leaching colour since Hannah died, each subsequent loss perforating further the membrane within which her glossy aspirations abide - husband William, then a long gap when she thought she might heal, and then Sally and Franny, tearing new holes. She bites a thumb nail, watching her eldest son cross the yard to the shop, brighter than the life around him, a patch of brilliance cresting dangerously the dreary morning.

In the shop, one of the apprentices has lined a piece up for Mellor. He checks it over while Sowden, the other apprentice, raises a piece on the nelly with Ben. Hall lifts a finished piece that has just been perched up onto his shoulder and hefts the heavy fabric out to the roadside where the jagger's packhorse awaits. Wood sets his hat straight, preparing to leave the shop in Mellor's care while he heads up to town for a look at the offerings in the Cloth Hall.

In previous years, Wood didn't need to spend much time at the Cloth Hall - business came to him. This year, he is feeling the pressure as the whole industry grinds towards a standstill. Cloth is still being produced at a phenomenal rate, but by big manufacturers who finish their own cloth and stockpile it in warehouses in the hopes of an imminent market recovery. Tuesday markets are a depressing experience these days, with far less cloth on display and less money to purchase it with. Still, the buyers are not that keen to take their cloth to mills for finishing if it won't be done by hand. They don't trust that the new shearing frames will give a good quality finish, and they are justified in this concern.

A good finish is what makes or breaks the end profit for a merchant. Once they've bought their cloth, they prefer to take it to whichever cropping shop they've trusted and used in the past, where the work is still done by hand. Wood has a good customer base, but he and Mellor both know that this could be undermined by the persistent undercutting of price offered by the mills. These mills offer hand finishing too, so what's to stop a man like Horsfall promising a quality cropping job for less money, when in actual fact he's secretly going to use frames? This is why Wood goes up into town these days - to catch the merchants who are wavering and remind them that they'll only get what they pay for from an honest clothier like himself.

Mellor goes when he can. He finds the exterior of the Cloth Hall oppressive; an elliptical fortress of red brick rising like a two-storey bruise in a town otherwise built of smooth ashlar stone. There are, by sensible design, no windows in the convex outer wall and the only indication that this is a living building and not some mute oval monument to the brick pits is given by the imposing and protruding square doorway which does thankfully have windows set either side, and is mounted with an incongruously pretty cupola and clock tower. The lack of windows reduces the threat of fire, and of vandalism or theft, but it gives it an unfortunately sinister aspect which Mellor can't quite put his finger on - like some kind of prison, but not of any type that he's seen before; Huddersfield's only gaol is a stinking couple of rooms too small to swing a cat in.

For an observer standing outside the White Hart or on Market Street, the Cloth Hall's grandiose entrance softens the effect of the harsh walls and the eye is drawn to the contrasting colours, where the wall edges and the arched door and windows are palely and decoratively delineated from the red brick in a more familiar stone. Like many features of Huddersfield, the building is a testament to the influence of the Ramsdens who built it almost fifty years ago to give the town a more modern and respectable hub for its most important trade. Before then, clothiers would pack the parish churchyard, draping cloth over the walls, and latterly, as things got busier, displaying their wares over the very tombstones themselves - neither a sustainable nor respectable practice for such a revered cloth centre as Huddersfield, though perhaps a fitting display of the ascendancy of practicality over sentimentality in this most successful of modern towns.

There is quite a difference now. The visitor to the

Cloth Hall, once he has been filtered in along dismal corridors that hug the outer wall and sweep away round shadowed bends, can move in and out of slim, bright, curved rooms - for here are the windows, fitted into the internal walls and drinking in copious illumination from the central courtyard onto which they cast an inward gaze. A long, straight, single-storey gallery bisects the courtyard, running like a wide street from the main entrance to the back of the building and within this grand space, high ceilings are supported by smooth, regular pillars set in a row down the centre.

The traders like to talk in whispers. Packed in close together along both the lower and upper galleries, their cloth almost touching, they lean across the wooden tables and put their ear close to the customer, listening to the offer and negotiating as necessary in a soft, low hum that their competitors won't pick up above the general noise of people pushing past and inspecting cloth. Merchants engage in a circuitous journey around the hall, glancing through doorways and dipping into the rooms that appeal, where a particular pattern catches their eye or matches the swatch they have brought as a guide.

Horsfall might be there already, Mellor imagines. He pictures the sturdy manufacturer pacing the flagged floors, checking that his cloth - if he is selling any today - has been laid out properly. He'll smooth a scruffy edge, fold back the cloth at the corner to show off the weave, glance at the neighbouring traders. Clothiers are allowed to arrive between half past eight and ten o'clock with their goods. A steady trickle of sellers will flow in, even in these slow months, to find a nicely lit space on a bench. In the curved corridors, they will pass each other with pieces of cloth on their shoulders, and they won't graze their elbows nor snag the fabric on the walls because when Ramsden built the place he specified that the width of these stone arteries should equal just a little more than two passing traders, each with their hefted pieces resting on shoulder and raised arm. The doors are promptly locked behind the sellers at ten, keeping eager buyers out until all the cloth is in place. Then in these optimistic men come, for several hours of satisfying perusal - if they should need so long to make their choices - until the market ends at twelve thirty and tens of thousands of pounds have changed hands.

Mellor can almost smell the cloth dust in the air of his conjured theatre, dancing on the shafts of sunlight that descend through the high bow-topped windows; Horsfall moves spectre-like to the west, along the main hall, checking he has secured his favourite place, and that his employees are laying the cloth out correctly.

One thing perhaps Mellor and Horsfall would agree on, if they were locked in a room and forced to find a commonality, is that the cloth made in Huddersfield is beautiful almost irrespective of which clothier it comes from. There are better and worse spinners, weavers, dyers, finishers, but even the worst in Huddersfield is a thousand times above anything Mellor - or Horsfall - has come across elsewhere. As such, the cloth demands unquestioned respect - hands must be clean before they stroke it, the pattern of the weave must be shown to its best effect, the quality and origin of each piece must be known, clarified, extolled. Tuesdays in the Cloth Hall are not just a weekly trading opportunity, they are a celebration of the industry and a chance to revel in the beauty of the fine woollen craft that has elevated Huddersfield to international renown.

When everyone spills from the Hall at the end of sales, those with sufficient status and earnings will stroll merrily along to The George Inn for the market day dinner. Others will visit the Packhorse Inn, The White Hart, The Queens Head or one of scores of public houses throughout the town. When they are done eating and drinking, they'll conduct other business in the banks, dyers, warehouses, dressers, packers and carriers. Around the heart of the Cloth Hall, an entire industrial eco-system flourishes and pulsates - slower this year than in others, it is true, but the steady beat is still there. The inns are crowded, the horses fill out the stables. Even men with nothing to do between market-end and collection time will find some way to spend their money.

At three o'clock, back come the buyers to load up their pieces onto horse, cart or human back. This is when the slow exodus from the town centre begins, with merchants calling in on cropping shops to deliver their newly purchased pieces for finishing. Those with goods to carry home are first to trudge along the byways. The manufacturers and clothiers now divested of their stock, are in no rush. They meet and greet each other, share news and begin discussions that will later resurface formally at minuted meetings of the Manufacturers and Merchants Committee. Business can go on well into the evening. The only limitation is how soon the night will draw in, and how far each man must travel to reach home.

And what has Mellor been doing, this long, drawn out market day? Exactly what Wood has told him to do - working hard and getting the shop straight. His perusals on the Cloth Hall and on what Horsfall might be doing at any particular time have given him the peculiar sensation that they are twinned. He didn't experience this altered awareness before his attempt on Cartwright. The surety with which he can visualize the other man's movements makes him feel that tonight he will be successful - that he is fated to kill Horsfall. The knowledge gives him a drowsy, distracted air. He is neither excited nor afraid. His eyes and hands move with artful deliberation. His narrow focus persists until the early afternoon, when the sharpness and clarity of his workmates voices begin to pierce his consciousness and he steps back into the fast flow of their conversation. Ben's father has called in bringing a friend, both of them twissed, along with James Varley, the journeyman who is chatting away with the group.

'Lads,' Mellor says, 'It's time to get moving. Are thi both still in?'

Tom Smith downs tools and wraps his arms around the back of his head, stretching out his chest. He looks sideways at Ben O' Bucks. O'Bucks stares straight at Mellor.

'I'm in,' he says.

'That's a good boy, Ben,' says his father, approvingly. 'The men's a menace. We'll be well rid!'

'An' thee, Tom, what does tha say?'

'I'm in, George, o' course I'm in.'

'Good lad. Na then, Ben, get thi sen up road and

199

fetch back the coits an' guns.'

'Reit.' Ben allows his face to crack into a smile as he leaves, bolstering himself - 'What a grand night it'll be, if we get the bugger!'

His father goes with him, issuing a merry wave of camaraderie at Mellor and Smith, and a mock salute. Varley, in the silence, seems about to say something.

'Tha's not coming,' Mellor forestalls. 'I sh'll have other jobs for thee, James. Reit, I've to go out. I sh'll be back soon.'

He leaves the shop before Varley can argue and walks to the Yews. It takes him less than five minutes, and when he arrives, William Hall has Mellor's old weapon all ready for him. It still needs to be loaded, but as Mellor turns the huge, wide-bored Russian pistol in his hands, he is glad he got it back. It's been, as they say, around the houses, and unsurprisingly so, since it is a fine pistol. The iron-tipped barrel is a foot long, and the attractive weapon is brass-mounted. A few months ago, Mellor was more in need of muskets for mill raids, so he sold this lovely souvenir to a man over near Mirfield who paid a pretty penny for it. But now the Ludding game has changed and a horse pistol like this is much more usable and accurate for shooting moving human targets. Hall, with his contacts over at Mirfield, has managed to track the gun down and buy it back and now here it is, newly brought back to Huddersfield by Hall when he returned on Sunday night from visiting his family in the Spen Valley.

'I'll come back wi' thi to t'shop,' says Hall. 'Listen, George, where did thi get this pistol any road? That felly in Mirfield says to me, George Mellor brought it from Russia his sen. I said, that cannot be true, for when would he o' gone, he's done a full 'prenticeship at Woods an' he never went to Russia by his sen afore he were fourteen!'

Mellor smiles non-committally. Russia, that distant land of ice and fur, a brooding and potent threat with which the United Kingdom is technically at war, has most beneficially cast her enigmatic sheen over Mellor. People will wonder if he went there, and why, and what he did.

He thinks of the men he knows who are still there. There is talk that this war with Russia will end soon - insofar as Mellor can tell, it's no real war at all; Napoleon took Russia by the scruff of her neck five years ago and demanded that she cease all trade with Britain, which Russia duly agreed to do, having established that France would give her a helping hand against the Ottomans. But Napoleon has failed to deliver that help, and Russia is sick of this little, noisy emperor.

That vast, inscrutable nation has played a long and patient game, avoiding all-out fighting with the United Kingdom and continuing, to the latter's relief, to engage in a good amount of discreet trade, and the time is coming when she will throw the French yoke from her shoulders altogether. Mellor is unsure who he prefers in that contest - Russia, their major partner in the wool trade or France, the bastion of Republicanism. His memory skips to Booth's passionate embrace of revolutionary politics, his young, slim face mirroring the enthusiasm of John Baines's rousing speeches in The Crispin. Yet however much he detests inequity, Mellor cannot reconcile himself to a Napoleonic future. What is Napoleon but a self-styled king? He knows he is no real thinker and he admits he cannot analyse politics, society and economics in the way a man like Baines can; he is unable to envisage a social model radically different from the one within which he lives. Mellor suspects, though, that there is a better way to live, some arrangement more fair and natural than the inheritance of feudalism - but he doesn't believe the guillotine will discover it; the path to liberty cannot be built entirely on human bones, even if some bodies must be felled on the way. Not for Mellor the lines of aristocrats jostled to the guillotine; a few manufacturers returned to the earth will do the job. The Luddites have given fair warning, and Horsfall was, after all, the first to make threats to spill blood.

Mellor has the Russian pistol hidden in a specially-sewn and reinforced inside pocket of his greatcoat. It juts from the opening, catching against his waistcoat, so long is the barrel. This is the gun that will kill Horsfall, he thinks, patting it fearlessly. This is no gravitational blade, indiscriminately severing a whole class from existence. This weapon has a single focus, and it will kill for a clear reason - an eye for an eye, it's simple enough. Soldiers are sent into battle and expected to kill to protect their country's interests; boys, shooting each other like puppets on a stage, anonymous and primed. Today's work is not even so bad as that; Mellor is fighting for precisely what makes this country great, the biggest interest of all - the sanctity of the cloth trade and the skill of the people who work within it - and he will point his weapon with great accuracy and inflict no collateral damage.

'Tha seems happy now,' Hall comments as they come to the shop, Mellor cheerfully steadying the foot-long barrel against his thigh.

'I've got good business to do today,' he replies.

Hall follows him inside, where William Thorp is already waiting. Work has dwindled to minor tasks. Buck's friend is messing about with the press and chewing on a liquorice root. James Varley wanders over to look at the pistol Mellor is laying on the bench. He picks it up, nodding appreciatively, stroking the glossy auburn stock.

'Aw look! Thi got it back,' Thorp beams, beginning to dig musket balls out of a small, grey sack.

'Hall got it for me. Pass us some o' them,' Mellor answers, gesturing to the dark spheres Thorp is handling, and hanging his greatcoat on a hook by the door.

Conversation dips as Mellor takes a short-handled hammer and brays two of the balls, distorting the soft lead into misshapen slugs. Nothing exists beyond the act they are all preparing for, beyond the watershed of assassination. The fear of discovery, of arrest, can wait until tomorrow. Sowden slinks through the workshop with wide eyes, his head bowed but face upturned, nervously hunchbacked as he surreptitiously notes the scene.

Despite his anxious appearance, Joe Sowden is not cowardly nor sheepish by nature. He's actually a bright lad of nineteen who works reasonably hard and has a healthy respect for Mellor. He mates about a bit with John Bower, another apprentice at Wood's, and he possesses a high, chuckling laugh that, when elicited, lifts his thin lips into a high cupids bow and crinkles his naturally large eyes. Starting work in Longroyd Bridge, Joe had high hopes of a good career - journeyman positions stretching before him, like stepping stones over a mill dyke, culminating, some day in the future, in his very own shop. This initial enthusiasm has waned. A comfortable ascent to success is no longer a viable daydream, not with the devastation caused by the Orders in Council, nor especially with the rise of militancy in the West Riding. The hoof on his wrist is well formed, though not complete, and his apprenticeship drags on irrelevantly. Joe believes cropping by hand has no future. He guesses that at some point he will take a job in one of the big mills, maybe working one of the frames his shop foreman is so intent on smashing. After all, Joe reasons, each machine takes only one out of every two jobs. Someone has to run the damned iron contraptions. If half the croppers lose their livelihood, he just needs to make sure he's in the half that doesn't.

He slips into the back room and Mellor lets him go without comment. He has his doubts about Sowden, but whatever that young lad thinks, he's twissed and he'd do well to remember it. It was, after all, Joseph Sowden's own house that John Walker had to rush into on the night they attacked Vickerman's - Walker used Sowden's firepote when the flintlock on his pistol failed. One could argue that without the ministrations of that red hot poker, the Ludds out at Taylor Hill would have had less forewarning about the advance of the patrol and may even have been apprehended by those soldiers. Sowden wasn't, as it happens, especially happy when they swore him in officially the next morning, but he must have known it was inevitable, sooner or later.

Mellor hits the slug harder. He wants pellets that will blast Horsfall to pieces and render surgical repair as impossible as it was for John Booth. He tips a generous quantity of powder into the barrel then takes a perfect ball and pushes it down the muzzle of his pistol, following it with a slug. Varley expects him to push some paper in now, but Mellor picks up the second slug, feeds it into the barrel and even tops it all off with a final musket ball. Fascinated and horrified, Varley can only stare. It's Hall who approaches Mellor and surveys the grossly over-loaded weapon with wary respect.

'Does tha really mean to fire that?'

'Aye. I mean to give this to Mr Horsfall,' vows Mellor, not taking his eyes from the vertical barrel as he pushes a scrap of cloth down. Hall passes him a ramrod without further comment, though his eyebrows are lifted high on his forehead. Mellor lines up the rod and feeds it elegantly down the long shaft. With a firm pressure, he backs the balls and slugs up until they will go no further. He removes the ramrod and passes it to Thorp who needs it to ready his own pistol. On the bench lay the slugs Thorp has created as spares. Mellor takes a few, along with some musket balls, and drops them into the hidden inner pocket of his greatcoat. It hangs awkwardly taut on the peg, unevenly weighed.

'I've done the twists.' Smith hands out the little packets of gunpowder, ready to arm the firing mechanisms at the scene. Mellor checks the tiny parcels that Smith plants in his palm. Just like little twists of sugar, he thinks, stuffing the packets in with the musket balls and running a finger along his own thick stitching to check for holes. He made this pocket strong enough to take a gun and ammunition, but his Russian pistol, designed to lay across a horse in front of the saddle, is heavier than most. He puts his coat back on and lifts the weapon. Imagining the gun accidentally falling to the floor, the impact driving the half-cocked hammer forwards to create a spark just lively enough to somehow light the barrel without powder in the pan, he double-checks the flintlock mechanism is properly un-cocked, handling the pregnant weapon with due reverence. Each man stows his gun, loaded and un-cocked under a fastened coat. 'Good luck to thi,' says Varley as he and Hall see them off. Their anxious wait for news begins the moment the shop door is closed.

Tom Smith and Ben O'Bucks make towards Crosland Moor on the Austerlands road, heads down, ready to detour along some of the tracks and byways if needs be. Mellor and Thorp take a less direct route, heading up Spider Alley and on through the Yews, then following an old lane along Dry Clough, up towards the sandstone quarry. The sky has the curious, blank emptiness of a canvas; white and endlessly still, yet as suffocating as an upturned ceramic bowl. Days of mild weather bore Thorp. He likes the broad blanket of sun burning the tenterfields or the bruising clouds that roll in on gusting winds to fill the valleys with rain. This nothing-weather leaves his soul cold. He follows Mellor along the track, avoiding conversation, knowing that careless chatter today will only serve to disturb Mellor's concentration.

The land slopes uphill, but the cant is gentle through the fields and pastures of Radcliffe's plantation and they veer north-west to meet the Austerlands turnpike that runs along the western edge of the plantation. Here they find O'Bucks and Smith waiting for them, skulking sulkily in a small copse that stands behind a high drystone wall.

'Been waiting ages,' mutters Bucks, kicking against a stump. Mellor ignores this complaint. He leans over the wall and looks up and down the road.

'We need to be further down. We won't get a clear shot from here. Anyone speak to you on the way up?'

'No, we didn't see anyone we know,' Smith answers, voice high and breathless.

'Come on then.' Mellor spits into the tufted grass and feels for his pistol as he walks.

Further downhill, he stops and assesses a mid-height point on the drystone wall. He pulls at a stone already jutting out. It feels loose but it won't give. 'Thorp, hold this one up,' he orders, tapping the one above, and between the pair of them they wangle the loose stone completely free. Mellor looks through the hole - thigh height and easily deep enough to poke and manipulate a pistol through. He rummages in his coat, produces his gun and tries the monstrous Russian barrel. It fits nicely.

'Ben, can thi shoot from here?'

Bucks bends down and puts his own pistol to the hole.

'I think the angle will do. Don't forget, George, he'll be on horseback. But I think it'll do.'

'Then you stay here, an' Tom, you behind. You

shoot over t'wall.'

Mellor feels along the wall, pushing and pulling at the stone, trying to find another opportunity to create a little embrasure. He's out of luck there - drystone walls are built to last hundreds of years - but the thinner capping stones, lined up on end, are slightly easier to shift. Thorp takes the strain, holding back the tilted row while Mellor, grunting, drags two from their place, letting each fall onto the grass with a heavy, muffled thud. Thorp lets go of the row, and it slams back into place. Where the two capstones have been removed, a small slanting triangle of light remains. Thorp stands back to let Mellor test it out, but Mellor shakes his head.

'You take it,' he says. 'I'll take a clear shot from up here,' and he stands straight and holds his pistol out at arm's length, pointed at the empty road.

'How long, does tha think?' Smith stands anxiously behind Bucks, shifting from foot to foot.

'Not above half an hour,' Thorp reassures them.

Bucks groans, rising up from the kneeling position in which he has been inspecting his aperture. Half an hour will feel like forever, standing openly in this field under the cool, milky sky. Smith bites at his lip, giving himself a peculiarly womanish aspect.

'It could be worse. At least it in't raining,' Mellor says. He roots about in his pocket for one of the powder twists, then levels his pistol and half-cocks the hammer. This action lifts the frizzen up, revealing the pan beneath. The paper unravels in his fingers and he tips the dusty contents into the pan and pulls the hammer fully back, ready to fire. Thorp leans on the wall, crossing one leg over the other and sucking on a sturdy piece of grass as he primes his own pistol. Exposed on the plantation with only the wall to shield them, they watch and wait. O'Bucks slumps back to the ground and wedges his pistol through the opening, leaving his hands free to wrap behind his head as he lays up against the wall and rests. Tom Smith still paces, gripping his gun, watching the road, watching Mellor. They're anxious - they all know they might have missed him if he passed by earlier than expected and the uncertainty of the wait is unsettling them all. The minutes drag by until finally Thorp breaks the silence.

'Shall I walk a way down, see if I can spot him?'

'Nay William,' Mellor holds his hand up at Thorp, 'I think I can hear hooves!'

They all press to the wall, looking over and straining to listen and, sure enough, there is a barely perceptible but rhythmic thudding, then the muffled sound of a man's voice, shouting at someone in the road.

'It's him, get down,' Mellor cries. He'd put money on the likelihood that Horsfall has just shooed some shit-shovelling kid out of the way. At any moment, the manufacturer will come into view. Thorp squats and shoves his pistol into the triangular gap in the capstones. Mellor is behind him, a hand on his friend's shoulder as he bends at the waist, keeping his eyes level with the top of the wall. He barely looks sideways at Ben and Tom, but has a vague peripheral impression that Ben is lining his pistol up through the wall and Tom is kneeling on the ground.

'We all shoot, reit?' Mellor doesn't take his eyes off the road. The steady clopping is getting louder.

The dark-coated figure sways into view. His yeomanry cavalry horse trots slowly, taking the long hill at a sensible pace. Horsfall is upright and relaxed, readily recognisable in his expensively cut outfit. Now that he has appeared, he closes the gap with disturbing speed, rolling inexorably towards them. His large figure, his tall steed, will make a good target for them. The others look towards Mellor, but Mellor watches Horsfall. When he begins to raise his Russian pistol, Tom licks his dry lips and forms a proper hold on his own pistol. Thorp listens to Mellor's steady breath and feels fingers grip into his shoulder as Mellor's anticipation grows.

Mellor stands up straight. He points the heavy pistol and fires. The crack rings out over the fields, sweeping a murmuration of starlings out of the trees and into the sky, a dark spray against the white, as the sharp retort mirrors itself in the bones of Mellor's hand.

Horsfall folds at the waist and Mellor recoils, finger broken. Thorp and Bucks fire a second later and at least one shot, like Mellor's first, finds its home. The horse rears and twists, spinning Horsfall from his seat. Mellor delves into his pocket, grasps the second twist, half-cocks his gun, tips powder down the barrel and a few grains into the pan. Thorp stands, takes aim, fires.

Lapwings circle overhead, their manic ascending cries competing with the bellow of gunshot. Mellor's groping fingers find a musket ball and he slams this into the pistol's muzzle, pressing the twist of paper in after it. Bucks is standing, elbows on the wall now, lining up to shoot again. Horsfall scrabbles, pulling himself upright with the aid of his horse's mane, then lurches sideways in his saddle, clutching at himself with one arm, trying to steer with the other. The mount rears for a second time, dislodging Horsfall and leaving him tangled and dangling helplessly at the flank. Mellor cocks his gun and scrambles up onto the wall, ready to fire again if necessary, but the beat of approaching horse hooves stops his progress.

A man on horseback gallops into the scene. Open-mouthed in horror, he swings down from his mount and runs to free the bleeding and gasping figure of Horsfall. The manufacturer is bumping on the floor by now, his leg caught up in the stirrup, his plans to ride up to his saddle girths in Luddite blood at a poor end. The stranger looks to the wall. Mellor is frozen in a dynamic posture, a heartbeat away from leaping down to finish Horsfall off. Poised on the top of the wall on his feet and one hand, the other arm held out for balance, he resembles some malevolent demon. The stranger waves his arms in fury.

'Go on with thee! What? Art tha not content, lad?' Instinctive anger makes this lone protector brave and he turns to Horsfall without considering the danger at his own back. As he untangles the injured man from the stirrup, Mellor drops back down on the safe side of the wall.

'He'll not live wi' them wounds. Come on.' Mellor sets off across the field. His heart is hammering so hard that he feels pressure in his throat. His damaged finger throbs. None of them speak, but Smith's silence carries an extra weight. Thorp cannot bear it. He releases his fury at Ben, the elder of the pair.

'Here, take this, I cannot carry it any further.' He

211

slams his pistol into Bucks's palm and strides ahead. 'Are thi goin' to say nowt, George?'

'Run, Will, that's what I say,' and with this, Mellor breaks into a sprint. If soldiers should arrive promptly, it will only take one witness to report their direction of travel and they will be outrun. They have to get rid of the weapons. Thorp is the fastest runner, overtaking Mellor and leading the way across the fields. They charge down into the woods but here they must slow down or risk broken ankles. Under cover of the trees, Mellor feels safer. He jogs down the hillside, sliding on the cold, dry ground, and only slips once, taking care to break his fall with his uninjured hand. Thorp is still ahead, picking out his way with a devil-may-care kind of efficiency. He swears loudly as a thin branch whips his cheek, and the hand he raises to it comes away with a faint smear of blood.

'Slow down,' shouts Mellor. 'They'll not catch up to us now.'

The four regroup, stumbling together downhill.

'You!' Thorp points, jabbing air at Smith, who hangs his head, full of shame.

'He'll take no lessons from thee, who can't bear t'weight of his own hot pistol!' Bucks starts, and he throws Thorp's weapon onto the ground as they walk. Mellor stops and picks it up. He points both pistols - his own and Thorp's - at the men now walking away from him. His own is still loaded with the second shot he put in. Thorp's is empty and warm. Above Mellor, the trees are in full bud, leaves unfurling and beginning to decorate the sparse canopy. Bare patches of milky sky wash the empty spaces that summer will block with dense foliage. Underfoot, old autumn leaves coat the floor and acorns crunch into the ground beneath the boots of Bucks and Smith, Thorp stamping along behind them.

'Wait,' Mellor calls and the three turn round to face the pointed pistols.

'Na then,' begins an alarmed Bucks, stepping in front of Smith, but Mellor waves a barrel to shut him up.

'I teld thee, Tom. We'd all to shoot.'

'I'm reit sorry, George. I meant to, I swear I did.' Smith stares plaintively, his arms drooping at his sides, a gun still gripped in his palm though he seems entirely unaware of it.

'Why didn't thee, then?'

'I don't know. I just got stuck, I couldn't move me arms.'

'Yer not new to this, kid!' shouts Thorp.

'I've nivver shot a man afore, or seen blood gush from a felly like that,' Smith yells back. 'It's no excuse, George, I know, but I'm just telling thee it were all a shock.'

'Aye, well.' Mellor looks to Thorp. 'It dun't change owt, does it?'

'Happen he gets took up - what's he goin' to say to Radcliffe, eh?' Thorp's truculence is rarely stoked to such vigour. Mellor suspects Thorp is fighting demons of his own, and that the shock which prevented Smith from firing his weapon is now steadily seeping through Thorp and seeking a convenient outlet.

'I wun't say nowt!' Smith declares, indignantly. 'I'd hang just for being 'ere, wun't I? So why would I say owt to t'Magistrate?'

'That's true, lad. Don't forget it,' Thorp growls.

213

'William, leave it now. Lad knows he's made a mess of it. He'll not talk out o' turn. Will thee, Tom?'

'Nay George. Thi can shoot me thi sen, if I do.'

There's no more time to waste. Mellor is conscious that they've spent too long talking as it is. He directs Bucks to take Smith for a drink out at Honley. He distrusts Smith's nerve, if not his resolve, and the last thing they want is for the shocked apprentice to get randomly picked up by a patrol on the road back to Huddersfield. Neither Bucks nor Smith has any money, so Mellor slips two shillings to Bucks and tells him to take Smith to the Coach and Horses Inn and sit tight there for a while until Smith has pulled himself together. 'Ditch t'guns in t'woods, we'll come back for them another day', is Mellor's parting instruction as they split up.

Thorp still has a streak of blood on his face and their greatcoats are smeared with dirt where they have skidded on the rough descent. Smith and Bucks are already out of sight as Mellor and Thorp complete their run to the tree line at the bottom of the woods.

'We can't go back to town looking like this,' Thorp says between breaths, his body still catching up with the effort of sprinting the past mile. He plants his hands on his thighs, groans and then stretches upwards, inhaling deeply.

'Let's go to Joseph's,' says Mellor, pointing towards the cluster of cottages a few hundred yards away. His cousin, Joseph Mellor, is twisted-in, as are a few of his apprentices. Mellor takes off his rough, green great coat and drapes it over his arm. He withdraws the two pistols that are severely straining the inner pocket of the coat and tucks them under his arm, pressed against his body and hidden by the thick folds of the coat.

They walk briskly along the quiet road to the yard behind Joseph Mellor's house and enter at the back through the open workshop door. No one is around, though they can hear young, male voices in the back room and the thwacking sound of cloth being beaten round the other side of the building. Thorp follows Mellor through the empty main workshop to a door at the far end that leads into the kitchen. The light gleams through the gap as Mellor nudges the door open, illuminating the roll and lift of thousands of shining filaments of cloth as the visitors disturb the still air.

'Oh George, thi startled me,' exclaims the young woman by the stove. She rubs her hands down her skirt front and comes cautiously over.

'Hello Martha. How are thee?'

'I'm well. Joe's not here, it's market day.'

'Can me friend have a quick wash? Passing horse threw up some muck.' They stare at one another – Mellor, frank and intense, a burning bright version of Martha's more even-tempered husband, and Martha, quick-witted and suspicious of this enigmatic cousin. She purses her lips and sighs, wrinkle-mouthed.

'Mm-hmm.'

Thorp goes to the wash bowl that she points to. He damps his face with wetted hands and dries himself carefully on a towel left on the sideboard. Mellor wanders to the table, looking about him, not noticing one of the apprentice boys through the open kitchen door. Joseph Oldham watches Mellor for a moment, ambling about with that big, dark coat over his arm; he sees a man in a drab-coloured top coat dabbing at his face with a towel. Then Martha spots the boy and fixes him with a glassy stare. He hurries off into the yard, before his sharp-eyed mistress can shout at him for nosiness.

'I wanted to see Joe about some work for me friend,' says Mellor, picking up a bread knife and balancing it point-down on the wooden table top, his index finger pressed on the end of the wooden handle. 'Well Joseph in't here,' says Martha, removing the knife from his hand and standing too close to him. She lays the serrated blade back on the board and is about to say more when the servant girl comes in from the milk room at the back. She takes in the scene - Mellor with a big coat over his arm and what she guesses must be a loaf of bread cradled beneath it, Martha standing close by him at the table, and a stranger in a drab coat gazing out of the small, stone mullioned window that looks over the yard - then she puts her butter on the table.

'How do,' she says.

'Grand, Maria. How about thee?'

Maria smiles at Mellor but doesn't reply. The prim set of Martha's face is enough to keep her quiet. She knows not to antagonise her mistress; though Maria is seventeen and Martha is only just twenty-one, making them of an age to be friends, Martha tolerates little familiarity. The mistress doesn't like Maria to assume a friendship between them, nor to fraternise with the apprentice boys or any male visitors. Maria forgives this because she believes Martha is jealous of her own youthful, unmarried, childless status. She risks a second peek at Mellor, whom she knows to be the master's cousin, and satisfies herself with a little rush of excitement when she sees that he is still watching her and that he has taken a step away from Martha.

'I don't think Joe'll have any work for thi,' Martha is saying now to Thorp. 'We've four apprentices already, or are thee a journeyman?' Thorp says something in reply and Mellor slips from the kitchen into the workshop, leaving his friend to hold his own for a while. Mellor has to deposit the guns, hopefully before either Martha or Maria see what he is carrying below his coat. In the workshop, he bumps immediately into another apprentice boy. Thomas Durrance has been in the back, cracking crude jokes with John Kinder when the pair of them should be working, but having returned to the front room he is surprised by Mellor's sudden appearance.

'Good day, lad,' says Mellor. 'It's a hot one, in't it?' Thomas looks at him dully - a bit like a cow, Mellor thinks, chewing the cud. Mellor carefully lays his coat on the brushing stone, taking care not to drop the two pistols as he draws them with one hand from underneath. Thomas gapes at the weapons. 'Got somewhere for these?' Mellor asks, motioning up the stairs with the barrel of his Russian gun. Thomas nods and rushes up the steps, pushing out of the way an excitable black Labrador that has come in from the back room. The dog bounds at Mellor, nearly taking him off balance mid-way up the steps, and then follows the two men to the upper rooms, nosing into Mellor's stockings and breeches, scenting leafmold and bracken, squirrel tracks and rabbit warrens. Thomas directs Mellor into the place where the flocks are stored.

'We can stick 'em under here,' he suggests, kicking

at the fleecy remnants, 'Can I have a look?'

Thomas holds out his hand. Mellor hands him Thorp's pistol and the boy fingers the barrel and grips the stock. He blows down the pan and a tiny amount of grey residue lifts and scatters. Mellor holds the flocks up and lays his big horse gun in the corner. Thomas places the second beside it and they lump the waste material back over the brace of pistols. The dog comes sniffing, wagging its tail so hard that its back end bangs hard into Mellor's calf. He uses both hands to steady the lively creature, stroking the smooth, shining fur with a firm, pressing motion.

'Come on,' he says, to both the boy and the dog and they follow him back down the stairs into the workshop. John Kinder is below - he's come out into the main shop from the back room after hearing the movement upstairs and he watches Mellor descend with open curiosity.

'A fine dog,' Mellor says, patting the muscled side of the animal.

'Aye,' Kinder replies.

'Best get back to work, yer don't want Joe to be mad wi' yer,' he tells them. They saunter hesitantly into the back, out of sight, the dog going with them and Mellor returns to the kitchen where Maria is still working on the butter and Martha is setting something to boil and checking on her sleeping infant in the crib. Thorp still hovers by the window, casting a long shadow over the stone floor. There is a welt of blood, fresh risen on his face as he turns.

'Where has tha been?' he asks impatiently. 'We should get going.'

'Went for a look at t'new dog. He's a lovely one.'

218

Then, in a lower voice, 'Thi face is still bleeding.'

'Oh hell,' grunts Thorp, touching his face. 'Mrs Mellor, can I borrow a handkerchief?'

Martha leaves her pot with a theatrical sigh. Maria is pushing the butter, drinking in a sideways view of Mellor. She barely registers his tall friend in the drab top-coat, who has hovered so quietly in the corner by the window, his cap pulled low enough that she has not even properly seen his face, only had the impression that he is ill-tempered and sour of countenance.

'Wait here,' Martha says, pressing close as she passes Mellor.

She goes off, into the workshop and returns barely a minute later brandishing a black silk handkerchief.

'I would lahk this back,' she enunciates slowly, dangling it in front of the pair of them. Thorp thanks her and takes the handkerchief, stepping out into the workshop, eager to be gone.

'When's Joe back?' Mellor asks Martha.

'After nine, afore ten. Why don't thi stay for a while? Thi must be hungry. I'll make thi summat.'

'No thanks, we've to be off. We'll like as not run into Joe - or we'll call again.'

'Oh, please stay,' she tries, regretting her earlier brusqueness. Behind her, Maria looks up with hopes of an entertaining evening, but she is to be disappointed.

'We can't. But we'll call again. He's back after nine?'

'That's reit,' Martha says.

'Oh, an' can I borrow a coit?'

'A coit? What are thi up to, George, pestering

women for coits an' hankys?' she laughs, pushing him into the workshop, pulling a dusty drab topcoat off a hook on the back of the door and throwing it at him. He can't honestly tell if his cousin's wife likes him or not. She switches from matronly contempt to flirtation so quickly, still so young despite her familial responsibilities. He waves her comment away with a grin and ushers Thorp out of the workshop door into the yard. It strikes him, belatedly, that he should have stuck his own coat up on the peg, out of the way, but he doesn't dwell on it. Someone will hang it up, when they find it on the brushing stone.

They walk back along the road to Huddersfield, reaching Lockwood Bar in little more than five minutes. There are people passing them now, the homeward-bound traffic picking up, on horseback and on foot, slow carts trundling on the cobbles away from town. Thorp occasionally gives his cheek a testing dab with the spit-dampened handkerchief, leaving tiny smears of blood shining on the black silk.

At Crosland Moor, Horsfall has been taken to The Warren House on the Austerlands road. News of his shooting is already rippling outwards, racing the assassins home.

7
The Perilous Situation of This Country

His prayers over, the Chaplain moves away. A door closed, a heavy lid slammed - an ark full of secrets instead of oats; Mellor's treasure, safe and untouched. And yet the aftermath is lonely, now his appeal is complete and interest has passed on to the next prisoner to take to his knees. Reverend Brown cannot disguise the resentful frustration with which he discards Mellor and sets his inquisitive sights on Thorp. There will be no earthly reward for Mellor's loyalty; no praise, no warm hand upon his shoulder. His lingering need for paternal approval galls him.

Thorp shuffles forward, chains clinking. He drops down to a kneeling position and begins to mumble a series of prayers under the Chaplain's subtle observation. The crowd concentrates on him, their rapier focus shifting by half a yard to Mellor's right, like the vivid sun rays of a changeable day, sweeping a hillside, picking out a ridge, a line of trees, a herd of cows and bathing them in splendour before abruptly abandoning them to the cold shade chasing in their wake.

Mellor holds the rapt attention of the West Riding at gun-point, head of an army whose bloodily successful manoeuvre has left it momentarily revealed above the parapet of shadows, yet still the bowl-shaped valley in which Huddersfield nestles retains a tense daytime calm. Manchester is crazed with riots, but Huddersfield simmers, a stew of furiously impotent magistrates and captains, seemingly chasing their own tails as one hundred stand of arms are stolen, no doubt to embolden the now undisputed network of Luddites within the town. The first blow has been struck, declare the voices of law and order in horror at Horsfall's downfall; but at the Luddite meetings men erupt in roars that the first foul blow was against them, and it took off Booth and Hartley.

Horsfall lasted a couple of days, dying before April was out, from a handful of shots to his lower body. Mellor read the piece in the paper, aloud as usual, and his colleagues applauded, much as they had when the news had originally swept downhill in whispers and shouts from The Warren House to Longroyd Bridge. Mellor half-expected an immediate crack-down - soldiers flooding the roads, croppers taken up summarily for questioning, residents required to hand over their weapons - but May has dawned with eerie quiet and the powers that be have looked first to their own protection, cowering within their properties and strengthening their defences. This has worked to Mellor's advantage, giving him time to put his own house in order.

He's in the back room of a small warehouse off Upperhead Row, sorting through muskets and boxes of ammunition with a gang of other men. Looking down the muzzles, trying to angle what small light is available into the dark barrels, the absence of moral conflict within him is pleasing. Beyond the confines of the law lies a new morality - a justified use of force. The precipice he, in the secret recesses of his heart, feared falling from upon shooting Horsfall has not materialised. Instead, freedom beckons - freedom from magistrates, generals, ministers, preachers and kings with their false claim to authority. The very fact of having got away with it is evidence of the sweetest kind that Mellor was right to do it - that the light still shines on him.

He wraps a tiny rag around the wormed end of a ramrod and carefully works it deep within a musket barrel. When the rag re-emerges, it brings with it the detritus of previous firings - paper fibres blackened with filth. These smooth-bored guns are easier to clean. Sometimes they come across rifled muskets - the type with ridges worked into the inside of the barrel - and these are harder to polish, more furred up with evidence of past activity. Occasionally they have to drag from the depths of a barrel an unfired musket ball. This they do with a screw-like attachment fitted to the end of the ramrod. It all takes time, but needs must. When they requisition or receive new weapons, they clean them and, if necessary, get them repaired. Mellor's friends, the Brooks, at Lockwood, take care of fixing them up. In fact, Mellor remembers, he left a gun there last week to have the stock fixed. He'll need to see about picking it up soon.

The hardest part is not the cleaning or the fixing but the laying of hands on enough weapons in the first place. Each one is a testament to the efforts of groups of Luddites who visit households late at night to demand guns from occupants who might just as easily shoot them through the windows. Clement Dyson, he recalls, had threatened exactly this when the Ludds paid him a visit the evening after Horsfall was shot. You would think the man would see sense, so recently having been apprised of the earnest intent of the movement, Horsfall still in his death throes at that very time, but Dyson blustered and puffed and tried to point his musket at twenty men who would easily have stormed his house before a second shot was fired. The man was evidently still sore that the Luddites had smashed his frames when he was away from home in March, and had resolved to restore his pride with a foolish show of resistance.

It took, as seems to Mellor so often the case, the good sense of his wife to resolve the situation. She disarmed her husband, quite literally, and threw the guns out of the door. This was much to the relief of Mellor's cousin, Joseph, who in the immediate aftermath of the shooting of Horsfall, had decided that his own involvement in Luddism did not rest well next door to an armed victim of their activities. A simple message to Mellor along the lines that Clement had a musket and a pistol was all it took to neutralize the situation. A good result, all round, Joseph declared, when next they met, but Mellor has reservations. Clement Dyson seems like trouble, and cousin Joseph has not attended all the meetings he should. These worries niggle, with a thousand others, in Mellor's over-worked mind.

Bandaged in stiff greyish linen, his right forefinger aches. Awkward bumps and catches hurt to high heaven, so his mother has shown him how to wrap it securely, keeping it lashed against its neighbour. When in brotherly company or the dressing shop, Mellor wears the bandage, but he must take it off in public. In the absence of any genuine information, the authorities search for signs and marks - not the boils, scabs and blemishes of witchcraft as in days of old, but the shattered bones and lacerated flesh resulting from musket fire. If combined with a cropper's hoof, the evidence, for Justice Radcliffe, borders on irrefutable. A hoofed cropper with a broken trigger finger in the weeks after Horsfall's death? Magnificent! The fear of such an arrest keeps Mellor from crying out when a button fastening goes awry or an acquaintance applies excess pressure during a handshake. Avoiding use of the hand would render as much suspicion as the strapping, so he forces it into work, accepting change from vendors into his right palm without a flinch and appearing to carry heavy items with both hands, when in fact his left is bearing nearly all the strain.

It's getting easier, as the bone heals. He doesn't have to grit his teeth quite so much. Betty makes a wet, green poultice of leaves and salt each evening and she packs it around his finger, leaving it there for an hour or so when the children have gone to bed. Mary was dubious, but Mellor has to admit it eases the unpleasant throb and the stiff ache, and if he needs any other remedy to chase away the nagging pain, he thinks of Jonathan Dean's hand, shot clean through.

More disabling than the minor damage to his digit is the nervous undercurrent within both the sworn Luddites and the wider community. The manufacturers are frightened, of course - that was the very aim - but other men of business are anxious too, from the merchants visiting the cropping shops with their pieces of cloth, to the publicans behind the bars of the town inns. An implicit sympathy with the Luddite rallying cry is a long way from overt approval of murderous tactics. He picks up the next musket, lays the slim, light weapon across his raised left forearm and examines the lock, wrinkling shut one softly lashed brown eye in order to focus with the other. The pan is gritty and black, the hole to the barrel probably caked. Years, decades may have drifted by since some of these guns were last cleaned or, indeed, fired.

In The Packhorse last night, Mellor left without a drink. It rankles, that these landlords so eager in past months to court his thirsty custom should now turn to judgemental wariness, but he understands the dual nature of their business, servicing the rich and poor alike. Rumours of Mellor's status have begun to crystallise into received fact. He will not be readily welcome everywhere - particularly not in those places where the proprietors were on speaking terms with the late Mr Horsfall. In death, even the most unpleasant characters can be more fondly remembered, and there is a touch of this theatrical sadness across the town - grief surfacing in even unlikely places for the loss of Horsfall's familiar figure, his steady routine. Thorp put his finger on it, when Mellor commented bitterly on the numbers of poor people who had turned out for the funeral. They're not mourning Horsfall, Thorp said, they're just scared of what's to come.

What had been a danger at arm's length, confined to moor and cropping shop, disturbing ordinary people only at a relatively safe remove, has descended to the streets, has killed a man whose face many knew and will remember. All of Marsden is in shock; Horsfall's mill at Wood Bottom is in a state of lock-down and is guarded zealously by workers who may indeed have Luddite tendencies but now fear a greater immediate threat to their livelihood than industrialisation. No one knows who will take over; William's father has visited, but they say he turned his horse about as the garrisoned walls of Ottiwells came into view, not being able to bear the sight. There, in the father at least, is some genuine grief for the man. Perhaps Mr Horsfall senior knows that as his bleeding son was transported roughly back to The Warren Inn, the people who came out to witness the commotion loudly castigated the victim for the greater harm he'd done to the town's poor.

Mellor can concede some slight sympathy for the father. It cannot be easy to live with the knowledge that your son has taken two days to die, under merciless ministrations of various surgeons, after earning the rebuke of the community. He expects old Mr Horsfall's face wears the same partly vacant bewilderment that old Mr Booth's does. This balance of suffering may not ease the pain of either man, but it restores Mellor's own equilibrium, removing the taint of responsibility he has carried in these past weeks for poor John. Can it still be measured in weeks, the endless time that has passed since that terrible smoke-filled pit at Rawfolds? If only they'd had all these muskets then! Not to mention the ammunition - under tables in this very room are piles of pipes, vessels, sheeting - all made from lead and all stolen to be melted down into bullets.

Mellor has had enough. He finishes the musket in his hands, leaving it passably clean, the barrel smooth and bare inside, and he stacks it with the ready weapons. Telling his friends he's off, he receives a chorus of goodbyes from the various men working in the gloomy light. He goes though a door into the outer warehouse, past a great pile of folded pieces and a table stacked with pattern books. High windows filter pale spring sunshine onto the grey floor and tiny silver particles stream above him, flocked by invading air currents. As he passes, he strokes the pile of cloth, lonely and forgotten. A thin veneer of furry dust transfers to his palm, softly reproachful.

Wiping it absent-mindedly away, he exits the warehouse into bright, mild air curling with the scents of horse shit, ale and that peculiarly sharp chemical odour drifting across town from all the dye-works. A high clanking echoes from the ironmongers. Women kall in the entrance to Dundas Street, their feathery voices pitched at a frequency that prevents Mellor's discernment of the words. Underfoot the cobbles are mostly dry, damp only in the crevices between, and the streets are not busy; just a trickle of people - a few ragged paupers lying up against a wall, a stained old man driving a couple of pigs ahead of him and a constable parading his irrelevance past a gang of soldiers who are loitering outside their billet.

It occurs to him, belatedly, that the apparent hostility of Beaumont, the Landlord at The Packhorse, may have been partly for his own benefit. Stuffed to the gills with soldiers, the town's public houses are balanced on a knife-edge. The landlords, never especially in favour of seditious discourse within their premises but inclined to tolerate some pointed banter, now find their own allegiance under scrutiny and measured by the behaviour they permit within their houses. Rooms formerly used for discreet gatherings now house units of militia, leaving the Luddites with fewer places of safety to meet. In the bar rooms, men lock arms with friends who have imbibed to excess, dragging them home before their inebriated tongues loosen - when even a jolly ditty about the mad king and his rascally son might land a man in grave trouble, a reference to Luddite activities is sure to bring an arresting constable sweeping in. Any man who'd happened to hear a rumour about Mellor could get over-excited, start buying him ale and thumping his shoulder. All it would take is a few careless words, a bit of praise, the mention of Horsfall's name.

Sworn men would die before they let such dangerous talk spill from their mouths, and most folk in Huddersfield are button-lipped, siding, as they do, with the Ludds and remaining safely uninformed about the particulars anyway. Stupid men are a different matter - they are the ones who swagger about uselessly, incapable of holding their alcohol without reeling about in an infantile pleasure, riling others for fun, starting fights with weaker men and, conversely, hero-worshipping the men they will never be. A buffoon like this, armed with a bit of gossip and unaware of his own hazardous laxity, can be found in every bar, in every town.

As he strolls down onto Manchester Street and towards Outcote, Mellor wonders whether he should stay away from the town pubs altogether - Longroyd has its own watering hole that does just fine for Mellor, and there are not so many soldiers there. He feels gritty resentment at being forced from his own territory, but the withdrawal is a tactical necessity. He can't afford to be provoked into rashness nor drawn too clearly into the open. He must embed himself in the defining advantage of Luddism - its binding and blanketing secrecy. The more Radcliffe attempts to uncover their network, the more transparently ephemeral they will become, hiding in broad daylight, striking fatally before blending back into normal life. With each action, their reputation will grow and the manufacturers will experience terror at the unending, invisible threat. Since no one can live in terror indefinitely, an end is inevitable, one way or another.

Mellor does not want escalation. He just wants the manufacturers to stop using the cropping frames. His demands are so simple, he cannot understand why Cartwright, Vickerman, Atkinson and the rest will not compromise, why they must push their profits ever higher and crush the workers so brutally. Do they not understand that they run the real risk that the Redressers will be overtaken by militant radicals? In shadowy corners of the entire kingdom, Jacobins are trembling in excitement and anticipation of the civil war they are sure will come. He cannot pretend to understand nor be in close contact with this vast, fractured, disillusioned strata of society, but he will make use of them, if it goes so far.

Back at the shop, Bucks asks him how it stands at the warehouse. A lot of good guns, Mellor tells him; go down there and take a look if you want. Bucks says he will, when he goes for his drink. John Wood glares at them through the doorway at the back of the shop. Elizabeth is working at a piece under the window, burling out the tiny lumps of fluff and loose threads. They have spoken too freely and Mellor nods apologetically to his step-father.

'Beautiful work,' Mellor says, leaning over Lizzie's shoulder. A dimple sinks into her cheek, signifying the smile she is hiding by keeping her head down. Her eyes flit to the back room where her father has turned away, then she dares to look up at Mellor.

'What's t'guns for, George? Are thi goin' to shoot somebody?' Her voice is a whisper, spoken into a cupped hand. From Betty, such a question would be abrasive, from Daniel, excited, from his mother, accusing. But from Lizzie, the inquiry is full of fear and her dimple is gone, drawn out by the way she has rolled both lips in between her teeth. The implication from her incredulous phrasing that she has no suspicion of his involvement with Horsfall, endears her to him. Almost fully grown she certainly is, but still she has that childish capacity to purposely fail to see what is right before her. He squats down, unsure what to tell her. He is not, by nature, a liar and he prefers not to dissemble.

'I'll not shoot anyone who doesn't rightly deserve it,' are the words he settles on.

'Feyther says yer just out drinking, when yer go. But I think yer off with t'Ludds,' she confesses.

'What does mam say?'

'She says not t'ask so many questions.'

'Mam's reit. Less tha knows, better it is. I'm just keeping us all safe, that's all.'

She looks unhappily at him and he laughs at the seriousness of her expression.

'I mean it about the cloth. You've done some good work there, lass.'

Moments like these allow him to forgive his step-father's calculating manner. No one could pin a thing on John Wood. Mellor has sometimes resented it, this cautious self-protection, but now he silently thanks the older man, who will always be there to make sure his

231

mother and brothers and sisters are taken care of. One day, a musket ball may fell Mellor, but he'll die knowing, at least, that everyone he loves is being looked after. How many others can say the same? Not Jonny Dean for one, hiding somewhere over in Lancashire - though with the riots in Manchester he may have moved on again.

Fleeing Huddersfield the day after Rawfolds, knowing that his reputation alone would see him picked up if he stayed, he told his wife he'd return when his hand was well healed. That assurance does not pay for Mrs Dean's bread and milk. The Brief Institution is doing that, discreetly slipping her money each week, and bringing her news of her husband if they can. But if he never comes back, what will pregnant Mrs Dean and her children do then?

The Brief can't pay her a living for ever. Mellor has been to see her, sitting quietly in her small kitchen while a toddler cried and yanked at the woman's arm, finally falling asleep in her lap. He told her how brave Jonathan had been, beating at the mill door even under fire, while she listened intently with her brow all screwed up as if the key to her salvation from this sorry mess lay in fully comprehending the necessity of that evil night. She still looked puzzled when he left.

Yet, while individuals mourn the losses that Luddism has brought upon them, the mood of the country sways to Mellor's bent. In the papers, discontent ripples the print; rioting across the north, fervent Luddism prevalent in Nottingham, army units being moved here, there and everywhere as Lord Lieutenants wake up to the lethal potential of their own populace. Through the lens of Horsfall's death, every minor occurrence takes on a more sinister hue. It takes just one further event to raise the nation to fever pitch.

On May 11, two hundred miles away from Huddersfield, a man walks into the House of Commons. He stands in the lobby with a pistol concealed in a purpose-sewn pocket inside his brown broadcloth coat.

The Prime Minister, Mr Spencer Perceval, enters. At fifty years old, the corners of his mouth lift in a sour smile. The father of twelve, sombrely clad and on his way to a meeting about the Luddites who are, to his intense irritation, refusing to be cowed by his frame-breaking bill, takes the final step of his life before his way is blocked. The rather unremarkable forty-something man waiting in the lobby, distinguished only by the flash of a caddish yellow and black waistcoat revealed as he pulls back his brown coat, exposes and points a pistol directly at Perceval's chest and fires, without words or hesitation. Perceval falls.

The various assembled people gape. Members of Parliament that are present collect themselves and apprehend the man with the gun, who has lowered his arm and is simply waiting to be taken away. Perceval is picked up and carried out, blood spilling from his mouth, to die swiftly in a nearby room. London constables dash into the lobby to remove the killer. They drag him outside, where a small crowd has already formed. As the shaken MP's stand about, reaching for their pipes and shaking their heads, staring in disbelief at the bloodstain on the lobby floor, someone shouts 'Burdett forever!'

Newspapers scream the story, in the days that follow - the Mercury is where Mellor obtains his account. He longs to know more - who is the man? Is he a Luddite? And if it has proved so easy to assassinate a Prime Minister, will someone attempt now to shoot the King, or his son? He also wonders if anything will change, now the hated Perceval is gone. Perhaps the Orders In Council will be repealed at long last. Maybe there is even a real possibility of parliamentary reform. But the shop copy of the broadsheet is frustratingly limited in detail.

Nothing can stop him from going out drinking the night the news reaches Huddersfield, despite his intentions of keeping his head down. He and Thorp visit a couple of pubs -The Golden Fleece, The White Lion - trailed by Ben O'Bucks, Smith, Varley, Hall, John Walker - practically the whole lot of their close associates.

In each pub, on each street, are more men they know and, Luddite or non-Luddite, they flow and coagulate in one celebratory organic mass. Even the soldiers are relaxed, drinking and laughing, no less pleased than any other working man to see Perceval brought down. Sitting with Thorp late into the evening he realises a deep feeling of contentment - an old, almost forgotten feeling of innocently and joyously drinking his night away. His own guilt (technical, he asserts, not emotional nor moral) has faded in the face of so grand an assassination. He hasn't worried once this evening about being taken up, and not one of the publicans has dared refuse to serve him. It is as if they and the laughing soldiers and the absent magistrates

234

and the hysterical papers perceive that the balance has shifted. Blind Justice wavers, her sword point hovering between the tiny group of rich landowners and lawmakers who think they own her, and the swathes of starving poor who have brought outrages to her feet in order to gain her attention. When an officer reported the shooting of Perceval to Pall Mall's Grenadier guard, the soldiers broke into spontaneous applause, such is the nature of the shift in sympathy.

'Here's to Bellingham,' says Thorp, yet again, clashing his mug against Mellor's.

'A good man,' answers Mellor, wondering what is happening to the mysterious John Bellingham now, whether he is interred in some dark cell and sleeping peacefully, or whether men of law are at work extracting from him the network of his associations.

'Will Burdett stand up for us now, does tha think?' Thorp slurps at his ale.

'I don't know. I think prob'ly not.'

'Why's that?' Thorp looks mildly disappointed, as if Mellor has upset some tidy arrangement.

'They're all friends,' says Mellor, simply, spreading his hands.

'Burdett's a reformer, Perceval were t'opposite.' corrects Thorp.

'An' both of 'em's Members o' Parliament an' Burdett's a rich man. It's lahk,' Mellor casts about him for an explanation, thinking aloud, 'It's lahk when a blacksmith comes to a cropper's meet. We're different, on t'surface, but underneath we're t'same. We want t'same things.'

'But they don't want t'same things.'

'Aye,' Mellor nods, 'underneath they do.'

'How does tha mean?'

'They've all got money, han't they? All got big houses, horses, carriages, servants. Those are things they mean to keep hold of. An' what they all fear from us is that we'll tek it away. Anyone who's got more 'na what he should have, fears that someone lahk us'll tek it away.'

'That's not what we want to do,' Thorp argues, shaking his inebriated head.

'That's what the Painers want. It's all bloody John Baines ever talks about! Does tha see? Burdett knows things in't fair and good on 'im, he wants parliamentary reform. But he doesn't want it to go too far. That's what they're all flaid of - that it'll go too far. Even Burdett. Even 'im.'

Thorp considers this for so long that Mellor thinks the conversation is at an end. He isn't even fully sure of what he's said, what exactly he means by it, or what it means for his own ambitions. He just knows he's stumbled on some kind of truth - that they must save themselves because no one else will do it for them - not Burdett, not Byron, not one of them.

'I thought this were good news for us, but nowt's lahk to change then, is it? They'll still not listen to us.'

The incongruity of the situation brushes Mellor, that two rough-born croppers in the West Riding should put themselves within the same sphere of action and importance as the murdered Prime Minister. The elevation of their own agency to that of their upper class governors is for a shocking second both comical and unnatural to Mellor's lurking class consciousness. The rarely felt taint of worthlessness settles lightly on his shoulder, dusting off malevolent

236

wings. It feeds on the gentle intoxication of Mellor's tired spirit. He senses the talons, slowly sinking in, and rouses, defiantly. He will not accept it, he will not give in. Liberty, equality, fraternity - if it is true in France, then why can it not be true here in England?

He has the right to be heard, he has the right to be warm, to be fed, to work. He has the right to go to work that he is trained for. He has the right to exist, to go on, to lay claim to his own small part of the world and announce that the life within it will not perish. He has the right to fight for that, no matter what the frame-breaking laws decree. And if this is true, then logic dictates that the laws and the Orders and the men who have written them are the real incongruity, the moral aberration, the unnatural authority and Mellor owes them no deference, no obedience, no mercy. He does not want the reformer's dream of equal representation in a skewed and distorted political hierarchy. His duty is simply to make himself an agent of God's justice, to strip the veneer of social convention and expose the true grain and the worms within.

This stranger, Bellingham, has seen the truth - that Perceval is just a man of no especial value, a man who can die like any other, whose death matters no more than any other, whose voice should, in life, have held no more sway than any other. In the lobby of the House of Commons that day, it was not Bellingham who was the interloper, but Perceval. Those halls of power, carved with the twin tools of taxation and poverty, permitted Bellingham to enter and escorted his target into range with all the ancient, hulking menace of a giant trampled goddess, silently biding her time.

'Don't be so gloomy, Will. Think on how flaid they'll all be now, looking abaht to see where't next pistol shot's coming from. There's two ways this could go, I reckon.' Mellor leans on his forearms across the table. 'Parliament might cave in an' repeal the frame-breaking bill - let the manufacturers know they've to ease up and act fair. But that's none too likely.'

'What's t'other way?'

'They'll come down hard. More soldiers, more men taken up, hangings, troops patrolling all t'time.'

'How the blummin' ummer is that good news for us?'

'Soonest torn, soonest mended.' Mellor grimaces. 'We're ready for it, an' now we can get on wi' it.'

'They've tekken up James Brook,' yells Varley, coming into the shop and throwing a basketful of teazels into the corner. 'He's at Milnsbridge House.'

The men down tools and lay into Varley with questions - when was he taken, why, what did the constables say? Mellor's stomach sinks, just as it does every time a Luddite is taken into Radcliffe's custody. He has such faith in these men, but who knows what pressure the magistrate is now free to apply? Rumours of the torture of Booth and Hartley have turned to legend within a month, and now people are talking of the sweating room in Milnsbridge House, where Radcliffe incarcerates his prisoners.

'They took 'im this morning, first thing. Constables are in Lockwood reit this minute, tearing t'house apart.'

'What they lookin' for?' asks Bower, the apprentice

lad.

'Guns, kid. Pistols an' muskets. An if they find any...' Varley shakes his head.

'They'll find nowt,' says Mellor. 'Anybody else been tekken up?'

'Just James, far as I know.'

'Reit, get thi sen up to town, find out what everyone's saying. But don't mek it bloody obvious.'

'Aye, all reit,' Varley settles his cap back on straight, happy to have an excuse to go out drinking early

'Rest o' thi, back to work.'

They creep back to their jobs, unsatisfied and anxious, but Mellor has at least some relief. He knows they'll find nothing at the Brook house that shouldn't be there - maybe a family-owned musket or two, a serviceable hatchet and the like, but no stolen guns - nothing that can tie the Brooks to any raids. Mellor knows this because he has just recently picked up a gun that needed its stock repairing, and he has taken nothing else there in the meantime. But if the Constables are looking for guns, that means someone has informed against them. Who? An insider or just a nosy onlooker? Mellor is thinking quickly now, as he brings the heavy blades of his shears together across a pale broadcloth. Does anyone have a grudge against James? Not that he's ever heard - the Brooks are well-connected and least-suspected. Thomas runs a tight ship at Lockwood and his father, William, tolerates and makes use of the company of men who might well find themselves on the wrong end of a Luddite musket. Mellor is as confident as he can be that the oath is holding and that it is no Luddite who has

239

handed James Brook to the authorities, but he has to wait until he catches up with Varley that evening to make the pieces of the story fit together.

Varley returns as they are pressing the final piece of the day and puts them all out of their misery.

'Anyone know a felly called Milns? That's who's done it,' he announces, proudly.

'The constable who lives reit by 'em?' Mellor asks.

'That's 'im. I've heard it were Constable Milns who went to Radcliffe wi' some tale or other an' then soldiers came an' took James off.'

'They've a Constable next door?' asks Sowden who, despite his natural reticence with the whole business, has been caught up in the suspense of the day.

'It in't uncommon, lad,' says O'Bucks, hanging up his shears. 'Everyone who in't a Ludd, an' even some who are, is getting listed as a special constable now. Mean's nowt. Half of 'ems just covering their own backs, mekking it look like they're good, law-abiding folk. They don't usually do a reit lot.'

'This one did,' says Tom Smith. 'What else does he know?'

'I've nobbut that,' answers Varley.

'That's good enough. If Milns had owt on anyone else, they'd've been tekken up already. All we've to hope for now is that James keeps 'is mouth shut. If they find nowt, an he says nowt, he'll be reit.' Mellor makes his voice sound entirely sure, for the sake of the other men. He doesn't mention to anyone else what he is thinking - that saying nothing is hard to do if someone pushes you in just the right way, and that evidence doesn't need to weigh very heavily for Justice Radcliffe these days.

8
The Footsteps of Justice

Betty arrives home hot and flustered. She drops her basket onto the kitchen table and stands slightly bent, both palms flat on the scarred wooden surface, catching her breath.

'Them bloody men,' she exclaims.

'What's happened, Bet?' he asks, getting up, fists clenching.

'Nay, George, sit thi sen back down. It's all reit, truly. Sit thi down.'

'I'll swing for 'em!'

'Nay, get back,' she orders, barring his way. 'I should think swinging for me alone would be a waste o' thi talents, lad. Just... get me some ale.'

He fetches her a mug of the rich drink. She takes it from him with shaking hands.

'Has thi been running?' he asks, taking in the ruffled, pink state of her.

'Walking fast. I don't run in skirts lahk these in this weather for any man, an' 'specially not when I'm carrying two pounds o' potaters. I should've fetched 'em a thump if they'd caught up.'

She sits down in the chair Mellor has vacated.

'Bloody rascals,' she says, gulping her ale. 'They've nowt better to do than pester women going abaht their own business. They said they'd push me in't river if I'd none give em a kiss. It were all talk, I dare say, but they say as that happened to a lass at Aspley. An' I nivver know, when they come bearing down in their little patrols, if they're really on for taking me up, making me talk; if they might have heard summat abaht thi. I shouldn't worry thi wi' all this,' she sighs.

'It's a worry to me, whether tha tells me or not. Just so long as they didn't touch yer?'

'Nay lad. I'm just angry, that's all. They ruined mi walk back from town, an' I were already mithered that tuppence only got me these few tatties. Used to get three times as much not so long back.'

The outer door opens as their mother returns from the privy still smoothing her skirts down, looking concerned at the raised voices.

'What's gone on? What's happened?' She goes to Betty's side, looks back at George.

'Calm down mam,' says Betty. 'It were just some soldiers shouting rude things.'

'Oh.' Mary looks from one to the other, disconcerted. 'Reit. Nowt more?'

'Nowt more, mam.'

Mary nods and fixes her stare downwards. She writhes a thumbnail into one of the thin crevices of the table-top and digs out a thin taper of grime. It balances for a second, a tiny dried corpse on her flat stubby nail, then she flicks it onto the stone floor, impatient with herself.

'I allus feel the pair o' thi are keeping secrets. Happen it's habit wi' you, boy, but don't be dragging thi sister into it.'

'Them soldiers start on her, an' somehow it's my fault?' he exclaims, as Betty simultaneously cries 'I'm not keeping secrets, mam!' but Mary raises a hand to demand silence. 'I don't care for it. I won't have it in my kitchen.'

'Won't have what?' Betty asks, bewildered.

'None of 'em,' her mother says with a finger pointed

at the small, mullioned window, 'would even be here now, if it weren't for your brother and his friends. First they were just up in town; now they're patrolling the roads, the river, the cut. How long afore they're here, eh George? How long afore Radcliffe pulls you in, an' all my house gets turned over?'

'That won't happen, mam. I'm not even a suspect, not really. Not more than any other cropper round here.'

'But for how long? People talk, everyone knows.'

'No one talks, everyone's under oath.'

'The women aren't. Didn't see fit to swear any of us in, did thi? And there's more harm done in idle kallin on the street than in a dozen o' your raids. How does tha know what them soldiers were up to? How long afore they grab our Betty here and drag her off to Radcliffe? Maybe they were thinking about doing that today.'

'Nay, they weren't, they were just mucking abaht,' Betty says, but her voice has shrunk.

'Mam, listen,' Mellor says, 'Stop frightening our Betty. Them soldiers didn't know her from any other lass. I know exactly what they were interested in, an' it were nowt to do wi' finding out abaht me. As for t'Ludds bringing all t'soldiers here wi'out cause, tha knows that's rubbish, mam. We're not going hungry yet, granted, but we will be in a few years when all t'cloth's goin' to t'manufactories to be finished. Which would thi rather have at thi door - soldiers now or starvation later?'

'Yer not at a p'litical meet now, boy,' Mary says. 'Tha dun't need to convince me that what's happening is wrong - all o' t'Riding's wi' thee on that score. But

243

tha's got thi sen reit in't middle o' t'stir, lad. Why can't thi do what other lads do - go along and march a bit and then come home? Why does it have to be you that's allus telling everybody else what to do an' fetching weapons abaht an' goin' off to break frames an' shooting folk?'

'Because I'm good at it, mam, that's why. There's nob'dy else to do it. An' I get tired of it too sometimes, but I've no choice now. It in't lahk I can just give it up an' go back to just cropping and drinking 'cause in a few more years, there'll be no more cropping and what'll I do then, when I've a wife an' kids an' I can't bring any money in? An' if I'm worrying abaht it now, think on all t'men who've already got wives an' kids an' how flaid they must be. I've only mi sen to worry abaht an' that meks it easier for me to do it, an' I can read an' I can understand what's goin' on, an' men listen to me an' trust me. I don't know why, but they do. So it can't be anyone else, an' I wouldn't want it to be anyone else. It has to be me. But if tha's worried, I' sh'll move out. I'd not bring trouble on you, mam, or on Betty.'

'Aye, well I'm not saying I want that,' she replies, with her head tipped up slightly and her eyes cast down, as though she is surveying Mellor's unexpectedly eloquent explanation through an invisible pair of pince-nez and finding it frustratingly watertight. She snatches up Betty's empty mug. 'Just be careful,' she says, in chastened defeat.

Mary's temper is subject to the atmosphere of precarious balance that pervades and defines these days of early summer and Mellor, his hands controlling the scales, is feeling the strain. Always, from all angles, he feels the pressure coming in on him, like a physical presence slowly buckling his strong body, but he knows that the force holding back this external pressure is his own resolve, his own faith and belief. If he were to admit a weakness, a doubt, then a part of him would cave in. He fixes firmly to his cause. Nothing else matters - not his own tiredness, not the fear that comes with every taking-up of a friend, not the obstacles to getting the Ludds twissed, equipped and trained. As long as he reminds himself that his choice is already made, his path clear, then none of that matters. He can act no differently than his cause allows - and thus, prevarication and vacillation removed from the equation, his confidence is restored.

Yet what he hates, what shakes him more than any occasional brush he might have with the authorities, is the threat against his family. He can barely stand the idea that they might suffer, so he has to remind himself that though his actions might single them out for the patrol's attention or might put them in front of Justice Radcliffe one day, his inaction could see them destitute and starving on the streets. Besides, he thinks, they have nothing on me. No one has come for me and it has been weeks since Horsfall was killed.

He walks to Lockwood, escaping the sullen mood of the kitchen, needing the open air and the warmth of the June sunshine on his pale face, leaving his greatcoat behind on the peg. His smallish pistol fits inside his breeches, strapped against his outer thigh under the stiff grey kersey. Where once the weight was an imposition, uncomfortable and irregular, now it has become a necessary appendage, without which his body feels unfinished. Who, exactly, he might be called upon to shoot on a such a pleasant and sunny afternoon is unclear. If the patrols tried to take him up, he could scarcely resist them alone. If he encountered news of a brother who had turned then he would not submit that treacherous man to justice without proper knowledge and planning. If the magistrate himself rode right alongside, would he shoot him? Maybe, but the chances of such an opportunity arising in which Mellor could be certain of success and therefore remain unidentified, are slim, and it would be a waste to end up in York through foolish spontaneity. There is so little chance of Mellor needing to fire his gun on this short outing that it can only be emotional need that impels him to carry it.

The distance from Longroyd Bridge to Lockwood is half a mile as the crow flies. He walks a longer route than necessary, going through Rashcliffe and over Mount Pleasant, enjoying the feel of baked earth under his boots, where churned, muddy footpaths of winter have hardened to even, grassy tracks. In the little yards and fields, resilient pieces of cloth stretch out on tenterhooks and children rattle around the rough streets, chasing dogs and each other with sharpened hazel sticks, casting as ammunition inedible berries stripped from hedges.

The packhorses trot at the same gait, come rain or shine, but he imagines that they, like himself, are happy to have a bit of sun on their back - or what part of their back is not covered by their heavy loads. The man drives them on casually, nodding at Mellor as he saunters with his animals towards town, the best part of the day still in front of him. The sky is blue, the flimsy cloud high and streaked and the afternoon stretches peacefully ahead.

A drystone wall wends alongside and Mellor skims the finger-pads of his left hand against the cool, gritty surface whose northerly aspect only receives the sun's rays in high summer. Stepping neatly over a pale grey dog turd perched on a clump of bright dandelions, he shades his eyes and looks towards the main street. A few soldiers on horseback trot out of sight towards town, and a small trap pulls in to one of the local yards.

There are more children playing, a few of them with the little carts they use for collecting horse muck. A little boy, four or five years old, picks up the sun-dried grassy dollops with practised ease, loading them haphazardly before lifting the back of the cart and swerving crazily on one buckled wheel to the next pile. This time last year, those dried dollops would have been soggy circles, melting into the road under the onslaught of almost daily rain, a rain that persisted until the country's whole harvest was washed away. Torrential rain assailed them by day, and at night the flaming streak of the comet stretched across the dark heavens. Summer of 1811 never happened at all. He remembers last year, and gives prayers that this year will be better and that the sun will continue to shine.

Mellor passes the children and follows the road into Lockwood. The trip is too short - this is a day for striding out to Castle Hill, or Blackmoorfoot, or following the canal all the way out to Tunnel End and picking up the Blake Lea track to Esther's Gate - but Varley passed him a message in the morning requesting his presence at the Brooks house at two o'clock, and so a simple stroll to their house must suffice.

He arrives in the middle of an argument. Voices lift and subside with his approach but he cannot make out the words. He glances next door, to Milns's place, where everything appears to be quiet, then raps briefly, interrupting the lively discussion within; someone swings the door open from inside and Mellor steps in with a smile and a hello.

'Put wood in t'oil,' calls Thomas, who is sat with his father, old William Brook, at the family's kitchen table. 'Happen thi can talk some sense into this 'un.'

Mellor closes the door behind him as instructed. James leans against the hearth and rolls his eyes at his older brother. The youngest, John - the door-opener - stands beside Mellor, as if, having repositioned himself opposite the men of his family, he too can enjoy the relief of being an onlooker.

'What's t'stir?' Mellor asks.

'This silly business wi' Milns,' James answers, dismissively.

'They've not been looking for you again?'

'Nay, George, quite the opposite, it's Milns in bother now.' James looks pleased but Thomas is stiffly upright in his chair, elbows on the table, fists steepled before him.

'Radcliffe's goin' after Milns for being drunk when he took up our James,' John helpfully explains. 'He's charging Constable Milns wi' acting maliciously.'

'Ha, he's never!' Mellor splutters.

'Oh aye, now we've another clever 'un,' spits Thomas, throwing his arms up in disgust and then folding them tightly across his expansive chest.

'All reit, all reit,' says Mellor, waving his hands as

248

if to erase his ebullience. 'Just tell me what's happening.'

James explains to Mellor that he has been to the magistrate, and that Radcliffe is so incensed with the wild goose chase he's been led on that he has actually countenanced a claim against Constable Milns. It wasn't that hard to convince him, James says. Apparently Milns had been drinking quite heavily before he bleated on James, and Joseph Radcliffe now considers that perhaps a malicious, drunken jealousy was what led Constable Milns to bring a half-baked tale of stolen guns and illegally coarse singing to his door. Perhaps, suggests James, cheekily, Radcliffe is losing his temper with all these men who are sworn in as Special Constables and then do absolutely nothing useful at all. Maybe Milns is the unfortunately recipient of Radcliffe's impotent fury.

'But why, James? Why would yer push this? I'd ha' thought yer wouldn't want to set a foot near Milnsbridge House ever again.'

'Oh, it weren't so bad. I were only in there overneet, an' Radcliffe only asked a load o' questions. Thing is, George, there's money in this. I've heard that if the Assize convicts 'im, I might get fifty pounds, even more.'

'I'll lose more value than that if the lot o' thee swing!' old William yells suddenly, making John jump at Mellor's side.

'I'm in t'clear, feyther,' says James, irritably.

'For how long?' asks Thomas. 'If owt else gets brought to t'attention o' t'magistrate, he'll remember all this an' he'll start adding it up.'

'Think what we can do wi' t'money,' pleads James.

Mellor must have his mouth pursed in consideration of the relief that fifty pounds - or more - would bring, because Thomas is nodding slyly at him.

'Aye, tha thinks it sounds good lad, but has thi asked him what it means for thee?'

'What's tha mean?'

'Well, see, thing is,' James squirms, 'I told 'im t'gun were yours an that we were just fixing it for thi.'

'What the blummin' ummer did thi do that for?'

'See, he gets it now,' mutters William to his eldest son Thomas. Mellor glares at them, then eyes James, shrinking against the hearth.

'Come on, let's 'ave it.'

'I 'ad to tell 'em summat. Yer see, it were Mrs Milns who said she saw t'gun, an' even if her husband were drunk, it wouldn't cancel out her having seen it. So I said it were your gun, we were repairing it for yer and Mrs Milns saw it. Then when she told her husband, he just made out it were a stolen gun because he were drunk and wanted to land us in it.'

'An' what did Radcliffe mek o' that story?' Mellor demands.

'He said, "George Mellor? I believe I know his step-father. A good sort." An' that were it. He 'ad this other felly mek a note abaht it an' he said as long as you'd speak as a witness, it'd be a straight-forrard case.'

Mellor exhales. 'A good sort?'

'That's exactly what he said.'

Thomas takes pity on Mellor and pulls out a stool from under the table. Mellor sits down and rests his arms on the pitted surface. William fixes him with a stare. Mellor ignores the father and looks up at James.

'How much more?'

'What?'

'How much more 'na fifty pounds might we mek?'

'Oh, ha, well Radcliffe's felly, what were tekkin down notes, said mebbe seventy five. Not likely to be more n' hundred though.'

'Reit.' Mellor smooths a hand over his raspy chin. James waits, biting at his lower lip.

'Will thi speak for 'im?' asks Thomas

'I've no choice, 'ave I? Aye, I'll be a witness. But if that Milns gets on mi back-'

'Nay, he'll not be interested in thee, George. It were me he had it in for.'

'That's as mebbe, James, but tha's drawn me inter summat an' tha shouldn't 'ave done it. Even for t'brass.' Mellor points his thick index finger at James as he speaks. 'I've more risk riding on it than thee. There's more they can pin on me, if they get wind of owt. I'm not pleased abaht it, but t'is done, an' I sh'll be a witness an' say no more. But that brass-' Mellor stabs the table with his finger, 'that brass comes into t'croppers fund.'

'Aye George, that were t'plan all along,' agrees James, but at this statement, William is looking amongst his sons like they've all lost their minds.

'It's reit, feyther,' says Thomas. 'George is reit that it should go in t'fund.' He ignores his father's rolling eyes and shakes hands with Mellor over the table.

'I'll be up an' see Radcliffe to give 'im 'is statement,' confirms Mellor. 'Hopefully that'll be it, job done.'

What real harm can it do? he asks himself on his way back to The Bridge, where he intends to have a swift pint before returning to work. He's slid past

Radcliffe's gaze before, though the threat of being taken up to answer questions remains high. The tight network of friendships across the finishing trade is both the obstacle and the key for Radcliffe. The pattern of association is there for all to see, in the chapels and the public houses, in the cropping shops and in the streets, but Radcliffe cannot commit men to York simply for sharing space at a bar or working in the same shop.

The problem for Radcliffe is that he floats above the town, however much he feels he is part of it. The ornate edifice of Milnsbridge House overlooks vast gardens and ornamental waters from a gable-ended frontage, the shallow triangular peak framing a single attic window that peers blindly but prettily over the tops of trees and mill roofs. The men that come and go, those who are called to answer questions and give statements, some of them politely required to exit afterwards in a locked carriage bound for York, are as alien to these extravagant surroundings as Radcliffe's own portly figure would appear should he choose to dismount his horse and stoop to enter a widow's hovel. Mellor has been on the grounds several times in order to observe Radcliffe's doings, and he felt as belittled and oppressed by the unnatural beauty of Radcliffe's home as any other ordinary man would.

This is not to say Radcliffe has the finest house nearby. There are other families - the Beaumonts, the Ramsdens, the Armytages and more - who have mansions and gardens to attest to a lineage of increasing power and wealth, but it is not these houses to which the suspected Luddites are brought. Only Milnsbridge House witnesses the steady flow of apprehended men and their apprehensive smiles as they are welcomed in, housed in the sweating room, brow-beaten by Radcliffe with their words committed to paper by the clerk, Allison. And still, with all the might of his ashlar sills and pointed mortar and five floors of residential prowess, Radcliffe cannot press hard enough upon the bodies of his prisoners to make their sealed lips come undone. With all this metaphorical weight proving so ineffective, Mellor has been worried that Radcliffe will be tempted into actual physical force, torturing men in the cellars of his home until they spew up names of Luddites and locations where weapons are stored, but the evidence of his own liberty would suggest that hasn't happened yet, and Mellor knows all he has to fear from Radcliffe is the emasculating effect of entering rooms of power and privilege, of the magistrate's invocation of all those archaic but ingrained artefacts of control - King, Church, law, justice, blessed are the meek, and if you only tell us the truth you'll save yourself and your family.

'It in't like I'm being tekken up,' he says to John Walker at The Bridge, swallowing thick, malty ale in one long, draining effort to quench the thirst that came upon him on the walk back from Lockwood. The landlord refills the tankard and takes Mellor's money. Outside, the sun is still cracking the cobbles. Walker follows Mellor from the gloom of the pub into bright daylight to sit on old barrels at the front and soak up the welcome rays of warmth.

'Nay, it's completely different lad. I've half a mind Radcliffe won't even waste time seeing yer. He'll just get his felly to write down what yer say.'

'Exactly. Still,' Mellor hesitates, takes another mouthful of ale, 'I'm not looking forrard to it.'

'Tha's nivver had a problem wi' being canny around them folks afore, George. I think it's summat more that's troubling thi.'

'What's tha mean?'

'Won't be easy, talking wi' a felly that yer planning to shoot dead.'

'Aye, well.' Mellor drinks again, emptying his tankard for the second time.

'That's it, in't it?'

'Happen tha's partly right,' he admits. 'But it'll not stop me shooting the bastard just because we've had a conversation. I spoke wi' Horsfall on occasion too an' it made no difference.'

John grins at him.

'That's first I've known for definite that it were thee,' he says, triumphantly.

'Who else would it be?' Mellor replies with a wry smile.

'Listen, don't worry abaht this visit to t'magistrate. It'll be nobbut a few minutes of effort and we'll all be better off, if James is reit abaht the money. Does tha want another?'

'Nay, I've to get back to t'shop,' Mellor says, handing his empty tankard to Walker to take back inside. 'I'll si thi soon.'

It all, he thinks, comes down to money in the end: who has it and who doesn't. Mellor understood some time ago that he was engaged primarily in a war of attrition, that the tactical advantage held by his highly mobile and motivated men with their local knowledge and widespread support, would begin eventually to be eroded by the basic disadvantages caused by lack of funds. The balance of men in and out of work was tipping - more subscribers to the fund were needing help. Ammunition must be stolen since there was no spare cash to buy it. Guns were needed, and men had to eat and drink properly if they were going to be fit to fight.

Yes, he'd go and see the fat old magistrate and give his statement about the gun. A hundred pounds would make it worthwhile, but Lord, how he resents it - the wealth of the country being stockpiled in the pockets of social climbers and aristocracy. How he despises the inequity of the fight, the might of the state to keep on and on sending more and more troops and to change laws as and when it suits them.

Even the preachers are against it - a minister called George Beaumont has been raising hackles, going round some of the manufacturers and trying to secure promises that they won't cut jobs or bring in new machines. He caused a bit of a scene in The George Inn when he suggested that the frame-breaking law was ungodly, murder the only crime that should warrant the taking of a life. They'd shoved Beaumont roughly back out onto the square with mingled outrage and laughter. A few of the Methodist minister's more moderate merchant friends quietly quit the premises in his wake, turning their backs on the ribald carousal with swelling discomfort. But those same powerful men who'd turned their ruffled and contemptuous backs on the earnest minister would sit in the Parish church the following Sunday and affect an attendance to the word of God, intentionally blind to their own mockery of scripture, entirely dismissive of their appalling behaviour towards a man of God. A funny, subverted world it is, where manufacturers toss ministers into the streets, and Luddites claim damages from special constables, but Mellor supposes he must make use of whatever small advantage he can find, even if it rankles.

Mellor waits at the door. The maid has rushed inside to report his arrival and all he can see is a slim wedge of hallway and an occasional table holding a vase of dessicated pink flowers. Beyond the hallway, a dog barks and then a second starts, high-pitched and chorusing towards a howl. There are footsteps, then a slamming door and voices - two or three, one of them a woman or a girl. He is straining to make out the words when the light-footed maid reappears and beckons him inside. He follows her down a narrow passage, watching the sway of her black skirts and when she stops and knocks sharply at an oak panelled door, he waits behind her until they both hear the summons from within.

'George Mellor?' asks a man sat at a desk, his back to the bright window so that he appears at first in silhouette against the square of daylight.

'That I am,' Mellor replies, moving closer to the desk and letting his eyes adjust. Behind him, the door closes softly and Jonas Allison, attorney-at-law, dips his quill into an almost empty ink jar and sighs.

'I've used more ink these past few months than- Ah well. Nivver mind. Mr Mellor, 'tis my understanding you're here to make a statement pertaining to the case of-' Allison consults a flurry of papers, '-Brook versus Milns. Forgive me if I hope your statement is a short one.'

'I'll keep it simple an' to t'point, Mr Allison,' smiles Mellor, knowing already the name of this harassed clerk who has interviewed so many of his friends.

'About this gun, then,' prompts Allison, clearing his documents away from his writing paper. The desktop is untidy - piles of paper, a rack of correspondence, a discarded blotter, several broken quills - and in the gaps between the detritus, the green leather inlay is faded and scuffed. The room itself is modestly grand. A rolling landscape in oils dominates the partitioning wall, competing unsuccessfully with the picturesque view from the window of green trimmed parkland. The rug covering the floor is of quality, but well-worn - russets and ceruleans trodden into mundane browns and blues. There is a second desk in the corner - a table, really. It has no drawers or ink well but is stacked with yet more piles of documents, wax and sealing stamps, and several volumes of some important-looking text. On the other side of the room, a dilapidated but ornate chaise-longue lies, loftily at odds with the rest of the study's functional apparatus. Mellor imagines Allison flopping down onto it at the end of a long day of scribing, flexing his aching fingers and laying his head back on the cream upholstery.

'Mi gun needed fixing,' Mellor begins, 'so I took it to t'Brook family to be repaired.'

Allison's quill scratches and strikes. He dips again, tilting the ink jar to soak up the last of the liquid.
'When exactly did you take it and when did they return it?'

Mellor supplies him with the dates. He confirms he

knows nothing about any involvement by the Brooks in Luddite outrages. When Allison passes the paper across, Mellor signs in neatly flowing script.

'That's you finished,' Allison decrees, wiping stained fingers on an already inky rag and coming round the desk to see Mellor out into the passageway. He yanks on a bell-pull and waits within the room while Mellor turns awkwardly in the passageway to face him.

'The maid will be along to show you out.' But they have to stand there for an uncomfortable moment until she arrives.

'Where's t'sweating room,' Mellor asks, on a dangerous impulse. 'Is it along here somewhere?'

'Best be hoping you never find out, lad,' Allison answers smartly. The maid comes round the corner and Allison closes his door.

'This way,' the girl says, coming straight past him. He walks behind her through some kind of drawing room, with an empty fire grate and unoccupied chairs and then they turn into what must be a servants area - the walls are grey, the windows tiny and the floor is bare stone. They pass a kitchen and he gets a brief glance of a huge hearth and pots and pans hanging from the beams, and a florid lady hammering at dough of some kind, before they arrive at an inconspicuous external door. The maid stands back, leaving him to let himself out, but as he does, she says very quickly, and in an anxiously excited way - as if she is tired of knowing secret things and never being able to share them - 'It's near where you were, the sweating room. Just further along. I've seen 'em leave men in there for hours.'

258

'Just a normal room, then?' he asks, carefully.

'More of a cupboard. We'd to move all t'silverware and t'linens. There's no windows.'

A spirited barking starts up somewhere above, and a rattle of footsteps as if people are on the move.

'Sir'll be tekking t'dogs out,' she says, looking up at the low, plain ceiling. 'I should get going if I were you - turn left up here, don't cut across t'gardens unless you're wanting to bump into t'master.'

'Ta,' says Mellor, slipping outside and keeping to the snicket that takes him away from the house, past the pair of soldiers guarding the gate who observe and log his expected departure, and back to the centre of Milnsbridge.

July dawns bright and gauzy. Britain's fair pastures are doused in the elusive golden warmth that fixes childhood memories fast, like dye in the wool. The newspapers are optimistic that trade will be on the upturn, that the economy will recover, now the Orders have been repealed; for yes, Lord Liverpool, the new prime minister, has seized the reins of government and dissolved the detested Orders, though whether this action will turn out to be too little too late is still to be seen.

The merchants are cautiously hopeful. It helps them to know that Bellingham, hanged on 18 May for murdering a prime minister that no one liked very much anyway, was acting alone out of a desperate sense of abandonment by the government when he had been persecuted and gaoled in Russia. But the buoyant spirit is confined to the south-east. In the north, the splendour of the summer sun serves only to stoke the restless masses. From the comfort of leather armchairs housed in rooms of grandeur splayed off from corridors of great power, politicians cannot quite believe that this trouble is still ongoing and that they are being pressed, provoked and harangued into providing more troops for whining Lord Lieutenants who are surely at fault for gross ineptitude.

How on earth a bunch of illiterate, potato-throwing brutes have not yet been brought under the whip is a mystery of infuriating proportions. Are the relevant authorities not equipped with gunpowder, muskets and horses? Must their military resources rival those of Lord Wellington before they can bring the law to bear in their home counties, for goodness' sake? Parliamentary impatience is showing - Viscount Sidmouth in his new role as Home Secretary has been quick to appoint Special Committees and the House eagerly awaits the spectacular debates that are sure to surround his Preservation of the Public Peace bill. If that succeeds, and there is really no question that it will, Britain will become a police state.

Mellor doesn't know it yet, but soon the Magistrates will not even need to read the Riot Act before they seize protesting members of the public, and Joseph Radcliffe will find, to his absolute delight, that geographical boundaries to his power no longer exist - he will be free to operate as a magistrate anywhere, if another magistrate is not on hand already.

Frightening as this new reality is, it does nothing to help the flummoxed Captains who are still, after all this time, chasing dark shadows around on the moors. By the time they arrive at a property, the owner usually ringing a bell like a madman and dogs barking and workshop doors all ajar and tangled ruins of frames cluttering the ground, the culprits are long gone and the soldiers on horseback become the unlucky target of a great deal of mixed emotion. It's a very different prospect to that facing the Captain approaching a traditional riot. At least in the besieged cities there is a protocol, an understanding of what should happen - but in the deep valleys and on the high passes of the West Riding, the people aren't rioting. There aren't great gatherings in Halifax or Huddersfield and daily life looks exceptionally normal. When the Luddites attack, it is so swift and unexpected that a billeted force of hundreds can make absolutely no difference at all, if that billet is beyond a mile away.

Yet the situation feels, to all concerned, like stalemate. No real gains are being made by either side. If Rawfolds had been a success, Mellor knows, that would have changed the whole game. What he needs is another Rawfolds where they actually make it inside. He needs to take down Bradley Mill or one of the other big players, but to do this, he needs arms. That's what Rawfolds taught him - more planning and more firearms. So the tactics, for the time being, have altered a little. No longer are his men targeting frames on their night-time expeditions; they are looking instead for guns - guns of any kind, doesn't matter what. Any homestead that might possess a musket or two is now under threat - and who doesn't have something, if only an old rusted firearm that hasn't been used in years? This new direction has caused some division.

'People are goin' to get twitchy,' Thomas Ellis

advises him. 'People who're on our side, who look t'other way when your men pass in t'night, they're goin' to be flaid it's them next.'

'So?' Mellor replies. 'If they're more flaid, they'll keep looking t'other way and keep their gobs shut an' all.'

'Mebbe.' Ellis leans back on the lang settle, positioned neatly under a clean kitchen window and examines his nails. It's early evening and they are in Ellis's home, a terraced cottage in Lockwood. 'On t'other hand, while they like thi, they're not goin' to spill tha name. But if tha teks from 'em, they're not goin' to like thee any more and then-' he sits forwards and points a long finger at Mellor, who is sat on a spindle chair opposite, 'they're not goin' to be so willing to cover up for thi. Sometimes, George, respect is more useful than fear. Not always, but sometimes.'

Ellis has piercing blue eyes and a nose that sits slightly out of alignment below the bridge. His hands are broad and smooth, a soft shine on the skin that comes from repeated handling of raw wool. He is physically smaller than Mellor in height and breadth, less intense in manner, more open in nature. Introduced by Thomas Brook, Mellor and Ellis are increasingly in one another's orbit, becoming friends as necessity develops into trust. Ellis is a wool stapler, working from premises in Lockwood, and the respectable and established nature of his business gives him power, influence, contacts and protection. He buys wool from the producers, sorts it into grades and sells it on to the manufacturers - men about whom the Luddites need all the information they can get.

That he wishes to ally himself with the Luddite cause is highly beneficial to the units of men operating around Huddersfield. Mellor has been quick to make use of Ellis's advantageous position, and of his perceptive and educated outlook. Ellis, for his part, enjoys the energy and activity which emanates from Mellor and hopes to exert a steadying influence on the cropper's aggressive fervour. He has watched master croppers like Hargreaves and Beaumont attempt to reign in the younger man at meetings and has seen the way their heavy-handed patronage has been rebuffed. That is not Ellis's way. He engages Mellor, advises him, learns from him.

Being a wool stapler, Ellis has precious little occupational connection to the majority of his Luddite brethren. His close friendship with the Brooks has greased his entry to the secret army and his passion is as strong as any other man's, but the croppers are a tight-knit breed; his presence within the ranks requires from him a greater level of attention and focus. Mellor obligingly fills in the references and connexions that he doesn't know or understand and he, in return, provides a tactical and strategic perspective that Mellor is free to accept or discount. On this current point concerning the thieving of guns from private homes, Ellis is genuinely worried and does not like to let the matter slide.

'It's only until we've enough weapons, then we can stop wi' all t'raids on people's homes,' Mellor argues.

'There'll nivver be enough,' Ellis counters, shaking his head, 'an' you've got another problem. There's a fair few fellys who tek it as an excuse. They'd be thieving any road, but it's fair useful to claim they're doing it for t'Ludds.'

'I'm not to blame for all t'thieving sods in Huddersfield!'

'Aye, fair enough, but happen another stern word to thi men might not go amiss.'

'They know t'rules already, Thomas, but I'll remind 'em.'

'I wonder if tha's missing a trick wi' all this stockpiling guns. Why not fire a few places instead? Yer don't need many guns for that.'

'I thought yer wanted people to like me?' Mellor laughs. 'They won't be very happy if I start burning all t'shops down.'

'Well, happen not the small places, most o' t'small masters are practically on our side any road. Some just need a bit o' persuading. But it's the bigger mills I'm talking about. Why aren't we trying to fire Bradley Mill? That'd be easier, surely, than trying to storm t'place wi' muskets.'

'Easy? Have you seen that place lately? Soldiers coming and going, guards in t'mill yard, workers all checked for flints an' guns afore they go in an' Christ only knows what they've got waiting on t'inside. Barrels of acid, spiked rollers, trapdoors, swinging blades. Dear Jesus, I've heard some foul tales Tom, o' some bloody awful things that they've been rigging up to disable any of us that gets in. Trying to get a fire to take means getting inside to set it, an' doing a proper job of it. T'int as easy as it sounds.'

'Aye, but even so. It's worth a go, in't it? A few men to try and start a blaze rather than three hundred to storm the place - less men at risk, less effort all round.'

'We keep looking for chances,' Mellor shrugs. He's

fairly sure that if there was a simple way to light up Bradley mill, his men would have found it by now, practised as they are in the commission of opportunistic attacks.

'Be careful wi' t'others at these meets,' Ellis says, straightening from his languid posture. 'They might not have t'same end in mind as thee.'

'What's tha mean?'

'I mean, think about what threatens their business, lad. It in't just frames, 'cause half of 'em are rushing out to buy 'em. When all's said an' done, it's the big manufactories that'll run the small masters out o' business, whither they've frames or not. Just you be careful, when the master dressers are lining up targets for thi, that the risks are worth taking.'

'I'm nobody's dog. I choose me own targets.'

There are footsteps out on the pavement followed by the squeak of Ellis's garden gate.

'Happen I'm speaking out o' turn. We all want t'same thing, roughly speaking. Just, have a care for thi sen.' Ellis rises and goes to open the door for Hargreaves, leaving Mellor unsettled and unable to pursue the conversation.

On pay day, Mellor takes his twenty shillings from Wood. 'I'm sorry, son,' Wood says, 'But t'cloth price is still dropping. It's thi five percent addlins, I promise.'

'There's men much worse off than me, John,' Mellor answers, putting the coins away, but it does rankle that over the last year his pay has dropped by a third. Anyone who depends on cloth for an income - which must be over ninety percent of the people in the West Riding - is enduring a similar drop, and many of

265

them are slipping from wages already low as sin. At least Mellor's starting point was high. Even on twenty shillings, he earns more than any labourer could dream of and he certainly earns enough to feed and clothe himself and give money back to his mother too. He has enough for the subs - he'd never let the Brief Institution down - but he is struggling to save money the way he used to. He has about a hundred pounds sitting in a bank account - a fact he is proud but tight-lipped about.

'John, there's something I've been meaning to ask.'

'Oh aye?' Wood takes in Mellor's strained face and makes a sudden and unusual decision. 'Let's go for a drink, lad.'

Mellor follows him out of the house and they walk together to the pub. It's busy, being a warm late afternoon, with all the workers knocking off around this time, so Wood buys a couple of pints and they stroll across the road and up the banking to a shaded stretch of wall where they can sit in peace and cradle their drinks.

'We haven't done this for a long time,' Wood says, supping at the lukewarm ale.

'Why would we?' asks Mellor, eyes fixed on his tankard.

'I've had the raising o' you from a nipper,' says Wood, 'An' there were many times I'd ha' liked to just come and have a drink wi' thi like this but thi never wanted to.'

'I don't remember thi asking.'

'Aye, well.' Wood doesn't want to get into it all. It's easier for him to recall the sulking, the moodiness, Mellor's refusal to call him father, than to pick apart the beatings, the meals withheld, the dirty jobs that went Mellor's way even though his mother said he was too young for it. Difficult years, Wood thinks, putting a mental lid back on it all. 'So what did thi want to ask me about?'

'The small masters,' Mellor says. 'I want to know why some o' them get frames an' some o' them don't. Why don't you want frames?'

'What a question to ask! Tha knows what I think. Frames put men out o' work.'

'Tha's a man o' business, that in't all it is.'

'Frames don't give so good a cut as a man does. My cloth's better finished by you lot than anything a machine can produce. It's a better product.'

'An' the masters who get frames in, why do they do it?'

'I make me money from quality, George, they make it from quantity. Stop talking so soft! Tha knows all this, what's tha getting at?'

'Well, I've been seeing it as t'same thing - whether it's big mills getting lots o' frames in or little shops getting one or two. A frame's a frame.' Mellor balances the imaginary iron on his upheld arms. 'But these two things,' he scrunches his fists and examines them, 'they're not the same at all.'

'How so?'

'This felly with two frames an' a small shop, he's probably not going to lay anybody off just yet. He's going to put a couple o' men on running the frames and keep the best croppers for hand-finishing. He'll end up wi' two different products - hand-finished best and a cheaper cloth, finished by machine. His customers will decide what they want, when they bring their cloth to him for finishing, an' he'll probably find that he makes a bit more money by being able to run off a quicker product for them as only need a cheap finish. Now, this felly over here,' Mellor holds up the other fist. 'He's doing something different. He's thinking: there's money at every stage in making cloth an' I've got a bloody big mill, so why don't I do everything here - spinning, weaving, finishing, all under one roof. An' he's thinking lets find the fastest, cheapest way of doing everything, so's he can squeeze every little bit o' money out of it.'

'Money from quantity, like I said, George. Tha's not telling me owt I don't know,' sighs Wood.

'But look at where it ends up. The small master over here, with his couple o' frames, he's still running a cropping shop. He's competing wi' all t'other cropping shops, same as always. But the manufacturer over here, he's taking over t'whole process. Why would anyone buy his cloth from t'mill an' then bring it to a cropping shop when t'mill can do that part too?'

'What's thi point?'

'My point is that we've got different enemies, John. Mine is the frame, because it's taking me job. And yet, there'll still be some jobs - someone's got to work t'frames. I could get a job doing that. Your enemy is t'manufacturing process, because it's taking yer trade. Yer can't compete, even if yer get a couple o' frames in - places like Atkinson's are just too big.'

'Yer mean I've got more to lose? Horse shit, lad! See them men, starving in gutters all over town? Them's men out o' work, and no jobs for 'em. Tha says "I could get a job working a frame" but there's no jobs to be had. Men like thee are starving to death.'

'All I'm saying is, even if we destroy all t'frames, the shops'll still be in trouble. They've been in trouble for years, ever since the old fulling mills started expanding.'

'I don't deny it. But I'll ask thee again lad - an' I warn thee, I'm starting to lose patience - what does it matter?'

'I don't know. I'm trying to get mi head round it all.' Mellor picks up his pint from beside him on the stone wall and takes a long drink. The clopping of a horse and cart passing by covers for the drop in conversation. Across the road, men are leaning back with their drinks in much the same manner as Mellor and Wood. Tall yellow irises and vivid pink foxgloves bask on the banking, soaking up the summer sun and swaying softly in the breeze. A home-time bell starts to ring in one of the small mills upriver towards Paddock.

'Are thi losing heart, George?'

'Nay. Never. I suppose I'm just trying to understand mi enemy.'

'Tha wants to know what makes me different to Joseph Hirst or Clement Dyson or any o' them small masters that's bought frames in? Well mebbe I'm old-fashioned, but I like t'old ways o' doing things. It used to work reit well - clothiers, millers, finishers, all doing their own bit. We'd hard times, o' course, but we lived a damned sight better than this. These paupers everywhere, up in town? It weren't a bit like that when I were a lad. You'd old Jimmy, dead-drunk on gin, and a few others t'toss coins to, but they were a rare sight. Not like now. And kiddies? Working in t'mills when they're nobbut babes in arms? Well kiddies allus used to help out; a bit o' spinning, cleaning up the looms, burling t'cloth an' that. But that were at home, wi' their mams an' dads, not under t'whip o' some overseer who dun't care if they've slept or eaten in hours. Using kiddies for their little hands where a grown-up's won't fit? An' just look at what Haigh's did - bringing up kiddies from London workhouses and not even paying 'em - an' then when t'mill shut, them 'at hadn't been worked to death were half-starved in t'streets until t'Marsden parish took 'em in. Slavery, that's what it is. An' every month brings some new machine, some felly who thinks his contraption can do t'work faster, cheaper. Nobody's bothered if its better or not. They're like dogs chasing their own tails.

'I'm not saying there's owt wrong wi' making a profit. Far from it. We do hard work an' we should be paid for it. We make good cloth, an' we make it fair an' square. But when a cloth dresser, big or small, buys frames, he's not thinking abaht the cloth, he's only thinking abaht the profit he'll make from getting rid o' men. Thi talks abaht having hand-finished an' machine-finished products, but what'll happen in t'long run? Merchants are canny, they'll get the cheapest job they think they can sell on. Afore long, they'll all be asking for machined cloth an' everyone will forget what proper, hand-finished cloth looks an' feels like.'

Wood's voice has risen. It echoes around Mellor, dissipating through the tree branches, carried away on the soft, warm air. Does it matter at all, the distinction Mellor thought he had made? Is there a difference? In the end, the manufacturing process is his enemy too. It will close the cropping shops one by one and perhaps give him a job, but it won't be a good job. It won't be one that satisfies his soul. He says, aloud, 'Why would a man make cloth when he has no care for it?' and Wood says, 'Them men don't make cloth, son, they make money.'

Across the carriageway, the tableaux remains unchanged - ten or fifteen people drinking, smoking and laughing in the sunshine, a heat haze shimmering on the dusty surface of the road in the distance, the glint of river and canal beyond workshops and houses. Bare patches of land, left over from when the canal was being constructed, are dotted with skipping children and sun-bathing dogs; brambles are beginning to assert themselves on the periphery and in the cracks.

'Yer mother wishes you'd find a lass.'

Mellor laughs dismissively. 'When would I find time?'

'Make time,' Wood says. 'A good woman makes life more bearable. Aren't thi lonely for a wife?'

'Lonely? In a house like ours?'

'I know yer busy, but there's never a good time. You've just to get on and do it.'

'Find me a good woman, an I'll think on it.'

'Yer on,' grins Wood.

When he smiles, Wood looks older. Mellor doesn't know why this should be - surely happiness should make a person more youthful? But Wood's smile is sad - a wistful lifting of the face that creases the skin and mists up the eyes. It comes to him suddenly that his own father never reached such an age, that in fact Mellor himself is approaching the age at which his own father died. The idea of outstripping his own father's existence - of becoming more worldly-wise and grey - is somehow appalling. How will they greet in the heavens, if he has entered a white-haired senescence and his father is eternally in his prime? Perhaps in death we change, he thinks, perhaps I'll be a little boy again when I meet him - but then, how will my children know me?

'I could sit here for hours,' Wood says, kicking a heel against the stone and dangling his empty tankard between his knees as he gazes up into the sun. 'But I'd best be getting back.'

'Aye, I've a meeting any road.'

'O' course, lad, o' course. I'll si thee.' And, with sudden feeling, he pats Mellor's leg as he dismounts the wall. Mellor, shocked by the unusual intimacy, watches him cross the carriageway and deposit his tankard on one of the pub's stone windowsills. He weaves past friends and acquaintances with a practised choreography, smiling and chatting, and although Mellor cannot hear the words from this distance, he can fill them in from imagination easily enough - 'How are thee? Nice weather, in't it? Come see me abaht that kersey. How's yon Mrs?' and then Wood slips out of view and Mellor is alone.

Mellor's personal possessions are meagre. He has a single drawer in which he keeps his timepiece, his handkerchiefs, his bible, a tiny bottle of ink and some feather quills. He has a small, sharp pocket knife, a limited supply of thin paper and an old children's book of parables. Rummaging around, he pulls out the ink, a quill and some sheets of paper. He knows he shouldn't commit thoughts in this way, but he can no longer fit all his plans inside his head. He feels as though the best ideas will leak away, that he'll lose his sense of purpose and that the internal arguments that rage in his mind will drive him into indecision. Not knowing how best to start his expulsion, he carefully writes the date at the top left of the page. The first line comes slowly, held back by the habitual avoidance of such incriminating self-expression, but then he scrawls faster, more urgently until his page is almost full - and still he doesn't stop, sliding the top page away and beginning on a second, cramping his lines together to make the best use of the precious space and drawing his quill from the pot so quickly that he speckles his own text with jewels of black. Even in his looping, practised calligraphy, he is only barely decipherable and by the third page his misspellings have multiplied and his lines have begun to slope untidily as if falling from the surface. He finishes with a stabbing full stop and signs his name in a grandly theatrical flourish.

The bizarre memorandum lays on the tabletop. Mellor spreads the three pages before him and tries to re-read his own words. It's not the deteriorating handwriting that forestalls him, but some sort of exhaustion. He can't bear to read it or even to look. He snatches it up and rolls it tight, then stows it beneath a splintered floorboard under his side of the bed.

The final meeting of the month is a largish gathering in a pub on the outskirts of Linthwaite. Twenty or so men dare to assemble to discuss tactics, but they are all on edge. The landlord's sympathies notwithstanding, they are now highly vulnerable when assembled in such numbers. Mellor leads the argument, pressing still for assassination of mill owners and although there is tacit agreement, no one seems willing to volunteer, nor even to make specific plans. He sees how it still shocks them, this murderous talk, no matter how reconciled they are to the inevitable escalation in hostilities. He tries another approach.

'We've not fired a mill for a long time. Since the Atkinsons are hard to catch off guard when they're out an' abaht, happen we'll have better luck burning their place down.' It's not for want of trying - Mellor has personally stalked Law Atkinson but been unable to define a point of weakness in the man's routine, and as for Thomas Atkinson, he hasn't even got close. They can't get at the men to shoot them, but firing Bradley's Mill would be a major victory.

'It's getting in that's the problem,' says Ellis. 'But it can be done, somehow or other. Do we know anyone there?'

'There's a few,' says John Walker, 'But we shall have to press 'em hard to make 'em do it. It'll put 'em out o' work as well as in danger o' being caught.'

'There's money yet, from the Brief. We can help 'em out if needs be.' Mellor points to Drake. 'Will thi go see these men?'

'I'll speak to 'em. Put a bit o' pressure on.'

Someone asks, 'Why don't we fire a few o' t'smaller shops? That'd be easier.'

'Who does tha mean? Blyth? Gairner? Not many troops out that way...'

'Aye, a rag in a bottle'd do it.'

'Na than,' says Mellor, waving his arms at the assembled Luddites, 'Firing a mill is one thing. Firing a man's home an' workshop is another. We're not trying to destroy the cropping shops, we just need to put 'em off using frames. The manufactories are different - everything about them is a threat to t'way we live. So I say, fire the mills but stick to breaking frames at t'smaller shops.'

'But nothing's happening,' John Walker complains. 'It's all going too slowly.'

'Aye, it feels that way. But we're building up arms an' we're in contact wi' more an' more Luddites over in Lancashire an' down in Derbyshire. Firing workshops won't speed things up, it'll just make us more enemies where we need friends.'

There are some noises of agreement, but a voice pipes up from the rear, 'Talking o' Lancashire, has thee heard about Captain Raynes?'

'Who?' Mellor asks, trying to make out the speaker in the gloaming light. It's about nine o'clock and even though the days are at their longest, only a dusky glow filters through the pub's grimy windowpanes. The speaker, realising that this is a name new to Mellor, stands up and lifts his cap awkwardly as faces turn to appraise him.

'Captain Raynes, Mr Mellor. Mi family lives over near Oldham. I go back regular, like, an' they've teld me abaht this army captain who's trying to round up Ludds by promising folk money.'

'That's nothing new. Even bloody tight-fisted Radcliffe keeps offering rewards for information.'

'Aye, but 'tis the way he's going abaht it,' emphasizes the man, who has removed his cap entirely and is twisting the rim between his fingers as he speaks. 'He comes late at neet, just a few soldiers wi' him, an he rides in fast, flicking his whip abaht an' pointing his musket, getting everyone flaid. In a pub like this he'd drive us all out onto t'street an' he'd order us to disperse. An' if we didn't, his troops'd start priming an' loading. He's going abaht, breaking up meetings and chasing down gangs who's out smashing frames. Almost caught a load red-handed t'other neet, me mam said. Her friend said her lad were there an' he slipped into t'ditch running away an' they'd ha' shot him, if they'd a' seen him but they didna.'

The man fumbles to a conclusion and awaits Mellor's response but Mellor is thinking about what this means and a long moment of silence ensues. William Thorp looks from Mellor's furrowed countenance to the worried faces around them, and gives Mellor a discreet nudge. Mellor lifts his eyes to stare directly at the speaker, who is looking like he wishes he'd kept quiet.

'This is important information, thanks for passing it on. It sounds like the army is copying what we're doing - small groups o' soldiers, acting fast... Did thi ever hear of an army working like that?' He looks to the trusted men at his side.

'Nay, they move abaht in big troops,' says Ellis, licking his lips and biting a thumb nail. 'What's this Raynes felly up to?'

'Folks is scared of him,' adds the speaker, 'reet scared of him. Beat at least one lad to death-'

'What's thi name?' Mellor interrupts

'Hoyle, Mr Mellor.'

'This Captain Raynes is over the Pennines. No need for him to interfere wi' what we're doing. But anything more, Hoyle, you come straight to me. An' anyone else who hears owt.' He sweeps his gaze around the room.

On home soil, Mellor feels confident. He knows the people to trust, the places he can hide and where to run to, but on the day following that meeting, Mellor has to make a journey beyond the safety of the Huddersfield basin, and Hoyle's words rattle with him as he sets out on the stagecoach towards York. James Brook, the man whose fault it is that Mellor must make this trip, sits alongside, companionably mute, while Mellor gazes out of the jiggling, boxy vehicle at the sun-dappled villages and homesteads that litter the land between his own town and the distant city of York. The road is rutted and stony and the iron wheels bounce the passengers in their seats - Mellor, Brook, a vicar with hands folded over a wrapped parcel and a middle-aged couple pressed into greater proximity with each other than they appear comfortable with. Brook has paid for the tickets. Mellor has agreed that he can take back the amount from whatever monies they are awarded today for they are en route to the nervously anticipated Assize court, where James Brook's suit against Constable Milns will be officially heard.

The lady opposite Mellor fidgets and picks at her gloves. Then she mumbles something to her husband. He ignores her, staring out of the window. She won't let it go and voices her worry again. Evidently this is a marital argument that was underway well before the coach journey. Her husband shrugs at her latest complaint and says, quite audibly, 'I wouldn't piss on your brother if he were afire.' She shrinks as far away from him as she can in the enclosed space and the vicar purses his lips. Brook looks down, embarrassed, but Mellor meets the woman's eyes and holds her gaze. He is curious, and a little sorry for her, but the husband senses disapproval. 'What's tha looking at?' He says, with a bullish toss of the head.

'Behold how good and pleasant it is for brethren to dwell together in unity,' smiles Mellor, mischievously.

'Psalms, 133,' nods the Vicar, with a forceful stare at the husband. 'And might I add, a friend loveth at all times and a brother is born for adversity. Proverbs, 17.'

'Si thi,' says the woman primly, pleased with the support. The carriage drops back into silence, if the grating clang of the wheels and the constant clop of horse hooves can be experienced as such. The couple disembark at Barwick in Elmet, for which Brook, at least, is grateful. While they drink pints in the coaching inn as the horses are changed, he laughs about the Vicar's delight in Mellor's easy citation of scripture.

'I'm a god-fearing man, James. What's funny about that?'

'Tha said it just to wind the bloke up.'

'He were an arse.'

'Mebbe his brother-in-law had done summat terrible.'

'Mebbe.'

'That felly might have clobbered thi.'

'Not likely.'

'Well I'm glad they're off. I should just like now for some lovely young governess to join us for the rest o' the ride.'

'That would be more agreeable,' Mellor laughs.

'Ey up, t'Vicar's getting back aboard,' Brook says, gesturing through the large, open doorway. 'Don't be goading 'im when we get back in, I don't want t'have to listen to a sermon for t'rest o' t'way.'

'He's not to my taste, neither,' Mellor agrees.

Methodists both, they climb back into the coach where the Anglican vicar is already engrossed in a small leather-bound book of psalms. Brook props his legs on the door sill and slides his cap over his eyes to take a nap. Mellor returns to gazing out of the window as the horses pull away. It wouldn't entirely trouble him to have a conversation with the minister opposite, but he senses that they would run into conflict before long.

Methodism in the West Riding crests high on the wave that John Wesley set in motion. The Church of England is involved in a rearguard action, conscious of dwindling congregations - the Anglicans have in recent years even attempted to mimic the Wesleyans by preaching outdoors and paying more attention to the needs and sufferings of the poor, but in these horrifically austere times, when people are actually starving to death in the North's most prosperous woollen towns, the message of the dissenting religions is stronger than ever. The Wesleyans and the Kilhamites speak the language of the destitute more fluently than does the Vicar of Huddersfield's Parish Church of St Peter - a building framed appropriately enough in a flimsy edifice of cheap masonry that threatens constantly to disintegrate.

It's a well-known story that once the church chancel actually did crumble, crushing the poor sixteenth century Parish Clerk who was about his business beneath, but the rest of the structure teeters on precariously, braced either by God's steadying hand or by a perverse Anglican obstinacy.

And yet how secure is Methodism truly, in the West Riding? The religion has already endured a major split, between the Wesleyans who espouse a more moderate line and the Kilhamites - or New Connexion - who embody a far more radical stance. A significant proportion of Old Bank's congregation are confirmed Luddites, a fact which would undoubtedly horrify the New Connexion ministry which is desperately scraping and scrabbling under the crushing pressure of a suspicious government. Methodism, at both ends of its spectrum, is anxious to appear respectable and to avoid sanction.

At the ground level, the Kilhamites might be supportive of Luddism, but officially they can in no way align themselves with riotous dissent. They exist in the middle of the industrial fiasco, attempting to both protect and censure their followers - an unsustainable position. If they make fully clear their disapproval of the Ludds, then the tenuous nature of their hold upon the congregation will be revealed. Mellor has firm faith, and Methodism suits his purpose, but the form and function of Methodism is merely a pattern to which the people of the West Riding are more readily suited. They imbibe its character only to the extent that the flavour is compatible with their essential nature. The ministry surely knows this.

Anglican, Wesleyan, Kilhamite; grappling pointlessly with each other, gnashing their teeth and stamping the ground, heedless of the giants beneath, the earth yet to shake them free. Mellor's faith in God is driven by a power deeper and older than these human convocations.

The carriage shudders into York, disgorging them within sight of Clifford's Tower, the limestone keep that rises on a motte above the castle bailey. James Brook looks nervous as they approach the grand compound on foot. There are three neoclassical buildings beyond the tower - the women's gaol on the left, the county gaol in front and the Assize court on the right, all three facing into the Eye of the Ridings, which is the name given to the grassed circle in the centre. Mellor leads the way towards the Assize court entrance and into the central lobby which gives access to the Crown court on the left and the Civil court on the right.

They find, to their relief, that their case has not yet been called, and the Civil court itself being quite packed, they sit and wait on a wooden pew just beyond the court doors. Somewhere in the bowels of the gaol next door, James Haigh is locked away, awaiting trial for his involvement in Rawfolds. It is unclear if he will be tried at these very Assizes. Discomfort at this knowledge keeps both men silent and time passes in a frozen kind of way, the ticking of a nearby cabinet clock marching on through the empty wait, until it is time to enter the court and for Brook to give his evidence. Nerves manifest as honest humility - Brook's retelling, clean and simple. Mellor's job is even easier. 'I know John Wood,' he says in answer to the Judge's prompt, 'I had broken a gun and carried it to the Brooks to be repaired,' and within minutes, a judgement is awarded against the fuming Constable Milns, of a hundred pounds in damages for his malicious behaviour. James Brook does a good job of looking earnest and grateful and the case is done. They leave the Castle premises with all possible speed, disbelief catching up with them. It seems impossible that they have actually done it - won the case and made a hundred pounds out of it - and there follows that natural fear that in skating on such thin ice, they cannot possibly escape unscathed.

In one of the little, winding streets of York, they find a pie house and buy one each, munching hungrily as they embark on the proprietor's directions to the most reliable coaching inn and, still on a wave of exhilarating adrenaline, they put their money down for the return journey to Huddersfield and await departure at the bar of the busy inn.

9
Under The Canopy of Heaven

The Assize court is behind the platform on which Mellor now stands, his back to the ancient castle walls, the open swell of St George's Field below him, people filling the green space right up to the banks of the Ouse and the Fosse. That cabinet clock ticks on incessantly within the court, he has no doubt. He was foolish to think he could outrun the steady pulse of this place, or shed the evanescent tendrils that must have smelt antagonism in his blood when first he entered the Eye of the Ridings. A reprieve from the grasp of this place was all he gained - the sojourn of high summer - before autumn felled his plans along with the leaves.

Smith is praying now. He won't take long; Tom's prayers, sometimes overheard at bedtime in the room they used to share, have never soared to ambitious heights and they show no signs of doing so now. The lad sounds strangled and inarticulate. Dancing time approaches and Mellor's throat is dry. No more ale, he abruptly realises; a thirst never to be quenched. He grits his teeth against suffocating panic - not the rising fear of death (though that is there, too) but the claustrophobic agony of imprisonment. Crashing upon him for the very first time is the true meaning of freedom - or rather the true horror of the lack of it. Liberty, the vague notion he has for so long held sacred, crystallises in a brutal and beautiful clarity, fathomed only in its total absence; it is the sharp and radiant opposite of the murky and changeable limits within which he has lived - that darkly opaque fiction of freedom to which the lower classes are subjected and to which most will submit and endure. His thrashing against the constraints of this world has been inevitable; those who most revere liberty and equality are the very people who will slam into the man-made walls around those unassailable diamonds, pressing for the emancipation that eludes them.

Maybe his is not much of a life to lose; maybe it is a glorious and transcendental truth that he has never been as close to Liberty as he is now, on the brink of the launch into eternity, but all of his being yearns for that life he has lived, in his town, in his home, with his family; the life he had before they caught him.

'Come for a picnic,' Elizabeth begs, while Betty packs food in a basket.

'Tha should come, George,' his mother says without looking up. 'It'll do thi good.'

Lizzie grabs at his wrist and he allows himself to be dragged out into the yard. They walk up towards Gledholt on the quiet footpaths and as they crest the hill, they can look back upon Longroyd Bridge and see their small empire - the shop, the house, the ribbons of river and canal threading past. Wood walks a little way behind with Mary. Mellor escorts Betty and Lizzie. Daniel is up ahead with a friend, the pair of them bumping shoulders and breaking sticks and kicking stones. Sweat forms where the edges of Mellor's cap press above his temples, the hair there turning damp and shiny, and Lizzie links his arm as she tires.

At the woods, they find a dappled place to sit, the stream trickling thinly by. Daniel and his friend start to build a dam; Lizzie pulls off boots and stockings and paddles tentatively while Betty lingers alongside on the bank. Mellor drops down by his mother and stepfather, and reaches into the basket for some bread.

'Is Brook's money in t'fund?' Wood asks. Mary sighs and looks over at the splashing children.

'It is,' Mellor confirms.

'A Dewsbury man got off same day as you were there. Charged wi' being at Rawfolds, but he'd an alibi.'

'Aye, I read abaht that. Din't see him - we din't stop longer than we had to.'

'What were York like?' his mother interrupts. 'I've nivver been.'

'Busy. A lot o' small streets. An' pretty - the river goes reit by t'old castle. We had a pie from a shop afore we left an' it were one o' t'nicest I've ever had.'

'Radcliffe's done wi thi now, is he?'

'Aye mam, it's done wi, now that Brook's got his damages.'

'Only... I've been trying to figure summat out.' Mary pauses. She looks between Mellor and Wood, biting her lip, and then commits herself to pulling a small handbill from the very bottom of the basket. It's pressed into a small square, battered and mucky as if she has carried it with her for a while, folding and unfolding the paper repeatedly, maybe getting a friend to read it for her since her own ability is so limited. She opens it out now in front of them, smoothing a hand across the ink, revealing the words with reluctance. Pardon of Illegal Oaths, it announces boldly, above a subtext in finer print below.

'Mary, thi shouldn't be worrying abaht this,' says

Wood, removing the handbill gently from her pincer grip.

'Why dun't tha do it, George?' she whispers. 'What if other men do it first an' tell on thee?'

He looks at the proclamation in Wood's hand, the Royal promise to Luddites that if they swear allegiance to the crown when confessing to having taken an illegal oath, then they will be pardoned. Already, in the Lancashire villages, a few men have given themselves in.

'Mam, let me explain something,' he murmurs, conscious of the children within earshot. She leans towards him, brow earnestly ruffled. 'This deal, it means a man gets off if he's taken the oath. That's all, nowt else. Most o' the men who've taken the Oath have done a lot more besides.

'If they go to t'magistrate an' turn 'emselves in, especially if they go to our Mr Radcliffe, he'll pardon 'em for the oath-taking, but he'll want to know their alibi for Rawfolds, an' where they were when Vickerman's got done, an' he'll dig away until he gets 'em for summat. The Ludds know that. They won't go to him. An' even if they do, they won't give names. Why should they? There's no reward for it, except in one or two cases. It's true that we might lose a few Ludds who've taken the oath but never seen action - them's the only men as can safely give 'emselves up - but there's not many o' them. We've made sure o' that. Does tha see? Being twissed means more 'na just taking t'Oath. It means tha's bound, in deed as well as word. In for a penny, in for a pound, that's how it works. An' even them as thinks they can go running to t'magistrate to get out of it have to think abaht what the brothers'll do to 'em for it.'

While Mellor has been speaking, Wood has folded the handbill into a passable paper boat and now holds it out to Mary. She smiles and takes it from him.

'I thought it were a way out but it's just a trap,' she says, turning the simple vessel about on her palm. 'I shall have to stop expecting an end to all this.'

'I'd call an end tomorrer if the manufacturers would see sense,' Mellor says. She hands him the boat. 'Take this to t'boys,' she tells him.

Mellor eats his bread and butter watching as the paper boat floats for a while, turning in crazy circles until Daniel and his friend lose patience and begin stirring up the dammed water with too much vigour, overwhelming the stern and collapsing the sides into pulp. Daniel swirls it about a bit, before hoisting the capsized craft out on the end of his stick and flinging it downstream. Lizzie shrieks at the splashing. Mellor's breeches are sprayed with water too and his back itches with sweat. He takes off his own boots and stockings and finds a rock to sit upon, from where his feet can dangle in the shallow flow, the skin turning milk-white, delicate bones shimmering under the surface. He rubs at the gravel and pebbles with his toes, raising clouds of dirt and the flash and shine of stones, so much prettier under the water than when they are lifted for examination.

Tossing the tiny artefacts at Daniel, aiming for his legs, he laughs at his brother's clumsy dance of avoidance, then waves his hands in surrender as Daniel threatens him with a rock the size of his fist. Backlit against a brilliant blue sky, the canopy of birch and beech overhead holds a fixed pattern. Mellor leans back and lets the filtered sunlight warm his face from above while the chilled water below sends a cooling swell through the core of his body.

He thinks about the Dewsbury man who was acquitted. Maybe he too is lying on the grass somewhere, counting his blessings in the summer sun. Things have not worked out so neatly for James Haigh; that damned musket wound is too hard to explain away. The authorities, he guesses, are whittling away at the likeliest suspects, dredging for evidence before bringing them to trial. They obviously had so little on this man from Dewsbury that it was easier to let him go, but Haigh's case is different.

When James Haigh went on the run, his employer, Joseph Ardron, got him to the house of a Mary and Joseph Culpin - friends of his he felt were trustworthy. The Culpins can give dates that correspond to the aftermath of Rawfolds. They can testify to the whispered explanations of Ardron, and to whatever unguarded comments Haigh, in his feverish pain, may have made. After the constables traced Haigh's movements to the Culpins, it became clear to the Brief that the couple were a liability and that friendship with Ardron alone might not keep their mouths shut.

A friend of Haigh's, a Luddite though not of Mellor's close acquaintance, had been to see them on several occasions and made the necessary threats - but the Culpins in their fear informed upon him, and Mellor has lately learned that this man - Pat Doring - was tried at the Assizes for his threats to kill and has now been sentenced to several years in York. The conviction of Doring dovetails perfectly with the postponement of Haigh's trial - the authorities will now press the Culpins for all their evidence against Haigh, confident that Doring's conviction proves the pair have genuinely damning evidence against the Dalton cropper. Mary and Joseph Culpin refused to go to the Assizes and testify against either Haigh or Doring, which represents at least some modicum of decency, but they won't get away with that again. They'll be arrested themselves if they do not attend a future trial of James Haigh. Mellor does not expect them to be capable of dissembling their way out of the fix. He knows they will incriminate Haigh. If only they had kept their mouths shut in the first place.

His reassurances to his mother were genuine; Mellor does not believe the Luddites will break ranks - even the two thousand pounds of reward money on offer for names of the Horsfall murderers has not teased a thread loose. The problem is the non-Ludds; the untwissed; the frayed edges where Luddism meets a sympathetic public, where practical judgements of trust and risk must be made is where the danger lies. The Culpins have proved that, as has the debacle with John Hinchcliffe over at Upperthong. Mellor has kept himself at a clear remove from that business, but he does know that two of the men under his command have shot Hinchcliffe in the eye.

They had been working on the clothier, wanting him to take the Oath, but it became clear he was more averse than they presumed and, having given themselves away, they sought to silence him. Unfortunate, that they blinded him in one eye and did not finish the job, for if Hinchcliffe can give evidence against them, they will be taken up. Schofield, one of the Ludds, has fled south already - he knew

Hinchcliffe had recognised him before the shot was fired.

Less than a year ago, the movement was able to expand with such relative ease. Angry talk in the friendly societies enabled large numbers of men to come to a common understanding without danger, and the Oath was widely taken in pubs and shops across the district. Luddism in the West Riding swelled to a buoyant mass and enabled Mellor and others to put the movement on a war footing against the mill owners.

He hadn't appreciated then that the numbers formed by spring also represented a critical mass, and that expanding further might destabilize the entire operation. Where whole units were formed over the course of a few days last winter, each single new addition this summer comes with enormous risk. Men give the impression of willingness, like Hinchcliffe, and then blab to the clergy or the constables. Men turn up at meetings looking keen and serious, but Mellor knows that spies - soldiers, officers, constables - are trying to infiltrate their meetings. He faces the same challenge as any insurrectionist - expanding his base of power whilst shielding it from overwhelmingly superior forces.

The rewards for information, to which he has just alluded in conversation with his mother, are indicative of the intelligence tactics the authorities have adopted. Just as Mellor knows the weak points of the operation, so too do the magistrates and they are making the most of them. The weak points are fear, greed and foolishness. And pride, for pride results in foolishness.

Four or five months ago, Mellor encountered a foundry man called Jonathan Brook on the Bridge.

'How do, Mr Brook,' Mellor had said, and the iron-worker had responded promptly that he was not doing well at all - that he was in fact in enormous fear of Luddite wrath for his previous efforts to manufacture cropping frames, and that he was in receipt of a terrible letter that threatened to lay his property and person to ashes if he so persisted. 'And so,' the man had confided, "I am off to the printers and shall get mi sen a batch of handbills to say that I've nowt more to do wi' making cropping frames.' 'Is that truly so?' Mellor had asked. 'Then go no further, tha need not go to t'expense of handbills. Word o' your sensible decision will soon reach the right ears.'

I meant it kindly, Mellor thinks; he was doing the right thing and I reassured him, and saved him money too. Pride, though, his conscience prods; you can't deny the satisfaction when his eyes registered the revelation, when his posture became that little bit more craven in your presence. What if Jonathan Brook remembers that conversation? There'd been a loud argument between the foundry man and Horsfall on account of Brook's decision not to manufacture frames. What if someone remembers that and points Justice Radcliffe in Brook's direction? What if Brook then recounts Mellor's words to Radcliffe?

What if, what if; Mellor removes his cap and ruffles the damp hair stuck to his scalp. It's not evidence, not even for Radcliffe whose benchmark is so low. Evidence would be, say, if Thorp or Walker or Smith went to Radcliffe and gave an eyewitness account, but none of them can - they are so very deeply implicated in Luddite activities that they could not possibly emerge unscathed.

He groans, lying there, propped back on his elbows, face tipped up to the quilting of leaves against the speedwell sky, wanting the world to be simple just for one afternoon. Squeezing his thoughts, like cheese in a cloth, to the farthest corner of his mind, he watches the damson fly skimming above him and the nuthatches and sparrows in the trees.

Two score men, at least, have had their guns removed by the special constables. Mellor receives this information in early August. It trickles through friends like Ellis, who know of men who have been required to submit their weaponry. There is a good deal of outrage, and understandably so, but those faithful to King and Church can hardly refuse the request. It is an interesting approach. The authorities fear the extent of weaponry being amassed by Luddites in house raids and so they are taking the guns before the Luddites can and storing them in a property on King Street where only the owner and the authorities can access them. Undaunted, Mellor orchestrates a raid in Sheepridge which he anticipates will be productive, though he does not take part himself.

In fact, his direct involvement has faded now that he has so much to coordinate. He's been on very few of the arms raids and hasn't broken a frame in weeks. He spends more time cloistered away with the master dressers, meeting go-betweens from Oldham, Manchester, Leeds, Sheffield, helping to dictate letters and planning which units will raid which villages and where the stolen lead and guns will be stored and prepared. It's been a while since he met with Baines over at Halifax, principally because he fears that the

Republican nest in The Crispin is too conspicuous to the authorities but also because he is being kept so busy in Huddersfield. The movement has a steady rumbling life of its own, cartwheeling gently now until they can really let the brakes off. He's running at the side of it, keeping everyone in the cart, watching for obstacles, nudging the vehicle back on track when it lurches.

Home seems quiet in comparison. Elizabeth and Daniel are carving out the beginnings of their adult lives, flitting in and out of the house, for food and sleep, but with the focus of their existence changed, Daniel concentrating on his apprenticeship and Lizzie training in the shop and looking to Wood for approval where before she was her mother's girl.

Both siblings are like small moons gradually breaking away from their orbit and Mary's adjustments to the growth of her youngest living children are visible to his eye. Sometimes she stills when they leave - a half-second of watching the space they have vacated - before her perpetual motion resumes and she picks up their bowls, wipes the table and turns away to the hundred and one tasks ahead of her. Sometimes she stops in the yard and stares up at the sky in a kind of confusion. Sometimes she stops right there in the kitchen, flat iron or wooden spoon in hand, and he backs soundlessly away, afraid to invade the privacy that such internal moments would seem to require.

Betty has no such compunction. 'Mam,' she snaps, 'art tha mixing or dreaming?' Once upon a time, their mam would have fetched Betty a smack for that sort of cheek, but now she accepts the rebuke almost gladly, as if the tether of Betty's bluntness prevents her from floating away altogether.

Mary-Ann visits Longroyd Bridge for a day in August. She works in service, sleeping in at the large home where she is employed, but every so often she comes back to see her parents. Elizabeth suggests a walk after supper and they beg Mellor to come along and make the most of the golden evening. He walks between them with his shirt sleeves rolled up, strolling in the fading warmth as charcoal shadows softly and slowly interpose.

'Will you always be a cropper, George?' Elizabeth asks, running her fingers over his hoofed wrist, feeling the raised welt and callused skin.

'Like as not,' he says. 'What will you be?'

'A publican,' she responds promptly. 'I'd like t'best pub in all Huddersfield, wi' dancing an' singing an' t'best ale.' She twirls on his arm, tripping on the cracks and laughing, knowing she'll burl cloth until she marries and has children.

'How about you, Mary-Ann, art thi satisfied wi thi job?'

'It's all reit.' She shrugs and lets her skirts swing as she walks.

'How did thi become a cropper, George?' Lizzie asks.

'Thi dad needed croppers, I needed an apprenticeship, an' that were that.'

He hands them one at a time onto a dry stone wall, then heaves himself up in between so that they sit in a line overlooking Rashcliffe.

'Why do yer say "thi dad" like that?' Lizzie bunches her skirts under her bottom as padding against the uneven capping stones of the wall.

'Well he in't my dad, is he?'

'Do yer remember yer own dad then?'

'A bit. Not much.'

'Did yer like 'im better than our dad?'

'Can't thi just enjoy this view?'

'She can't shut up for two minutes,' grumbles Mary-Ann.

'Do yer like cropping now or would yer rather be doing something different?' Lizzie persists.

'I like it, I suppose - especially now I get paid reit for it. It weren't much fun when mi wrist were bleeding every day an' I'd only a few shillings a week to show for it.'

'I remember,' says Lizzie, 'an' I remember you an' feyther going at it hammer an' tongs at times.'

'I remember too,' Mary-Ann echoes, looking away. Lizzie frowns and sighs.

'I'm not surprised thi dun't call him dad. He were fair mean to thi back then, afore thi went away.'

'Yer remember all that? Yer weren't so old.'

'Old enough. He made mam cry a few times an' I recall as that made yer fair mad, an' then he cracked yer for it, didn't he?'

'Blummin' ummer kid, yer remember things I'd forgot.' he says, shaking his head. 'He only hit me a few times an' I probably deserved it. It in't easy for a man to take on someone else's kids an' raise 'em. An then to train 'em an' give 'em work as well - yer dad did a good thing, even if he were a bit heavy-handed at times.'

They all sit silent now, digesting this statement. Mellor feels he should qualify or explain further, but the more he analyses it, the more it seems the most fitting summary of those turbulent years. Each argument, each fight, each raising of a hand can be distilled into that simple framework - Wood was doing his best and Mellor is grateful they both came through those times relatively unscathed. His younger self would recoil in disgust at this interpretation, but that self is gone, moulded out of existence, and Mellor would not be what he is without Wood's influence. He cannot unravel their relationship or wish away the past without unravelling himself.

'He got so mad one day,' Mellor chuckles, remembering, 'that he chased me round t'yard wi' a rolled up newspaper. I got away but I din't dare come back till it were pitch black. An' all 'cause he said I weren't properly listening to him reading.'

'Why, what were he reading that were so important?' Lizzie asks.

'That's the funny thing, I can hear it clear as day, his voice, the words - so I *was* listening, I was just pretending not to be, to wind 'im up. He were trying to tell me about what were happening in Leeds, wi' Gott's croppers.' Mellor nods to himself, picturing Wood's thick fingers curled around the edges of the newspaper, the pages drooping at the outer corners, the sudden break in Wood's narration as his temper fled, the speed with which a young Mellor had to skip backwards to avoid a blow.

'Who's Gott?'

So Mellor, basking in the slow, lilting sunset with his two young sisters, tells the story of Mr Gott's croppers. Benjamin Gott, he explains, had a huge manufactory over in Leeds, and back when Mellor himself was about twelve years old, Gott decided to hire some new apprentices. The problem was, he took on lads that were too old. It mattered, because they'd still to serve their seven years on low wages, but for the last few years of that they'd be grown men working for a boy's rate. Cheap labour. Apprentices have to start under fourteen, that's the rule, so that when they turn twenty-one, they can earn a proper rate.

On top of that, the gig mills and frames were being installed, even back then, which was putting the hackles up, and so the croppers quit. They just walked out - all eighty or so that Gott employed - and they refused to come back until he promised to stick to the law. Gott thought they'd give in once their money ran out, but the manufacturer had underestimated the croppers association - in fact, like most of the other men at the top, he thought it had been severely weakened by the Combination Acts. He hadn't realised that the Brief Institution had carried on as strong as before, with all the national links still in place, but under cover of friendly societies and sick clubs. The accumulated subs of hundreds of Yorkshire croppers kept Gott's employees afloat until Gott himself was the one to give in.

'What's subs?' Mary-Ann asks.

'The money we pay to belong. It all gets saved up, an' then when there's a need...' Mellor unfolds his palms in explanation.

'So why did feyther get so mad abaht thi not listening?' she presses.

'That's clear enough,' answers Lizzie. 'Yer said he wanted yer to be a cropper for him. He were probably trying to show yer how much power the croppers had. He were trying to persuade yer into it.'

'Aye lass, tha's bang on there. That were exactly it.' Mellor is surprised at how quickly she understands something that took him years to realise.

While he was running round the yard and out of the gate, all he could think of was avoiding a beating. He didn't trouble to wonder why Wood was so frustrated with him.

Later, when he paid his first subs at one of the meets, he remembered how collections like these had forced Gott to back down, and he grasped the enormity of what his step-father had been trying to teach him. But so many things cannot be taught - they must be allowed to soak in until they are deeply and devoutly felt.

Misunderstandings are such a tragedy, a misalignment of timing. We are forever arriving at the truth too early or too late, barrelling through life like a shuttle on a loom, barely seeing the warp threads, only gradually becoming aware of their significance. Surely, by the end, we will be allowed to see the pattern in full, to study all the long ends and floating places - all the mistakes in the weave - and do our best to mend them, re-threading the missing colours, working the intricate arrangement back into perfection. Or maybe the flaws in the cloth are what distinguishes our lives from a thousand million others. Maybe only the worst patches must be repaired. Mellor remembers Wood patting his knee just weeks ago, sitting opposite the Bridge with a mug of ale - he can feel the shockingly paternal hand print still, a warm and unexpected pressure, spanning ripped parts of the past and darning them back together.

'Feyther must be happy then, that yer did become a cropper, an' that yer run the shop so well for him,' says Lizzie, her brow bunched up in worry at the melancholy in his face.

'That he is,' he answers and he smiles at them both to dispel the solemn mood. 'We're a lucky family, all of us doing so well now.'

He slides off the wall and lifts them down onto the grass. The grand sunset burns fiercely near the end then winks out as silent and small as a match flame. They walk home through the gloaming, the burnished world turning to full shadow in their wake.

For months now the troop numbers in Huddersfield have been growing. Regiments of militia are converging on the whole of the North of England and other regions certainly have their share of soldiers, but a glance around the streets of this jewel in England's cloth-producing crown alerts any onlooker that this is where the vortex has formed - the eye of the storm glares upon these recalcitrant streets and the influx of armed forces has become a torrent.

Mellor surveys the market place on the first day of September and considers his next move. Beside him, Thomas Ellis bites at the end of an empty pipe. In front of them, carts, baggage and soldiers fill the space. There are so many soldiers that the overcrowded inns are having to extend their sleeping facilities into barns and stalls. The publicans cannot refuse - by law they must provide straw and candles to the army, as well as food and drink, for which they are entitled to, and yet mostly denied, adequate reimbursement. Thousands of outsiders occupy the town, all sent here for the sole purpose of crushing Luddism. Nottingham did not get this. Leeds, Manchester, Oldham, Sheffield - none of them have seen anything like this.

The viciousness feels personal, malevolent - a new harrying. He understands the tactic. General Maitland, named by the papers as the man in charge, wishes to terrify them. Such enormous numbers of men are a clear signal that Huddersfield has become the most successful seat of dissent. The government means, by brute force and fear, to suppress them at all costs. Mellor and Ellis walk on, picking out a path among the packed streets.

'We want to do as many raids as we can afore they get a proper foothold,' says Mellor, thinking rapidly. 'afore they get to know all t'tracks an' paths, afore they get comfortable in our pubs an' friendly wi' all t'manufacturers. Give 'em a fortnight an' this lot'll know their patrols an' they'll have the guts to start dragging us in off o' t'streets.'

'What's tha thinking? Get as much cash an' arms as we can now, then lay low for a bit?' Ellis asks.

'Cash an' guns, aye. I want small groups out raiding everywhere, all this week. An' all t'stashes have to be small, split up all over. Thank God we moved all them muskets from t'warehouse. We'd never get 'em out past this lot now.'

'Sometimes, George, I swear tha sees what's coming. This in't a surprise to thi, is it?'

'It's a shock o' sorts,' qualifies Mellor. 'I never imagined mi town looking like this. But I s'pose thi could say I expected summat like this from 'em. Ludds have brayed an' beaten manufacturers in Nottingham, Oldham an' all over, but nobody's had the balls to shoot one, except here in our neck o' t'woods. Until somebody swings for Horsfall, they'll bear a grudge. What's it now? Four months? An' we're all still out there raiding an' breaking. We're an embarrassment to 'em, Thomas. We're a serious threat. But I'll be honest wi' thi, I'm not reit sure what we do next.'

'Lay low,' suggests Ellis again.

'To what purpose? Nay,' Mellor demurs, 'We've set summat in motion, an' we've not to let it slow down. We've to find a way, even against these odds, to keep attacking.'

Ellis goes quiet. Mellor feels the pregnant silence but doesn't disturb it. He is sure he can find a way, if he only thinks hard enough, but hiding out and waiting for the militia to go away just won't work. The stakes have risen to a critical point where both sides require a denouement. It is the nature of this final resolution that is in question, not the resolution itself.

He rolls scenes around in his mind - Bradley Mills on fire, Vickerman in a blood-riddled ditch, a pile of broken frames jammed up against the doors of Milnsbridge House while Radcliffe whimpers inside - but he cannot hold the images, nor make them resolve the situation. His brain refuses to comply with the logical demands he makes of it. It won't think it through, because it can't- because maybe there is no way, ever, to stop the mills using shearing frames. If each side will stop at nothing, then the Ludds will run out of men, guns and options first. He rubs at his face and clears his head, quashing the dissenting voice within himself. He trusts in something bigger. He

301

knows he is right. The Lord will give him a way to make his stand against the callous, self-serving greed of the manufacturers and against the inequity of a system which grinds profit and supposed progress from the bones of human suffering.

It becomes clear in coming days that Huddersfield's flooding by militia has coincided with significant developments across the Pennines. Thirty nine men in Manchester, accused of illegal oath-taking, have been acquitted in the Assize courts, assisted by excellent representation from Henry Brougham - a name that surfaces in the papers from time to time as a champion of the poor and the oppressed.

The result is a victory for Luddism but a blow to the authorities, who must have been hoping that some transportations and hangings over in Lancashire would subdue all the other regions. Maitland, already funnelling his troops to the hotbed of the West Riding, now has extra motivation to move swiftly and decisively. If the judicial system cannot get Luddism under control, the government will act directly through its army and impose martial law. The papers won't call it that - not yet - but Mellor laughs bitterly when he walks the uniform-thronged streets of his town to think that anyone could doubt the facts. Martial law governs in Huddersfield already.

Even so, the raids continue. By the end of the week, muskets and pistols have been gathered from scores of homesteads and the soldiers have caught no one. It's the most successful raiding week by far and spirits are high. Ben O'Bucks whistles as he dresses cloth in the shop. Tom Smith has asked Nan to marry him. Ordinary people walk around with tight-lipped smiles, holding precious secrets in their native hearts as they bypass troops and patrols. Nothing unifies the town so much as invasion, and they all, Luddite-sympathiser or not, feel invaded - all except the Merchants and Manufacturers Committee members, who liaise with the Captains and Generals and spit out every malicious rumour they possess in the hopes that a live Ludd will be caught on the army's hook. Everyone else holds fast. There are people still living who can remember their grandparents' fear of Scottish invasion - Huddersfield's whole architectural web of inward-facing homes over small, fortress-style yards is the historic legacy of a town that knows how to defend itself and how to go to ground. That the threat now comes from their own government makes little difference.

The Oath is just one thread binding the Luddites together, a thread which in the face of such military hostility has become almost redundant. A bigger loyalty than the Oath holds sway in the town. The drama and the danger has merely tightened the stitches of a town so closely knit that only something very sharp and determined will stand a chance of undoing it.

10
Veil In Sunder

Last night a minister came to see him. He was a Methodist, come all the way from Huddersfield. He stooped as he stepped inside the condemned cell, though he cleared the doorway easily. It had that effect, the poky, damp, dark space; it made men bend and shrink, the way an altar makes men genuflect. Mellor knelt on the grubby stone floor and prayed under the guidance of the minister for a good while. The minister asked him to confess his sins, and Mellor obliged, listing every flaw in his character until the minister became impatient.

'Has thi nothing to say about the crime that has brought thi here?' he pressed. Mellor sighed. He was so tired of finding ways to answer such questions, of being evasive and aloof.

'Do not ask me about that,' he had said, shaking his head.

'Look around thi, lad. See what an awful end tha's come to. Has thi nowt to say to me, to the Lord, afore the time o' reckoning comes?'

Mellor had taken a full, deep breath, drawing the stale air into his lungs and then exhaling steadily, his eyes flickering closed. He could see Horsfall: the blood, the stricken eyes, the sideways fall from the saddle; the girl with coal under her threadbare dress; the beggars in the gutter on the day John Booth was buried; Betty, red in the face from the soldiers' taunts; the flogged militiaman's blood-soaked back. He'd pressed fingers into his eye sockets to stem the parade of pictures.

'I'd rather be here,' he had said at last, 'in this cell, waiting to be hanged - dreadful though that surely is - than have to answer for the crimes o' me accuser. I wouldn't change places wi' him for anything - not for liberty, not even for two thousand pounds. That's what I've to say to thi, an' to the Lord.'

The minister had ruminated on these words and nodded slowly, as ministers often do. Mellor had no idea whether he understood, whether he empathised or whether he had merely given up on getting a detailed confession. They prayed together some more before the minister left, the man of God no better informed than he had been when the York Castle chaplain eagerly ushered him inside. It was later that Mellor collapsed, after the preacher had gone and he was alone and the weight of all those memories became too great - an avalanche of the past driving him hard into the dead end of a future.

His brain had tried to burrow backwards, curled itself up into a ball in an attempt to leave his body behind, but still he finds himself here, alive and fresh this cold morning, thrown up onto the scaffold like a piece of rock spewed out onto a glacier's terminal moraine. He can, as he told the minister, accept death, but death does not accept him. It had its chance to take him last night, in the depths of his sudden fever, and it cast him back; and now time is bending about him awkwardly - a trajectory that once existed is being erased by man's hand and nature submits truculently, with a pursed, unchanging sky and a silent crowd and a feeling of grief and unease that hangs suspended in the air, palpable even to the attendant military guarding the bottom of the drop.

The prayers are over. Tom Smith gets up from his knees. Mellor sees him running his eyes over the crowd, no doubt looking for his parents and his lass. Mellor is equally horrified and unsurprised that no mercy has been shown. We live in an age, he thinks, where the horrific has become unsurprising. The judges refused, when the contrite jury asked for clemency for Smith. Hang one, hang all, the judges decreed - even a young man whose chief accuser admitted was not responsible for firing a shot. Mellor remembers the four of them in the woods; Smith's hands trembling as he confessed his failure, O'Bucks stepping forward to protect the younger man from Mellor's pistol. And yet I was never a danger to that lad, Mellor thinks sadly; it was you, Bucks, who brought him here - you and that spineless cousin of mine.

They are led to the trapdoor, a distance of only a few steps, so that the ropes can be secured about their necks. Their shackles are left in place. Mellor, Thorp and Smith will be on full bodily display as they die, since the authorities have purposefully removed the usual shielding to maximise the awful spectacle. The shackles will not only hinder any possible rescue attempt, but will also restrict some of the twitching which might otherwise prove unseemly if it is protracted. There is, after all, a fine line to be observed between deterrent and incitement, and the government have put a lot of thought into getting the balance just right.

Somewhere out of Mellor's sight, Radcliffe is nodding with satisfaction. The way this is going, he reckons he might end up being the hero of the piece

306

after all. He apprehended all these men - he is the only magistrate to get results like this. If you think about it, he might be responsible for preventing an entire revolution. Maybe - could he wangle it? - maybe he'll be in the running for a baronetcy... He won't count his chickens yet though, not with the rest of the Special Commission to get through, but the signs are promising, and there's still all the Rawfolds lot to go. There's sure to be more hangings out of them. Radcliffe picks his teeth with a sharp fingernail and hopes the rest of the executions aren't like this one. So sombre and downcast! Where are the usual bun-sellers and music-makers? Where is the revelry, the mockery, the good-natured banter? It isn't like a proper hanging at all. Shifting his weight uncomfortably, he finds himself wishing this one over and done with.

It is the third day of Honley Feast and the centre of the village is thronged with stalls and games. He squeezes through the crowds to get to Joseph on the other side of the street.

'Thought we'd lost yer,' his cousin calls. 'We were just abaht to go wi'out yer.'

They pass a troop of dancers, a juggler, a table full of muffin bread and jugs of milk, and a table where the pans from the hot-porridge eating competition are being sided away. Homes have their doors wide open and piles of sliced roast beef and pickled red cabbage are on sale from every kitchen. Mellor already has a parcel of beef and cabbage. He eats some as they walk back along the road towards Dungeon. Needless to say, he has already had plenty of home-brewed ale from various kitchens in the village, and he strides

307

along so lustily that Joseph has to ask him to slow down for Martha's sake, since she is carrying the baby strapped within a shawl. She tries to walk abreast of them both, but something about her manner aggravates Mellor and he prefers to keep her behind them as he talks to her husband.

There is only a year between the cousins - George was born to William Mellor a year after Joseph had been born to William's brother, John. Both fathers are dead and buried. Both sons run cropping businesses, though Joseph is his own master, while George runs the shop for his step-father. In appearance, they have a vague resemblance, but nothing too close - too much of their mothers in each of them - and in character, too, they diverge. Respectability is important to Joseph, and though he is twisted-in, rule-breaking and disorder don't sit easy with him. The sphere of his concerns extends only around his Dungeon cropping shop and he is well aware that he has a wife, a baby and numerous apprentices and servants who are dependent upon his making a success of the business. To keep things safe, he talks with George about the cloth orders he currently has, and what the market over in Lancashire is like, and to his relief George seems happy to stick to these subjects.

Back at the house, they invite him in, and Mellor is persuaded without difficulty into the kitchen for a sit down after their walk.

'How was the feast?' Maria asks, from the floor in the corner. Monday is wash day, and now that the clothes are all washed, mangled, rinsed, mangled again and now hung on the hedge outside, she has tipped the used bucket of soapy water over the flags

308

inside and is scrubbing the final bit of the kitchen floor, her hands red and swollen.

'Still busy. Won't calm down till Wednesday, I shouldn't think,' Martha answers, depositing her child in the wooden crib and going out to check the clothes are properly clean. Maria struggles up from her knees as her mistress steps past, stretching out her back and wiping her hands down her underskirts. Mellor watches her pick up the empty bucket and take it out to the little room at the back.

'Let the lass sit down, Joe, she looks done in.'

'Soft spot for our Maria, has thi?' grins Joseph. 'Oi, Maria, come an' try some o' George's cabbage.'

She comes back shyly, unsure whether she is being teased, but Mellor kicks a buffit out from under the table and pushes what's left in his paper parcel across to her.

'Oh I'm famished, I don't mind admitting,' she says, sitting down on the buffit and snatching up a mouthful. 'An' they don't do cabbage as good as this anywhere but t'feast.'

'Floor's looking clean,' Joseph says, pouring some ale into jars for them all. 'Good day's work, lass.'

'Has thi been to t'feast?' Mellor asks her.

'Went yesterday, wi' one o' me brothers an' me mam,' she answers, mouth still full of cabbage. 'Hoping Mrs Mellor will let me go again tomorrow, now I've done all t'wash.'

'She can go, can't she?' Joseph asks as his wife comes back in to see the child who has started to give gargling, hungry cries.

'Aye, I suppose. Look in that basket, Joe, I've fetched some beef back, an' there's bread an' all. May as well eat it as let it go off.'

Joseph puts the food out on the table, tearing the bread into chunks.

'None o' thi friends wi' thi today, then?' Maria asks, putting some tender shreds of beef on her bread and taking a large bite. It's a treat to have meat this good - a speciality of the feast. The September run-up to the Honley feast is the busiest time of the year for the butchers in the neighbourhood.

'Saw one or two there,' Mellor says.

'More 'na one or two, George here knows half o' town,' Martha laughs, putting the baby to her breast. 'Can't move two foot wi'out him stopping to chellep.'

When he leaves, Mellor is mildly drunk and happily relaxed. He exits through the workshop and, unseen by the others in the kitchen, reaches up behind the door and retrieves his old bottle-green greatcoat, left there to gather dust almost five months before.

Midday, a Saturday, and Mellor sits with Thorp in The Bridge drinking ale. Ellis is supposed to join them, but there is no sign of him. Thorp glances at a battered pocket watch and then at the door. Mellor sups slowly.

'I'm none waiting all day for him,' Thorp says. Saturday is a working day, though the croppers set their own rules. They could drink all afternoon if they wanted. It would take a horsewhip to fetch them out of the pub if they wanted to stay. But neither man is in the mood to loiter, and in any case, Thorp has further to walk back to work now - he changed jobs in July, leaving Fisher's place at Longroyd Bridge and taking a position at Lockwood's shop up on New Street, nearer to Cropper's Row where he lives. The position he left behind at Fisher's has been filled by William Hall, who has moved out of Wood's. Sometimes it's useful to work in a few different shops under different masters, especially when they are still so young and learning about the trade. Tom Smith will move on very soon, his apprenticeship just about over. Mellor wonders if Wood will take on more men, or if the current shedding of employees is a permanent slimming down of the business.

'Give it five and twenty,' says Mellor, looking at the clock face in his friend's hand.

'What time did Varley leave her?'

'Ten o'clock, or thereabouts.'

'He should've followed her all t'way,' Thorp says.

'We'll find out where she's been.'

'But too late, she'll have said all she's to say by then.'

'She would ha' said it any road. An' trying to waylay the lass, or question her would ha' looked worse for us.'

'I would not have been asking questions,' Thorp enunciates, slipping his watch away and hunching over the table with folded arms and clenched fists.

'Nay, not little Maria Dyson,' Mellor admonishes. 'She'll not do for us. She knows nowt.'

'Should ha' given her what they gave that Armstrong bitch - a stone to t'bloody skull afore she could say owt at all.'

'It in't same. Maria's been summoned - if that's where she's gone. She wouldn't go looking to get men in trouble out o' choice.'

'Then why are thi so worried, George. An don't tell me tha's not,' he points across the table, 'because I can see that look on thi face. This is bad news for us an' tha knows it.'

'If Maria's talking to Radcliffe - if that's even where she went - then all she can say is that I was at Dungeon that day. She never saw t'guns, she hardly knows thee.'

'It in't Maria tha's worried abaht,' Thorp realises, sitting back abruptly.

'Nay,' Mellor whispers, 'I'm worried abaht who sent her to Radcliffe, who's kallin in her ear. Summat's brewing, Will. Summat's gathering, like a big old storm cloud. I can feel it. I wanted to find out from Ellis what he's heard but it looks like he's been held up. There's these rumours that Vickerman's been over in Lancashire, hob-nobbing with t'lawyers and magistrates over there. An' wi' this Lloyd felly coming over t'Pennines an' running interrogations at Milnsbridge, and that Captain Raynes flitting all over t'borders, catching people off guard, well, tha starts to add it all together an' I won't lie to thi, it makes me worried.'

'Good old Clement Dyson's pally wi' Vickerman,' Thorp observes, and Mellor nods, making silent eye contact. They are both wondering if Clement, the target of several Luddite raids, has been squeezing his niece Maria for information about the comings and goings at Joseph Mellor's house. If he has, then he could be passing whatever he has learned directly to Francis Vickerman - a man with an even larger grudge against the Luddites than Clement himself has.

Their particular cause for concern began earlier that morning, when James Varley happened to notice a young woman turning off the Meltham turnpike up

312

towards the Yews.

The journeyman was returning from Honley, making his way back to Longroyd Bridge, and as he slowly caught up to the figure ahead, he recognised her as Maria Dyson, the servant girl he had met a few times when running errands between Wood's cropping shop and Joseph Mellor's. He expected she was running an errand herself, maybe even to Longroyd Bridge, since she appeared to be anticipating his route, but when she turned off unexpectedly onto a dirt track that lead up over Crosland Moor, his interest was piqued.

On impulse he decided to follow, and, keeping a discreet distance, he shadowed her all the way past Barton on pathways and lanes, taking him about a mile off his own course, until they came out on the open hillside and started the descent into Milnsbridge. Varley stopped there and watched her until she was out of sight and then he turned tail and strode back to Longroyd, full of foreboding. He remembered that when he had called in at Dungeon the morning after Horsfall was shot, and had quite a heated conversation with Joseph on the doorstep, Maria had been present in the kitchen. She had stared right at him, that foggy early morning, when Horsfall was teetering on the edge of consciousness in the Warren House and Varley was arguing with Joseph about where to store the guns.

It is entirely conceivable that she is in Milnsbridge House right now, answering questions put by the formidable magistrate and his newly acquired colleague, the odious Mr Lloyd - a conniving clerk from Stockport. Why else would Maria Dyson walk over to Milnsbridge? She has no family there, and as Varley pointed out when he reported all this to Wood and Mellor, she carried no basket - she was neither delivering nor collecting anything.

When they leave the pub, Mellor and Thorp are no wiser. Ellis has not made an appearance. Mellor wonders what has detained him, but isn't unduly worried. He returns to the shop and works until mid-afternoon, pouring his mental energy into the physical labour until Wood suggests he should go up to the sale at Joseph Hirst's shop.

Eager to get out and stretch his legs, he obliges. He can kill two birds with one stone - see if there's anything worth buying, and catch a word with a fair few people who might have heard recent rumours. The last person he is expecting to see is Maria herself, and the sight of her milling about and chatting confounds him.

For a few moments he thinks maybe she was not going to the Magistrate after all, maybe she was coming here, maybe she was doing all sorts of things other than giving his name to Radcliffe. The air is suddenly very bright around her and his skin prickles with the potential of all the hours left in this beautiful autumn day, all the things that could be done, all the secrets that have held fast. Then she catches his eyes locked onto hers, and her mouth breaks into a desperate, cornered smile. He knows right then that he is in trouble. She comes to him, not trying to avoid him.

'How do, George?'

'Fair, and how are thee, Maria?'

'I'm not so bad.'

314

'Where's tha been, lass?'

'Oh George, tha knows where I went. I cannot lie to thee. I've been to see Mr Radcliffe an' I've told him what I remember about the day Mr Horsfall was shot.' She pulls at the corners of her shawl, draped across her small, high chest and looks down at her feet in their shabby clogs.

'Did thi tell the truth?'

'Oh yes, George,' she insists, 'I teld him exactly what happened - how thi called in with another felly that day.'

'And thi remembered how the other felly wanted work? That's why we called,' he presses her, 'because he wanted work.'

'I remember, George, I do.'

'Well just so long as yer tell the truth, it'll be fine. Not to worry.' He smiles at her and then turns clumsily on his heel and away, ignoring the quick intake of breath, her mouth open with the start of a sentence that he doesn't want to hear. He can't go on looking at her eager, hopeful face. Why should she care what becomes of him? Why should he care to reassure her?

No matter what she does now, something has been set in motion, like a wheel slowly turning, or a thread end being drawn carefully loose. Trying to persuade himself that he and his friends have nothing to fear and that they are well-prepared to defend themselves with alibis and obfuscation, he peruses the goods at Hirst's but he can't focus and his acquaintances fail to spark any conversation with him. He pushes past people, he runs a hand along a piece of cloth entirely oblivious to its weave. The world reduces to shapes - to blurring shades and colours - and he longs to see

315

Maria again - to make out her clear face, eyes so huge and honest, but she is gone. He stays about half an hour longer thinking about what he should do, before deciding he must talk to Joseph.

Striding in the direction of Dungeon, his mind weighing all the implications of what Maria has done, he catches up with the girl on the road, blessedly alone and also walking back toward the Dungeon shop.

'All reit, George?' She asks, startled and flushed at his unexpected approach.

'Thi left a long while back to only have got this far,' he says, clumsily.

'I called in on mi brothers,' she explains.

'I'll walk thi back to Dungeon.' He gestures that they should keep walking. She falls into step at his side, daring to glance up at him once or twice. His stride is so much longer than hers that she has to scurry to keep up and when he realises her discomfort, he slows down, until they are ambling, like lovers on a stroll. His chest gradually loses the tightness that came on at the sale and he becomes conscious of his balled fists, flexing his fingers out in surprise and tipping his head from one side to the other to stretch his neck muscles.

'I'm sorry, George,' Maria whispers after five minutes or so. He tells her again that it will be all right. They don't speak again until they pass her uncle, Clement Dyson, stood talking with a friend on the other side of the road. Dyson eyeballs Mellor and glares at Maria but she keeps in step, sending only a perfunctory nod in her uncle's direction. When they are a little way past and Clement can no longer see them, Mellor says 'Was it him? Did he send thi to

Radcliffe?' and Maria answers in a little voice, 'Yes.'

'Has anyone else gone?' He asks.

'Not apart from Joe.' He looks at her, uncomprehending, thinking at first she means her cousin, but she quickly corrects him. 'The apprentice Joseph Oldham,' she says, 'Tha knows that he went in afore me?' She clutches him suddenly, tight fingers gripping urgently onto his wrist, the pad of her little finger pressing into the hoof. She doesn't flinch from the calloused skin, doesn't purse her lips at the hardened scar tissue like most women do. 'Joe went in this morning. I haven't seen him since, I don't know what he said.'

'He hasn't talked to yer at all?' Mellor asks.

'Not abaht this. Is there something more that he knows that I don't?' She looks away, as if she doesn't want to be told, but her hand is still wrapped around his wrist.

'I don't think so,' he says, but he isn't sure at all. He doesn't know Joseph Oldham. He can't say if Oldham was the boy who helped him hide the guns, but he doesn't think so. He thinks that boy was called Tom. He needs to speak with his cousin. Joe Mellor will know what's going on, since two of his employees have been called in to talk to Radcliffe. 'Let's get back to Dungeon and find out what's behind all this,' he says, stroking his free hand over her raised knuckles, curled white on his wrist. She lets go, reluctantly, her palm scraping the hoof, soft skin snagging over the thick raised scar.

'Does that still hurt?' She asks. They fall back into step and he runs his hand absent-mindedly over the place where her fingers have been, a memory of the pressure rippling up his forearm, a dreadful thrill quivering between his shoulder blades.

'Nay, not for years.'

'Good. I'm glad,' she says. 'The lads have 'em, Martha showed me how to make a poultice for 'em, when they're sore.'

She twitters on, sparrow-like, her nervousness increasing with their proximity to Dungeon, telling him about what it's like to work for the Mellors and how she has some fine cloth but no time to make a dress with it, and where would she wear it anyway? - a high, tinkling laugh - Chapel is the only place she goes, except when she visits her family, which isn't often. She talks until she runs into empty, circular observations, until she is worried she has bored or irritated him, and then she drops into silence and bites at her chapped lower lip and pulls leaves from the tall, bedraggled weeds that are slowly toppling under October's damp, cold onslaught.

'I like the woods,' he says, gesturing at the looming Dungeon sprawl over the hillside. 'The colours at this time o' year, I could just stand here an' look for hours.' Daubs and flashes of lime green, yellow, firelight orange - a penultimate stand of colour, glowing and still. The next stage will be the darker reds, the golden-browns as the leaves bleed back into their trunks, the parent trees sucking them dry. Before that, all the zest is on display, the swan song of the leaves, vivid and tart, mouth-wateringly fresh.

'It's beautiful,' she agrees. Autumn touches him too - the light as kind to his auburn hair where it peeks from his cap as it is to the dazzling foliage in the tall trees. She had thought his hair an ordinary brown when previously they have met, but now it glints like boiling syrup.

Risking a longer look, fearing the burn of his intense gaze, she finds he is still fixated on the woods, his gait slowing almost to a halt. He has a hollowness to his cheek, a level jawbone and long eyelashes - longer even than her own; they flash dark-gold when he blinks. Has she never looked at him properly before, on those times he called into the dreary workshop? Does one man's figure become the same as any other in the dusty press of trestles and shears?

Her limited interactions with him - tiny flirtations, conversations in miniature, spread so very thinly across many months - skip across the canvas of her mind's eye and make her blush, so artless do they seem now, when he is talking of the colour of the trees and walking as if he doesn't really want to arrive at his cousin's house anytime soon. She is afraid to speak and to ruin the calm he has spun around them.

Later, she will wish she had told him all sorts of things - her dreams for the future, her favourite bird, the names she thought would be nice for her babies - things she could never have told him, things he would have laughed at. Except, she knew, he wouldn't have laughed. He would have listened without comment and she would never have known what he was thinking. Would that be better or worse?

She touches her skinny pale face as they walk, conscious of her unlovely appearance - the cheekbones that sharpen her, the wide eyes that counterbalance the edginess: making her look, as her father used to say in unkind moments, like a starved dog expecting a kick. He mistakes the lifting of her hand to her cheek for fatigue and asks if she needs to sit down. Reflexively she says no, embarrassed by his misinterpretation, realising too late that she has missed her chance to prolong this time together - they are almost home. Her awkwardness is an agony - if there was time to think, she would arrange her words to properly engineer the situation. 'Can we sit? I'm tired after all,' she would say, and they would spend an age resting on a wall, indulging in all the conversation that will have to be so unsatisfactorily imagined later on. But she chokes on the words, caught in a web of indecision - Uncle Clement's warnings and Martha's whispered hints about Mellor's crude and dangerous character conspiring with her graceless manner to deliver her right to the door of her employer without further intimacy.

Angry at herself, she sighs - a bitter, audible breath. He catches her, so swiftly that she gasps, the stubble of his jaw grazing the downy area of skin just by her right ear, his breath warm down her neck. There is a fecund pause - a millisecond in which she feels him wrestle with something; that fractional hesitation enough to spawn a thousand imaginings over countless, aching months - and then he lets go of her without speaking at all, almost pushing her into the workshop.

'I'll get Joseph,' she says, stumbling backwards, feeling her way around the bench and the cloth press. He's outlined in the doorway, the light stark behind him, and she turns and scuttles away before her eyes have adjusted, the dark silhouette filling her vision. He watches her disappear through to the kitchen. Standing motionless on the step, he waits for his cousin. All around him feels empty, as if he could swing his arms and find nothing there - the door frame insubstantial, the stone walls an illusion, the cloth press a compelling fiction through which his entire body could pass unhindered. Unwilling to test this dislocation of his being, he stays very still and yet feels entirely untethered, his mind blank as new snowfall, his limbs afraid to shift in case they disrupt this vacant, easy state. Not even at his highest level of inebriation has he experienced such weightlessness. From a long, long distance away comes the sound of Martha's raised voice, then Joseph's, followed by footsteps muffled on the flagged floor, the quick tread reeling Mellor in. He breaks the spell, steps inside.

'Na then, what's to do?' Joseph says, rounding the bench and squaring up purposefully to Mellor.

'Yer can tell me, Joe. What's this abaht Maria an' one o' yer apprentices going to see Radcliffe?'

'I'm in t'dark mi sen, George. All as I know is they got summoned by a constable.'

'It's Clement Dyson, I know it's that felly, Maria's teld me he put her up to it. But why has he begun the stir? Why now, after all these months?'

'I don't know. But I'll find out.' He claps George on the back, steering him out into the yard. 'Meantime, why don't thi get back home. Happen he sees me an' thee talking now - it'll only make things worse.'

'We're cousins, Joe, I come over all o' t'time. Why shouldn't I be seen here talking wi' yer?' Mellor asks, incredulously.

'Aye, aye,' placates Joseph, backing away from him. 'Look. Leave it wi' me, I'll go an' see him now.'

'Let me know what yer find out,' says Mellor

glancing past him to where Maria lingers, her fox-like face and worried eyes fixed on him. Not now, he decides - he has to get back to the shop and talk to Wood and the others. He'll call again, he thinks, and take her out walking when things have settled down, when this latest yoke has been thrown from his neck.

He strides home at a wappy pace and explains to Wood that Maria and an apprentice have both spoken to Radcliffe and placed him at Dungeon on 28 April. Ben Walker, pressing cloth with William Hall, listens intently and checks that his own name has not been mentioned.

'You've been called in before, lad, this'll be just the same,' says Wood.

In the kitchen, his mother puts a meat stew on the table and stares as Mellor silently empties his bowl. Betty is fretful too. They sense, with their blood-born instinct for Mellor's shifting moods, that something is slipping dangerously out of kilter. Thorp comes over just as Mellor is finishing. He puts his head round the door and says 'How do?' and Mary manages a weak smile at her son's best friend. Mellor grabs his coat and takes Thorp to sit on the riverbank where they can talk privately.

'She knows nowt,' Mellor insists, after filling Thorp in. 'She can't name yer, she didn't see t'guns, she's only teld 'em that I brought a friend round looking for work at abaht five o'clock.'

'That's summat, then,' Thorp agrees.

'But-' he hesitates. It's hard to voice the fear. He doesn't want to, but he must be honest with Thorp. Both their necks are on the line. 'I don't know what

322

this Oldham kid has said. I'm guessing he knows abaht the guns, an' mebbe he'll give a different time. But still, it's only me they can name, not thee.'

'What's Joseph say abaht it?'

'He were on his way to talk to Clement Dyson when I left.'

'What good will that do? Damage is done - no point shutting t'stable door now.'

Mellor exhales into his hand, gripping his lower face in concentration.

'Joe were a bit off,' he admits. 'Didn't want me there today.'

'He's going to drop us in t'shit,' says Thorp, his voice rising unsteadily. 'That fucking arsehole.'

'I don't know, Will. Mightn't be as bad as that. But he's covering his sen, that's for definite.'

'What abaht the Oath? He in't supposed to be covering his sen, he's supposed to keep his bloody mouth shut.'

'He'll keep quiet,' says Mellor. 'He's mi cousin.'
Thorp shakes his head.

'He's mi mate, I knock abaht with him, tha knows I do - but I don't trust him, not like I trust thee. He's got a wife, a baby - it makes a difference to what a man will risk. I think we've to get ready for some hard questioning, George. Happen Radcliffe in't going to go so easy on us this time. Happen Joe'll give 'em just enough to get his sen in t'clear.'

'Yer might not even get called. No one knows it were thee wi' mi, apart from Joseph.'

'Aye,' says Thorp. 'So we've to wait an' see what happens.'

They sit and watch the river until the sky deepens

and the first stars begin winking in the heavens.

'I'll si thi tomorrow at Chapel,' are Thorp's parting words as he leaves, hoisting himself off the damp grassy mound and drawing his coat about him as he crosses through the yard and back to the road. Mellor listens to the water, the way it gushes and glugs, thirsty in the blackness, and above the suck of the water, a cantering of horse hooves, drawing ever nearer, as he had always known that they would.

They are to take him to Milnsbridge, the constables who have come. Unhurried, even-tempered, they allow him to say goodbye to his mother, running through the yard towards them. Daniel and Lizzie follow, but he has to be brief. Lizzie wraps her arms around him and Betty has to pull her away. 'Don't be soft,' she berates, 'he'll be back come the morning.'

At the magistrate's house, they take him in by a side door and through a passageway to a small plain room into which he is directed. He expects the door to be closed, the lock to turn, given the lateness of the hour, but Mr Lloyd attends within minutes.

'So, so,' he says, looking Mellor up and down, 'This is he?'

'George Mellor, sir,' says one of the special constables, and Lloyd semi-circles him, as if he were an exhibit.

'Your name has come up in relation to the murder of Mr William Horsfall. A number of people say you were in the vicinity, and not only there, but carrying and hiding guns. What have you to say about that?'

Mellor regards the clerk with interest. It is helpful to be told something of the evidence against him. Mr

Allison would not have made that mistake. Lloyd prowls about him with the eagerness of the hound after its quarry; tongue salivating, ears slicked back, a bright sheen on the eyes.

'Can you deny it? That you murdered Mr Horsfall, then disposed of guns at your own cousin's house?'

Mellor studies the raised furrows around the outer corners of Lloyd's eyebrows. Excitement and expectation chase across the man's features, frustration running close behind. Lloyd sighs and wheels about on his feet.

'Dumb creature,' he motions, talking to an invisible audience, or perhaps to the constables who remain, intrigued, beyond the open door. 'You won't get anywhere with this attitude. Tell me,' he whispers, darting up close, 'Who was with you? Tell me now, save yourself, lad. We know there were four, we know you were one. Give us the others and save yourself from the noose!'

Pleased with himself he steps away and faces the wall with his head bowed. He gives it a moment then turns back, hands on hips, lowered head shaking from side to side. 'You know, George, we've rather got off on the wrong foot. I can see you're a good man - a strong, young man. You have a job, come from a decent family. Why let all that go to waste? I'm offering you something here, George. Give me the names. Just give me them, and maybe you'll live. What matters now is looking after yourself, not the fellows who got you into all this. Start with one - just give me one name, we'll take it from there.'

And so it goes on, for minute after minute, hour after hour. Sometimes Lloyd leaves the room, locking the door and leaving him in pitch darkness, then bursts in to waken Mellor from a doze with a kick to his ribs. Theatrical, conspiratorial kindness follows outbursts of furious frustration. Lloyd hops about like a malevolent Mr Punch, unpredictable and unnerving, full to the brim of questions and unwittingly scattering the tiny droplets of information that nourish Mellor's last remaining hopes. He grasps at each one - Thorp, Smith and Bucks have not been named, there is confusion about what time he visited Dungeon, confusion about the colour of greatcoat he wore and who was with him when he called into the workshop. Throughout the long night, he maintains a perfect silence - the silence to which his Oath binds him, in the simplicity of which he finds enormous strength. There is no other option - he will not name a brother. Finally, the clerk leaves him and does not come back. Lloyd must need his own sleep. Mellor gets a couple of hours, curled uncomfortably on the cold, hard floor.

In the morning, they enter abruptly - this time Allison is at the door, backed by soldiers.

'Owt to say?' he barks, and the dismissive contempt feels worse than any of Lloyd's interrogative tactics.

'Nowt,' Mellor spits back.

'Thought as much. Put the irons on him.' He leads off down the passageway as the soldiers fumble with a set of chains, clamping Mellor's wrists but leaving his legs free. They follow the clerk outside, round the building to where several soldiers are patrolling and a carriage awaits. On the driveway ahead, two figures, a man and a woman, approach on foot. They stop, as they see Mellor in chains, and he realises it's Joseph and Martha, no doubt come to swear their statements.

The soldiers propel him onwards and Mr Allison veers off to greet the couple.

'Where?' he asks, stupidly, as they force him up and into the seat. 'Where am I going?'

'Town,' the clean-faced, stern figure holding his shoulder says in a Scots accent, 'to catch the stagecoach to York.'

York Castle Gaol is a little like the squalor Mellor has witnessed in the slum yards of Huddersfield. The food is thin, rotting and weak. The flags are coated with decades of filth. Ablutions are conducted outside in the freezing yard, with cold water in scummy barrels. Inside, a pungent, greasy odour strangles the air and a dismal twilight persists throughout the day. He yearns for his own rickety bed under the bronzed beams, the warmth of the hearth and the taste of his mother's meals, wholesome and plain; the privations are deeply unpleasant, but he bears them more easily than he thought he would.

Inside the walls of the gaol, he has seen Haigh for the first time in many months. Haigh is ailing and sallow. His arm hangs limply by his side, the shoulder wound healed but still painful. He doesn't speak much when they pass, just dredges up a grimace of recognition and tips a nod. Baines, the old republican from Halifax, is here too; a dead man walking, skeletally thin and losing his wispy white hair by the day. 'They brought in my sons,' he says, in bewilderment, when he and Mellor find themselves side by side at the wash barrel. Mellor remembers them - another John, full grown, and the boy Zachariah, who might have been mistaken for a grandson. 'What charge?' asks Mellor. 'Oath swearing, same as me,' Baines replies, 'Do you remember your Oath, lad?'

'Always,' Mellor answers.

The words of the Oath are his prayer, spoken direct to God daily: I, George Mellor, of my own voluntary will, do declare and solemnly swear that I never will reveal to any person or persons under the canopy of heaven, the names of the persons who comprise this secret committee - their proceedings, meetings, places of abode, dress, features, complexion - or anything else that might lead to a discovery of the same, either by word, deed or sign, under the penalty of being sent out of the world by the first brother who shall meet me, and my name and character blotted out of existence and never to be remembered but with contempt and abhorrence - and I further do swear to use my best endeavours to punish by death any traitor, should any rise up among us, wherever I can find him, and though he should fly to the verge of nature I will pursue him with unceasing vengeance, so help me God and bless me, to keep this - my Oath - inviolate. Amen.

There are other twissed men in here - a few from over Thornhill way and thereabouts. Mellor notices a morbid interest from all the men around him, charged as he is with murder. They regard him with a respectful kind of pity, which seems incongruous as they face the rope or the boat for their crimes too. A sheep or a lamb, Mellor's roving mind sings, on the bad nights when he cannot sleep: for which would I rather hang? Smashing a window or shooting a man? The dazed and hunted expression in James Haigh's eyes suggests that it is worse to face the rope for smashing a few windows. Then again, Haigh has been imprisoned for months - plenty of time to go mad with fear. Mellor is only a few weeks in, and none of them know when their cases will be heard. Maybe he too will have begun to lose his mind by then.

The hardest part to bear is when they bring in Thorp and Smith. He hears the news from another inmate - men pass information along like tobacco, snippets of news greedily fingered and slowly, surreptitiously shared. 'More Ludds,' comes the whisper, 'men from Huddersfield.' He can hardly bear the waiting; watching in the yard for new figures to appear, simultaneously hoping and not hoping to see friends. When Thorp emerges, Mellor is engulfed by a wave of pure sadness that pins his feet to the ground for whole seconds until he resurfaces and pushes past men to get to his friend. A guard is taking off Thorp's chains - they don't have to wear them in the yard; the irons are only clamped back on when they return inside. Mellor waits until Thorp is freed and the guard moves on, before taking Thorp by the arm and steering him towards the wall.

'Yer look well, George,' Thorp says.

Mellor still has hold of his friend's arm and he squeezes it. 'It's not so bad in here, Will. You'll be all reit.'

'O'Bucks has turned,' Thorp says. 'He were questioned same as me, but they've not brought him. Smith's wi' me - look, he's here now - but Buck's weren't in t'coach. They know stuff they could only have got from him.'

Mellor and Thorp watch the guards pull Smith into

the yard and begin releasing his ankles and wrists. The nineteen year old rubs the reddened skin and looks about him like a new child at Sunday school. Mellor gestures and Smith wanders over in bewildered relief.

'Jesus save us,' Smith says, looking around the yard at the bedraggled inhabitants shivering in ragged clothes, baring their bony rib-cages to soap away the grime.

'It's no worse than Shitten Lane at bottom o' town,' Mellor points out, and Thorp smirks.

'Did he tell thi 'bout Bucks?' Smith asks.

'In't just Bucks,' Thorp interrupts. 'I'm damned if I'm not sure that Joseph's given us away too.'

'Bloody hell fire,' says Mellor. He bites at his lip and rocks on his feet, shaking his head. 'But it's down to t'trial, lads. Nowt's proved yet. I'll write to me cousin.'

'Nay, don't,' says Thorp in alarm, 'I'm telling thi he's dangerous. Write to someone who can speak to Joe for thi, happen turn him back.'

'They give yer paper an' that in here?' Smith asks, doubtfully.

'If yer know the reit way to ask. They're allus hoping for a slip up or a confession. Come to it, they'll prob'ly open me letter an' read it afore they send it.'

'Then write it carefully, George.'

'Have you two said owt?'

'Nowt,' swears Smith. Thorp looks uncomfortable under Mellor's gaze.

'What has tha said, Will?'

'I gave a statement to Radcliffe. It were when they called me in, same as always, asking this an' that, an I've allus talked mi way out afore. Once I knew they'd

330

got me proper, I said no more.'

'So what did thi say afore then?' Mellor persists.

'It were over me blue jacket - yer remember that one I got rid of after a month 'cause it were too small? Mr Allison asked me abaht whether I'd left it at Joe's on the day Horsfall were shot. I teld him nay, I din't even have that coit then. He wanted proof, an' when he called me in again, I thought that's what it were for. I brung him t'receipt for t'tailoring - remember I had it made up at start o' summer? Din't even have it back in April - that coit din't bloody exist till June. But does tha know what I think?

'I think yer cousin Joseph wants to pin all this on us an' mek sure none o' t'shit falls on his sen. So he's remembered that blue coit an' he's thought to his sen, eh that coit stood out a mile - I'll just slip that into mi statement an' it'll add up against Thorp. Any road, I brung me receipt into Radcliffe's place an' I answered a few questions abaht where I were on t'day o' t'shooting an' I were expecting to be off home afterwards, but that nasty felly Lloyd were rubbing his hands together after they'd finished wi' t'questions, an' he said I were being committed on t'word of a witness. Now, whether it's Bucks or Joe, I couldn't say. Might be both.'

'It's all reit,' Mellor says, when Thorp stops to breathe. 'There's no damage done. But we've all to be silent abaht it now - just let the alibis speak for us. They can't convict us if we've solid alibis - but if we say anything, we don't know what harm we'll do.'

'I din't say owt any road,' says Smith, under his breath. Thorp looks away.

*

Silence. Mellor imagines what that would be like. It didn't exist in bed at home - the creaks, the snores, the cats and dogs, the carts, the wind; in the fields as a child, there was the rustle of breeze through the grass heads, the frogs and toads, the crows, the sparrows, the distant rumble at Engine Bridge from where the water was pumped up to town; the empty shop was quiet, but still the clock ticked and the traffic passed by on the bridge and a child's voice would always break the calm.

In the womb? Not even there - he imagines the softly thudding world beyond a crimson gauze, muted but ever-present. True silence means complete stillness. It means lack of life. It is why when we speak of silencing a person, there is such implied threat. Life is noise, whether made or heard. He rolls off the rough cot and stretches up to the low, vaulted ceiling, thinking about the Oath. They had all promised to pursue any brother to the very verge of nature if he broke his Oath. He remembers the two figures on Radcliffe's driveway, over a month ago now. He hadn't even been close enough to make out their features before the guards carted him away - had simply recognised in those few seconds his cousin Joseph's build and coat, and the scant frame of Martha by his side. He went to their wedding, not so long back. She stood against Joe's arm in just that same way then. How old is she now? Twenty? They are all so young. He tries to forgive them. Someone may yet chase Joseph Mellor down with a pistol.

Ben O'Bucks is lost, he knows that. Thorp says that Radcliffe and Lloyd held Ben for six days at Milnsbridge House and worked on him continuously.

They must have sensed the weaknesses that Mellor did months ago - that nervousness, that dependent need for security and comfort. They knew they could crack him eventually - probably they promised him the two thousand pounds of reward money too, though Mellor would bet his life that Ben will never see a penny of it. He can't do anything about Ben's testimony, but his advantage is that Ben is tainted. He may have turned King's evidence, but his credibility, as a self-confessed Luddite, is greatly lessened. The real threat is Joe Mellor, whose words, as a witness of apparently good character, will be taken more seriously.

At the ancient table, grimy and rocking on the uneven floor, he regards the words already on the paper. 'I now take the liberty,' the letter reads, 'of informing you that I am in good health, as, by the blessing of God, I hope this will find you all.' That's the easy bit done. He threads his fingers together behind his head as he contemplates how best to proceed. Please visit my cousin and ask him to remember his promise? No. Please persuade my cousin of the need to be careful? No. Mellor rubs his face. He picks the quill from the tiny cracked pot, catching the nib on the neck to take off the excess ink. He hesitates above the page, like a boy preparing to dive into a river. 'Please do give my respects to my cousin,' he writes, refilling the nib, 'and tell him to stick fast by what he swore the first time before Radcliffe and I hope his wife will do the same-' Mellor is taking a guess, but it is an educated one. He has had plenty of time to process everything Lloyd said to him in that airless, windowless little cell in Milnsbridge House; plenty of time to piece it all together and to make sense of who has said what. He presses the nib back to the paper - 'that I left their house before 5 o'clock and I did not leave anything at their house, and if the boy swore anything tell my cousin to contradict him and say he told him a different story, that there had been a man and left them, and he did not know him, and as for the girl-' The words tumble from his fingers, the ink staining his skin as he tries to remove Maria from the eye of the storm, '-she cannot swear anything, I know, that will harm me, and tell the boys to stick by what they said the first time if not they are proven foresworn. Tell him and his wife, I hope they will befriend me and never mind their work for if I come home I will do my best for them. Remember, a soul is of more value than work or gold.'

His hand is a vein-knotted claw upon the quill. He drops the pen into the ink well and grasps at his wrist with his left hand, turning the tense joint in his grip. Your soul and mine, Joseph, he thinks. We are both worth more than this. His meaning is as clear as he can make it - neither the lure of two thousand pounds reward money, nor the threat of losing his livelihood and liberty must tempt Joseph to break his Oath. The evil work that Joseph and Martha have done will not matter, if they get Mellor off, as he will prevent the Luddites taking their revenge. That is what he means by saying he will do his best for them. It's the safest way to word his threat that Joseph will be hunted down if he gives the Crown evidence that convicts Mellor. He cannot bring himself to dwell on the possibility that Joseph has already irretrievably succumbed, and that whatever his cousin has said, that sent Thorp here to York, cannot now be undone.

By the time he finishes the letter, there is only a tiny sputtering of light left from the rancid candle. His spelling has gone to pot and his writing sinks to the right-hand side of the page, but this final part has been easier to set down. 'I have heard you are petitioning for parliamentary reform,' he has written, 'and I wish these names to be given as follows.' Beyond that, a simple list of names staggers down the page, beginning with his own initials. He glances over his work in the failing light; messy, but it will have to do. He folds the paper roughly into thirds and daubs a scalding smear of dirty wax across the join, then he puts Ellis's name and address in larger script on the outside.

He has little confidence that these petitions for parliamentary reform will make any real difference, but it cannot hurt now, to add himself to those calls for change, and it gives a legitimate reason for the letter, should it be intercepted by the warden or the postal service. Ellis is, he thinks, a perfect choice of recipient. If Joe won't listen to Thomas Ellis, he won't listen to anyone. Ellis has a way of persuading others and people tend to trust him. He is also a sworn-in Luddite, and surely Joe will understand the danger to himself if he refuses the request in Mellor's letter. Ellis himself could give the order for Joe to be shot.

Mellor tries to convince himself of these things but truthfully he doesn't know what good this letter will do. It feels like dropping a stone into a pond - he can be fairly confident of the ripples, but not whether they will reach the shore with any force. In his dreams, that night, the names he has written for the petition parade down a grand avenue, strips of paper lined in row and gliding silently onwards, until the gusting wind sweeps them away with the fallen leaves.

The thickness of winter seeps into the old gaol. Outside, the fields lay bare and horse dung freezes to the carriageways overnight. In the woods at Dungeon, the native birds flit in the empty spaces between naked branches and a carpet of leaves mulches the steep hillside above Joseph's shop. Wash days are painful; the handling of sodden linen and dripping cotton chafes Mary's hands in the little yard at Longroyd Bridge, and Betty works the mangle with a fierce, blind purpose.

The streets of Huddersfield shine with cold; pack horses snort steam and tap hooves impatiently and the pubs are busy both with locals looking to warm up and with soldiers who still fill the eaves. Mellor closes his eyes and breathes the memory of his home. From the prison yard, he looks up at the lowering sky and hopes for snow. It would be nice to taste a snowflake, to feel the soft sting of falling snow on his face, to gaze up into the infinite rush of snowfall, refulgent against the pewter clouds, and to feel himself drawn into the speeding flow - no longer the snowflakes falling, but him racing upwards through them. The snow comes to pass, a gift of the freezing December, numbing their exercise in the yard.

On Twelfth Night, 6 January, the guards give them a football and allow them to play in the yard. They kick it awkwardly between them, slowly growing into the game. It feels strange at first, to be so confined when football should be played across miles of open land, but they evolve a pattern, dribbling the heavy leather bag around the water pump, each man playing for time with the ball, poising and thumping assailants until a tackle is successful and the ball passes on. Mellor hoots and shouts with the rest of them, many of them men he knows.

A steady stream of Luddites has trickled into the gaol over the few months of his imprisonment. Mellor is surrounded by friends - the Brook brothers, Jonathan Dean, James Haigh (who, after his longer confinement, has rallied a little in the presence of brethren), Mark Hill, James Varley, John Walker, John Ogden and more. Ogden is making a half-hearted attempt for the ball, having been shoved sideways a couple of times.

Mellor pushes into the throng and trips the runner, giving Ogden possession. 'Go on, John, go on,' he yells and Ogden kicks onward with a strangled cry of triumph. Poor John, he's not even twissed. How he came to be picked up by the constables is a mystery. Someone must have mistaken him for Jem, and now John must either let the misapprehension persist or condemn his younger brother. He will not speak about it - will accept neither praise nor ministration from anyone - and so they simply accept him as one of their own, though he fights against this inclusion, blanking their approaches and averting his eyes. The man can resent Mellor all he likes, but Mellor will only ever feel a warm regard for John Ogden.

It doesn't surprise Mellor to receive no visitors that day, even though it is the highlight of the festive season and other prisoners are brought cake and new shirts by their families. He tells himself that his mother and Betty are wise to stay away from this place, with its dangerously enveloping aura. A persistent and foolish notion that intrudes into his daydreams, is that he might have been safe had he not come here to the Assizes in July - that the Castle scented his nature and fixed an invisible tentacle to his soul and that he was already captured long before the constables came for him.

It's ridiculous, and yet he is glad his family are well distant of the gaol, no matter how much he wishes to see his mother and Betty or to reassure his siblings. Wood probably advised them to stay away - he would have seen no sense in them making a long and expensive trip just to pass on a bit of cake and some useless platitudes. Good, Mellor thinks, it's for the best. In the night he whispers a prayer for them and for himself. It's best they didn't come, he insists to God; it's for the best, I understand, I do.

In the morning, after the awful slop of breakfast, Thorp shares the cake his sister has brought.

'How are Mary and Abe?' Mellor asks, licking the sweet, buttery crumbs from his palm.

'Safe,' Thorp answers. 'But she's taking it hard. She came over wi' Ogden's wife an' his sister. Yer can imagine what that were like.'

Mellor nods.

'Ever think mebbe it's worse for them out there than for us in here?'

Thorp appraises him steadily from his seat on the narrow bed. 'I think it's shit all round,' he says, at last. He wipes his hands on the legs of his breeches and pulls a bundle of crochet from his sleeve. It unrolls on his lap - a tidy with a hanging handle at the top and three descending pockets increasing in size, the whole thing measuring the width of his large hand and the length of his forearm. On each pocket front, carefully stitched into the design, is the shape of a heart. The remainder of the ball of yarn is umbilically attached to the unfinished bottom edge, shrinking as the stitches gradually absorb it.

'I wish I'd had it ready yesterday, I could have given it to her then,' Thorp sighs, setting to with his wooden hook.

'For yer sister?' Mellor asks, briefly touching the knitted creation in Thorp's hands

'For mi niece, Annie,' Thorp corrects. 'She turns four at the end o' this month.'

'Kind o' thing girls like,' Mellor says.

There are other men who knit or crochet as a way of passing time in the gaol. Some write letters, though most of the inmates are illiterate. They are allowed to read from a bible, if they can, and sometimes Mellor does. But gaol is mostly about surviving the hunger and the cold and the stifling boredom. It's about washing when he must wash, no matter the iciness of the water, and swallowing food that tastes like leavings, and forcing himself to sleep though his blanket has lice in it. Gaol is the monotony of the prison yard and the shabbiness of unclean clothes and the smell of hemmed-in desperation. He has barely scratched the surface of what being in gaol does to a man, when the Special Commission is begun.

They hear of it first through the Huddersfield solicitor that Mellor has hired with his savings. The solicitor is called Blackburn and he meets with them in the week before the trial, explaining that all the Luddite activity will be tried by the Commission over a couple of weeks. He spends an hour or so trying to build some kind of defence and leaves with papers listing names - all the alibis the men can give him. Mellor's list fills a sheet. Thorp has three or four. Smith has two lonely names. They tell Blackburn they're not guilty and he nods impassively. He shakes their hands when he leaves but Mellor senses the man's eagerness to be gone. On Blackburn's second visit to the gaol, he tells Mellor, Thorp and Smith that their case will not be the first that the Special Commission hears, although it is the most serious. 'We've asked for more time,' he explains, 'since Mr Brougham is only just arrived in York and requires time to familiarise with your case.'

'And how is Mr Brougham minded to proceed?' Mellor asks.

'We'll concentrate on the alibis,' Blackburn says. 'We've got a lot of defence witnesses to present. Whatever the prosecution argue, it comes to nothing if we can show you were elsewhere at the time of the murder.'

It sounds simple and straight-forward. The men give their assent. Blackburn has already been paid his fee and all they need do is sit back and let the lawyers get on with it. What does Mellor know of courtrooms and defence arguments? He allows the following two days to drift past him.

On Wednesday, the fifteenth day of of the new year, they are taken in their chains to the Assize court and led to the bench where they must sit. The press of the crowds is tremendous. They pack the court, squeezed in along walls and rammed into pews, and the guards have to push their weight against the doors to close

340

them against the crowd outside still trying to get it. The ushers look perturbed. Blackburn keeps clearing his throat and shuffling papers and when Brougham turns up, Blackburn assumes a deferential and submissive attitude, quietly pointing to notes on his papers and nodding in agreement when Brougham shakes his head or strikes something out with his quill. He leans forward and looks round Blackburn at the three defendants and briefly raises his eyebrows.

That's it - just an eyebrow raise. It should be Mellor's first clue that things are going to go very badly, but he is distracted by the noise of the crammed room behind him and by the sight of the prosecution solicitor and the jury who are taking their seats; and besides, he trusts Brougham. This is the man who has represented the poor and disadvantaged before. He's been celebrated in the papers for it. Mellor genuinely believes the man will do his job properly. It's just like when you shear the cloth - you do it properly no matter the client; respect for the craft comes first.

He watches the jury filing into position, and then everyone stands while the judges enter and take their places and the room drops into silence. He works out, by both the whispers and the official prattle, who all these people are. Judge Thomson and Judge Le Blanc both sat at Chester Assizes; he remembers their names from the newspapers, when the earlier Special Commission was held. The judgements were listed in the papers - young people transported, others hanged for stealing a few bits of silver, a woman in her fifties condemned to death for forcing a merchant to sell his butter to a crowd at two-thirds the price he was originally asking. That is the nature of the justice that

Thomson and Le Blanc see fit to dispense.

To his right, the Prosecutor, Mr Park, is taking to his feet. Hobhouse, the solicitor from the Treasury looks eager, and beside him, seated, are the two attorneys employed to assist Park. Mellor is acquainted with both - Mr Lloyd and Mr Allison. Allison barely looks in their direction but Lloyd takes a good, long gaze, the satisfaction clear in his face. Mellor tries to concentrate on Park's words but it's hard to catch them and even harder to decipher their meaning. Long after Park has moved on, Mellor recalls a phrase over and again, trying to make sense of it - '...nothing could be more ill-founded than the idea that the introduction of machinery into our manufactures lessens the quantity of human labour and abridges the means of subsistence.'

But it does, Mellor screams in his head. That's exactly what it means. That's why croppers are losing their jobs and families are starving. If it didn't save the manufacturers any money in wages, why the hell would they buy the machines in the first place? All the while, he keeps his face plain and still. He bites at the inside of his cheek. There is a man before him, scribbling away in a notebook - a journalist, he guesses. He knows his demeanour will be recorded. He makes fists in his lap and keeps the rest of himself steady and unmoved.

Park is describing Horsfall as greatly beloved. Mellor blinks slowly, savouring a few seconds of darkness and reminding himself that Horsfall drew a hostile crowd as he was transported, dying, back to the Warren House, while Mellor was quietly celebrated across the town. I am the one who is beloved, he thinks, and it doesn't feel arrogant to believe it. It feels honest - not a symptom of ego, but a truth welling up from within and without. He lets it come, lets it flood over him and allows Park's words to pass by. Whatever this man says, it doesn't matter.

In fact, he mostly daydreams until Henry Parr takes the stand. This is the man who came to Horsfall's aid and Mellor remembers being atop the wall while Parr shouted at him, weaponless and brave. Parr gives his evidence cleanly and honestly. He says he has lived in Huddersfield for five years. Mellor can see no proper recognition in Parr's face as he looks back at them, though of course, Parr knows they are the accused.

Mellor frowns for a second in the grip of a fleeting moment of clarity as Parr descends from the witness stand - that man, Mellor realises, could not identify them. If he could, why did Park not ask him? Why did Park not say, 'Point to the man who got up on the wall in front of you'? If Parr pointed at Mellor and said, 'It was he,' the case would be half-won for the prosecution. The fact that Park has not asked it means he knows that Parr cannot do it.

Mellor turns to Blackburn intending to whisper something to this effect, but Blackburn shushes him as the next witness approaches and the moment is lost. I don't understand all this, Mellor thinks, I should leave it to Brougham and Blackburn. They know what they are doing. Perhaps Brougham, like Park, cannot risk what Parr might say if called on to make an identification. Yet this whole drama feels incomplete - as if parts are missing and no one cares. It feels like a decision was made long before this day about the necessary outcome and that the wheels are turning

343

automatically. Questions that should be asked are being ignored. The process that should occur has been subverted.

Mellor breathes slowly through the medical evidence and the descriptions of Horsfall's wounds. Booth and Hartley had worse, he thinks, and I bet no one gave them anything for the pain at the end. Worse than hearing any of this, far worse, is when Ben O'Bucks takes the stand.

He looks pale and malnourished and his voice is reedy and high. He gazes at Park with over-large eyes, fixated, as though he is frightened to look anywhere else.

Under prompting, he tells a rich story, full of detail and Mellor listens as the whole of that April day is evoked, from the cropping in the shop beforehand, to the sprint down to Dungeon after. Mellor had expected to feel anger. That would have been easier. Instead he feels loss and sadness. He wonders if someone will shoot O'Bucks for what he has done here today. He remembers Betty saying she would smash her lover's legs if he betrayed her brother. A picture comes, unbidden, of her raising the deadly Russian pistol and firing it into Ben Walker's Oath-breaking heart...but the picture brings no relief, only emptiness.

A strong cross-examination could tear holes in Walker's story, especially as Walker has entirely invented some details to improve his own standing, but Brougham stays seated and lets a junior colleague ask a few pointless questions. Both Parr and Walker are prosecution witnesses and yet their testimony conflicts, Mellor realises. Parr says he saw all four men by the wall after the shots rang out, but Bucks has told the court that he and Smith remained hidden in the copse. The timings in Ben's story don't work either. With the palpable hatred in the room and the inconsistencies in his story, Ben O'Bucks is vulnerable and Mellor wonders why Brougham does not capitalise on this. When Bucks steps down he staggers, as if his legs are numb and Mellor has to look away. From then on, it's a torture. First there is Hall, the man with whom he shared a bed only months ago, talking of how Mellor rammed that gun full of slugs. Hall, like O'Bucks has turned King's evidence. It will save them both from the gallows. Sowden, the apprentice from his own shop, is up next - a lesser betrayal - and then Martha.

Martha takes her seat delicately, smiling nervously at Park, but with a sickly set to her jaw, as if she were tasting lemons. She describes Mellor's visit to the shop - the black handkerchief, the drab topcoat he borrowed. Such banal details with which to capture anyone - like Thomas Brook, taken up on account of his blasted hat, found floating in the mill race at Rawfolds. Just leave out the times, Martha, he pleads silently, and all will be well. But she doesn't.

She tells the packed court that he came with his friend at a quarter past six, and anyone knows that, allowing a little room for error in everyone's pocket-watches, he could have shot Horsfall at six o'clock, or five past, and still made it at a sprint from Crosland to Dungeon by that time. Yet he knows that Maria told the magistrate that he came at five o'clock. Perhaps she will be summoned and cast doubt on Martha's testimony? All of a sudden, he wishes they would call her and that he could see her again. He didn't name her, on the alibi list for Blackburn - it never really occurred to him to use her in that way, and part of him is glad it didn't. But maybe the prosecution will bring her out? He is disappointed by the appearance of Durrance the apprentice next, and then Kinder, and by the time his cousin Joseph has been called, he knows that Maria is not here.

Joseph tries to limit his answers. Someone has already tried to shoot him, in his own yard at Dungeon on New Year's Eve, the bullet lodging in the stone wall as he fled indoors, and he fears that he will pay a heavy price yet for this testimony, but he is relieved that Walker and Hall have already given such damning evidence. People will blame them and hopefully forget that, if not for his own connivances, Walker and Hall would probably not have been identified in the first place.

He looks directly and apologetically at Mellor several times as he gives his evidence and he refuses to identify Mellor's dark green greatcoat that the gaoler, Mr Staveley, has brought to court as part of the evidence. For Mellor, it is too little too late. Joseph could have done more - he had only to dispute his wife's timings to trip up the prosecution, but Joe will not go this far. He is sliding through this Special Commission as a witness by the skin of his teeth. He could so easily have been taken up as an accomplice.

There are a few more witnesses for the prosecution - men who saw Horsfall's murderers running away down the plantation - and then comes the turn of the defence witnesses. Mellor, Thorp and Smith are asked if they want to speak, and though they are each wondering at the lacklustre approach of Brougham, they still have some faith in him and don't want to undermine anything the alibi witnesses might say. 'We leave it to our counsel,' Mellor tells the court, believing that in the elicitation of alibi evidence, Brougham will find the many opportunities to shred the prosecution case. One after another, trusted men and women step up and say where and when they saw Mellor on the day Horsfall was murdered - William Hanson, John Womersley, William Battersby, John Thorpe, Jonathan Battersby and the Armitage brothers. William Hirst, the lodger in Wood's house who Mellor knows well, gets up and says he saw Ben Walker in the yard at seven o'clock, directly contradicting the account O'Bucks has given. Mellor knows that his step-father must have orchestrated this claim and it is a careful, subtle attempt at undermining the prosecution's star witness, but subtlety is lost on the increasingly bewildered jurors.

Later, after all the evidence has been given and it is left for him to sum up the case, Park mocks the defence witnesses - the defence counsel is, of course, not allowed to state its case or address the jury, only to examine witnesses. It's easy for Park to lead the jury, and Brougham's complete silence through the whole trial almost lends a weight to the indictment.

It might be an honest tale each of the witnesses for the defence gave, Park says, if you only substitute a different date or time. He casts all the defence witnesses as liars and yet he never suggests they be tried for perjury. He knows he cannot prove they are lying, he knows his case is not really strong enough for that, so he must plant the suggestion and allow the judges to make what they want of it. Mellor can see exactly what they are making of it - the day is nearly over and they wish to quickly pass sentence before their evening meal.

At five minutes before eight o'clock, Justice Le Blanc sends the jury out, with an instruction to resolve the different accounts given by all the witnesses. He asks them to consider, in any case, whether people would honestly remember the events of a nondescript day so many months ago. It sounds to Mellor as if he is telling them not to actually bother paying any attention to the discrepancies at all. Twenty five minutes pass and the courtroom fills with a low chatter but the defendants' bench remains quiet - a hollow space with hope and despair circling the periphery. What could they say to one another? There is nothing now but the wait. Then the jury file back into their places and the room drops to dead silence. Guilty, the foreman says, and his word drops into an ocean of nothingness; no movement, no sound, like the end of all things.

Justice Le Blanc's voice cuts into the void. He asks the prisoners why he should not pass a death sentence. Blackburn twitches, surprised, and he looks to Brougham, though Brougham just sits a little straighter and purses his lips. In the previous two days of the Special Commission, sentencing has been withheld and Blackburn has already told the defendants that they will not be sentenced until all the cases have been heard. This manoeuvre by the judges is unexpected. Mellor realises himself addressed. He has had seconds to process the knowledge of his fate.

'I have nothing to say, only I am not guilty,' he says, and Thorp says 'I am not guilty, sir, evidence has been given false against me, that I declare,' and Smith says 'Not guilty, sir', as if the energy and life is draining from him already in his shrunken, defeated reply. Le Blanc reaches for his black cap and launches into a hefty sermon against the wickedness of the men at the bar. You bastard, thinks Mellor, but he means Brougham, who sits with his legs crossed and arms folded and does not speak up at all, even though he could appeal to the Crown for clemency. One hang, all hang - Justice Le Blanc told the jury this before they went off to deliberate, meaning that despite all evidence agreeing Smith had not fired, he was still guilty if he had been present. Mellor remembers Smith saying 'I'd hang just for being here,' and yet they could appeal. Brougham could beg mercy for Smith; Le Blanc could sentence him to transportation instead.

'...there to be hanged by the neck until death, and thereafter, your bodies to be delivered for dissection and anatomisation,' Le Blanc is saying. He tells them they will die on Friday morning, just thirty six hours away, and Mellor thinks how strange that is, to know how and when one will die. Blackburn whispers to Brougham, 'But they're indicted for Rawfolds, they're meant to stand trial for it,' and Brougham, breathy and irritated, murmurs 'We don't need them. Better for the others if they're gone.' Then the machinery of the courtroom packs up, the Judges departing and the jury following on their heels and the shocked crowds spilling from the doorway, and Mellor, Thorp and Smith are led in their irons back to the cells.

The Shameful Tree

Everyone is waiting. Mellor has been asked for his final words and he knows he must not prolong the agony - not for himself, nor for Thorp and Smith, nor for the watching crowd who sway in a sickly, silent swell all across St George's Field.

He does have something ready. The words came to him early in the morning, when he awoke from strange dreams of playing cobnuts on strings with Thorp while seven angels seemed to dance in his vision. He thinks of his father and his three dead sisters and of Booth and Hartley, and of the way death comes so slowly and yet so suddenly - never either one speed or the other but somehow both at once, as though the passage of time ceases to have meaning or form on the verge of existence.

'Some of my enemies may be here,' he calls out. 'If there be, I freely forgive them, and all the world, and I hope the world will forgive me.'

Thorp gives Mellor and Smith the ghost of a smile and adds, 'I hope none of those who are now before me will ever come to this place.'

The sky is still white, no shape of the sun behind the high sheet of cloud, but it fills Mellor's vision with light as the noose is drawn tight on his neck.

Then the drop, the agony and the futile fight - and then, once more, the light.

Author's Postscript

In anticipation that readers may want more factual detail, the following is a summary of my findings from genealogy research, along with a quick look at the unanswered questions of the whole episode.

It was reported that Mellor, Thorp and Smith appeared convulsed for a few moments when they were hanged. Immediately after the hanging, the bodies were taken to a York surgeon for dissection - a tactic planned before the Special Commision had even begun and therefore long before a jury had even found them guilty.

This appallingly premature decision was designed to prevent tensions from boiling over into riots in Huddersfield, should the bodies have returned for burial there. The remains of Mellor, Thorp and Smith are most likely buried under Dog Yard at the rear of the Debtor's Prison within the York Castle museum site, but no memorial site exists for them.

William Thorp (the legal paperwork naming him 'Thorpe' was in error) was said to have two sisters, but parish records show he had a brother, John (about whom nothing seems to be known) and a sister, Mary. Mary and her husband Abraham Ashton went on to have six children - all girls apart from the fifth. They named this solitary son William Thorp Ashton. He, like his father and uncle before him, became a cloth dresser; he married a cloth dresser's daughter and they had a large family. His grandson also bore the name (with the 'e' now added) of William Thorpe Ashton, taking the name right through into the twentieth century.

William Thorp did in fact crochet a beautiful hair tidy while he was in York gaol, just as he does in my story. It is in the possession of Tolson Museum, Huddersfield, where is appears sometimes on display, though no one knows for whom he made it. He had no wife, so it is feasible to think it may have been intended for Mary or for her daughter, Ann (a toddler at the time), and that a family member later donated it to the museum.

Fourteen further men were hanged in scenes described as 'inexpressibly awful' by Edward Baines. These were John Ogden (who died for his brother), John Walker (of Longroyd Bridge), Jonathan Dean (whose hand was shot through at Rawfolds), Thomas Brook (who lost his hat in the mill stream), James Haigh (who went on the run with his wounded shoulder), Nathan Hoyle, Joseph Crowther, John Hill, William Hartley, John Swallow, John Batley, Joseph Fisher, James Hey and Job Hey. They approached the gallows (in two separate groups of seven) singing the Methodist hymn, Behold the Saviour of Mankind - a hymn from which I have taken several of my chapter headings.

The entry in the Parish register for John Ogden's death contains a separate note in a later hand describing how he died to protect a brother. My parish records research shows that John did indeed have a younger brother, Jeremiah. Jeremiah went on to marry Maria Townend in 1815, and in 1816 they named their first child John.

Seven men were transported. These were John Baines (the elderly republican who frequented The Crispin), John Baines the younger, William

Blakeborough, George Duckworth, John Eaden, John Lumb and Charles Milnes. Zachariah Baines, a boy of only fifteen years, was, like his brother and father, charged with administering an illegal oath but some fleeting moment of sense and mercy prevailed, and he was acquitted.

Ben Walker - Ben O'Bucks as he was equally known - was held for six days in October by John Lloyd, whose questionable interrogative techniques caused consternation at the highest levels of the military and judiciary. Lloyd had begun to apply pressure to Ben's mother, and did eventually kidnap a female witness and secure her within his Chester home, but whether this female witness was Mrs Walker or Maria Dyson, I find inconclusive. Most presume it to be Mrs Walker, though there are semantic discrepancies in a close reading of Lloyd's letter of 20 October that, to me, make it more likely to be Maria. In any case, Ben was protecting not just himself but his family when he turned King's evidence, and he paid dearly for this decision.

The two thousand pounds reward promised to him was never forthcoming, though it had been offered by the magistrate and he was entitled to it. He spent time away from Huddersfield and desperately petitioned government for his reward. When he returned to his home town, he cut a miserable figure, destitute and friendless. The saddest account is of his state directly after the executions. The Quakers who visited him found that his countenance was pale and ghastly and that his joints were loosened as if they were scarcely able to support his body.

Joseph Mellor, rather than Ben, gave the crucial

incriminating evidence against his cousin George and his role and involvement remains a frustrating mystery. That his 19 year old servant, Maria Dyson (named 'Mary' in many sources, but baptised Maria and named as Maria on her official statement to the magistrate), disappeared in quite surprising fashion casts even more confusion. Joseph Mellor said a constable came and took her away from his shop during all the October upheaval, and this might suggest she was indeed abducted by John Lloyd. A magistrate from Lascelles Hall who knew the Mellors tried to track her down, believing her witness statement was important, but he got nowhere. Joseph Oldham, the apprentice from Joseph Mellor's shop, also disappeared, apparently dismissed for misbehaviour, so neither Maria Dyson nor Joseph Oldham gave evidence at the trial. I cannot find any further evidence for Maria, either by way of marriage or death record and her fate is very unclear.

It is troubling, also, that her account as given to Justice Radcliffe differs so greatly from Martha's, especially as James Varley's statement mentions that Maria witnessed his visit to Joseph Mellor's shop the day after the shooting. It seems that she may twice or more have been a witness to events and conversations that Martha and Joseph may have needed to obfuscate. Whether her employers or the zealous clerk Lloyd were the bigger threat to her safety may never be known, but it seems highly likely that Joseph Mellor was himself a Luddite.

Joseph and Martha Mellor went on to have at least two sons. After Joseph died, Martha moved in with one of them (also named Joseph), and she lived until at least seventy, becoming a grandmother. My research suggests that Martha herself was the daughter of Luke Bradley of Taylor Hill. A Luke Bradley was identified by Francis Vickerman as a leading Luddite in the area, suggesting, again, that the Mellors were far more complicit in Luddism than was revealed at the time.

Of the Woods, there is little evidence. They told Thomas Shillitoe (the visiting Quaker) that they had thought about leaving Huddersfield, but that the compassion they were receiving had made them reconsider. There is a death record for a 64 year old Mary Wood of Longroyd Bridge in 1829 that would suggest they did indeed live out their lives there, but nothing conclusive for John Wood. The trail for Mellor's half-siblings is also cold - there is nothing that I have been able to identify with any certainty in the parish registers for William, Mary-Ann, Elizabeth or Daniel. It is true that Frances (Franny) and Sarah (Sally) died as infants, and that Mellor's full sister, Hannah, died when Mellor was just a toddler.

For Mellor's sister, Betty, there is just one possible record that I have found besides that of her 1787 baptism - a death in 1832 at the age of 45. of a Betty Mellor of Moor Croft. She was buried at Linthwaite Church but there is no surviving memorial inscription. If she is the correct woman, this record suggests she died without marrying.

Of Mellor himself, of course, there is nothing more. He left no wife and no children. Given the extreme poverty and misery to which the state abandoned the hanged Luddites' many dependents (including 57 children and 8 orphans), that might be considered a blessing.

Acknowledgements

This being a work of fiction, I don't intend to provide a full bibliography of the extensive range of sources used, but I must acknowledge my particular indebtedness to the works of Edward Baines; Thomas Shillitoe; Frank Peel; D.F.E. Sykes; Mrs (Isabella) G.L. Banks; Gertrude Ghorbal (nee Humberstone) and co-author W.B. Crump; Lesley Kipling; Alan Brooke; Kevin Binfield; and to the team who have created ludditebicentenary.blogspot.co.uk. (on which exists a vast amount of excellently organised information).

My huge appreciation also to the Public Records Office resources (specifically Home Office correspondences for the period); the West Yorkshire Archive Service; Huddersfield Central Library; and the Huddersfield and District Family History Society 'Root Cellar' facility in Meltham.

A massive thank you to Steaven Heppener whose design for the book cover so beautifully captures the spirit of the story, and my warmest thanks to all who have supported and encouraged my endeavour to do justice to this story.

Glossary of West Riding Dialect

(Some of these terms are archaic, but many are still in common use)

addle/addlins = earn/earnings
buffit = low stool, often with three legs
chelp = yelp
chellep = chatter
claggy = sticky like clay
flaid = afraid
fain = glad
fair = very
fast = puzzled
felly = a man, similar to modern 'fella' or 'bloke'
grand = fine
kall = talk idly, gossip
laik = to play
nobbut = only, nothing but
poise = kick (often with hard boot/clog)
reit = right, proper
si thi = common exclamation
skaddle = scare, frighten
snicket = short cut, narrow passage/path
sup = drink
t' = a glottal stop, made in place of 'the'
tha/thi/thee = used interchangeably for you/yours
throng = busy, crowded
ummer = Hell (often in exclamation, e.g. 'blummin ummer' meaning 'bloody hell')
wappy = quick

Made in the USA
San Bernardino, CA
01 May 2020

70603004R00224